JAMES W. NICHOL

TRANSGRESSION

A NOVEL

McArthur & Company
Toronto

This edition published in Canada in 2008 by
McArthur & Company
322 King St. West, Suite 402
Toronto, ON
M5V 1J2
www.mcarthur-co.com

Library and Archives Canada Cataloguing in Publication

    Nichol, James W., 1940-
    Transgression : a novel / James W. Nichol.

    ISBN 978-1-55278-717-5

    I. Title.

PS8577.I18T73 2008   C813'.54   C2008-900302-0

Cover and text design by ASAP Design

The publisher would like to acknowledge the financial support of the Government
of Canada through the Book Publishing Industry Development Program (BPIDP)
and the Canada Council for our publishing activities. The publisher further
wishes to acknowledge the financial support of the Ontario Arts Council for
our publishing program.

10 9 8 7 6 5 4 3 2 1

For all my family, big and small

TRANSGRESSION

• • •

FRANCE, 1941

CHAPTER ONE

• • •

A burst of pigeons flew up off the narrow cobblestone street, cleared the roof of the nearest building and scattered across the grey sky. Hands fleeing in front of the Germans, Adele Georges thought to herself. It was a futile gesture; they'd already been chopped off.

Adele was given to such thoughts and visions. They visited her mind, filled her eyes, sometimes invited, sometimes not, but always more vividly than she'd expected.

"Adele is blessed with an imagination that would rival Dante's," her father had remarked many times. "She'll be a great artist."

"She's empty-headed" – this from her mother. "Any absurd idea can fly in there and find a home. She should live in the real world." And on the tip of Madame Georges' tongue, "And so should you."

During the first weeks of the Occupation this hand story had swept the country but it had turned out not to be true. The Germans were not cutting off the hands of hundreds of young men to make a future resistance impossible. Nevertheless darkness had come to France the year before, and death, and mind-numbing fear.

Adele walked on toward the Domestic Population Bureau of Information and took her place at the end of a long queue. The line shuffled slowly and silently ahead. Finally she reached the open door. Rising up on her toes, she could see a Wehrmacht officer in his field-green uniform talking to an old lady. She wondered if he was wearing one of her trousers. She thought it was quite possible, because that's what she did every night now, sit in a long dimly lit room in the middle of a row of rough women and sew seams on an endless procession of Wehrmacht pants.

The queue divided into two beyond the doorway, the right tributary heading off toward another officer. Unlike the Wehrmacht man, this one was sitting rigidly at his desk, his eyes fixed on a tall, frail-looking individual who was standing in front of him kneading his cap in his hands. His uniform was black.

Adele's body went rigid.

Just that morning, René had screamed at her not to go to the Domestic Population Bureau of Information.

"It's a Wehrmacht office," she'd stubbornly yelled back. "They don't know anything! Besides, I have to!"

Adele aimed herself at the tributary to the left. After another half-hour of shuffling, she sat down and asked her question.

"Perhaps your father is dead," the middle-aged officer replied in a reasonable tone. "So many soldiers couldn't be identified."

"Yes." Adele was trying to keep her voice low without whispering, so that the young SS officer sitting only twenty feet away wouldn't overhear, but wouldn't become suspicious either. "But my father wasn't a soldier. He was a doctor. He was serving in the medical corps."

The man smiled sadly at the naiveté of this remark, particularly coming from such a diminutive and sweet-looking girl. It was all Adele could do not to spit in his face. She hated him, she hated every German on the face of the earth. She kept her expression set and blank.

"How old are you, dear?" he asked in his raspy French.

"Sixteen."

"In time of war, front lines collapse back on themselves, even safe positions can be over-run. Bombs fall, shells explode. You say your father was stationed near Arras?"

He was still speaking kindly enough. Tears, unplanned for and unwanted, burned in Adele's eyes. "That's the last we heard from him."

The officer reached for a cigarette and lit it. "Very high casualties there. And it wasn't until after the Armistice was signed that we allowed French authorities on to the battlefields. Many weeks under a very hot sun, a hundred thousand French soldiers strewn everywhere. Very difficult to identify."

"We have heard that a million of our soldiers were taken prisoner and transported. We think our father is in your country."

They felt the SS officer's eyes fall on them at the same moment. The older man shifted in his chair. "Why haven't you made inquiries to your own authorities?" he said more sharply.

Adele leaned forward – there was no stopping now. "We have. Every week for months but they have no information about prisoners in Germany. They said we should come here."

Adele could see the young man rising like a black cloud in the corner of her eye.

"May I ask this young lady a question?" He had excellent French.

"Certainly, Captain."

Adele looked up.

The young man's pale eyes were fixed on hers. "Tell me, why did you wait so long to make this inquiry?"

"We were waiting for our father to return home. We hoped he'd just been wounded."

"How long did you wait? Two months? Four?"

He sat down on the corner of the desk. His black pants, flaring out at the thighs, were tucked neatly inside the tops of his gleaming boots. Adele tried to concentrate on the seams.

"We made repeated inquiries, we went to our town hall, we wrote to hospitals, to the special centres of information in Paris. No one's lists are complete. They always say we have to wait for more information to come in."

"So you find no information from French sources, but you hope for the best, that your father has been transported to Germany. And now, almost a year later, you come here to inquire if this is indeed true. I ask you again, what took you so long?"

"We were told complete lists of prisoners would be made available to our officials, but to this day they have not been made available. We waited and prayed."

The young SS captain stared at her in silence.

Adele examined her bruised hands and broken fingernails.

"What is your father's name?"

"Henri Paul-Louis Georges."

"What was his occupation?"

"She says he was a medical doctor." The Wehrmacht officer answered for her.

"It is always of interest when people seem slow to bring a name to our attention, particularly in a matter that seems so routine. We have to wonder why. But we have your father's name now. Thank you."

Adele nodded, got up and walked out of the Domestic Population Bureau of Information. She couldn't feel her legs.

• • •

René was waiting for her, sitting at the kitchen table smoking one of his black-market Turkish cigarettes. His dark hair was uncut and wild-looking, his fingernails were black with grease, and he was trying to grow a beard. He glared at Adele through a cloud of blue smoke when she opened the back door.

René was older than Adele by only thirteen months but already her head barely reached his shoulder. For some infuriating reason her body was refusing to grow at an acceptable rate. Her hair was black and thick and wild about her head. They both had prominent eyebrows, high cheekbones, and the same dark eyes, though Adele's eyes were larger and more luminous and projected an appealing vulnerability. With no effort at all they seemed to be able to draw all kinds of people to her. Adele and René had been in a heightened state of competition all their lives, whether it was to demonstrate who could balance a spoon on the end of their nose the longest, who could make the funniest remarks at the dinner table or who could deliver to their father the most impressive school report. After the first few grades, Adele wasn't really in the running when it came to school.

"René has such a conventional mind," Adele had remarked to her father one day in an attempt to account for why her reports were full of four point fives and fives, while René's reports glowed with columns of sixes. "I'm going to be an artist." It had been a blatant attempt to use her father's best thoughts about her as a defence.

Henri Paul-Louis Georges had smiled at this, though whether it was because he was slightly appalled or slightly amused, it was difficult to tell. No doubt his school reports had once glowed with straight sixes, too.

"Then you must decide what kind of artist you're going to be – run-of-the-mill, like this report, or exceptional. Be exceptional, Adele. Become well-educated, think deeply on all things, and then turn and show the world its true face. Like Dante." He'd smiled and squeezed her hands. "Dante aside, whatever you do, you must try your best to be of service to your fellow man. That's the most important thing in life. Isn't it?"

"Yes," Adele had replied.

"Then you must acquire an education."

Now Adele closed the back door and decided to ignore René for as long as possible. She put the kettle on to boil and began to rummage through the cupboards to see what Old Raymond, the family's chauffeur when they still had their touring car, their gardener when they still paid attention to the gardens, had managed to buy with that day's quota of food tickets.

She could hear her other brothers, Bibi the youngest at four, and Jean six, playing loudly somewhere in the house.

"So," René said, "what happened?"

Adele looked into the tea jar. It had been empty that morning, but now there was a little pyramid of black tea leaves sitting in the bottom. God bless Raymond.

"What did you find out?" René persisted.

"Nothing." Adele tried to sound as casual as possible. "This Wehrmacht officer looked up Father's name. But their lists aren't complete either. It's very slow, getting information out of Germany, even for them. He said I should come back in two weeks' time."

René held his cigarette between his teeth and clapped his hands together in a slow show of appreciation. Adele knew her brother very well. The sound hurt her ears. She braced herself.

"Well done. Well done! And the SS officer, what did he say?"

"What SS officer?"

"You stupid little shit!" René yelled at her.

"Why did you follow me?" Adele yelled back.

René raised one of his greasy hands and rubbed it against his face as if he were trying to rub off her indirect admission of guilt. Adele could see a purple vein on his forehead pumping blood. He got up slowly and moved around the table. "I didn't follow you. One of my men did."

"Ha!" Adele retorted, her voice, she hoped, ringing with sharp scorn and ridicule. One of his men, what a dreamer.

"What did you tell the SS officer and what did he say to you?"

"He doesn't suspect anything. They always ask questions, that's all they do. They don't follow everything up."

René clasped the edge of the sink and closed his eyes. When he opened them again and turned her way, his eyes looked bloodshot. "Did you give him our father's name?"

"What other name would I give him? What good would it do to give him a fictitious name, so we could find a fictitious father?"

René's hand shot out, grabbed Adele's thin arm and in one swift motion slammed her up against the cupboard. "I told you not to go there, I forbade it, and now you've given him away!"

"That's all in your head! He's waiting for us to find him. He needs us to help him. He needs to come home!"

"He'll never come home now!"

"He will, he will, he will!"

"Murderer!" René's mouth opened in a scream.

He let Adele's arm go and leaned against the wall. He turned his face away and started to cry.

Adele couldn't have been more surprised if he'd pulled out a gun and shot her. Great wrenching sobs shook his body.

Adele reached up to him, held his head. "René," she whispered, "dear René."

René pulled away from her and rushed out the door.

CANADA, 1946

CHAPTER TWO

· · ·

There were dead children hanging in the woods.

At first Madeleine hadn't noticed them because it was wet over there and full of mosquitoes and she was concentrating on finding the cows, and then she'd seen them. Three of them. They had looked like dried bunches of grapes.

"You remember how Father and Andrew and Uncle Matt strung up the pig last fall?"

Jenny had nodded.

"And you remember how Uncle Matt hangs up ducks in the garage to ripen them?"

Jenny had nodded again.

"That's what she was doing. She was ripening them."

"W-w-why?" Jenny had been afflicted with a terrible stutter since she'd learned to talk.

"You know why. She eats them."

Jenny's breath had caught in her throat.

"She looks for ones she can catch. Lame ones and half-blind ones and ones who can't hear so good. Ones who are defective."

"D-d-defective?" Jenny had said.

Two months had passed and Jenny had almost forgotten her big sister's story when Madeleine came into the bedroom they shared and caught her. "What are you doing looking at my things?" Madeleine screamed.

"I'm not hurting anyth-th-th…"

Thing, Jenny raged in her head, *thing.* But the word wouldn't come out of her mouth.

"Stay out!" Madeleine snatched back her small cedar chest full of dirty jokes and notes from boys and other private treasures.

"I was just looking for the c-c-c..." *Coins,* Jenny wanted to say, *the coins from Great Britain Grandma Jenkins gave you,* but she found it particularly difficult to speak when she was caught red-handed.

Her sister gave her a violent push. "Why don't you just g-g-g-go outside and g-g-g-get lost?"

Jenny ran through the back kitchen, past the lilacs and the privy and headed out into the buzzing sun-scorched world.

She made up an escape plan as she ran. She knew what she'd do – she'd cut through the woods to the other side and wade through Mr. Timmon's oat field to the road. It was just a short walk from there to the trestle bridge. The railway under the bridge was on an up-hill grade that slowed the trains down to a walk. This was where the farm boys gathered in the warm summer evenings to ride the freights all the way to the Township Line. This was where Madeleine would sit on the railway bank and watch them. Sometimes, if she was in a good mood, which was rare, she'd let Jenny watch, too.

Jenny began to wonder if she was strong enough, if she could run fast enough through all the steam and noise, if she was tall enough to reach the bottom rung and haul herself up on the iron ladder and ride past the Township Line, past everything and away from everyone she ever knew.

She could still hear Madeleine taunting her and it wasn't the first time, either, it was about the millionth. She would do it. She would hitch a ride on a train. She'd run away.

And then she remembered the story.

The wagon trail she was walking along had disappeared into a towering mass of trees. Everything was still. There wasn't a hint of a breeze. She could skirt around the woods, but it would take longer and it was swampy at the one end. Her father's wagon trail was dry and ran almost perfectly straight through to the back field.

Jenny stared at the opening into the woods.

If the witch did live in a deep cave under a tree, as Madeleine had said, maybe she was asleep. It was the middle of the day and it was scorching hot. Hell's own kitchen, her father would have said to her. If he had been standing there beside her. If he were holding her hand.

The longer Jenny stared at the opening, the more tempting it became. Her heart raced. It would only take a few moments and she'd be through. The lane soon narrowed and darkened. She began to walk up on her toes like a water bird, ready to take flight at the crack of a twig, at anything. She could hear the lonely clang of a cowbell somewhere. Her father was over at Uncle Matt's, three miles away, helping out with the threshing. So was her big brother Andrew.

Dark corridors opened up on either side of her. Vines hung down from dead trees. Jenny kept her eyes straight ahead. A shadow was moving somewhere, it was moving toward her. She began to run. Something was running between the trees, she could hear some horrible, panting noise.

Jenny flew out of the woods and into her father's back field. Stubble began to cut into her bare feet. She slowed down, stopped.

There was no creature standing on the trail behind her, nothing to be seen at all, just the still green woods and the cloudless, sun-seared sky.

Jenny picked her way carefully across the stubble toward Mr. Timmon's oat field and began to rethink this idea of running away. Maybe she'd just hide under the railway bridge all night instead. Everyone would be scared out of their wits. Everyone would be searching for her. Her mother would be turning insane. Her father and Andrew would be running around in the dark. Madeleine might even feel sorry for what she'd done.

Ahead of her, puffs of dust began to rise in the air like small explosions. She'd never seen anything like that before. They were rising out of the weedy fenceline between her father's field and Mr. Timmon's. She went up on her toes again. Another puff of dust. She could see something moving, a shifting of light, a copper-coloured rustling.

Jenny stepped closer. Something as startlingly white as a snake's belly flew up in the air and then fell back down again. Jenny stuck her foot out cautiously and parted the tall dusty grass. One of her mother's hens was staring up at her. She recognized it right away – it was the one whose eggs she could never collect, the one who'd chased her across the barnyard on numerous occasions. It bobbed its head and again something white flew up in an explosion of dust.

A garter snake, she thought, but it seemed too stubby for a garter snake. Whatever it was, it had disappeared into the grass again. The hen began to peck and peck.

"D-d-damn you, g-g-go away!"

Jenny kicked at the bird. The bird shied off a few steps. Jenny knelt down and parted the weeds. The thing the hen had been worrying was puffy and milky-looking, its one end rough and black. She picked up a twig and poked at it. The thing rolled over, dragging something behind on a long sinuous thread, something thinly curved and as shiny as coal.

A faint smell, both sweet and repugnant, reached Jenny's nostrils. And now she knew that Madeleine's story had been true. And now she knew that the witch was close by.

She was looking down at a finger.

FRANCE, 1941

CHAPTER THREE

• • •

Adele queued up in front of the Domestic Population Bureau of Information again, since she couldn't see how she could make things worse. She wondered if they'd already looked up her father's name, if they knew where he was being held.

And she wondered if they knew who he was.

Henri Paul-Louis had been a Democratic Socialist. His patients knew this, because in mid-treatment or even in mid-trauma he'd often engage them in annoying political discussions. All Rouen knew this, too, because in the elections of 1936 he'd been the campaign manager for one of the party's local candidates. When the Front Populaire won and Leon Blum formed the government, Henri Paul-Louis had declared it the happiest day of his life. He'd made this declaration, not to his political cronies, but at the family dinner table. It had come as a shock. Adele had immediately thought, What about me, what about when I was born, weren't you happier then? And Adele could tell by the sour look on her mother's face that she was thinking similar thoughts. Twelve-year-old René, however, had nodded wisely. He, too, was deliriously happy that the Socialists had won.

But what if Adele's inquiry had caused a curious official to check their father's name against some political list? What if the list recorded *Henri Paul-Louis Georges, Socialist and political organizer*, which would mean Bolshevik to the Nazis, which would mean he'd become a political prisoner and no longer be under the protection of the conventions of war? They would torture him as they did all their political prisoners and when he had nothing left to tell they would kill him.

This possibility had terrified Adele as much as it had René, but finally she'd convinced herself that even the SS knew the difference between a Socialist and a Bolshevik, and as far as being a Socialist went, her father hadn't even been a member of Leon Blum's government. He'd simply been a supporter as millions of others had. How else could Blum have won the election? The SS weren't running around persecuting everyone who had ever voted or worked for the Front Populaire.

Adele had tried this Socialist vs. Bolshevik line of reasoning out on René one night. She might as well have been talking to a stone.

The queue to the Domestic Population Bureau of Information seemed even slower than the previous day. Finally Adele reached the open door. A different Wehrmacht officer was sitting behind the desk to the left. The desk to the right was unoccupied.

Adele's body unclenched.

She gave her father's name once again. The new officer didn't seem forewarned or suspicious. He got up from his desk, pulled a thick ledger down from a shelf and began leafing through it. Adele's cheeks felt hot for no good reason. She looked around. A German clerk was standing at the back of the office looking at her. He seemed very young, almost as young as she was. And then he smiled.

Adele could hardly believe it. She turned away.

"There is no such name as this on our lists. Perhaps you will come back in two weeks." The officer sat back down at his desk.

"Thank you," Adele said, and keeping her face down so she wouldn't look at the young clerk again, even by accident, she escaped out the open door.

Adele saw girls with German soldiers all the time, standing in crowds together on street corners, or being overly noisy and obnoxious at the back of buses, arms around each other, mushy kissing, shrieks of laughter. Empty-headed girls with bullet-headed Boche soldiers. Everybody hated those girls.

She hurried along the street toward her home. She didn't bother announcing her arrival, because for the last year her mother had taken to her bedroom and had remained there unresponsive.

Like everyone else in town, the Georges family had fled before the German advance and had straggled back only after countless Stukas had screamed over their heads and Panzers had rumbled by and an endless procession of grey trucks full of double rows of soldiers had over-run them. Pushing open her broken front door, Madame Georges had discovered that her silverware had been stolen by local thieves. All Henri Paul-Louis's medicines had, too, and every scrap of food in the house. These final insults had seemed a small thing to Adele compared to the hardships they'd endured during the weeks they'd spent wandering the countryside, including having to abandon the family's touring car, but they had broken Madame Georges' spirit. She slept her days away and in the evenings she wrote letters to ever more distant relatives, informing them that the Georges family of Rouen was husbandless and starving and needed immediate assistance. So far there'd been no replies.

Adele closed the back door. She climbed up the stairs, walked as silently as she could past her mother's closed door and sprawled across her bed.

A shaft of sunlight pierced her dormer window and fell on a picture of a boy sitting on a grey-dappled rocking horse. He was dressed in some kind of shiny blue material – perhaps it was meant to be silk. He was staring over his shoulder at Adele. He'd been staring at her just like that for as long as she could remember. She didn't particularly like that picture. He seemed too old to be on a rocking horse for one thing. Once she'd taken it down and put it in the back of her wardrobe but her mother had hung it up again.

Soon Bibi and Jean would be home from school. It would be time to try to scrounge something up for supper. This duty had fallen on her shoulders. Since the family's return from the great exodus, all domestic duties had fallen on her shoulders.

For some annoying reason Adele couldn't get the young German clerk out of her mind. She knew why. He might as well have reached out and touched her with a live wire of electricity.

All he did was smile.

Who was he, anyway? Who were any of them? They were just Huns, as scary and foreign as a herd of rhinoceros, always bleating on the radio about the glorious New European Order, unknowable creatures puffed up in their various uniforms and marching past the towering spires of Notre Dame cathedral and through the narrow cobblestone streets with their brass bands blaring and their flags flying, the city's fine old buildings suddenly smothered in black and red and white.

And this young man had smiled at her and it had hurt her heart.

It wasn't as if boys her own age and even men didn't pay her any attention. They did. More than she wanted sometimes but she'd never felt like she was being electrocuted before.

The house remained silent. Silence wherever she looked, in everything she saw. It rang through the house like a great lonely bell. Adele closed her eyes. Every day for a year now the front door was going to open. Every day Henri Paul-Louis was going to return home.

She began to bite at her ruined fingernails. She rolled over on her side. She stared at the rocking-horse boy. He stared back.

Adele tried to remember the young German's face. Dark eyes. Hair shaved down to his skull, possibly dark, too. Most certainly dark, because his arching eyebrows were dark. Pale skin. Not very tall. Almost frail-looking, like some of the boys she knew who sat in coffee houses for far too long and smoked far too many cigarettes. Handsome, but it wasn't that. The electricity was in his smile, a loneliness so directly communicated that she'd recognized it instantly. And longing, a searing longing for a different situation, as if he and she were part of the same heartache.

Adele closed her eyes again, squeezed them painfully tight as if to close out any more disgusting and dangerous thoughts. When she opened them, her father was sitting on the edge of a cot where her wall used to be.

His head was down, his shoulders were sticking out of a torn and muddy uniform. In the distance other prisoners were opening packages from home. Her father had none to open. No one knew where he was.

• • •

When Adele returned to the Domestic Population Bureau of Information two weeks' later, her heart was beating too fast. She told herself that it was because she was afraid the SS officer would be sitting at the desk to the right. He wasn't. She told herself that it was because she was anticipating good news, that her father's name had finally appeared on a list. But there was no good news, no news at all. She could try again in two more weeks if she liked.

The boy was still there, though, the clerk, the Boche. He was sitting at a long desk at the back of the room busy matching documents to towers of files. He didn't look up this time.

Adele felt both relieved and disappointed. She wanted to see his face again, have him smile, test herself. She was sure there would be no effect this time. She had something to prove to herself and to her missing father, perhaps even to God.

She thanked the officer who was sitting in front of her, another new man. They must switch them all the time, she thought, and left. Less than a block away she felt a brisk tap on her shoulder.

"Hello," the young clerk said, "do you have this moment?"

Adele was surprised not so much by his sudden appearance but by the almost overwhelming anger that welled up inside her. "I suppose I have to. Don't I? I don't have any choice. Do I?" Her voice rang through the street.

The young German was either hard of hearing or chose to ignore her tone. He came up close, as if trying to shield her from the stares of the people in the queue. He pulled out a crumpled package of cigarettes and offered her one.

Adele shook her head.

He turned a little away, struck a match and lit up a smoke. Despite his average height and the fact that she was looking at her feet, she could tell that she came up to only just past his shoulder.

"I could help, I would like very much."

His French was ridiculous. "Help what?"

"My name is Manfred Halder. I live in Dresden. This is in Germany."

Adele couldn't keep her head down any longer. She looked up at him. "You're living here now," she replied darkly.

Manfred glanced along the street and back toward the open office doors. "I have only one moment. You are searching for your father."

Adele's heart jumped at this.

"This office is not good. It is provincial. You understand? Paris has everything."

"What do you mean?"

"Paris. Everything is there. All major bureaus of information. I worked in Paris. Information is not shared. Communication is not good. We get reports that are not complete here. Old reports. No reports. It's very bad here. Do you understand?"

"I think so."

And then he smiled his sad, terrifying smile again. Adele could feel her body flinch.

"You must go to Paris."

"Where would I go?"

"Yes, I will tell you. I will write a letter. I have a friend, an officer. He will search for your father. Do you understand?"

"Yes."

"You come here tomorrow. I will give you a letter."

"What time tomorrow?"

"Yes, I will see you at the door. I will have everything ready. I very much hope you find your father."

Manfred Halder looked toward his office again and then with a quick nod hurried away. When he reached the open door, he turned back.

All the townspeople in the queue were looking in Adele's direction. She knew what was expected of her: she should put on a sour face and turn briskly away to show that she'd been forced to communicate against her will.

Manfred pinched off the lighted end of his cigarette and tucked the rest of it inside his Wehrmacht jacket. He glanced at her one more time and hurried inside.

And then Adele turned away.

Canada, 1946

Chapter Four

• • •

J enny stared at the puffy white finger and its trailing blackened fingernail for the longest time. She could see tiny splits in the skin where an
iridescent purple showed through. The smell of it was faint and familiar,
like the smell of the groundhogs that Brandy would catch on occasion, and
shake and leave stinking out in the sun.

Jenny looked toward the edge of the woods. She couldn't see the witch
anywhere. Maybe her stomach was full now. Maybe she was having an after-
dinner nap in her cave.

Jenny looked down at the finger again. She knew she had to do something. But what? Maybe she could take the finger with her and then when her
family found her hiding under the bridge she could prove how horrible
Madeleine had been. Madeleine had been so horrible that she'd had to risk
being eaten by a witch. That's how much Madeleine's teasing had hurt her.

The more Jenny stared down at the swollen finger, the more it seemed
to pulse with some kind of ominous magical power. It hushed all the sounds
in the world, it stopped the sound of her own breathing.

Witches could smell children from a long way away. Jenny knew this.
Her heart was beginning to race again.

A tall dusty weed stood beside her, its broad leaves pierced through
with a myriad of tiny holes She plucked off two leaves, rolled the finger into
them, stuffed everything into her dress pocket and, ducking through a hole
in the wire fence, began to run. The farther she travelled into Mr. Timmon's

oats the safer she felt but she didn't stop running until she'd reached the embankment on the other side.

She climbed up to the edge of the road. The dust there felt deep and soft as powder on her stinging feet. It felt warm and comforting. She hurried along, trailing a little dust cloud behind her.

By the time Jenny reached the wooden trestle bridge, she'd developed an alternative plan. There was something so profoundly bad in her pocket, something so beyond any words of explanation she might manage to get out of her mouth that it would make her bad, too. Just the sight of it would sicken her mother. It would sicken everyone but Madeleine.

After tiptoeing up the thick scorched planks to the bridge's highest point and crouching by the rusty iron railing, she settled down to wait for a passing train. It could come from either direction, it really didn't matter. Madeleine dropped things like stones and old school books off the bridge into open freight cars all the time. That's what Jenny would do with the rolled-up finger. And the train would carry this bad thing away. And no one would hate her.

Jenny waited. It seemed to be taking a long time for a train to come by. The smell of tar from the planks on the bridge filled her nose and made her stomach feel sick. The sun danced everywhere and dazzled everything.

After what seemed a long time, she noticed a plume of dust coming along the road from the other direction. She wasn't sure whether to run and hide in the shadows under the bridge or stay where she was and pretend she wasn't doing anything of any importance. Maybe whoever was coming along would wave at her and drive by. But it was too late. She recognized her father's battered yellow truck. She knew he'd already seen her.

Jenny stood up and waited for her father to close the distance. The truck rattled up on the bridge and came to a stop. Her father's face was speckled with flakes of silvery straw and looked sweaty and hot. His large tanned arm rested on the edge of the rolled-down window.

"What are you doing back here?" he asked.

Without a word and contrary to her plan and against her very best judgment, she pulled the bunched-up leaves out of her pocket and held them out.

Her father's tired eyes went from her face to the leaves, now partially unfurling in her hands, and back to her face again. "What have you got there, Jen?" he asked, pushing open the door and getting out, which was an amazing thing because normally he would have stayed in the cab. Jenny took it as a sign that her father somehow knew that a shadow was falling.

She remained silent.

Her father parted the leaves. The finger, just as milky-white as before and emitting its faint, frightening smell, rolled a little inside the cup of leaves. She could hear her father's breath come to a stop.

Jenny found her voice.

"There's a w-w-witch in our w-w-woods," she said.

FRANCE, 1941

CHAPTER FIVE

• • •

A dele waited under the trees in the small park across from her old school for Simone Ducharme. Unlike Adele's situation, Simone's family remained well-to-do, so she could afford to stay in school.

Adele was beginning to feel a small wave of nostalgia for her lost scholastic life by the time Simone came out carrying an armful of books. It lasted only a moment, though, for she had much more important business on her mind.

"Lend me some money?" she said, falling into step with her friend and taking a few books to lighten her load. Simone always carried home more books from school than anyone else. They'd been best friends since the age of six. By the time they were twelve, Simone could see over Adele's head but Adele, despite her small size, was the superior athlete. Simone, among all of her other achievements, was the most uncoordinated girl in the school.

"All right," Simone replied. She didn't ask why. That was part of their secret code. All their lives people had been interrogating them: the nuns at school, priests at confession, the other girls, and in Simone's case a mother who had nothing better to do with her time than attempt to know every detail of the private lives of her seven children.

"I have to go to Paris," Adele added.

Any information had to be voluntarily offered between the two of them, which made having a conversation difficult but kept them intensely interested in each other. They walked along together in their usual comfortable silence. When they reached the iron gate in front of the Ducharme house,

Adele further added, "A German clerk has given me the name of an officer in Paris who might have some information about my father."

Simone turned to look at Adele, her eyes instantly quizzical and on guard behind their shiny plates of glass. "What German clerk?"

Simone had broken the code.

At first Adele thought she wouldn't respond, and then she knew she would, surprised to realize that this was what she'd had in mind all along, to ask to borrow money, yes, but also to tell Simone about Manfred Halder. She could count on Simone to be appropriately horrified. Simone was always appropriately horrified about everything. But why would she think, even for one moment, that she might need some bulwark against Manfred Halder?

"He's just this stupid clerk," she said.

"How did you meet him?" Simone was really breaking the rules now.

"He met me. He came out on the street. I couldn't do anything about it. But he wants to help me."

"Why?"

"I don't know."

"I do. Wake up!" Simone's angular face looked fierce and full of virtue.

Adele tried to look fierce, too. "There's no question of that," she said.

Avoiding Madame Ducharme, the two girls snuck up the back stairs to Simone's bedroom. Simone took down a carved wooden box from inside a mahogany armoire, placed it on her canopied bed and counted out enough money for three nights' lodging in Paris, or as close as they could estimate. Adele thought she had enough money hidden in her dresser drawer at home for the train fare and for food.

Simone knew that Adele's mother was in a fragile condition, at least that's how her own mother expressed it, so she didn't question Adele's need to keep her trip to Paris a secret. They made a plan. Simone would drop in on Madame Georges to ask if Adele could stay with her for a few days. Because Madame Georges had always been impressed by the Ducharme's money, and in her current penurious situation would be even more anxious to keep the lines of communication open, she'd be sure to come out of her bedroom and agree, just as long as Old Raymond took care of Bibi and Jean. And Adele would talk Old Raymond into walking across town to the factory where she worked to tell her foreman that she was sick and must stay in bed for a few days. Given any chance of finding his beloved Dr. Georges, Old Raymond could be talked into most anything.

René was a more serious problem. He'd found work in a scrapyard and lived apart from the family, but he continued to come around to the house. All she could do was pray that he'd stay away for now, at least until she could tell him the glorious news, that despite the risks she'd taken she'd found out that their father was alive.

"I couldn't stand it if my father was missing for a year." Lately Simone had been keeping the long velvet drapes on her two windows drawn, no matter how many times her mother opened them. Now she was poised like a tremulous deer in the middle of the large shadowy room. "Do you think there'll be a price to pay?"

Simone's father owned the largest tool and die shop in the district, and if he'd been wealthy before the Germans occupied the city he was even more wealthy now – up to his neck in German contracts, people were saying.

"For what?"

"For dealing with the Germans."

Adele was well aware of what was being said about Monsieur Ducharme's growing financial health, but what was the similarity with her situation? How could Simone compare the two?

"Whatever the price, I'm willing to pay it," Adele said. And she would, any sacrifice at all for her father. She expected to feel brave and proud, a kind of exhilarating rush in the blood, but all she felt was a sense of foreboding.

• • •

It was raining hard when Adele jumped the queue and stuck her head inside the open doorway. Manfred, working at the back of the room, saw her almost immediately. He whispered something to a fellow clerk and hurried toward the door.

"Come this way," he said, running down the steps. He waited until Adele had caught up and then he ducked under her umbrella. She had to lift it a foot higher to accommodate him.

They began to walk down the cobbled street together. Manfred lit a cigarette. Water splashed noisily down drainpipes and ran off the edge of the umbrella. Manfred's one shoulder was getting soaked. He turned and smiled at her.

"Have you got the papers?" Adele asked sharply, averting her eyes.

Manfred pulled out an envelope from inside his jacket. "I have drawn you a map of Paris."

Such a German, Adele thought.

"You will go to see Lieutenant Max Oberg. Show him my letter. He is a kind man. He will do everything to locate your father. I have given you the name of Madame Germaine Bouchard. Please stay there. I know you will be safe there."

Adele took the envelope and tucked it inside her coat.

"Good luck," Manfred said.

Adele didn't reply.

They'd come to a stop under a streaming awning. Adele kept her eyes fixed on her wet shoes as if they were the most amazing sight in the world. Rain clattered everywhere. She could smell his cigarette smoke.

"I would like to apologize," Manfred said.

Adele looked up at him. His face seemed even paler than usual, his dark eyes uncertain. He turned away and walked quickly through the rain.

CANADA, 1946

CHAPTER SIX

• • •

As Chief of Police Jack Cullen drove along the road, a fine dust began to cover his windshield and collect on his windshield wiper blades. He turned on the wipers. Only one worked, the one on the passenger side.

"Goddamn it to hell," Jack muttered to himself, trying to peer through the dust. The town council was out to get him and, in particular, the mayor. The one police car the town owned, the one he was currently driving, was old, and he was old, too. The mayor and council were waiting for both of them to fall apart.

Jack allowed himself a tight smile. The car might be at the wreckers by the end of the year, but he wouldn't be. He turned into Clarence Broome's lane and raced up to the house like a minor dust storm. The car came to a halt and Jack, all six foot three of him, six foot five in the black regulation boots he never failed to polish to a high shine every working day of his life, stepped out.

It was close to a hundred degrees but it didn't make any difference. Grey face as tough as a side of old beef, silver hair buzzed into a brush cut, in full uniform, blue shirt, necktie, jacket and pants, he reached back into the car and put his cap on his head at a snappy angle.

A wiry-looking farmer came down the steps of his side porch. "Hello, Chief. Clarence Broome," he said, walking across the yard.

"Where's it at?" Jack replied.

"In the drive shed. Wife wouldn't have it in the house."

Jack looked toward the porch.

A woman and two girls were watching him through a screen door. The woman opened the door. "Good afternoon, Chief," she called out, and though she tried a welcoming smile her face looked strained. The smaller of the two girls followed her out on to the porch and clung to her dress. The older one hung back in the shadow of the kitchen.

Jack touched the brim of his cap but didn't return the salutation. "Show me," he said to Clarence.

The finger was under an oil-stained rag on a workbench in the drive shed. When Jack saw the rag with the little bump under it, it was all he could do not to break out in a cock-eyed grin. Clarence Broome, out of some sense of decorum, had covered it up as if it were a corpse. It told Jack something important about the man in front of him, though. It told him, if a crime had been committed, this squeamish fellow hadn't likely done it. But then you could never be absolutely sure.

Jack picked up a corner of the rag and pulled it aside. A detached finger, luminously white, lay there in front of him. He pressed down on it, testing its sponginess, its condition of decay. The finger curled a little into itself as if he'd just touched a caterpillar.

"Anybody lose a finger around here, Mr. Broome?"

"Not that I know of."

"Somebody's hired hand, maybe?"

"Hired hand?" Clarence wasn't sure whether the chief was making a joke. "No. I would have heard, for sure."

"People lose fingers in machinery all the time, don't they?"

"Sometimes."

"Is there a cemetery close by?"

"Behind the stone church, but that's a good four miles away."

"Anybody buried there lately?"

"Old Mrs. Waggson. In the spring. She was ninety-four."

Jack picked up the coal-black nail. The finger spun below on its sinewy string. He held the fingernail close up, examining its shape and its size.

"I didn't have the heart to look at it much," Clarence said. "Maybe it's a tramp's finger. We're close to the railroad here. Or maybe one of those Europeans."

"The DP camp, you mean?"

"It's just a couple of miles down the tracks."

"I wonder if there are any displaced women out there," Jack said, but more to himself than to Clarence. He went back to examining the finger.

Clarence could feel his throat tightening. "Could that be a woman's?"

"Maybe."

Clarence stared at the disgusting thing. He wished it off his farm, he wished it as far away from his family as possible, he wished it to perdition.

"I hope it's not a woman's finger," Clarence said.

FRANCE, 1941

CHAPTER SEVEN

• • •

Adele had never seen such a tall man in all her life. When Lieutenant Max Oberg stood up to receive her, his sandy hair brushed the ceiling of his windowless office, and when he sat down after reading Manfred's introductory note, he seemed to do so in stages. He had a long face the shape of a prow of a ship, and his eyes were small and set close together, which gave him a kind of perpetually perplexed look. Anyway, he seemed perplexed now. He put the note aside.

"Is Manfred your friend?"

"No." Adele felt a sudden hot glow in her cheeks. "He just knows my situation. He wants to help."

Lieutenant Oberg nodded. "Yes, that would be our Manfred all right." He fell silent, looking at the other papers Manfred had placed in the envelope, shuffling through them with his large freckled hands.

Adele studied him. He looked like a kind man, as Manfred had said.

"He has set me a very difficult task. No one knows just how complete our lists are, but my guess would be that we have the names of only one out of a hundred of your soldiers, of which there are a million and a half being held in Germany."

Adele kept her eyes on Lieutenant Oberg and clung to a diminishing hope.

"Why this slowness in processing, I have no idea. Perhaps our officials are slow because it doesn't really matter. Soon all these soldiers will be set free. And your father," he glanced down at the papers again and said in his almost perfect French, "Doctor Henri Paul-Louis Georges, among them."

He looked up at her and smiled. A small, careful smile for such a tall man. He pressed a button on the top of his desk and almost immediately a woman in a grey uniform came in.

"We'll check our records now, if you can wait." He handed the papers to the woman and gave her a brief instruction. She nodded and went out the door. "I will also telegraph a few people back in Germany. Perhaps someone is sitting on a complete list. Who knows? I will inform Manfred immediately, if such is the case."

"Thank you so much, Lieutenant Oberg," Adele said.

Oberg nodded. "Perhaps it is deliberate."

"What is?"

"This use of psychology. I can't believe that they're so slow because of inefficient organization. They must see an advantage in sustaining uncertainty here in France. After all, it has been over a year."

"Who are 'they'?"

The lieutenant looked a little surprised.

"You said 'they'," Adele added quietly.

"We. I meant to say we, of course. From the very beginning, the Party has employed psychology in the most up-to-date manner."

Oberg shifted in his chair, picked up his pen. He tapped it against the desk and smiled at Adele again, a less careful smile this time. "I can see why you and Manfred are friends."

Adele had worn her best suit and the blue shoes that matched, even though they pinched her feet. They were pinching her feet now.

"Did Manfred tell you that he'd shot himself?"

"No."

"Only slightly but it was enough to get him out of active duty."

The phone rang. Oberg picked it up, nodded, put it back down. "The name Georges appears only once in our lists, Pierre Jean Georges, Infantryman, Third French Army, captured at Verdun."

Adele shook her head. Her father wasn't at Verdun, and anyway if he'd wanted to hide his identity why would he give the Germans his correct surname? She felt suddenly hopeless. The small windowless room trembled.

"I will wire an inquiry to my contacts in Germany."

Adele nodded and whispered a thank you.

"This is all I can do," Max Oberg said.

The interview was over.

• • •

It was the lack of motion and sound that Adele had noticed when she'd first arrived that morning. Now, suitcase in hand, she noticed it again. Rows of flags emblazoned with swastikas waved gently from grand buildings as far as she could see but only a few vehicles were making their way along the Champs-Élysées. No bustling crowds, no shouts, no displays of Parisian temperament.

Adele looked at her watch. A train left for Rouen at 2:20 p.m. daily. Lieutenant Oberg had kept her waiting for some time. It was too late now.

Adele sat down on a bench in a small park. After a while, she took Manfred's map out of her purse. For some reason the sight of his straight pencil lines, his crisply drawn arrows, his street notations gave her a feeling of comfort. But her father remained lost. He remained a fleeting ghost.

St. Augustine Street turned out to be only a few blocks away, and Madame Bouchard's house seemed decent enough. Adele climbed the steps and knocked on the door. A middle-aged woman peered out. Adele could hear German voices chatting somewhere in the deeper recesses of the house.

"Madame Bouchard?"

The woman nodded. A pair of sharp eyes studied her.

"I am looking for a room for the night."

"Are your papers in order?"

Adele passed her identity papers through the open door.

Madame Bouchard glanced at them. "So you are from Rouen."

"I've come to Paris looking for records pertaining to my father. He's a prisoner of war. A Corporal Manfred Halder recommended your *pension*. I believe he stayed here."

Madame Bouchard's eyes seemed to grow even sharper. She moved aside to allow Adele into a gleaming front hallway. Short and round and wearing a voluminous black dress, she glanced back in the direction of the German voices. "I remember him. The only one with a soul."

Madame Bouchard led Adele up a series of steep stairs, puffing and wheezing all the way. The room Adele had engaged proved to be on the top floor and was very small and very warm and also very expensive, despite Manfred having been the only one with a soul. Madame Bouchard handed her a key, told her not to disturb the Germans and, with the same amount of puffing and sighing, began her descent.

Adele stood inside the doorway and stared at the iron bed. She wondered if Manfred had slept there. The emptiness of the bed seemed somehow the perfect evidence that he had. If that was the case, then she couldn't use it.

She sat down on the one chair in the room. She could see his body stretched out before her, his dark hair, his eyes closed, hear the soft sound of his breathing. His hair was still wet from the rain.

She sat there for a long time, until the light began to fade outside the tiny window.

• • •

A week later at just past six o'clock in the morning, Adele was leaving work. She crossed the narrow footbridge that spanned the factory's raceway. The air was cool and a soft mist was rising up off the water. Manfred Halder, dressed in his Wehrmacht uniform, was standing on the other side of the road.

Adele slowed down. The rest of the women coming off the night shift pushed past her. She came to a stop and tried to control her panic. These women couldn't possibly see her meet a soldier. Military trousers half-seamed would be pulled away from her machine. She'd be bumped into, horrible notes would be stuffed into her pockets, terrible words whispered in her ears, excrement smeared on her chair. She'd seen all this happen to another girl, plump and red-faced and frightened.

Adele hurried off the end of the bridge and turned down a cinder path that led along the bank of the raceway. She came to the corner of the factory. She could see the path continuing on toward three abandoned warehouses.

Surely he'd know enough not to follow her. Surely he'd have at least some brains in his head.

She held her breath and turned around. The last few women were straggling across the bridge and none of them were looking her way. There was no one else in sight.

She kept walking along the cinder path. She didn't know what else to do. Manfred had said, "I would like to apologize." What could be more useless, more insulting, more obscene than to apologize for a slaughter, for a blood-soaked atrocity?

Adele approached the first warehouse. It looked medieval, its bricks chipped and blackened with layers of coal smoke, its roof swaying and covered in moss. She walked behind it and stopped. She could see where the raceway rejoined the river, splashing a little in its eagerness, dancing in the early morning light.

"Hello," Manfred said. He was standing some ways off, almost lost in the sun and waist high in weeds. He stepped out on to the path. His pants and boots were soaked from the dew that was sparkling everywhere. "Why do you run away?"

"How do you know where I work?"

"I looked up in your file."

"Leave me alone!" Adele turned to walk back the way she'd come and then realized she couldn't. What if he followed her? She turned to look at him again. She had to put her hand up to shade her eyes.

"I think," Manfred said, "if you had received good news in Paris, you would have told me. I am sorry."

"I don't care if you're sorry."

"You are a very rude girl."

"I apologize if I hurt your feelings. You march into our country, you kill everyone, but I shouldn't be rude." Adele could feel her chin beginning to quiver.

"I thought to buy you breakfast," Manfred persisted, "I know a café."

"I can't be seen with you."

"It is dangerous?"

"It is disgusting!" She expected him to swear at her and walk away, perhaps even strike her across the face. She wanted him to strike her across the face, that was exactly what she wanted him to do.

Instead, he smiled. "You remind me of Ingrid when she is difficult."

"Who is Ingrid?"

"She is my niece. She is eight years old."

Adele could feel her face go red. "Lieutenant Oberg said you shot yourself."

"Did he?"

"Was it an accident or did you do it on purpose so you wouldn't have to fight? If you shot yourself on purpose that makes you a coward, doesn't it? And if it is against your principles to fight you should say so and refuse to fight, even if that means you'll go to prison."

"I was not wounded badly," Manfred replied, somewhat beside the point. "I thought to make a very loud but wordless protest. In my barracks, every voice declares that what we do is just. Our generation will redeem the past. But I only hear madness in this. I do not want to be part of this."

But you are a part of it, Adele thought, you are.

"You cannot say you are against war. There is no such thing as a conscientious objector in my country, only the grave for such people. You do not know this?"

And now he was looking at her with such intensity, such a lost loneliness, that Adele felt almost overwhelmed. She had to turn away. "I would have told you what happened in Paris soon enough. I have to visit your office to see if Lieutenant Oberg has sent any new information, don't I?" Then she said, "Why are you interested in me?"

The question was out of her mouth before she even knew it was in her head, like a small bird flying before a storm. She had a quick vision of an outraged Simone Ducharme, her eyes widening behind her round glasses.

"Because I saw you that first time."

Adele could hear him walking up behind her, his boots crunching down on the cinders.

"What first time?"

"When you were interrogated by the SS officer. You have to help me with this phrase. How do you say '"such a large asshole' in French?"

"Just like you said it."

"I thought you were very brave. I admired your bravery very much. And I thought you were really, very, extremely pretty."

In the not-too-distant past several boys had told Adele that she was pretty, and she'd supposed she was in some sort of way with her tangle of black hair going every which way and her large dark eyes, but all it had seemed to mean was that these same boys were angling to put their sloppy mouths all over her face and wiggle their hands up inside her blouse until she had to shout out as loudly as she could right in their ears, "Stop it!"

"There are lots of girls who will let you buy them breakfast. Or even just cigarettes and candy. And then let you do whatever dirty thing you want. Why don't you find one of them?"

"Because they are not you." Manfred reached out and touched her hand. "I have no one to talk to. Not like this."

"Leave me alone." Adele pulled her hand back. She walked over to the scarred brick wall. She could feel Manfred watching her. She touched the brick, and the soot of generations blackened her fingers.

"I am not your friend," she said.

Adele knew that all she had to do now was walk away and whatever this was, at least it would be over. Nothing would have happened. "I have one best friend I can tell everything to," she said, and immediately thought to herself, But not this, not this.

"You are very fortunate."

Adele stared at the brick. "Where do you live?"

"In a house on Ducrot Street. There are many of us. We have cooks and housekeepers."

"I live with my mother and my two younger brothers."

"I know."

"I am only sixteen."

"I am nineteen."

Adele turned toward him.

As she did, Manfred put his hands in his pockets, perhaps a gesture to quiet her fears. "I am an only son, an only child. When I lived with my parents in Dresden, I was very happy. But it is not good there now. My mother is

Polish and she is very afraid. She hears news about Poland from our relatives there and she has to remain silent. My father has to remain silent, too. Everyone is afraid."

"I can't have anything to do with a German soldier," Adele said, "even a harmless one."

Manfred smiled softly. "Yes." And he kept staring at her with his dark deep eyes. "I should go back now before I am missed."

"You should."

"I could come and see you tonight."

"No."

"I have no one to talk to."

"Why is that my problem? I can't have anything to do with you."

"There is a park near Ducrot Street, by the river. Do you know this place? What if I was to go there tonight? What if I was to sit on a bench there?"

"You'd still be lonely."

"What time do you start work?"

"I don't know."

"I'll be there at eight. I'll be there every night at eight."

Manfred began to walk back into the weeds. He waded toward a steep embankment and a road beyond. He made a wake in the dew. Iridescent insects whirled up in front of him. The early morning sun poured gold over everything.

CANADA, 1946

CHAPTER EIGHT

• • •

Jack rolled the finger into the farmer's oily rag and tucked it inside the breast pocket of his police jacket as casually as if he'd just purchased a five-cent cigar. "Do you think you could keep this to yourself for a day or two?"

"I'd like to forget it altogether," Clarence replied. "It doesn't have anything to do with us."

A large yellow dog, old and mangy, was stretched out in the doorway of the drive shed. He lifted up his head and watched the two men.

"It was on your property," Jack said.

"On the line between our place and Alf Timmon's to be exact, Chief."

"Whose side of the line?"

Clarence already knew it was on his side, but according to Jenny only by a yardstick or so. "It could have come from anywhere."

"Wife, two daughters and a son. Is that what you said?"

"That's right."

"How old is your son?" Jack could see a wave of anger colour Clarence's tanned face, which was just what he wanted.

"Why?"

"Just asking."

"Seventeen."

Jack nodded. He moved toward the open doorway, stepped around the dog and walked out into the bright sunlight.

Clarence, feeling more desperate than he wanted to, followed him.

"Mr. Broome," Jack said, "what I've learned about police work is this, you should always look for the most obvious solution. Do you know where I picked that up?"

"No."

"Sherlock Holmes." Jack's tough face broke into a grin. "This is what I think. Someone had a break-down. Maybe a farm wagon, maybe a car. Something. They jacked it up, the jack slipped, and bang. Pinched off a finger."

"That could be it, all right," Clarence replied, looking relieved. "The side road's just one field over."

"Because of the pain, shock," Jack went on, "they forgot about the damn thing. Or couldn't find it. I'm going to stop in at the hospital. I'm betting that a week or so ago some stranger came in to the emergency department with a bloody hand wrapped in a bloody shirt." He patted his breast pocket where the finger was bulging out. "I hope I have your word that no one here will say anything about this for now."

"You've got my word, Chief," Clarence said.

His wife and the younger girl were still standing on the side porch. Jack's grey eyes, cold now, looked them over. He could see the other girl lurking in the kitchen. "How old's your older daughter?"

"Madeleine? She's thirteen."

She'll be blabbing to her friends within the hour, Jack thought to himself. He walked to the battered cruiser and opened the door with a hand criss-crossed with a multitude of old battle scars. "I'll let you know how I make out in a day or two."

"Thanks for coming out, Chief," Clarence said.

• • •

The finger lay on a white saucer beside the sink in Jack's kitchen. The house was silent, just the far-away ticking of the mantle clock in the den. His wife was not there, which simplified things. She wouldn't have appreciated what Jack was up to – she wouldn't have understood it.

He'd thought of dropping in at the hospital on the way back, though not to inquire about some stranger's injured hand – he already knew the answer to that one – but to look in on his wife. Instead he'd driven by, staring resolutely down the street, not even looking at the place. For one thing, he could hardly visit with a detached finger in his pocket, though he supposed he could easily have locked it in the glove compartment. It was more that he wanted to sustain his buoyant mood. For the first time in a long while, he could feel the blood pumping through his veins.

Jack turned the water on, just enough so there was a steady dripping in the sink. He wetted an old toothbrush and began to clean off the knuckle end of the finger. The faint sweetish smell of carrion wafted up into his nostrils. That was the other reason for not going into the hospital. Ruth was all eyes now, the familiar plump flesh that used to define her face gone, her body withering away except for her lower torso. That's where the cancer was, a growing mass of useless bone-white cells. The smell of death was in her room.

Jack winced a little. He'd make sure to visit her that evening, just as he'd been visiting her faithfully every evening for over a month, but he couldn't do it that afternoon. He just couldn't.

Bits of dirt and black caked-on blood began to wash away. He held the bone end up into the sunlight and examined it closely. There were several score marks on its shiny surface, as if someone had been working away trying to detach it with a tiny chisel. This was what he'd suspected all along. The splits in the skin where the purple flesh showed through hadn't been made by pecks from the hen, they were too old-looking, and they weren't the result of decay, either. They were tiny bite marks. The finger had been gnawed off the hand it had been attached to, either by mice or a wayward rat. That's what had set his pulse racing the moment he'd seen it. Either by homicide or by accident, there was a very dead body out there somewhere.

Was it male or female? Jack studied the nail and the puffy white flesh for some time. Even cleaned up a little, he couldn't tell. Not a scrap of nail polish. But then, not one hair, either. It was too far gone.

Jack wrapped it up in waxed paper and put it in the refrigerator. Ruth had replaced the old icebox just after the close of the war. She'd done it on her own in a fit of compensation for her grief, Jack had assumed. The new refrigerator had a freezer compartment, too, but he wasn't sure about freezing the finger, at least not yet.

He washed his hands and wandered back toward the den. He'd avoided that room for about the last four years, but now that he was alone in the house he'd often find himself in there. Ruth had rearranged it about a month after receiving the telegram. Regret to inform you. What? That your twenty-seven-year-old son, flesh of your flesh, heart of your heart, had died somewhere near a place called Dieppe.

Jack had looked it up on a map. Dead. Witnessed by a fellow soldier to be dead. Buried hurriedly during a full-scale retreat and presumably still interred there somewhere, lying peacefully by the French seaside. That's what Ruth liked to think. Jack knew better. Food for the gulls a long time ago, for a myriad of insects and scuttling creatures.

Jack stood in the doorway and contemplated the arrangement of photographs. Kyle in his Royal Hamilton Light Infantry uniform, Kyle on parade, Kyle on leave with his buddies in England. Kyle as a two-year-old holding on to a tasselled cushion in a photographer's studio. At four looking all alone and tiny on an eight-seater toboggan. A variety of school pictures. Lots of pictures of Ruth with Kyle. Two tattered ribbons that Ruth had resurrected, a blue for second, a white for third. Jack didn't even know what they were for.

There were no photographs of Kyle with Jack on display, though Jack thought there must be at least a few somewhere. Jack and Kyle had not been close, and he knew the absence of pictures was meant by Ruth as a silent rebuke, a rebuke that had lasted four years.

He had acknowledged it without a word in his own defence. He didn't even know what his defence might be.

FRANCE, 1941

CHAPTER NINE

• • •

After Adele returned home from work, she lay on her bed and tried to will herself to sleep, but she couldn't.

Manfred Halder. When she whispered those words and conjured up a picture of him standing in the glare of the sun, his pensive face, the dew sparkling like diamonds all around him, everything now more vivid in her mind than when it was actually happening, what she felt most was a paralyzing fear. What would happen to her if they became friends, if they shared secrets, if they were seen together?

She drew up her knees. Unthinkable things.

There was a temptation, too, though, she had to admit this, and almost because of the danger. To be attracted to a German felt perverse and strange – it shortened her breath.

What was there to hope for in her life? Nothing.

Of course this wasn't true. There was hope for her father, more than hope, an absolute certainty that he was alive and that he would be returning to her soon. She could almost see him limping up the street. The neighbours would stream out of their houses to greet him. Adele would fly out the door.

She finally fell into a fitful sleep. She was roused four hours later by the shrill sounds of Bibi and Jean bursting into the house from school.

This was meat day. Two days a week the shops were supposed to have meat and you could use tickets to purchase the allowable ration, which had been reduced by the local commandant to enough for only one meal, possibly two, if you ate a translucent portion. With some luck, Old Raymond might have managed two vile-looking blueish sausages with the family's five tickets, or a piece of blotchy green beef she would have to boil and boil.

When Adele reached the kitchen, the racket was even louder than usual. Short and pudgy Bibi was standing on top of the table, and Jean, lankier and even more excitable than his younger brother, had attached himself to Old Raymond's neck and was hanging down his back.

"Hurrah, hurrah!" they both cried. "Raymond has got a chicken!"

Old Raymond, with Jean still attached, held up a scrawny old hen.

"My God, it's beautiful." Adele touched its feathers. "How did you manage this?"

Old Raymond's rheumy eyes lit up. "Ask me no questions," he said, and Jean and Bibi chimed in, "I'll tell you no lies!"

Adele knew the answer anyway: purchased on the black market.

Old Raymond stretched the chicken out on the counter so everyone could have a turn squeezing its legs and poking its feathery breast. Having secured the bird, and since meat tickets were good only for the day, he'd also traded the family's tickets for a bag of macaroni, five eggs and a piece of cheese. These transactions were illegal, as well.

Adele kissed him on his soft velvety cheeks. "You are a genius," she said.

"Thank you, Madame Downstairs," Old Raymond replied.

Jean and Bibi hooted to hear Adele called such a funny name. Old Raymond had taken to calling their absentee mother Madame Upstairs. Out of sheer exuberance, Jean seized Bibi in a headlock. Bibi started to kick and scream. Adele put some water on the stove and tried to ignore them. Old Raymond retreated out the back door toward the small stone cottage in the centre of the Georges' gardens. He'd occupied it since before Adele could remember. He'd take a nap there now, as was his custom. It was up to Adele to prepare the meal.

• • •

Adele stood in her room and stared at her unmade bed. Everyone had been fed, including Madame Upstairs, all the pots and plates had been washed and put away, and she still had time to take a nap before going off to work. In fact, she had two hours.

Adele walked around the room, trailing her hand along the wall. She stopped in front of the mirror over her dresser and studied her face. Some unknown girl, rash and stupid, was staring back at her.

She rearranged the clothes in her drawers. She took her sweaters out, refolded them and put them back again.

She stared at the boy sitting on his rocking horse. She came up so close to him that his face seemed as large as a normal face and blurred in her eyes. She could feel his breath on her skin. She knew she couldn't help herself.

Five minutes later Adele was hurrying through the back garden and was about to reach the wooden gate when she heard Jean's voice call out, "Where are you going?"

"To work," she answered, looking around, trying to see him.

For reasons known only to himself, he'd shinnied to the top of a tall slender pole that at one time had supported a birdhouse. Clinging there with his hair dishevelled and bathed in red from the setting sun, he seemed to Adele like a sprite from the underworld. "It's not time yet," he said.

"They're calling everybody in early."

Adele pushed open the gate and hurried away. The sun had disappeared and the clouds were turning deep mauve by the time she reached the park off Ducrot Street. The air felt surprisingly cool blowing off the river. It smelled fishy and brackish. Some children were playing on swings down the hill from where she stood. Dusk was falling quickly – all she could see was their dark shapes flying.

Adele walked to the secluded end of the park. Manfred was nowhere in sight. She sat down on a bench under a tree. She told herself she wouldn't wait very long. She'd count up to a hundred and then she'd leave. She started to count.

She was back behind the warehouse again. The early morning sun was shining down. She could feel its heat on her arms and on her face. She leaned close to Manfred Halder. She could smell his smoky smell. "I can't be with you. Stay away from me," she whispered.

When Adele came out of her daydream, Manfred was standing on the stone wall that ran along the edge of the river. It was even darker than before. His back was toward her and he was looking out across the water.

Adele remained sitting under her tree. She could see the running lights of boats bobbing up and down on the far side of the river. Manfred seemed to be moving a little, too, drifting along, but perhaps it was only the glint of the waves behind him that gave that illusion. She didn't know what to do.

"It smells fishy here," she said, coming up behind him.

Manfred turned and scooped his army cap off his shaved head. He seemed amazed. "I am so glad for me that you have come."

"I am glad for you, too," Adele said.

Manfred didn't get the joke, or didn't let on if he did. He jumped off the wall and said again, "You are here."

"I have to go to work soon."

"We can walk," Manfred said.

They walked beside the wall until Adele could once again hear the sound of the children on the swings in the dark. She turned away and walked up the hill. Manfred followed her. She turned again and headed back to the secluded end of the park.

"I have to inform you that there was no letter from Max Oberg today concerning your father," Manfred announced.

"Yes."

"I will keep watching."

"Yes."

Manfred stopped to light a cigarette. In the flare of the match, Adele watched his face.

"How do you come to speak French?"

"My major in Stuttgart University. I am a language student. First year. And then I wasn't. I was a soldier." He smiled. The match went out and it was dark again. "Your father, he was a doctor, wasn't he?"

"He still is." There was a quavering edge to Adele's voice. She hadn't meant it to be there.

"Yes, of course," Manfred replied.

Adele felt suddenly cold and lost. She began to walk toward a street lamp glowing at the edge of the park. Ducrot Street was just beyond, and a bus stop.

Manfred caught up to her. "My father is an electrician. He used to work in building houses. Now he works in making aeroplanes. He writes to tell me that they make hundreds of aeroplanes night and day. That's what he does."

To bomb and strafe and kill us, Adele thought.

"He fought in the other war. The insane asylum war. That's his name for it. Since I was little he has told me everything about his experience in the insane asylum war. He lost every friend." Manfred caught her arm. "I am afraid I will frighten you."

"How?"

Manfred took off his cap again and bent down and kissed her. His lips felt cool.

This came as a surprise to Adele because when she'd allowed herself to imagine what it might be like to be kissed by Manfred Halder, she'd felt his lips particularly warm on hers, and infinitely gentle. Instead they felt real and insistent, but almost at once this sweet, physical pressing became a source of pleasure, too. Muscular. Vital. And yes, smoky.

Adele let her mouth open a little. She felt his hand brush against her neck, touch her hair. An unfamiliar rush of blood stirred deep inside her. And now Manfred's lips were turning warm. She pushed away. "I have to go to work."

Adele hurried toward the light shining at the edge of the park. Before she reached it, she began to run.

• • •

Adele and Manfred continued to meet in the park. They walked hand in hand. They told each other everything. They kissed. Nothing more, but it proved enough to divert Adele's growing desperation about her father, enough to give her something to look forward to every day with a pounding heart.

"I think I'm going to be an artist," Adele announced one night. She and Manfred were sitting on their special bench under the tree. The air had turned cold. Adele could see her breath in the dark.

"What kind?" Manfred's breath billowed out toward her, it touched her breath.

"I haven't made up my mind yet."

"Do you draw?"

"Sometimes."

"Do you write?"

"Sometimes. I did at school. I just feel like I'm going to be an artist, that's all."

"I think you will," Manfred said.

I'll write a poem for you, Adele thought to herself, a love poem. She knew she loved him. She had to admit it to herself and she did, often, while visiting with Simone or sitting beside the rough women in the factory. I love Manfred Halder, she said secretly, silently. She wanted to tell Simone about him. She almost did, riding on a bus one day, but just as she was about to say, "Remember that German clerk?" Simone had pointed to something out the window. A tall girl was kissing her soldier boyfriend.

"Look at that." Simone had made a face. "Why doesn't she just pull down her pants and take a shit in the middle of the road."

Adele had felt numb.

When the cold weather came to stay, Manfred supplied extra food for the Georges family's pantry and coal for their heating stove. Under cover of darkness, he'd drop his secret gifts off in potato sacks at the edge of the back lane and Adele would drag them up the path past Old Raymond's cottage and down the cellar steps.

Old Raymond was becoming increasingly frail, and then he fell too ill to do anything, lying in bed in his cottage most of the time, uncommunicative and with his eyes closed. Adele knew what his trouble was. He'd been forced to wait too long for Henri Paul-Louis.

Adele was sitting in the kitchen one day watching wet snowflakes fall by the window when René walked into view through the back gate. Though it was cold outside, he was only wearing a sweater, his hands plunged inside his threadbare trousers, his long hair frosted and soaked.

Adele felt immediately nervous. She moved to the sink and filled up the kettle. "I'll make you some almost-as-good-as-coffee," she said as René pushed through the door. "I bought it from this woman. It's made out of ground-up chestnuts and lupin seeds and God knows what else. It's good, though. It'll warm you up."

René stamped a rim of slush off his shoes and sat down on a chair. His hair was plastered to his forehead, his thin silky beard was full of silvery rain drops. "I don't have a job any more."

"Oh, no." Adele sat down at the opposite end of the table.

René's eyes darted here and there as if he were half-starved and looking for food. "They took it away." He patted his pockets.

"Who did?"

René pulled out a damp-looking package and laid three cigarettes on the table to dry. "They came in trucks and took everything out of the scrapyard. Jews aren't allowed to own businesses any more. Sam's locked himself in his room. He won't come out."

Adele wondered if René was ill – he looked ill, his face had a strange flush to it. At first, she'd thought it was just from the cold but in the warmth of the kitchen it hadn't disappeared. It was all she could do not to reach out and touch his cheek to see if he had a fever.

"He won't eat. We've been leaving bits of food outside his door. Now his neighbours are stealing it." René looked up and grinned at her, but it was more like a grimace.

"That's awful." Adele knew better than to say that René should call the police, for everyone knew the police were in the Germans' pockets. "You'll have to break down his door, René, you'll have to make him eat."

Adele was about to get up and measure out the coffee when René said, "I heard something." Carefully he picked up one of his soggy cigarettes. "Someone said he saw you with a German soldier."

Adele's body froze.

René's eyes weren't darting hungrily here and there any more. He was looking straight at her.

"As if I would," Adele cried out with all the indignation she could muster. "What idiot-friend of yours told you that?"

"He was passing on a bus. It was dark. He just said this girl looked a little like you."

"The stupid fool! The nerve of him!"

René would never have understood if she'd sat there and explained to him for a hundred years how Manfred could be one of them and at the same

45

time not be one of them at all, in his soul, in his mind, in his heart. She knew she loved Manfred for who he really was. Her father would have understood this in an instant. But not René. All he would bullheadedly see was Manfred's uniform. It would set him off. God only knew in what manner it would set him off, though.

Adele stole a glance at her brother. He looked like a tramp, he was losing weight, he never talked about their father any more, refused to even mention his name. Adele wondered how much more he could stand.

"I would never do that," she said, her voice sounding to her as faint as if she were standing in another room.

"That's what I told him." René smiled at her warmly now, a brother's loving smile. "I'll find other work somewhere else." He touched her hand. "I'll keep helping out. I know it's difficult for you here."

"I'm all right," Adele said.

René nodded. He put the cigarette in his mouth and started to search in his pockets for matches.

Adele got up from the table hoping the kettle had already started to boil. She felt desperate to turn her face away.

FRANCE, 1941

CHAPTER TEN

• • •

No one in Rouen had ever experienced such a cold winter, at least that's what people were constantly saying.

The Wehrmacht were everywhere, bundled up in their greatcoats, faces swathed in scarves, their breath billowing into the crystalline air.

Soulless beasts from some ice-filled hell, they'd brought this winter with them. That's what the women at the factory were muttering, and with such a ring of certainty there could be no possible doubt about it.

The massive woman who sat next to Adele and tirelessly stitched buttons on the nightly parade of Wehrmacht pants thought Adele was shy because Adele never joined in any of their conversations. She teased her about it and called her Buttercup. The woman working on Adele's other side, all bony arms and legs, her sharp nose almost touching her sewing machine in near-sighted concentration, allowed that she was just as shy as Adele when she was Adele's age. It took a husband and five children for her to get over it.

"A man's big sausage is the best way to get over shyness," the huge woman agreed.

"Tsk tsk," the spidery woman replied.

"Big hard sausage," the huge woman repeated, smacking her lips and looking at Adele.

All the women close to them laughed. The spidery woman crossed herself. Adele continued sewing seams, trying to keep them straight. Not saying anything. Not giving anything away.

Adele and Manfred sat on the swings in the park. Even in the dark they could see the river, frozen solid, stretching out whitely. No one could remember the river ever having been completely frozen before.

Manfred tilted his face up to the sky, opened his mouth and caught a random snowflake. Adele laughed and did the same. It became a contest. They leaned far back, their mouths open, swinging back and forth. Snow began to pelt down. They lost count. Snowflakes landed in their mouths, on their eyes, on their cheeks.

Manfred caught her swing and drew her close. He took off his cap. They kissed and kissed. Manfred had snowflakes melting on his eyebrows, his eyelashes, Adele could see them. She put her hands up to his close-cropped hair. She could feel snow melting on her fingertips. She could feel Manfred's hand slip inside her coat, press coldly against her breast, cover her heart.

"No," she said, but without conviction.

His hand grew warmer there, and his fingers slipped under her bra.

"No," Adele whispered again, but there wasn't really anything she could do about it. Just stay there, lean against Manfred, kiss Manfred, and try not to think about anything.

· · ·

Adele had brought Old Raymond in from the cottage, setting up a bed close to the stove in the kitchen, but his condition had not improved. He was breathing in shallow gulps now interrupted by long staccato bouts of coughing.

She sent Jean to the hospital to fetch a doctor. A half-hour later Jean returned with one in tow. He was young and looked exhausted. His diagnosis was pleurisy, his prescription bed rest along with the consumption of great quantities of hot soup and to wait for spring. By then, the pleurisy would either be better or it would be worse.

Adele could feel her blood heating up in outrage at such a cavalier bedside manner. Her father would never have been so off-hand. "Surely there must be some medicine."

"What medicine? The Germans have taken the little we had and shipped it off to the Russian front. We take temperatures, we pat our patients' hands and advise the application of home-made compresses and soups."

Old Raymond turned his face away and stared at the wall.

That evening, much to everyone's surprise, Madame Georges descended the stairs and, instead of making a circle and ascending again, sat down beside Old Raymond's bed. "You're coughing too much," she observed.

Old Raymond nodded. His face was a brilliant red, his brow beaded in sweat.

Madame Georges got up, prepared a cool cloth and put it on his forehead.

"I've been doing that," Adele remarked, feeling defensive.

Madame Georges ignored her. "You're very sick."

Old Raymond nodded.

"Don't worry, dearest," she said.

Madame Georges took over the care of Old Raymond from that night on. She sat beside his bed and read to him. She made him tea when there was any, soup when Adele had something to make it from, and cups of boiling water the rest of the time. She laid an endless series of cooling cloths on his forehead and rubbed the inside of his wrists with her bony hands to coax better circulation. She got dressed. She brushed her hair.

At first, Jean and Bibi were confused. They stood in the hallway and stared at their resurrected mother. Then they dared to creep closer. Finally they sat on the floor beside her and leaned against the hem of her dress. Once in a while, in the middle of reading some passage or other to Old Raymond, she'd reach down and twirl her fingers absent-mindedly in their hair.

"I'm glad you're feeling better," Adele said to her mother one day.

Madame Georges was standing in the little room off the kitchen searching through some old magazines for anything she hadn't read before. She looked up and regarded Adele for a moment with her remarkably opaque eyes. Adele had always regarded her mother's eyes as slightly strange, but over the past year they'd got worse. She couldn't see into them any more – it was like looking into a mirror.

"One gets used to widowhood," her mother said. "You miss the physical comfort, of course. I'm sure you must find that, as well. Don't you?"

"What do you mean?"

Her mother smiled. It was the most terrible smile Adele had ever seen. "I know what went on," she said.

Adele couldn't reply. She couldn't find the words, nothing to express the gushing wound, the devastation she was feeling. What in God's name was her mother talking about?

All Adele could think to do was to walk away.

It had begun to snow again. It snowed all that day and into the evening. Adele made supper in a trance. No one seemed to notice. She cleaned up afterwards and then slipped unseen out the back door. She had to pick up the potato sack full of coal and two cans of bully beef that Manfred had promised to steal that night from his billet on Ducrot Street.

When she pushed open the gate, Manfred was standing there. This was not possible. He was supposed to hide the sack and leave. That was their arrangement. They met only in the park. Nowhere else. Ever.

"Hello," Manfred said, the word a puff of frost floating in the air.

"What are you doing here?"

He didn't answer.

Adele looked in a panic up and down the dark lane. Manfred tramped across the snow and held her against his great army coat. He pressed his icy face against her cheek, her hair, her neck.

"What's the matter?" Adele whispered.

"I could not stay away."

"But you have to!"

"All I can think of is you."

Adele relented a little, leaning against him. "All I can think of is you."

"I love you," Manfred said, almost sobbed, kissing with lips that felt unnaturally warm despite the frigid air.

Manfred had never said those words before. Such words. Adele felt as fluid as a sea, a warm sea rushing in. "I love you, too," she said, and instantly thought of her mad mother. "I love you," she whispered, but it sounded like a cry.

"Where can we go?" Manfred's eyes looked enormous in the dark, his lips a startling red, his beautiful face suffused with some kind of soft-glowing agony. "Where can we go?"

Adele pushed open the door that led into Old Raymond's cottage. It was as dark and cold as a cave.

Manfred began to unbutton his greatcoat. He opened it and they pressed together and began to kiss again. Adele could feel his hand moving outside her clothes, slipping inside her clothes, touching everywhere.

Although she'd successfully avoided thinking about it, she'd always known that the preceding days of kissing, embracing, touching, trembling would inevitably lead to this, and now it had. She must stop it somehow.

She could feel Manfred lift her up as if she weighed nothing at all, and then let her down again on Old Raymond's mattress. It felt like being put on a patch of ice. She'd only thrown a sweater over her shoulders for the short run out for the potato sack.

She began to shiver. She watched the dark wings of Manfred's coat open and spread above her. A giant bird. A winged god from Dresden.

He slipped out of his coat, and half-resting on top of her and half beside her, he pulled the coat over both of them. Now they were hidden from everyone. Adele closed her eyes. Soon she felt Manfred's hand again, and his hungry mouth, and now she knew with a fateful certainty that she wanted his hand, wanted his mouth. It was hopeless to fight against such feelings, hopeless to struggle against such an over-whelming, exquisite thing.

It didn't surprise her when it hurt, it just made her more aware of what he was doing, what they were both doing. She bit his ear in token reprisal, she scratched his neck.

And it didn't really hurt all that much, either, or for all that long. Manfred trembled, moaned, froze in mid-air as if he'd been transfixed by an invisible arrow, and then slowly sank down on top of her.

They lay quietly for some time. Adele began to feel a raw hurting between her legs and something trickling, warm and wet, as if they'd melted something down there in all their exertion. They'd melted together, slippery and warm.

Adele kissed Manfred's closed eyes.

"I am sorry," he said.

"Don't be," she whispered.

"Yes." Manfred raised himself on one elbow and kissed her gently all over her face. "Forgive me."

"There's nothing to forgive," Adele said, wishing that he'd just shut up about it. "Manfred, I have to go to work."

Adele asked him to try to find the cupboard that stood near the foot of the bed. She knew that there was an old quilt in there. She told him that she wanted to stay where she was until he left. When Manfred asked why, she said she just did.

Adele could hear him fumbling around in the dark. Finally he came back with the quilt. When he picked up his coat to put it back on, she drew the quilt quickly over herself so he wouldn't be able to see what he'd already felt.

Manfred crossed the room, opened the door and looked out. Past his dark shape, Adele could see tall dry stalks of flowers and a white patch of snow.

"Are you all right?" Manfred asked. She didn't answer. "We will meet tomorrow?" He sounded a little uncertain.

"Yes," Adele said.

Manfred hesitated as if he wanted to say he was sorry again, and then he went out, closing the door behind him.

Adele turned away and pressed her face against Old Raymond's mattress. She'd betrayed her dear father, betrayed one hundred thousand of her countrymen slaughtered at the hands of the Boche, betrayed the nuns at school. And René. And God. Why hadn't she stopped him?

Manfred would have stopped, if she'd just said something. He would have. But she didn't say a word, not one word.

Tears began to run down her face. A voice in her head screamed for her to hurry into the house, run up to the toilet, clean herself, wash herself, kill everything inside. It sounded like her own voice. It sounded like a girl she didn't know.

Adele curled up under the quilt. She could still feel Manfred's whiskers rubbing against her cheeks. She could feel the weight of his body on hers. She pressed her face down hard against the cold of the mattress and tried to choke off a cry.

She had let a Boche fuck her.

CANADA, 1946

CHAPTER ELEVEN

• • •

J ack stood on the steep approach, watching Clarence's seventeen-year-old son pitch hay from the floor of the barn high into the mow.

The day was airless, as hot as the one before even though the sky was hidden behind a low-lying blanket of grey. Everything felt pressed down. A storm would be a relief, Jack thought.

His pant legs and boots were smeared with mud from searching through the woods most of the day. His feet ached. He'd walked every field on the farm, the neighbouring farms, alongside the road, the railway track. Nothing.

"What's your name, son?" Jack called out.

The pitchfork arced through the shadows in the barn, a load of hay was tossed neatly to the top of the mow, the pitchfork came down to rest against the boy's slim waist. "Andrew," he called back and swiftly dug the pitchfork into the hay again.

A demon for work, Jack thought to himself, doesn't want to talk, doesn't like me looking at him, either.

Everything depended on something else, Jack knew this. If this boy in front of him, the Broomes' strong and handsome son, had killed a girlfriend, say, then he was acting suspiciously. If he was just a typical self-conscious farm boy, then he wasn't. A farm boy trying not to look suspicious, which was making him look suspicious.

Jack's own son was dead. Why was that? Because he was unfortunate enough to be in an infantry company chosen to prod the German defences along the coast of France. But why was he in the army in the first place, why had he been in such a damn hurry to join up? After all, he'd had a wife and a little kid by that time.

Jack knew the answer. The answer was Jack. Everything depended on something else.

He looked back toward the woods. The clouds seemed to hang just above the tops of the trees. Steam rose up from the intervening field. Jack's body felt as heavy as lead.

"Did you see it?" Jack said.

The boy stopped work again but still didn't look at Jack. He stared at a spot on the barn's hay-strewn floor mid-way between the two of them.

"What your sister found?" Jack went on.

Andrew shook his head. "I was over at Uncle Matt's."

Jack stepped up into the barn, stood there in the wide doorway. "Any idea where a thing like that could have come from?"

"No, sir," Andrew said, still not looking up.

"No one's missing from around here, are they, Andrew? No pretty young girl, say?"

Andrew's head came up, his tanned face flushing even darker than it already was. "No, sir," he said. He looked stunned, as if the thought had never occurred to him.

"That finger must belong to someone. We can agree on that much, can't we?"

The boy nodded carefully. At that instant, Jack wished that he was his son. He wished that his son was still alive. The wish burned through his heart like a drop of molten iron.

"Okay," Jack said and turned away.

Jesus God, he said to himself as he walked half-blind down the barn approach. What the hell was getting into him these days? Betrayed by quick uncertain emotions. Whatever it was, he didn't like it.

The chief of police strode across the farmyard. About ten that morning he'd driven up to the Broomes' house and hidden his cruiser from prying eyes behind a hay wagon. Mrs. Broome and the older daughter were sitting in the kitchen working on some sewing, but he had no doubt the daughter, a saucy-looking little blonde, had been talking up a storm all the previous day. He knew that he had only so much time before the news got back to the mayor and the rest of them. He could almost hear Mayor Westland now.

"What's this about a finger, Jack?" he'd say, having summoned him upstairs to his office in the town hall. He'd never once visited Jack's office in the basement. And he'd say, "We'll have to call in the Ontario Provincial Police if there's a body. That's the rule, isn't it? And what are you doing outside the town line, anyway, Jack? That's not your jurisdiction, is it?"

Westland always gave directives with questions attached, so that whatever the ensuing results might be, he could never be held directly responsible. And the thing was, he was scheming to replace Jack with his nephew. Everyone in town knew that. It was all Jack could do not to lean over the mayor's desk and throttle the little bastard.

Jack was the head of a three-man force. He'd hired Jock White because he'd liked him. He'd hired the mayor's pea-brained nephew, Todd Westland, under duress. It had been a big mistake.

He needed to find the body, he needed to identify it and he needed to be half-way toward solving the thing before the mayor even thought of calling in the provincial police. It would be his case by then, he'd solve it and everyone in town would hold him a little in awe again, like they used to. And then let the mayor try to replace him.

Jack looked fiercely around the yard. He half-expected to see Jenny, but she wasn't in sight. Earlier that day she'd walked between him and her father back to the neighbour's fence.

"Right here," she'd said, pointing to a spot in the tall dusty weeds and without a stutter to be heard. When they'd returned to the house, Clarence had said he had to go to town for something. He hadn't yet returned. Jack was beginning to wonder if he'd snuck off to talk to the mayor.

The family's old dog seemed to be waiting for his master, too, lying halfway between the stable door and the water trough and watching Jack go by. His name was Brandy. Jack had asked Jenny when he'd first met her, just to break the ice.

B-B-B..." Jenny had said.

"Brandy." Her father had helped her out.

Jack hadn't wanted the dog to mess anything up so he'd ask Clarence to lock him in the barn before walking back to the fence. He was out of the barn now, though, getting up and sitting on his worn haunches.

Jack walked over to the hay wagon, hitched himself slowly up on the edge of it and thought of Ruth. He'd visited her the previous evening, as he always did, sitting there watching the shadows creep across the hospital wall and trying to make a little conversation. He might as well have been talking to himself. She'd stopped responding about ten days before, though the doctor had said at the time that there was no physical reason for it. None of the nurses could get her to respond, either. She'd just closed down.

Once in a while on his visits, when it was almost dark, Jack would turn on a lamp and open a magazine for something to do, though he had no interest in actually reading. And every once in a while she'd groan sharply, clench her teeth, and Jack would lean over her, stroke her forehead, her hair.

"Ruth," he'd whisper, "Ruth."

Jack shifted on the edge of the wagon and tried to turn his mind back to the investigation. He was making a mess of it, stumbling around the farm like a blind man. Something was eluding him, but what the hell was it?

It had to do with the spot Jenny had pointed out. How far would a rat carry a chewed-off finger? That was the riddle.

Along the fenceline, for certain, or across Clarence's field, or maybe the neighbour's field, and from somewhere near the edge of the woods. But no farther. So where was the corpse? He'd been over all the nearby ground and most everywhere else within a reasonable distance, and no newly turned earth, no decaying smell, no suspicious mound anywhere. But what was a reasonable distance? Maybe he had the wrong animal.

How far might a weasel travel carrying the finger in its mouth? Or a fox?

Or maybe a bird flew off with it in its beak and then dropped it. A hawk, maybe? Crow? Owl?

Or a dog?

How far would a dog carry a finger?

Brandy got up and wagged his tail. He started to walk stiffly over to Jack. He looked for all the world like he knew the answer.

France, 1942

Chapter Twelve

• • •

Adele didn't return to the park for three weeks, or to Manfred. She went directly to work at exactly twenty minutes to ten and she stayed away from Simone, too. When her period finally arrived, it seemed like a last-minute reprieve on the steps of a gallows, it seemed like a bright red miracle.

Adele moved through a sea of votive lights and lit a candle at the foot of the Blessed Virgin. She pressed her forehead against the Virgin's cool bare feet and prayed to be forgiven. She vowed never to see or even to think of Manfred Halder again.

She'd been living a kind of frozen terror. What in the world would she have done if she had been pregnant? There was nothing she could have done, and nowhere she could have turned except to the steep bank of the river.

A priest stepped into a confessional at the side of the cathedral. When he closed the door, it made a sharp sound like a gunshot in the huge vaulted space. It echoed around Adele's head.

An old woman struggled to her feet from where she'd been praying and disappeared behind the velvet curtain on the other side of the confessional. Adele sat down on a pew to wait her turn.

The woman seemed to be taking a maddeningly long time.

Adele fingered nervously through her rosary, reciting her prayers. She closed her eyes, and as she prayed she could see the priest's face behind a criss-cross of shadows, she could see a glint of light from off his glasses.

"Father, forgive me." Perhaps he wouldn't ask her to go into details. But he would. They always liked to question young girls about those kinds of things. "For I have sinned."

The face in the confessional was Manfred's now. It was Manfred. She touched her hand to the metal grille between them. She slipped her fingers through. She ached just to touch his face. "Manfred," she said.

But it wasn't Manfred. It was the priest again. "God knows your heart and your heart is Sin," he said.

Adele put her rosary away and fled out a side door.

At six o'clock that same evening, Adele was standing in the doorway of an empty building on Ducrot Street, shivering in the cold and waiting for Manfred. A half-hour later she saw him walking from his work with a group of young soldiers. She stepped out from her hiding place.

Manfred looked shocked to see her, but pleased, too, so pleased and relieved his eyes immediately reddened.

All the soldiers stopped.

Manfred came up to her. She leaned against him. He wrapped his arms around her.

"Hello," she said.

• • •

"Do you go over to Simone's very often?" René asked.

He was leaning against the counter watching Adele scrub three potatoes. Every time he appeared and wandered about the house, he made her nervous. She had a stash of canned goods from the Wehrmacht hidden under an old coat in a corner of the root cellar right below his feet.

"I don't have the time," Adele replied.

René's eyes fell on the plump potatoes, fat and juicy. They'd been stolen just the other night from Manfred's pantry. Adele shifted a little, trying to shield them from her brother's sight.

"Nice potatoes," René said.

"I traded a sweater for them." Adele sliced one and gave him a piece to distract him.

René stuck it in his mouth. "So you don't see Simone very much any more? When was the last time?"

"I don't know. Two months ago. Why?"

"I haven't seen Edouard since we started fighting this war."

"The war is over," Adele reminded him. "Our so-called government signed a peace treaty with Germany, remember?"

Edouard was Simone's older brother. René had been a friend of his, but not as close a friend as Adele had been of Simone. René looked at Adele more closely, as if he were making some kind of important assessment. Apparently she passed because he continued. "I guess their father is still making a lot of money."

"Why does that matter?"

"Dirty money? Of course it matters. Have you seen anyone inside the house beside the Ducharmes? Anyone standing guard? You'd think the Germans would want to look after him, his plant does such important work."

"How would I know? Why are you asking?"

"The least he could have done was refuse to co-operate."

Adele turned to face her brother. "And then what? They'd have taken over his business, anyway, no matter what he did. He was just protecting his family."

René smiled at her.

"René, the war is over."

"You're right. Where's Mother?"

"She's taken Old Raymond out for a walk."

"I'll go look for them," René said.

. . .

Adele and Manfred strolled in among the trees at the far end of the park. The path was wet. Most of the snow had melted. Though they'd been seeing each other almost every day throughout the winter, they hadn't discussed what had taken place in Old Raymond's cottage and they hadn't repeated it. It was always on Adele's mind, though. She thought she knew why Manfred wasn't pressing for more – he was afraid she'd disappear again and this time she'd stay away forever. She loved him for thinking this, for putting her before what he must want.

For Adele, it was enough just to walk beside him, hear his sweet voice, hold his hand, kiss his warm mouth. He was a strange drug, so powerful he even made her forget her great guilt, at least for the time she spent near him.

Manfred reached into his coat pocket and pulled out something and handed it to her. It looked like a large gold coin except it seemed too light and its gold was just bright foil. Or like a brightly wrapped chocolate wafer.

Adele peeled off the covering. There was a balloon inside.

Moonlight filtered through the stark leafless woods. Remnants of snowbanks marched up the steep dark hill. The air felt warm and cold all at the same time and smelled like primeval mud, like the world just waking up.

"That is a condom," Manfred said.

Adele stared down at it. She'd heard of condoms before, though she'd never seen one.

"Do you know what it's for?"

"Yes."

"It's to keep the..."

"Shut up," Adele said, her emotions racing, her head swimming. She walked on through the trees.

Manfred followed her. "What do you think of it?"

"I don't think of it," Adele replied.

Manfred caught up to her and closed his hand over her hand. "I think of it all the time."

Please God, don't let me do this, Adele thought.

Manfred began to kiss her, his hand slipping inside her coat, trailing down her stomach.

She could feel tears burn in her eyes.

"If you don't want me to..." Manfred whispered.

Adele was shocked to feel how urgently her body had responded to his slightest touch. How immediately. Completely. "If you do anything more, I'll run away forever this time," she said.

Manfred groaned and kissed her tears. "If you don't want me to," he repeated, breathless.

Adele kissed his lips – they were wet and salty now. She held on to his face. He touched her between her legs, the most gentle touch. Her knees gave way.

"I don't want you to," Adele said, and reached down and touched him where he was already hard, where she knew he was already aching as she ached.

She knew she was lost.

After that night, they made love whenever and wherever they could, in the woods, on the park's cold bench, in the long grass beside the river when the warmer weather arrived. Manfred seemed to have an inexhaustible supply of condoms, and Adele kept up to him, loving him hopelessly, giving herself to him with a kind of blind and fatalistic abandonment.

One spring night as they were walking along the top of the stone wall overlooking the river, Manfred announced that he had a plan.

The warm air was full of strange and exotic smells Adele couldn't identify. Barges visible only by their running lights were moving along the far shore.

"What plan?"

"We will run away together."

Adele jumped down from the wall and began to walk away.

Manfred caught up to her. "I am perfectly serious," he said, and with one motion took off his army cap and flung it into the night sky. "I have retired from this war." It sailed back toward the river and disappeared into the darkness.

Adele ran back to the wall and looked down into the swirling water.

"Do you see it?" Manfred asked.

"You stupid dumb ass!"

"Good. You don't see it." Manfred started unbuttoning his jacket.

"Stop!" Adele grabbed his wrists. He freed himself. She seized his lapels and forced his jacket closed. "You'll be punished even for a missing cap. Do you think you can go back to your barracks naked?"

Manfred struggled with her for a little while, gave up and rested his face against her face. "Adele, listen, we must run away. There is nothing else for us to do."

"Run away?" Adele repeated, and again, "Run away?" as if he'd just suggested they take a stroll to the moon. "How?" She knew there could be no answer. There was no possible answer.

"I will tell you. Bring some of your brother's clothes to this park. He has some clothes left in your house. Yes?"

No, Adele felt like saying, even though René had left some old clothes he'd outgrown. She didn't reply.

"Bring some pants, a shirt, boots, a coat. We can hide them in the trees. In the middle of the night I will come here and exchange my uniform. We will disappear from this place before anyone is awake. We will travel to the south."

"Yes? And how will we live?"

"We will work on farms."

"Haven't you forgotten something? You're a German."

"Only if I open my mouth am I a German, and I can assure you that I will not. I am your half-wit brother. I am a mute. You must do all the talking for me."

Dear Jesus, Adele thought to herself.

"We are searching for our father," Manfred went on, "that is why we are travelling. Don't you see? You will do all the talking."

What Adele saw was nothing but scenes of disaster no matter which way she looked. "Manfred, my family depends on me for almost everything. They won't survive without me. Bibi and Jean are just small. You know this. I can't just leave!"

Manfred looked away. After a while he nodded. "Yes," he said with a sigh, "of course." He gazed off across the river, dappled shadows and watery light rippling over his face. "You are a good person. This is what I would expect you to say."

Adele watched him. He looked like he was drifting away from her, moving down-river.

Sometimes after making love Adele would trace Manfred's scar with her finger tips. The path the bullet had made ran from near the middle of his stomach almost to his hip, like an appendix scar except it was on the other side. It had become as familiar to her as everything else about him.

"Don't do that again," she'd whispered the first time her fingers had travelled that route.

Manfred had pretended she was referring to what they'd just done together. "We cannot do it just one more time?" But his eyes had told her the truth. He would do it again, if he was forced to choose between shooting himself or killing some faceless someone in an insane asylum war.

Now Adele took his hand and pressed up against him. "Manfred, when we were running from your soldiers, so many thousands of us, we had to depend on the farmers along the way. Even mothers with babies in their arms. Some were kind. But some stood at the end of their lanes and sold cups of water at one hundred francs a cup. These are the people you want to depend on to hide us and save our lives."

"We will find the kind ones," Manfred said.

"I can't run away," Adele whispered. "You're safe here right now and we're together. Things will change. We have to believe they will. We can out-wait anything."

She looked up at Manfred.

His face continued to float away.

FRANCE, 1942

CHAPTER THIRTEEN

• • •

Adele had just arrived home from work the next morning and was still thinking about Manfred's desperate plan to run away, when Old Raymond told her the news. He had heard it from Madame Georges, who had been told by one of the neighbours.

Monsieur Ducharme had been shot. He was dead.

Adele sat beside Simone's bed all that day and held her hand. She didn't try to think of anything comforting to say because she knew by her own experience that there was nothing to be said that would relieve the hurt in her friend's heart. Besides, Simone was receiving enough useless words of comfort from sombre relatives, priests, friends of the family, her mother to last a lifetime.

Candles were burning on the dresser. Shadowy figures came and went in the curtained and hushed room. Adele remained sitting there. She could see the limousine as clearly as if she were standing outside on the driveway looking at it, though it had been removed by the police the night before, as had the two bodies. Monsieur Ducharme's and his German chauffeur's.

The car shone in her mind. Monsieur Ducharme's brains were splattered across its shiny surface like pieces of pink blotting paper. She could see René standing there.

Adele felt sick to the bottom of her soul.

"You are the lucky one now," Adele heard Simone say, her voice faint and hoarse from all her crying.

"Why?"

"You can still hope to see your father."

Yes. Her father. Better that her father be dead than come home to this. An assassin for a son.

And his daughter? What was she?

Adele looked at Simone. She was lost in her own misery again – her eyes looked drowned.

Nothing appeared in the local newspapers concerning Monsieur Ducharme's death except a small notice that the police were continuing to investigate and had determined that the motivation was robbery. No one in Rouen believed this. Everyone knew Monsieur Ducharme had been executed by the Underground. It was meant to send a message: *The war continues.*

Given the enemy's over-whelming presence, it seemed more a piece of inconsequential street theatre, more a whimsical act than a serious action. A few hearts quickened with renewed hope, more were glad that Ducharme got what was coming to him, but most simply worried that such an affront would bring the wrath of the army down on the city. And it did. New curfews were enforced to the letter. Trucks rumbled through the streets at all hours. The SS escalated their random and terrifying midnight visits.

A month passed before Simone felt sufficiently recovered to return to school. Adele had kept her company as much as she could during this time, but now she avoided going over to the Ducharme house. It upset her to see the change in her friend. Simone wrapped herself in long silences. She rarely smiled and when she did it seemed to cost her a great effort. She walked more slowly than before and with her shoulders hunched over a little, as if she were protecting her heart.

Adele had waited for René to show up at the house but he hadn't. She'd wanted to see his face, look into his eyes, she'd wanted to ask him a question. And then she'd wanted to strangle him.

Adele told Manfred about her suspicions. They were sitting on their bench at the far end of the park under their tree. It was her night off and they were ignoring the new curfews. The sky was full of stars.

She said she could both believe that René was capable of such a thing and that he was not capable of such a thing. She could hold these contra-dictory thoughts in her mind at the same instant. The only thing she knew for certain was that somewhere inside herself she still loved her brother. She found that the strangest thing of all.

"What are we to do?" Manfred said. It didn't sound so much like a question – it sounded like a prayer.

Later that night Adele woke up to see a light shining in her room. René was standing behind it, watching her.

Adele sat up, her heart pounding so loudly she could actually hear it.

René was holding a candle. Adele could see where the wax had run down over his fingers. He must have been watching her for some time.

"What is it?" she whispered.

René just stood there.

"Why are you here? Are you all right?"

"It smells like a German whorehouse in here," René said.

Adele got up on her knees and gathered her covers in front of her like a shield.

"You diseased cunt. You filthy cunt. May God in Heaven strike you down," René said.

A hand clamped roughly over Adele's mouth. She struggled and tried to scream. A muscular arm was clasped tightly around, drawing her back hard against a broad chest. She couldn't see who it was, she couldn't move or make a sound.

René came toward her, aiming the candle at her face. Adele could feel its growing heat.

"May our poor father be at peace. May he be dead. May he never have to look at you!" René looked half-mad.

He's going to burn my eyes, Adele thought. She could see nothing but explosions of light, she could smell her singed hair.

Whoever was holding her let her go. She scrambled off the bed and into a corner.

A man she'd never seen before was regarding her with a kind of unnerving detachment. He was considerably older than her brother and was dressed in soiled coveralls like a workman. René leaned over her empty bed and held up the candle so the stranger could get a better look.

"I have a difficult problem," the man said in a quiet voice. Adele could see that he'd taken off his shoes and was standing in his stocking feet. "René wants to kill your boyfriend." He began to close the distance between them. "Your brother is an excellent soldier. He has more important things to do than eliminate a low-level clerk by the name of Manfred Halder who happens to work in the Domestic Population Bureau of Information and lives at 26 Ducrot Street."

Adele could feel herself about to faint. The man reached out and grabbed her by her chin.

"Too many of Manfred's friends know your secret. It wouldn't take the SS any time to connect your dead little lover to you, and you to an avenging brother. And then what do you think would happen? They'd torture René, wouldn't they? And when he talked, as he would eventually, what about the security of our future operations?" His fingers began to dig their way into Adele's jaw. "I have given René permission to kill your German if you ever see him again. And then, in turn, we will have to kill René." The man put his face close to hers. Adele could smell the faint scent of alcohol. His fiery eyes consumed her. "A high price for a snuggle, wouldn't you say? I hope to God you understand."

The man let her go and silently walked away and out the door.

René was still staring at her. He wasn't looking so much deranged now, though. He looked more as if he'd just received a wound to the heart that was beyond repair. And then he followed the man out the door.

• • •

Adele stayed away from the park the next day. At three o'clock in the morning, she made her way between the long lines of working women and walked toward the toilet in the hallway. Instead of turning in, she ran down three flights of stairs and hurried along a narrow corridor toward the loading docks. If René were watching her every move, and she was sure he was crazed enough to do just that, he'd position himself near the bridge by the women's entrance.

Adele slipped past the waiting trucks and disappeared into the dark.

The mansion on Ducrot Street looked fast asleep. All the windows were dark and only a single lamp illuminated the front door. Adele crept along the side of the building, picked up some pebbles from the drive and chose a window at random on the second floor. She threw a pebble at it. It fell short. She threw the whole handful and a few of them clattered sharply against the glass. A face appeared. Adele waved up at it. A young blond soldier pushed open the window.

"Manfred Halder," Adele whispered up to him, "I must see Manfred Halder."

The soldier studied her for a moment, then pulled the window closed again.

Adele backed under a tree and waited in the shadows for either an angry officer to come charging out of the building, or for Manfred. A side door opened and Manfred stepped out into the moonlight carrying his boots in his hand. Adele looked back up at the window. Three young soldiers were staring down at her.

Adele and Manfred hurried silently along Ducrot Street. When they reached the passageway to the abandoned house, Adele collapsed against him.

"What is it?" Manfred asked urgently. "What's wrong?"

"We can't see each other!" Adele was crying now. She had promised herself that she wouldn't. She wanted to be firm. Determined. Sensible. "My brother's found out about us. He knows where you stay. If we ever see each other again, he's sworn to kill you. He has permission to kill you!"

"Permission from who?"

"The Resistance. The Underground!"

Adele expected Manfred to go deathly pale at this news. Instead, he smiled and looked hopeful. "Is this so?"

"Yes, it's so," Adele cried out. "It's true, Manfred!" She felt like shaking him.

"But listen," he said, "your brother might kill me anyway, whether we see each other or not. He's already killed your friend's father."

"I don't know that!"

"But there is no guarantee that even if we did stay away, your brother would follow orders. For the sake of the family's honour, he might kill me anyway."

"He won't!"

"You don't know that. You can't possibly know that. You don't know anything about your brother."

This was true. Adele realized it with devastating certainty.

"Where is he now?"

Adele shook her head. "I don't know."

"What is he doing?"

Adele shook her head.

"Adele, we have to escape." Manfred held her more tightly, pressing her against his slender body.

"You have to escape! You have to!"

"No. I will go nowhere without you. What's here for you now? To be treated like filth under people's feet? Everyone will soon know. Your brother knows. What kind of life is here for you now?"

Adele closed her eyes and buried her face in his undershirt. Even in the middle of the night he smelled like smoke. And he was right. There was no life possible for her. Not any more.

"We need a plan. Some good plan, that is all," Manfred was saying, "nothing to do with farmers. What else? Think, Adele."

Manfred wouldn't survive if he tried to run on his own, she knew that. And if she did go away, perhaps it would be the kindest thing she could do. It would be a gift to everyone. Her mother was looking after Old Raymond. René would look after Jean and Bibi, he would take her place because that's what their father would have wanted him to do. She thought she knew that much about him.

"Remember the old warehouse where we met that first day?" Adele could hardly hear herself. It was barely a whisper.

"Yes."

"Meet me there. Meet me Thursday night. When you do, I'll have a plan."

"Adele," Manfred sighed.

She could feel his hand in her hair. It felt as familiar to her as her own hand. "The middle of the night. Three o'clock," she whispered.

She could hardly believe what she'd just said.

Adele arrived back at her sewing machine at ten after four.

The big woman looked up. "Buttercup? Did you fall down the hole?"

The spidery woman stopped her work. So did the women nearby, their clattering machines falling silent.

"I felt sick," Adele replied, pulling a face she hoped made her look sick, "maybe from something I ate. I lay down in the storage room."

"The foreman's been looking for you." The big woman's black button eyes searched Adele's eyes. Her meaty red slab of a face was on alert and terrifying.

"I could hardly stand up, my head was so dizzy," Adele said.

The big woman leaned closer. "What are you going to call it? Herman? Dietrich? Gretel if it's a girl?"

All the women burst out laughing, even the demure, spidery one.

Adele smiled wanly, prayed that the big woman was only making another one of her jokes and began to sort through the mound of pants that had piled up in front of her.

Three nights later, at ten to three, Adele got up from her sewing machine, walked calmly between the women and ran down the stairs.

"Mademoiselle, hello," a flirty young man called out, doffing his cap. Two older men were off-loading a large truck. They turned to look and laugh.

Adele held her head high, remained aloof and crossed to the other side of the loading docks, pushing through a pair of swinging doors. She had no idea where she was going.

The inside wall of the hallway vibrated with the thunderous and sweeping din of unseen machinery. Bits of wool floated like snow in the air. She saw a small door set in the brick wall opposite and pushed it open. It was raining outside. The sky had been clear when she'd walked to work. Adele peered out into the murky dark. Rain streamed down through the yellow lamp lights into the truck yard.

If she got soaking wet, how could she claim she'd been lying down in the storage room feeling sick again? Her question had no answer.

Adele put her head down and ran across the truck bridge and down the path along the bank of the raceway. A streaming silver darkness greeted her. She slowed down and began to drag her feet along the cinder path so she could tell where she was going. She looked back toward the factory. With all its lighted windows, it looked like an ocean liner disappearing out to sea.

The rain pelted down. Adele continued on, soaked through to her skin, going over her plan. She'd travel back to Paris and lose herself somewhere in its sprawling outskirts, she'd find an obscure room on a nondescript street and, under another name, secure work in a shop that wasn't particular about identity papers. She'd often heard the women in the factory talk of such places. And then when it was safe, she'd send a note to Manfred at a post box in Rouen. The trains were always filled with soldiers on furlough. All Manfred needed to do was wait for her to mail him the Paris address and then on his next leave he could come to her. She would hide him in her secret room. René would never find them. The German army would never find them. Days would go by, nights and days stretching out forever. And they could forget everything.

A dark shape loomed up in the rain. Adele reached out and felt a slippery chipped surface.

"Manfred! Manfred!" she called out.

Rain lashed against the warehouse and water ran off its swayed roof as loud as a waterfall. Adele felt her way around the corner to get out of the wind.

"Manfred!"

She stood in the teeming dark and listened for an answering voice. Every few moments she called out his name. Ice water streamed from her hair. "Manfred!"

Adele began to shiver. What if she had the wrong night? Or the wrong time? She called out again. The rain and wind seemed to snatch her voice away as soon as it left her frozen lips. What if René wasn't guarding the factory tonight? What if he'd watched the Wehrmacht house on Ducrot Street, instead? He'd have seen Manfred leave. He would have followed him. Adele took a few steps out of her shelter, trying to see past the glistening curtain of rain in front of her. She waded into the weeds.

Manfred was hurrying through the streets and past the factory, she could see him in her mind. He was running down the embankment into the weeds. A shot echoed in the rain, a sheet of blood fanned out from his forehead.

"Manfred!"

Something seemed to move in front of her. A wave of rain swept out of the darkness. And then another wave.

Adele retreated back to the wall. She gave up calling. She had no idea how much time had passed. A half-hour? An hour? All night? She couldn't see her watch. For all she knew, Manfred was lying dead in the weeds in front of her. For all she knew, he had changed his mind. He hadn't come at all.

Adele didn't return to the factory, and it was almost six in the morning by the time she reached home. Old Raymond was asleep by the stove. The sound of his breathing filled the shadowy room, coming in shallow and hoarse gasps like a child with the croup.

Adele walked along the hallway past the parlour. She crept up the stairs and into her bedroom. She fumbled off her wet clothes, crawled under her covers and curled up in a ball. She couldn't seem to get warm.

By nine o'clock that morning, Adele was standing in front of the Domestic Population Bureau of Information. She hadn't been there for a long time. She didn't need to go there because Manfred would have told her any news if there had been any news to tell. All she wanted was to see him sitting safely at his long table working on his files. They wouldn't need to exchange a word. He wouldn't even need to look up. It wouldn't take a moment.

The queue inched inside the door. Manfred was nowhere in sight. Adele couldn't see any of the usual clerks, or any men at all. The room was full of uniformed women. Adele waited her turn.

"Corporal Manfred Halder?" A middle-aged officer was sitting behind the desk, her face almost perfectly round and apple-cheeked, her uniform dove grey, her cap secured by a long straight pin that pierced her tight blond hair.

"He's a clerk here," Adele said.

"I thought you said you were inquiring after your father?"

"Corporal Halder has been very kind to our family. He told us that he would get in touch with some office in Paris and report back, but I don't see him."

"Corporal Halder has been reassigned."

"Where?"

The woman stared coldly at Adele.

"I'm sorry," Adele murmured, "thank you."

She got up and hurried out the door expecting at every step to hear a shouted order for someone to stop that woman, that spy. Spy!

Adele ran toward Ducrot Street. When she reached the house, a few uniformed women were coming out the heavy front doors talking among themselves.

"Do you speak French?" Adele asked the one in the lead. The woman ignored her and walked on. The second one shook her head. The third stopped. Adele was struck by how young she looked, no older than a schoolgirl.

"A little," she said.

"Where are all the soldiers?"

The young German looked uncertain.

"Men," Adele said, "all the men soldiers. Where are they?"

"Gone."

"Gone where?"

"Gone to..." The girl searched a moment for the right word. "To Russia. To the Front," she said.

CANADA, 1946

CHAPTER FOURTEEN

• • •

J ack and Brandy walked along the path through the woods together. Jack had tied a length of rope loosely around Brandy's neck because the dog didn't have a collar. For the first time that day, Jack was feeling slightly hopeful. Maybe the dog did know something.

At first, Brandy had headed for every tree, fence post and tuft of grass in sight, but by the time they'd reached the woods the dog had settled into a stiff-jointed, purposeful gait.

Jack glanced down at him. How would you really tell what a dog was thinking? Some people claimed they could tell, at least with their own dogs. He'd never had a dog, or a pet of any kind. His father, a cobalt miner and as tough as they came, wouldn't hear of keeping any animal in the house, it was damn foolishness and Jack had always felt the same way.

The closest his own son had come to having a pet was when he'd traded his bicycle for a rabbit. It was a deal only a moron would make and Jack had told him so. Nevertheless the boy had kept his pet in a hutch behind the garage. The arrangement had lasted only until the winter. The hybrid rabbit wouldn't have survived outside and Jack wouldn't allow it inside and he wouldn't pay to heat the hutch, either. His son had to give it away. At the time, because the boy had ended up with no bicycle and no rabbit, Jack had thought he'd taught his son a valuable lesson.

The chief reached down and touched Brandy's head. He wondered what he would do now if he had the chance to do it over again. He looked around at the trees crowding in, the leafy vines hanging down, the mist scurrying through the uppermost branches.

What would he do if he had a chance to do it all over again? Such goddamn foolish thoughts.

Jack hurried along and soon he and Brandy were emerging into the clearing on the other side of the woods. They walked over to the spot Jenny had pointed out earlier that morning. Jack let the rope go and the dog sniffed along the fenceline.

"You were here a week or so ago. Remember? You were carrying that finger up to the house," he said hopefully.

Maybe he'd carried it as far as he could stand and spit it out in disgust, Jack thought. Or maybe he'd got interested in something else, a jack rabbit or a fox crossing in front of him and forgot what he'd intended to do. Or maybe Jack himself was going crazy, pinning his hopes on a fucking dog.

He looked across the stubble field toward the railway cut. Beyond it, he could just see the top of a row of trees as the land fell sharply away toward the river.

Brandy was still plowing through the weeds in a kind of aimless fashion. Jack picked up the end of the rope again and yanked it.

"Where do you want to go?" Jack asked.

Brandy looked around for a moment and sat down on his haunches. Nowhere, apparently.

Jack began to go through all the possibilities again. The surrounding fields. Hidden somewhere in the woods. In an out-building maybe, an old chicken coop, an abandoned barn. In a ditch alongside the road. Or hit by a train, the body lying for a week near the tracks.

Or drowned in the river.

He hadn't thought of that possibility before. He wondered why he hadn't. Given what he knew, it made the most sense. For one thing that's where the rats were. Admittedly most of them were massed downriver toward the town. Twice a week a truck would back up to the edge of a high cliff and cascade the town's garbage down the bank and into the water below. But some of them must have ranged upriver as well just to get some elbow room. There were thousands of rats.

No one had reported anyone missing, man or woman, which fit if the body was a tramp's. Jack wasn't sure if the men out in the DP camp would report anyone missing. Probably not. Might not even know. They were on the move, too, hitching rides on freight trains and crossing the country looking for work, but for some reason a group of them had decided to settle down for a time and had built a makeshift camp just past the dump. They'd nearly given the mayor a heart attack.

"Do you think we should move them on?" he'd said to Jack.

"Can't," Jack had replied, "they're outside the town line."

He hadn't wanted to move them on, anyway. Poor foreign flotsam left over from the war. Poles mostly. Hungarians. Survivors of some fearsome, faraway hell, half wild looking and haunted by secrets. He could tell by their eyes.

For chrissake, he'd wanted to say to the mayor, why can't you allow them a little rest?

Jack started off across the field, dragging the dog behind him. When they reached the steep embankment down to the railway, Brandy seemed to pick up both interest and speed. He passed Jack going downhill and pulled him along a path. They crossed a double set of railway tracks and headed down into some trees, Brandy remaining in the lead.

In unison they stepped out onto a riverbank. The water was exceptionally low even for the end of summer and seemed to be at a stand-still. There were no sounds at all.

A drop of rain as big as a quarter struck Jack in the face. The surface of the water began to dimple in a sporadic sort of way. And still no sound. Jack stood there for a long moment in a cone of silence. He could have stayed that way forever.

Brandy was straining on the rope, anxious to move downriver. Jack gave him his head and followed through the chest-high grass. After a time, for easier walking they slid down the bank to the riverbed below. It was dry along the shore, the cracked pans of mud as smooth as concrete.

After a while, Brandy wanted to scramble up the bank again. Jack dropped the rope and hauled himself up the steep slope. It was easy to follow the silvery path through the tall grass the dog had made. Jack could hear him somewhere up ahead thrashing in among some trees. The huge raindrops began to come down harder.

Jack stopped.

There was something suspended in the air, something faintly stirred up by the rain. He wasn't sure what it was. He moved forward again, and now it wasn't a faint intimation of something but the thing itself, over-whelming and invasive, so sweetly sickening and gag-inducing he could feel his insides begin to lurch.

Jack reached the edge of the trees. He could see the big dog crouched down out of the rain. He stepped closer. Something was on the ground. It looked like a pool of mud had erupted. His eyes began to run with tears from the smell and now he could see for a fact what he'd already seen in his mind, a swarm of white maggots, a puddle of greenish intestines and beside them and reaching out of the earth, a bloated hand.

It was missing two fingers.

FRANCE, 1942

CHAPTER FIFTEEN

• • •

The first week was the worst. Every inch of Adele's body ached. She had to fight for each breath. She hadn't known that love could be such a treacherous presence, weigh a thousand pounds, turn on you like a disease. In the past she'd let herself wonder just how deeply she loved Manfred. She had no doubt now. Two had become one, one flesh, one shattered heart.

Each day brought the same test of strength. Get up. Dress. Procure food. Cook the food. Go to work. Sit dazed in a dream space. Floating Wehrmacht pants. The distorted sounds of gossip and harsh laughter. Return home. Try to fall asleep.

She began to wait by the front door for the mail. Even marching through Russia, between bombs and bullets, Manfred might have a chance to at least scribble down a few lines she could cling to with all her might. This idea quickened her. It encouraged her to comb her hair, give some notice to the clothes she was pulling on, take at least a sideways glance at herself in the mirror. No letter arrived.

She felt nothing her hands touched, saw nothing her eyes saw, heard nothing that anyone said to her. She wondered if Manfred, in a fit of despair, had killed himself.

René stayed away. Adele didn't know whether she was relieved or not. It meant no more accusations, at least for the present, but it also made it seem as if Manfred had never existed, as if nothing had happened to her and nothing had changed. Everything had changed.

The women at the factory had accepted her explanation for the night she went missing, that she'd become suddenly and violently ill, and frightened by it, she'd gone home. But as summer approached and finally settled over the town, it seemed to Adele that the women in the factory were looking at her strangely.

By the end of July, Old Raymond was feeling well enough to shuffle out of the house. Jabbing his cane at an army of waist-high weeds, he demanded that Jean and Bibi begin to pull them out. "Pull!" Old Raymond shouted and coughed and wheezed.

Startled, Jean and Bibi began to pull out fistfuls of weeds as if the old man's life depended on them.

By the end of August he'd failed a little, but every day, weather permitting, he'd still totter outside and sit on an old painted chair under the grape arbour. Adele kept an eye on him from the kitchen window. It bothered her to see him sitting there, as if he were hiding from some hooded spectre he feared was about to call in at the house and ask for him by name.

Old Raymond was staring at his hands, turning them over and over, examining both sides as if they'd never cease to amaze him. Sun filtered through the vines and speckled his skin with spots of light. They used to be calloused, the fingers broad and strong. Now they looked soft and translucent, their backs laced with delicate blue veins.

"I'll read your fortune," Adele said, having come out of the house to sit beside him. She picked up one of his hands just to stop its ceaseless turning. "This line says that you were very foolish as a young man, Raymond, but that you are much wiser now."

Old Raymond nodded as if this wasn't news to him.

"This line says that you're going to come into money soon."

"Am I going to meet a woman?"

"Well, let's see." Adele picked up his other hand and pretended to study them both closely. "There's a woman with dark hair."

"That would be your mother."

"No," Adele said quickly, "Mother's hair is turning white."

"Your mother is a wonderful woman." Old Raymond's anxious, rheumy eyes turned to look at Adele.

"Yes, she is," Adele replied against her better instincts.

"She kisses me like a lover," Old Raymond said.

Adele could feel her blood turning cold. "What do you mean?"

"Sometimes she rests her face against my face, sometimes she cries. Sometimes she kisses me." He looked confused, as if he were asking her a question.

"I don't know," Adele said, getting up quickly and moving away. Small bunches of stunted grapes were hiding among the leaves. Adele reached up and touched one. "Raymond, when does she kiss you?"

"She comes into the kitchen at night. When you're at work."

"Do you think these grapes will ever get ripe?" Adele asked, afraid to ask anything else, and not waiting for an answer turned away and walked quickly toward the house.

Some days later Adele arrived home from work at her usual time. Old Raymond was still sleeping in the kitchen because her mother wouldn't hear of him moving back to the cottage, even though Adele had become quite insistent lately that he should be moved.

Adele closed the door quietly. By the time it clicked shut, even before she turned to look toward him, she knew.

Old Raymond had worn his navy blue beret in bed all winter and it had become such a habit that even when the warm weather had arrived he couldn't fall asleep without it. His beret was lying on the floor and his right arm was suspended above his head. It must have been resting against the headboard, or perhaps he'd reached up for some support at his very last breath and then during the night it had moved forward a little. With his wispy white hair standing up on end and his raised hand frozen in mid-air, it looked to Adele as if Old Raymond was waving goodbye.

• • •

Pain radiated from Madame Georges' face, her body, in the air, it was everywhere palpable. Adele was stunned by it, her mother was bereft.

The evening before the funeral, the family sat together in the parlour beside Old Raymond's casket. Jean and Bibi were dressed in the dark grey suits they wore to Mass and looked almost civilized. Adele wore a navy blue dress close to the colour of Old Raymond's beret. She'd picked it out of her closet on purpose. Madame Georges was dressed in black, her face as shockingly white as if it had turned to alabaster.

A few neighbours called in to sit with them, and Father Salles, their parish priest, always a jovial man no matter the circumstances, made everyone feel reasonably comfortable despite Madame Georges' unnerving silence. Adele couldn't take her eyes off her. This was the funeral she'd never had, Adele realized with some shock. This was Henri Paul-Louis' funeral.

Adele had been expecting René to walk into the room at any moment. Surely her mother had managed to communicate the sad news to him, wherever he lived or wherever he was hiding. So far he hadn't appeared.

Madame Georges was accepting her neighbours' whispered expressions of condolences with strained tolerance. Sometimes she extended her hand in a stilted fashion and let someone grasp it. Her mind seemed shut down, though, Adele thought, her eyes that could look so hard and glittery at times, so insane, seemed expressionless. They caught the light from the candles but gave none back.

In the early days, when the family had first returned to Rouen after the German army had passed them by, her mother had roamed through the house restlessly and endlessly, so much so that her nightly promenades had become one of the routine sounds of the house, like rain tapping on the roof or the wind rattling Adele's window.

One night Adele had decided to follow her.

Madame Georges was standing by the parlour window, her face stark and quite beautiful in the moonlight. She seemed to be gazing expectantly down the street, as if she were waiting for someone she was sure would appear. She touched Henri Paul-Louis' chair, his disreputable, thread-bare, lumpy chair, the chair he'd collapse into every night after making his hospital rounds, the chair she'd kept threatening to throw out.

She ran her hands across the back of it and down its cool wooden arms, she pressed her body against it, put her head down, her hair tumbled loose.

Adele hadn't been able to watch any more, she'd retreated back up the stairs. Now she looked at her mother sitting across the room and felt for the first time in almost forever that she actually understood her. Their hearts had been similarly broken, the men they'd loved had been wrenched away from them in the same way, except that her mother had been driven mad by it.

She must be mad, Adele thought, to say the awful thing she'd said. What could have driven her to say it? What terrible will was driving her to destroy everything?

Simone came through the front door looking appropriately sad. Adele helped her off with her light coat, grateful that she'd come despite Adele not having made any attempt to see her in weeks.

"I'm leaving school," Simone said.

"Why?"

"Everyone hates me."

Adele didn't ask her why she'd think that. Her late father was a topic Adele would just as soon avoid. "What are you going to do, Simone?"

Simone peered through her glasses toward Father Salles, who was comfortably ensconced in Henri Paul-Louis' old chair and surrounded by a cluster of appreciative women. Simone seemed even more hunched over than the last time Adele had seen her. Her slim shoulders were sticking out of her dress.

"I'm thinking of becoming a bride of Christ," she said.

Adele looked at her in amazement.

"What?" Simone asked defensively.

"Nothing," Adele replied.

They'd spent half their lives ridiculing every sister who'd ever taught them, corrected them, pulled gum out of their mouths, cuffed them on the back of their smart-alecky heads.

"What kind? A teacher?" Adele asked, breaking their rule.

"No. Cloistered," Simone said.

• • •

After Old Raymond's funeral, Adele sought out Simone's company. There was a comfort in being with her, a going back to an innocent time, as if nothing had actually happened. No René standing in the dark. No dead Monsieur Ducharme. No Manfred Halder.

One afternoon Adele found herself walking with Simone in the same park she and Manfred had frequented. They sat down on a cold bench, the one Adele and Manfred had made love on more than once, and looked out over the river. The view was achingly familiar to Adele. She wondered why she had led Simone there. She began to bite her fingernails.

"Why don't you put salt on them?" Simone asked.

"I like them plain." Adele stuck her hands in her pockets. "When are you going into a convent?"

"I don't know. My mother's against it. She doesn't understand. Why do you ask? Do you want to get rid of me?"

"I don't want you to go anywhere."

They sat there a little longer looking out over the river. The air felt cold coming off the water. One day soon it would begin to snow. Adele would have to manage to get her mother and her two brothers and herself through another winter without Manfred's help. No potato sacks half full of potatoes, apples, carrots, spiced beef, appearing against the back wall. No more coal.

"You don't talk about René," Simone said.

"No."

"He wasn't at Old Raymond's funeral."

"We don't know where he is these days. We think he's working somewhere outside Rouen. He doesn't say where."

"That's mysterious."

"Not really. He always manages to send Mother some money. It's difficult to find any kind of work."

"Yes," Simone agreed. After a few moments of silence, tears began to trickle down Simone's face. This was not unusual.

"Simone, don't," Adele said softly.

"I hate everything," Simone wept, "I don't know how to live in this world. People kill people. No one is left in peace." She blew her nose. "The only way to live is away from people. You know those nuns that pray all the time? You send in requests to them and they pray?"

"Yes."

"That's as much as I can manage. I have a gift for prayer, I think. And it's helping people, so that's good, isn't it? I've been reading my book of martyrs.

So often they say they're overwhelmed by a distaste for this life and they're eager to move on to the next one. I feel just the same way."

Adele touched Simone's hand. "That's because you'll meet your father."

"He was a good man." Fresh tears shone on Simone's face. "He wasn't bad!"

Adele was walking with Henri Paul-Louis under an avenue of trees. Above her, she could see every bright yellow leaf. She could see the sun streaming through. She could feel his strong hand holding on to hers.

"What's better? To lead life with your heart or your head?" he asked. He was always testing her.

"Your head," her eight-year-old self replied, thinking this was the answer that would best please him.

"No."

"Your heart, then."

Henri Paul-Louis smiled. "Both," he said, "but in the service of other people."

Adele was still sitting beside Simone. The river still looked like slate. Most of the trees were barren of leaves. The air felt even colder now.

"We have to try," Adele said quietly.

"What?"

"To love this world."

CHAPTER SIXTEEN

• • •

Winter descended. The ration tickets Adele queued up for every day no longer guaranteed any food in the shops. She counted herself lucky if she actually found the one egg a month she was allowed or the one bucket of coal. For the Georges family, and for most everyone else, life became a steady diet of rutabagas cooked every way imaginable over a small wood fire, the odd carrot or black potato thrown in, countless bowls of macaroni, and sitting in grey rooms, wrapped in blankets.

Despite this general deprivation, the spidery woman who worked beside Adele left the factory to have another baby. Her job was immediately filled by the young wife of a soldier who'd been killed in the first days of the war. She talked excitedly about the Russian front. She said she'd heard it was going badly, not for the Russians, but for the Krauts. Every time Adele dared to glance her way, the woman seemed to be looking straight at her.

In February, Madame Théberge arrived. She showed up at the Georges' front door with everything she owned stuffed inside a large paisley-covered portmanteau.

An elderly aunt of Madame Georges from the district of Bretagne, she was a tall woman with large bones that pushed out from under her thin black coat at strange angles, and with hands that looked like they'd been digging up potatoes from time immemorial.

As soon as Madame Théberge and her portmanteau were settled inside the front hallway, she announced that her husband of forty-six years had died from a broken neck. Apparently he'd fallen on a piece of ice at the beginning of the previous winter, though she spoke as if it had just happened. Another relative in Bretagne, a recipient of Madame Georges' begging letters, had suggested that the widow Georges in Rouen might appreciate another widow's company.

Madame Georges had never seen the old woman in her life. She led her up the stairs with an obvious lack of enthusiasm and gave her René's old room on a temporary basis. All Adele could see was another mouth to feed, another burden, but this turned out not to be the case.

In the first week, Madame Théberge cleaned through all the house. The second week she took over queueing up for food. The third week she started pulling up the floor boards in Old Raymond's cottage, cutting them to length and splitting them for firewood.

Adele had never met such a person – the woman seemed incapable of sitting still. She took over most of the cooking. She did the washing, too, and subdued Bibi and Jean with threats of eternal damnation. She even seemed to be making friends with Madame Georges. It wasn't too long before Adele had to admit to Simone that her relentless presence was turning out to be a great relief. All Adele had to do any more was go to work and every two weeks hand her pay packet over to Madame Théberge.

Spring finally came and then the sudden heat of summer. Adele was walking home from Simone's place one particularly close and humid day when she saw a young woman standing in front of her house.

When Adele came up to her, the woman smiled and said, "Hello."

"Hello," Adele replied and moved to go by.

"Are you Adele Georges?"

"Yes." Adele looked at her more closely. She seemed about Adele's age, or perhaps she was a year or two older, nineteen or twenty. She was quite plump and, in the humidity, the thin cotton dress she was wearing was clinging to her soft body in all the wrong places. She had a perfectly round face.

"My Wilhelm told me to give you this." She held out a folded piece of paper. "I've already read it. All us girls share everything. It's like a family. We have to, don't we?"

Adele hesitated. "What is it?"

"Here," she said, pressing the paper into Adele's hand.

Adele unfolded it. The first thing she saw was *"Dear Adele."* She looked at the bottom. *"Manfred."*

"Oh!" Adele cried out.

"He says he's sorry for not seeing you, but then he doesn't say how long he's stayed away."

"A year," Adele managed to say.

The woman shook her head. "That seems like a long time."

A long time, yes. "He's fighting in Russia."

"Russia? God, no! He's on the Channel. He's not forty miles from here."

Adele looked at the woman's indignant face. She looked back at the faint pencil scrawl.

> *Dear Adele,*
> *The village of La Bouille, three days, August 25, 26, 27.*
> *Trust our friends. Forgive me this long time. Manfred.*

"Some of them can be real bastards," the woman said.

Tears were scalding Adele's eyes. "What's your name?"

"Lucille. Lucille Rocque. It would be different if he was like my Wilhelm. He can't write French, he can hardly speak it, but your soldier could have been writing you all along. It would be censored and everything, but still, a year and not to hear."

"He must have had his reasons," Adele said, and thought, What reason? What possible reason? "These dates he's written, what do they mean?"

"That's his three-day leave. Wilhelm's, too. All the girls go down to La Bouille to see their men. I can take you."

Adele looked at Lucille Rocque again. She had pleasant eyes, large, hazel, almond-shaped. They dominated her round, plain face. She looked harmless enough.

"Do you want to go?"

"Yes," Adele said.

• • •

The train to La Bouille was full of young women, thirty or forty of them at least, a few carrying babies or balancing small children on their laps. Adele sat beside Lucille, who had applied too much make-up, her face looked painted on. Two other soldiers' girlfriends were sitting opposite.

An elderly conductor swayed down the aisle. He seemed to know all about these dressed-up, chattering female traitors. He didn't call for tickets as he normally would, but instead just thrust his hand out, and whenever the lurching coach threatened to push him against one of them, he braced himself as if he were about to fall into a fire.

Adele watched the old man, and the women laughing and smiling up at him. She looked out the window. Rouen was fast disappearing behind her. She felt sick to her stomach.

It had taken her almost the entire morning to decide what to wear. For one thing she could hardly face herself in the mirror. She'd lost weight, she was sure of it, and she hadn't even grown one centimetre – if anything, she'd shrunk. Her hair had become more unruly than ever, her skin dry and pale, shadows of exhaustion showed under her eyes like blue half-moons. What would Manfred think?

And how could he not have written?

Adele had to delay leaving the house until Madame Théberge was off somewhere queueing up and her mother had finally left on one of her daily walks. For some reason, Madame Georges had become health-conscious under Madame Théberge's regime.

One of the young women sitting opposite touched Adele on her knee. She couldn't have been a day over fifteen. "I understand this is your first time. Me, too," she said. "I'm a bit scared, I mean about staying away for two nights. I don't know what lie I'm going to tell my father."

"I'm not telling my mother anything," Adele replied, and smiled kindly at the girl and tried to convince herself that she wasn't like any of these women at all. They were carrying on as if everything was normal, as if their lives would just continue on like this forever, that this riding back and forth on a train was more than good enough for them. Her situation was entirely different. She was meeting Manfred to plan their escape.

Lucille leaned forward. She had a suggestion for the girl. "Why don't you tell your father that the police arrested you for being out after curfew and wouldn't let you go home?"

"That's perfect," the girl said. She looked grateful.

Poor thing, Adele thought.

Lucille began to talk about her Wilhelm. She went on for half an hour. When she stopped to take a breath, the fourth woman spoke up. She'd been smoking one cigarette after the other and staring out the window.

"I'm telling Jakob I'm through."

"Through?" Lucille's large hazel eyes, encircled in charcoal, grew even larger. "What do you mean, through?"

"I'm getting married."

"What?" Lucille screeched.

Almost immediately half the women in the carriage moved over to where Adele was sitting. They hung over the back of the seats and began to interrogate the cigarette smoker. In response, the interrogated one blew smoke out of her nose in ever more vicious streams.

She seemed about twenty-one and a bottle-blonde by the look of her roots. She was certainly one of the toughest-looking women on the train, but nevertheless, under the barrage of questioning Adele could see that her eyes were beginning to shine.

"I'm pregnant," she said.

The carriage went deathly silent. No one had to ask any more questions now that bit of news had escaped into the air, all they had to do was wait. The announcement itself would supply its own momentum.

"This fellow at work, he's in love with me," the woman finally said. "I've taken him on, if you know what I mean, and I said I'd marry him. I'm going to tell him the baby's his, he'll never know the difference."

"What about, you know, just doing something about it?" someone suggested.

"An abortion? I have a friend who did that," the blonde replied. "She nearly bled to death."

Some others nodded. "There're different ways," another one said.

The blonde shook her head.

"Why don't you do the same as Maddy?" Lucille asked.

Everyone looked toward a woman sitting at the front of the coach cradling a small child.

The blonde shook her head again.

"But you love Jakob," Lucille pressed on.

Tears began to push through the powder on the blonde's face.

Adele looked out the window and tried once again to convince herself that these women had nothing to do with her.

The train kept coming to unscheduled stops. She began to see soldiers high up on the riverbanks. They looked like they were building an endless series of thick concrete walls. La Bouille was still some distance from the sea and just outside the Forbidden Zone. No one could travel inside the twenty-mile strip running inland from the coast without special papers. But clearly, even this far away from the Channel, the Germans were expecting something.

The tiny platform at La Bouille was jammed full of young men. They crowded forward and gazed up at the windows as the train slowed down.

Adele searched for Manfred's face. She couldn't see him. Lucille was already up and hurrying along the aisle. So were all the other women. Adele continued to sit there, watching her fellow passengers step off the train and push into the crowd.

When the coach was finally empty, Adele got up and walked down the aisle. As she stepped onto the platform, a wall of laughter and shouting in both German and French pressed her back against the side of the train. Women and soldiers were embracing all around her, kissing as desperately as if they'd been separated for a life time.

Still no Manfred. Adele started to make her way through the crowd toward the station. When she emerged on the other side, she saw a soldier who looked familiar sitting on a bench by the station door. When he saw her, he slowly stood up and took off his cap. The sun shone off his naked skull, there were long, deep shadows where his cheeks used to be. He looked ten years older. Adele couldn't make her feet move.

Manfred came up to her.

She reached up and touched his face. She kissed his mouth, his cheeks, his reddening eyes.

"I'm here," she said.

CANADA, 1946

CHAPTER SEVENTEEN

• • •

It began to rain hard, huge drops pounding through the over-hanging branches. They scattered the maggots and made the green intestines shine.

Jack held his handkerchief up to the rain until it was thoroughly soaked and, pressing it against his nose, circled around the corpse looking for a stick. He found a sturdy-enough one and, kneeling down, began to dig one-handed where he assumed the head should be.

A tangle of black hair came up out of the mud.

Jack dropped the stick and began to probe around with his hand. One of his fingers pushed through into something soft and mushy. He knew he was making a mess of things but he couldn't stop, he had to see the face. He began to push handfuls of mud aside. A white eye appeared. It had been punctured and pushed back so that it was turned half-way around. It looked blind. He knew that he'd just done that in his frantic, stupid haste. He began to push at the mud some more. A strip of skin peeled away.

Jack sat back on his heels. The rain thundered down around him. He looked toward Brandy but he couldn't see him any more. He knew he was disgracing himself, had disgraced himself already, and for what good reason? For the slight chance he might recognize this stinking, rotting thing and he could get a jump on the Ontario Provincial Police.

"Jesus God," Jack said.

The intestines had a pool of water in them. The maggots were drowning. It occurred to Jack that at some time something had dug into the shallow grave and opened the body up.

Dogs, probably, he thought. Not good old Brandy, though. Feral dogs. There were plenty of them running around the countryside killing sheep and scaring people half to death.

Jack looked at the solitary hand more closely. The rain had washed it a ghostly white. It didn't seem to be a large hand even in its bloated condition. There were little flaps of punctured skin all over it. At least this went some distance in proving his theory about the rats.

Water was running in a steady stream between the stumps of the fourth and fifth fingers. If the little finger was in his refrigerator, the corpse was probably a man. If it was the fourth finger, then maybe he was looking down at a woman.

He couldn't make himself touch the black muck any more. And he couldn't tell.

● ● ●

Clarence Broome's face went instantly pale when Jack asked him if he had a tarpaulin. Jack and Brandy were standing just inside the stable door – they both looked drowned.

The rain was still coming down, though not as hard as it had before. It was only mid-afternoon but it seemed like dusk, all the light had faded from the sky.

"Why?" Clarence asked.

"I found it," the chief said.

Clarence nodded. He didn't have to ask what Jack had found. He took a deep breath. "Where?"

"Near the river. About a hundred feet or so up from the bank. In a grove of trees."

"Not on my property then." Clarence looked relieved.

Some hay fell through an open trap door on the floor above them and landed with a soft hiss. The men could hear boots shuffling above their heads.

"That's just Andrew," Clarence said, "getting ready to feed the cows."

Jack shifted his eyes upward and then back to Clarence. His wet granite face remained expressionless. It gave Clarence a chill.

"There's a tarp in the drive shed," Clarence said.

• • •

Jack made the inevitable phone call from the Broomes' kitchen. Three hours later an unmarked car with two young detectives and a truck clearly marked *Ontario Provincial Police* and carrying two uniformed officers pulled into the lane.

The Broomes had invited Jack in to eat something after he'd come back from covering up the corpse with the tarpaulin, but Jack had said he wasn't hungry, even though he was, and that he'd prefer to sit out in his car and make notes.

He didn't make any notes. He just sat there in the rain listening to the ball game broadcast from far away Wrigley Field and tried not to think about anything to do with the case. He had fucked up the crime scene. It was a holy mess.

Eventually Mrs. Broome came out of the house, a raincoat draped over her shoulders and carrying a Thermos of tea and a cold roast beef sandwich. She looked pale and nervous.

Jack rolled down the window and smiled. He could be almost charming when he wanted to be.

"Much appreciated," he'd said.

Harold Miles was the provincial detective in charge, though he didn't look much older than Jack's son had been when he'd left for the war. There was one difference, though. Miles was almost as tall as Jack and cut an impressive figure in his fedora and a long tan raincoat. Jack's son had been quite a bit shorter than his father and slightly built, and he'd never cut an impressive figure in all his life.

After introductions and a conversation off to the side between Harold Miles and Clarence Broome, Clarence climbed up on his tractor and led the truck along the muddy trail between the front fields. They were heading toward the woods.

Miles sauntered back to Jack and said that his detective partner, who seemed even younger, would drive their car around the concession and park by the railway bridge. His partner would walk in along the tracks. He himself, however, wouldn't mind the opportunity to stretch his legs by taking a hike through the farm if Jack didn't mind the trek back.

The rain had eased off to a steady drizzle. Jack nodded. He'd already been chilled straight through once. Why not one more time?

"They'll be waiting for us near the railway tracks," Miles said as they headed along the flooded wagon trail. "I guess you're the only one who knows where the body is, exactly."

Jack nodded again and thought to himself, Me and Brandy, actually, sonny boy. And whoever laid the corpse in the ground – because it didn't bury itself.

Jack knew why Miles had decided to stretch his legs despite the drizzle and the water lying all over the place. It was perfectly natural and it was perfectly obvious. He wanted time to question the local cop.

"Clarence said something about a finger. I guess that's what got you out here in the first place."

Jack strode along in silence, going straight through a puddle. His feet had been soaked for hours, it didn't matter to him. Miles skirted around it.

"When was that, chief?"

"When was what?"

"When Clarence's daughter found the detached finger? When Clarence called?"

"That would be yesterday," Jack replied.

"And where is it now?"

"Where is what now?"

"The finger."

Jack turned and grinned at Harold Miles. "It's in my refrigerator."

There was no use playing a cat and mouse game. The best thing to do was to partner up with this young detective, make a friend out of him and proceed as if something like this happened in Jack's jurisdiction every day. Not that he was in his jurisdiction, but he was only a mile and half out of it.

"It could have been the result of an accident, the severed finger, I suppose," the young detective was saying. "Is that what you were thinking?"

"That's exactly what I was thinking."

"You know different now, though."

Jack didn't think it was necessary to reply to that question. The answer was obvious.

"You did the right thing, as soon as you found the body, calling us in. You didn't disturb anything, did you?"

Jack didn't look at Miles this time. He seemed to be addressing the soggy field in front of them. "I've been a police chief for twenty-eight years," he said, and that was all he said.

Jack marched grimly on. There would be no more questions.

It didn't take the Provincials long to get organized. As soon as Jack had pointed out Clarence's tarpaulin, they drove six-foot stakes into the ground near the four corners of the grave and hung a tarp for a roof to keep off the rain. They pitched a large tent just beyond the tree line. They set up lights and fired up a gas generator. More police arrived. A coroner arrived, one whom Jack had never seen before.

When he asked one of the cops who he was, Jack was told that the coroner had driven in from Hamilton, a city some forty miles distant. In fact, the whole forensic team had come in from Hamilton.

Clarence's tarp was finally pulled away. Dusk had settled into the trees and a pool of light flooded the gravesite. A plain-clothes cop began to take pictures, his flashbulb popping again and again.

Jack stood some distance off rigid as a tree. He was soaked through once more but he refused to shiver.

The picture-taking came to an end and some gnome-like characters in rain suits crouched down beside the grave and began to brush away meticulously at the mud. Every once in a while young Harold Miles's face would come up out of the crowd and look over at Jack in a kind of disbelieving way. Once he even shook his head. The chief stared back at him, never changing his expression. The generator filled the trees with a steady, nerve-jangling racket. Beyond the floodlights, the night moved steadily in.

It was almost midnight before the body was lifted into a long canvas bag and removed from the grave. And it was two o'clock by the time Jack reached his home, opened up the refrigerator and handed over the pungent and shrivelled finger to Miles's detective partner. Neither man exchanged a word.

Jack sat alone in his kitchen and downed a half bottle of rye. He climbed the stairs, remembered he hadn't taken off his wet clothes, let them drop in the hallway and drew himself a bath. He sat in it bleary-eyed and unthinking until the water had turned cold, until the phone rang down in the kitchen.

It was Detective Harold Miles. He asked the chief of police if he'd had a good sleep. Jack stood there naked and dripping and said, "So-so."

"There's a few things I'd like you to examine. I've got a room down at the Arlington Hotel. Have you got a minute?"

Jack stood there in the dark holding the telephone to his ear. He didn't know exactly what he had. He knew what he wanted to avoid, a public humiliation. At the same time Miles seemed to be suggesting some kind of collaboration. Or was he?

Jack felt emptied-out. That was all he felt.

"Chief Cullen." The young man's voice seemed a bit testy at the other end of the line. "Are you there? Will I see you this morning?"

Jack was trying to shift his brain into gear. What the hell time was it? He switched on the light. Almost five. Maybe he could establish a relationship with this young punk after all, maybe he could tease some information out of him, maybe he could manage to get one step ahead of the whole goddamn Provincial Police force.

"I'll be right down," Jack said.

He didn't go right down. He took all the time he needed to shave and press out his spare uniform until the various creases were just so. He put on a fresh blue shirt and a fresh blue tie, polished his second pair of boots until they shone with a high gloss, swallowed some milk so his breath wouldn't betray the presence of alcohol, and then he went downtown.

Harold Miles was waiting for him in a small room on the second floor of the hotel. He was in shirt sleeves and didn't look like he'd had any sleep, either. The bed was untouched, except for an open suitcase full of clothes sitting on top of it. He shook Jack's hand unenthusiastically, sat down in a chair and motioned for Jack to sit down on the other one.

Jack thought about it. If he remained standing he'd tower over Miles, which was good, but standing also suggested a subordinate position. Jack sat down. He took off his cap and laid it on the writing desk. Taking his cap off seemed to even things out. Two equals, face to face, ready to collaborate.

"There were lots of boot tracks all over the grave," young Miles said, "all made by the same pair of boots. I assume they were yours."

Jack stared at him for a moment. "What is it you want to show me?"

"And I suppose it would also be safe to assume that you were the individual digging at the grave with a stick, and also with your hands?"

Jack didn't answer.

"What happened to the eye, chief? It would be useful to know if it was damaged before the body was laid in the ground or during the course of your investigation. We noticed there was some wet mud pushed into the socket."

Jack continued to stare at Harold Miles but if the young man felt intimidated he wasn't showing it.

Jack picked up his cap and put it carefully back on his head, taking the time to tilt it just so. "I'll tell you," he finally said. "Not having a crew of ten at my disposal and in the middle of one hell of a storm, I took it upon myself to have a look at the body before the rain did irreparable damage. However, as soon as I'd determined that putrefaction had set in to such an extent it wouldn't make any difference, in fact might make identification even more difficult, given the force of the rain, you see, then of course I stopped."

"And the eye?"

"I didn't notice the eye."

"Until you pushed it in?"

"No. I didn't notice the eye. Full stop," Jack said.

"You should have left the site untouched, chief. You should have backed off and called us right away. It just makes our job a little more difficult."

Your job, that's what the fuck you think, Jack thought to himself. He could feel his adrenalin percolating and blood rushing into his chest and into the large muscles in his arms. It was an old and familiar feeling.

Miles got up from his chair before the chief could rise out of his.

"I wanted to talk to you about this before it went into my report. That's the way I do things, it's only fair." He walked over to a corner of the room and picked up a large satchel smeared with mud.

Jack had been about to open the goddamn door and just walk the hell out of there but the sight of the satchel had changed his mind.

Miles put it on the desk and drew back the zipper. "There's a few things I wanted to show you before I sent them off to the lab. Just in case you had any ideas."

The young detective pulled a jacket out of the satchel, a brown tweed smeared with mud. And a tattered plaid shirt. A pair of trousers. Wool socks with holes. Underwear. A leather belt. And two worn-out dress shoes.

A man, then, Jack thought.

"This stuff should be reasonably free of maggots." Miles smiled at Jack. Jack didn't return the smile. Miles flipped open the jacket. There was a label sewn inside. "Made in Toronto," Miles said, "not bad quality. Nothing in any of the pockets, of course."

Jack picked up the belt. It was worn and cracked and somebody had punched an extra hole in it some distance inside the regular holes.

"The pants are rough," Miles said, fingering them, "worsted. Never were much. Worn down to nothing now. The shoes were half-decent, though, at one time."

Jack put the belt down and picked up one of the shoes, the lace untied and hanging down, the black leather barely discernible below a smear of reddish mud. The lace was a make-shift length of sturdy twine. Jack turned the shoe over. More mud, and caught between the worn heel and the sole, he could see a thin bluish seam of clay.

"The clothes are cast-offs, in our opinion," Miles said, "probably a charity case. You don't know anyone around town who dresses like this, do you?"

Jack shook his head.

"A transient then," Miles went on, "a hobo. Someone like that?"

"Hmm," Jack said.

Miles began to put the clothing back into the satchel. "He was shot."

"Was he?"

"Yes." Miles's alert blue eyes were even more so now, inquisitive, searching, staring directly at the chief. "In the back of the head. Execution-style."

FRANCE, 1943

CHAPTER EIGHTEEN

. . .

Adele and Manfred walked hand in hand up the narrow road toward the village of La Bouille. His hand felt as rough as the scales on a fish. Adele had planned to admonish him immediately and severely for not writing, but she couldn't. Not the way he looked. Not now. They walked along in silence.

Most of the couples turned in at the side of a rambling white-washed hotel, climbing down some steps to a large stone terrace that over-looked the river. Manfred and Adele followed them. The bright air was full of laughter. Nervous waiters ran back and forth. Girlfriends sat on boyfriends' laps. Drinks were ordered, cigarettes were smoked, young children were lifted up and dangled over the smiling faces of their fathers.

Adele and Manfred sat at a small table on the edge of the crowd. Manfred lit a cigarette. His hands shook. Two of his fingernails were black and a thumbnail was missing. He ordered two glasses of beer.

Adele waited for him to tell her what had happened. She wondered how long she'd have to wait.

"They came for us in trucks," Manfred finally said. "This was two days before we were to meet." He looked apologetic. "I could send you no word."

"I nearly drowned."

Manfred looked surprised.

"The night we were supposed to meet. It rained."

"I am so very sorry," Manfred said.

"Why didn't you write me?" She tried not to sound accusatory.

"I could not."

"Why not? I was told you were in Russia, I thought you might be dead. How could you go away like that and only be forty miles away and not write?"

"It was dangerous."

"Dangerous? Do you know what's dangerous? Not knowing what's happened to you and going mad, that's what's dangerous!"

Manfred glanced toward the other soldiers. "I apologize."

"That's not an explanation!" Adele shouted.

Manfred leaned toward her as if he were going to kiss her, his face only an inch away. "I could not write a letter, I was planning to run. The censors record all addresses. Once I disappeared, their records would lead to you."

"So why didn't you run? Why didn't you come for me?"

"I could not. So many patrols, I did not think I could make it."

"Then why didn't you write?"

Adele didn't know why she was going on like this, around and around as if she were stupidly stuck on one thing, like Lucille Rocque or someone.

Lucille was one of the girls sitting on a soldier's lap. Her soldier, her famous Wilhelm, had coarse peasant features and a head that looked like a boulder. Right now he seemed very pleased with himself. Lucille's lipstick was smeared all over his cheeks and mouth.

Manfred shifted back in his chair. He rolled his cigarette around between his ruined thumb and fingers. "Every day I thought, This is the day I go." His dark eyes lit up for a moment with their familiar warmth and then the light went out again. "I shovel and build scaffolds and pour concrete up and down the coast. Sometimes I drive a truck. I have travelled many miles pursuing this new profession. Clerks are beasts of burden now so the real soldiers can reinforce the Eastern Front."

He can't do this work, Adele thought, he's not like the others, he's too intelligent, it's too much for someone like him.

They strolled around the village arm in arm, wandering down the back lanes and along the riverbank. Adele worked at carrying on a one-sided conversation, telling Manfred about Old Raymond's death and the arrival of Madame Théberge and anything else she could think of and all the time feeling increasingly nervous about his long silences.

When it began to get dark, he led her up a winding laneway to a small stone inn poised above La Bouille. He'd already arranged for a tiny room on the top floor.

They had kissed only once, really kissed, strolling by the river, and then they'd walked on. It was as if they'd forgotten who they were.

Manfred climbed over the bed and pushed open the window. It was hot under the eaves, there seemed no air to breathe at all. He came back to Adele. He kissed her, the softest of kisses. They leaned against each other. Manfred began to undo the buttons on her blouse, gently one by one. It had been a year since they'd made love.

Adele began to shiver, really shiver, as if it were the middle of winter, as if she were freezing cold.

"Would you like me to close the window?"

"No."

"What is it?"

"I don't know."

Manfred slipped out of his uniform and out of his underclothes. Adele smiled at him. This was gallant, he was going first. He wrapped his arms around her to warm her, she kissed his neck, he undressed her, he kissed her breasts, moved close against her. And it all became familiar again, it all became like remembering again, discovering and rediscovering and shattering again.

Adele and Manfred rested on the bed beside each other, sweaty now in the oppressive heat, listening to each other's breathing slow down, become quiet, still.

Adele trailed her hand over his body. He was much thinner. She could feel each rib. She traced along his jagged scar. She kissed his chest, his stomach, came back up and kissed his stubbly chin. "Do you want me to tell you my plan?"

Manfred smiled. "I have been waiting."

She told him about her Paris plan.

"How would I find you?"

"We'd have to trust Lucille Rocque. I would mail her a letter when I had a safe place in Paris and she would tell you."

"What if she told Wilhelm instead?"

"We would just have to trust her not to tell him." Adele shifted a little on her hip so she could see him better. "Manfred, when Lucille gave me your note, at first I thought you could wait for another leave and then slip away from here. La Bouille is outside the Forbidden Zone and so it should be easier, but I saw so many fortifications being built between here and Rouen. So many soldiers. I think you were right all along. You can't escape." She pressed her face against his neck. "It's impossible. My plan won't work." She could feel the pulse of his blood against her lips. "Don't even think about it, it's too dangerous," she whispered, not knowing whether she wanted him to risk it or not.

He pulled her closer. His thin sinewy arms. His bruised hands.

"I will think about it," he said.

The next morning they went for another walk along the river. The sluggish water smelled more brackish in La Bouille than it did in Rouen; here it smelled of the sea.

"We stop our work to watch the aeroplanes." Manfred was standing on top of a rock in shallow water. "They fly from England so very high. Do you see them in Rouen?"

"Yes."

"They fly during the day now. Day and night. We hear that Berlin has been bombed." He began stepping from stone to stone. "Hamburg. Cologne. Dusseldorf."

Adele sat down on the riverbank. "People are saying that the war will be over soon."

"What people?" Manfred put his arms out like a teetering bomber, balancing precariously.

"Everyone. At the factory where I work. In the queues. All we have to do is wait. Everything will change."

"How do you suppose it will change? Do you think Germany will wave a white flag and that will be the end of it? Do you think Germany will not fight to the death?"

"I don't know. I only know that we must make it our business to survive. You and me." She looked away from him. She had no desire to pursue a conversation about war and desolation.

She could hear Manfred climbing up the bank toward her. When she turned back, he broke into his famous smile. He looked better today. His eyes had a stronger light in them. She knew it was only because of her, simply because she had held him, because she was there. It made her feel extraordinarily happy but it was such an enormous responsibility, too. It frightened her.

"I have been thinking of something all night to tell you," Adele said.

Manfred sat down beside her. "What is that?"

"We are the New European Order."

"Ha! We are?"

"Yes. Don't laugh. Not what Adolf Hitler says. But you and I."

Light was reflecting off the river, it was dancing on Manfred's face.

"We will help to build a world where this can't happen any more," Adele said. "The two of us. French and German together. We are very necessary people."

Manfred stared at the river. He tugged at some grass between his boots.

"This would be my dream, also," he said.

• • •

That night Adele and Manfred went to a dance at the white hotel. Everyone was there, including Lucille and Wilhelm, and the bottle-blonde, who was in the company of a thin, ramrod soldier with a strikingly handsome face, and the fifteen-year-old clinging to a soldier who looked no older than she did herself. Heavy boots and small dancing shoes stomped out the time while a local band of nervous musicians tried to keep up to the barbarians.

Everyone joined in the dance, whooping and whirling around the hall. It seemed to Adele that each set of partners was trying to make as much noise as possible, to demonstrate unbounded confidence to everyone else in the room, to chase away the shadows that seemed to lurk in all the corners.

Up to now, the only dances Adele had gone to had been patrolled by the nuns at her school. She and Manfred had never danced together before. They were awkward at first, but soon they were whirling around with the rest, Adele clinging to Manfred's neck, concentrating as furiously as if she were in the middle of a spelling bee. And then they just melted into each other, and then they just danced.

Sometime after midnight the musicians got up the courage to sneak off into the night. A soldier older than the rest began to play an accordion. The men put their arms around each other's shoulders and, swaying back and forth, sang patriotic songs and marching songs and songs of glory. Manfred joined in because he had to.

Adele stood in the crowd of women and watched him. Instead of good cheer and comradeship, foreboding began to fill the hall. Everyone had seen the bombers crossing overhead during the day and heard them droning by at night. And no response from the German side. Nothing.

After the singing was over, everyone got drunk.

Adele had never been drunk before. She couldn't believe how dislocated she felt and how disgustingly sick she was on the way back to their room. They made love, anyway. They made love all night long, and in the first light of dawn they were still sprawled across each other's bodies, fast asleep like two abandoned children on a raft at sea, their arms and legs entwined.

FRANCE, 1944

CHAPTER NINETEEN

• • •

A dele made friends with Lucille. They met twice a week at a café a few blocks from the city's main square. She knew she was taking a risk, for there would be people in town who knew Lucille was one of those girls. In addition, she was hardly the discreet type, but Adele felt she had no choice.

Manfred hadn't said that they should activate her Paris plan, but he hadn't said they shouldn't, either. Just as she was about to climb up the steps of the train to return to Rouen, he'd pulled her close.

"The New European Order may be here more quickly than you think," he'd said.

"What do you mean?" Adele had whispered, trying to cling to him in the crush of the other women but she was pushed up into the train.

There was no news of the men all through the autumn. Nor in January. Or February. The pain came back. Adele walked in a daze through the snowy streets, pushed herself through her shifts during the night, barricaded herself in her room away from her mother and Madame Théberge during the day. On a rainy morning at the end of March, Adele came out of the factory and saw Lucille standing in the middle of the road.

"They're working near Dieppe," Lucille shouted at her, "they've got a two-day leave."

Adele hurried up to Lucille and, taking her by the arm, swung her away from the other women. "What do you mean?

"They're coming by train. The whole company."

"To La Bouille?"

"No." Lucille's enormous eyes lit up. "Rouen! Here!"

"When?"

"Tonight!"

The same La Bouille crowd of soldiers and women gathered at a public hall on the edge of the city. There were long tables to sit at and copious steins of beer to drink and a waxed floor to dance on. A four-piece Wehrmacht band sat on a small platform at the end of the room and played four polkas and four waltzes in an unvarying cycle all night long. Adele recognized most everyone.

Manfred looked even thinner and more worn out than he had before, and he was either uninterested in dancing or he'd forgotten how. He kept losing time. He was too busy whispering in her ear about the planes. Fighter planes. They were appearing out of nowhere, coming in so low they were hardly above the ground, blowing up supply depots and bridges, roads, railroad tracks. The officers in charge were in a frenzy, driving the men on like slaves. They had to camouflage everything, sirens kept interrupting, they were constantly running into their bunkers and out again. And all the while the grey sea stretched out before them all the way to England like a silent threat. It filled their eyes.

The men had only one night to spend in Rouen. Lucille and Wilhelm invited Adele and Manfred and two of the other couples back to Lucille's place. Manfred and Adele were the only couple who could communicate to any degree. The others shouted at each other in a babble of French and German.

The four couples, more than a little drunk and holding on to each other for support, started off into the windy dark. The men began to sing a marching song. Adele noticed that Manfred was at least one word behind the others. She wondered how drunk he was as he leaned against her – she was holding up most of his weight.

As they turned a corner, laughing and stumbling along, Adele saw a woman coming toward them. When the woman saw the soldiers, she pressed meekly against a wall to let them pass.

"Adele," she said.

It was the spidery woman.

Adele turned her face away.

Lucille lived in three small rooms over an abandoned dress shop. She and Wilhelm disappeared into the bedroom. The cushions were taken off a battered couch and laid on the floor. Then the lights were turned off. Adele and Manfred somehow ended up occupying the couch, Adele lying under him against the bare springs. Manfred fell instantly asleep. Adele stroked his skull and listened to the muffled sounds of love-making. One of the women giggled. The other one began to cry softly.

Manfred's sleeping face looked as fragile as glass in the dark.

Adele thought about the spidery woman. It had been almost a year since the woman had left the factory. She'd been the only one who had shown any kindness to Adele, and Adele had often seen her touch the small crucifix she wore around her neck and kiss it. Her lips would move in silent Ave Maria's while she worked.

Adele wished she could pray that the woman would continue to be kind but she hadn't been able to pray for a long time. God could see the sin that was going on all around her in that beery, smoky room. He knew who she was.

Adele fell asleep. When she heard Manfred's voice, she thought she was dreaming.

"Adele. We have no more time," he was whispering, "Adele, wake up. We can't trust Lucille."

Adele opened her eyes. Someone was snoring loudly in the dark.

"We just don't know what Lucille might do. We don't know. I will run. I will find you." Manfred was resting on his elbow looking down at her.

Adele touched his cheek. "But all those fortifications. The patrols. They'll catch you."

"They won't."

"And they'll shoot you for being a deserter!"

"Shhh. No." Manfred pressed down closer. "Go to Paris when you are able. Rent the secret room. And then go to St. Augustine Street. Madame Bouchard's *pension*, remember? But don't go inside and don't let her see you. Whatever she might say about it, she's still making money from Germans. She's dangerous. Just walk past each day. I will know you are walking there. One day you will see me there."

"I'm afraid for you."

"Don't be afraid."

"When will you run? Don't run from the coast. Wait until your next leave."

"Yes," Manfred said.

The next day all the company's soldiers and all their girlfriends made their way to the main station in Rouen. A train was waiting to take the men back to their frantic labours on the coast. Manfred and Adele said nothing more about their plans but when they kissed goodbye, they pressed their mouths so hard together it hurt them both.

That night Adele walked slowly to her place at the long sewing tables. No one said a word. All the women looked just as they always did, even the huge button-eyed one and the new woman, the fierce blitzkrieg widow, her hair caught up in a net, her hands flying.

The spidery woman had apparently not been talking to anyone.

Adele spent the week trying to stay calm and plot her strategy. She needed to save money to rent a room. This was the first thing. The only problem was she'd been handing her pay packet over to Madame Théberge and holding back only a small allowance for herself. On the next payday Adele hid half her money under a loose floorboard in her bedroom closet. When Madame Théberge questioned her about this sudden shortfall, Adele told her that they were cutting back the rate of pay at the factory. The old woman's shrewd peasant eyes looked straight through her.

She met Lucille at the café every other day, but there was no message from Wilhelm of an up-coming leave. She spent more time than usual with Jean and Bibi, joining in their imaginary games, racing through the house, putting head locks on them. They pretended to complain that she was hugging and kissing them too much. One day they asked her why she looked like she was about to cry. Adele got them both down and bounced their heads off the wood floor. "You see? I'm not," she said.

On her next payday, she held back two-thirds of her money. When she gave Madame Théberge what was left, the old woman grabbed her by the collar.

"Give me the rest," she hissed.

"Let go," Adele cried, grabbing a fistful of the old woman's black dress. They stood there in the gloom of the upstairs hallway glaring at each other.

"I need it." Madame Théberge gave Adele a shake.

"They cut our pay back again." Adele twisted the old woman's bodice.

"Liar."

"Old bitch! Let go of me or I'll fetch René and have him kick you out of our house!"

Adele wasn't sure why she'd said that. René was the last person on earth she wanted to see, but it seemed to have the desired effect. Madame Théberge let her go, and Adele released her grip.

"And me, coming here, slaving to keep your family together. How can you treat a body like that?" Madame Théberge had softened her tone but her eyes were just as relentless as ever.

"You live here for free. Isn't that enough?"

"What do you want with so much money?"

"What money? There is no money. They hardly pay us!"

The old woman regarded Adele for a moment. "You're up to no good," she said.

Adele brushed past her and hurried down the stairs.

That night on her way to work, Adele lifted up the floorboard and transferred her money to her childhood treasury behind a loose foundation stone in Old Raymond's cottage. She knew that while she was away Madame Théberge would search her room.

Adele pushed through the back gate and walked toward the factory. The time had come for her to leave. She'd wait until the next day when the house was empty of Madame Théberge and her mother and Jean and Bibi, and she'd pack her clothes. She couldn't stand to wait any longer.

That night seemed to take an excruciatingly long time but now, near the end of her shift, a feeble light was creeping in the long row of dusty windows. The sewing machines continued to chatter, the line of Wehrmacht pants continued to flow.

I'll be in Paris by tonight, Adele thought to herself.

• • •

Manfred was just waking up. He pulled on his trousers, ducked through the low door in the concrete bunker and hurried along the sandy cliff toward the latrine. Out of the stuffy air in the bunker, the morning air felt chilly. He hunched his shoulders against it and glanced out over the water and wondered what Adele was doing.

The sky was white as milk. Far out, barely discernible, a black line stretched across the sea exactly where the horizon should have been. Lightning seemed to race along the length of it, and then race back again.

Manfred stood frozen in the expectant air until he heard the scream of the incoming shells and then he turned and began to run.

It seemed to him that he had a mile to go to reach the bunker. It seemed to him that he was running in slow motion, like a man in a dream.

• • •

Within the hour, everyone had heard the news: there had been a massive landing on a sixty-mile front from east of Cherbourg to Caen. The radio kept telling everyone to stay calm, that this was similar to Dieppe, that a glorious victory was assured, but the signals beaming out of England and being picked up by clandestine radio sets all over town were telling a different story.

The news flew through the streets and shops and factories. General de Gaulle had landed. The Free French army had landed. The British, the Americans, the Poles, the Canadians.

Adele's first thought was to run to the coast and try to rescue Manfred. All the women felt the same way. They met at the dance hall that night. Babies were crying, a few two- and three-year-olds were running around. Some of the women sat off to the side wanting to be alone. Others stood in groups and whispered like mourners at a funeral. They all look stunned. They all looked terrified.

On the way home Adele came to a decision – she would stay where she was. Rouen was only forty miles from the coast, Paris was at least one hundred. She was sure that Manfred had already slipped away from the battle, and since it had only been a few weeks since his last leave he would assume that she was still in Rouen. This was where he'd come to look for her.

Adele continued to go to work every evening, and every evening she expected to see Manfred standing by the back gate, dusty and worn from travelling, perhaps even wounded. When the days went by and he hadn't appeared, she began to fear that she'd made a terrible mistake. He must have assumed she was in Paris already, waiting for him, walking every day in front of Madame Bouchard's *pension*. But she wasn't. She'd let him down and now it was too late. There were no trains available to carry passengers anywhere. Every piece of rolling stock had been commandeered to carry German troops from the interior to the coast.

The horizon began to light up at night. It throbbed and flashed like a ferocious storm too far off to be heard. People stood on their rooftops to watch. German officials loaded documents into trucks, preparing to flee. Silent crowds gathered in the streets and watched. Some people dared to whisper the word liberation, though it still seemed like a far away dream.

One night bombs began to fall all around the city, blowing up the railroad tracks and bridges and roads, lighting up the cathedral and the river and the statue of Joan of Arc standing where, so many years before, she had been tied to a stake and burned. Adele huddled under her work table in the factory. The lights went out. Windows blew in. Everyone crept through the exploding dark and down the stairs to the first floor.

The bombardment lasted for three hours. At four o'clock, it stopped. At ten minutes after the hour, the lights miraculously flickered and came back on.

Adele blinked her eyes. It looked like it had snowed. Everyone was covered in plaster dust.

Some local men burst in, brandishing ancient rifles and shotguns and clubs. "The Germans are leaving," they shouted jubilantly, "every last one! Running! Pulling out!"

One of the men scrambled up on top of a table. "Officers! Troops! Even the goddamn prefect of police, the goddamn coward!"

A great cheer filled the long room, an exaltation like a huge breath, a roar. And shouts and cries.

People began to kiss and hug each other. Someone started singing La Marseillaise and everyone joined in. No one had heard it in years. Men and women began to scramble up on chairs and tables and on the top of the machines; women whipped their kerchiefs in the air, men flung their caps across the room.

Adele backed along the wall. She wanted to join in, too – it was her country, too, and she had suffered just as everyone had suffered – but something deep inside her chest was warning her to get out of there, get away.

She turned and walked as calmly as she could toward the loading docks. The massive woman who'd sat beside her was coming toward her, surging through the crowd. Adele didn't know whether to run or to stop, and then it didn't matter. Someone kicked her feet out from under her. She fell hard to the floor.

The young widow was standing over her. "Stay down where you belong," she said, but the massive woman had reached her and, grabbing a handful of Adele's hair, yanked her up on her feet.

"Buttercup," she said.

She began to drag Adele through the crowd. The young woman followed along. "My husband was killed in Charleville-Mézières! In Charleville-Mézières, I tell you!" she screamed. "Make way for a whore of a German cunt! Make way for a filthy Boche cunt!"

The men stared and gave way but the women didn't. They surged forward, a terrible light in their eyes, eager to see the whore. Adele tried not to be there. She tried to go somewhere else in her mind.

The big woman thrust Adele through the door that led outside. A crowd pushed out after them. The woman marched her across the footbridge, still holding her by the hair, forcing her up on her toes. A larger crowd was waiting on the other side. Adele could see two women down on their knees but she didn't recognize either one of them.

A mass of people began to walk through the acrid haze left over from the bombs, picking their way around scattered debris, moving under flickering, uncertain street lamps.

"Oh, Butter, Butter, Buttercup," the massive woman kept saying, yanking Adele back and forth from time to time as if she were afraid Adele might fall asleep.

The marchers became silent. Soon all Adele could hear was the shuffling sound of what seemed like hundreds of pairs of feet. People began to run out of their homes and gather in the dark to watch. Adele could feel a warm liquid trickling down between her legs.

She was in her father's garden, though she couldn't see him. He must have been keeping busy though, because it was in good order and all the flowers were in bloom. She was sitting on the wooden bench that rested against Old Raymond's cottage. It was always pleasant sitting there, the air sweet and drowsy-making, the sun radiating warmth off the stone walls. Old Raymond sat beside her on the step. She could see his lined velvety face. He held a frightened bird. He was smoothing its feathers with his broad finger. Adele set her mind to examining every feather, every ruffle and distinguishing mark, every flash of reflected light.

She couldn't stay there. Angry faces were intruding. Filthy words. Faces and words, coming closer, pressing forward. Someone threw a punch. It grazed her face. Someone spit. It hit her.

A woman carrying a child had positioned herself in the middle of the street. She stared at Adele as Adele was being dragged by. It was the spidery woman.

Adele began to pray. She prayed for everything to be over. She prayed for God to swallow the world. She prayed to be dead.

The procession turned a corner, marched into the main square and pushed into an even larger crowd. It seemed that half the city was there. Lucille Rocque was there, sitting on a chair and holding her cut hair in her lap. When she looked up at Adele, Adele could see that a swastika had been painted on her forehead and had run down her face like a stream of black tears.

The big woman pressed Adele down into another chair and backed away, playing to the crowd, wiping her hands on her dress as if to get rid of all traces of disease. Adele's underwear felt soaked. Her dress, no doubt, was soaked through, too. Everyone would know.

She looked around hoping there was no one she would recognize and no one to recognize her, but she knew that there would be, some of them would, the only daughter of dear Dr. Henri Paul-Louis, who had delivered their children, who had supported their workers' politics, who had gone missing in action against the Germans.

A man began to shave her head, pressing her face hard against his stomach. Adele could feel the cold metal humming against her skull. Her hair began to fall past her eyes.

Someone somewhere began to pound a drum.

A woman came forward and painted her skull in a cold, wet criss-crossing.

Someone began to bang on a tambourine.

The man lifted Adele to her feet. She could see the others now, perhaps fifteen in all, freshly shaved skulls startling white, new swastikas gleaming.

A corridor opened up through the middle of the crowd. The women walked toward it as if they knew what they had to do, as if they'd known that this would be what they would have to do for a long time.

Adele walked toward it.

The drum and tambourine continued to bang and clash. Bang and clash. And another sound. It started low, a kind of hum, rising to a sigh, an abandonment, a throaty whine until all the crowd began to groan and sway.

A woman punched Lucille in the face. Lucille fell down. A man emptied a pail of kitchen slop over her head. The groan rose to a wail. The rest of the women kept walking. Adele kept walking. The crowd surged forward, plucking at the women's clothes, pulling, tugging. The women pulled back. The crowd roared. A man grabbed Adele by the throat, a woman ripped at her blouse. She could feel hands everywhere, she stumbled, felt herself being dragged over the cobblestones, spun around, her clothes pulled away, her underclothes ripped away.

Everyone fell silent. Everyone shuffled back a little.

Adele crouched down on the road.

She could hear the sound of someone approaching. She could feel a cold boot push against her side, forcing her over slowly and firmly.

Adele rolled over on her back, exposed for all the world to see.

CHAPTER TWENTY

• • •

A man had been shot, execution-style. Jack considered this bit of news.

"How do you figure?" Jack said.

"Close up, back of the head, blew out a piece of skull just above his right eye," Harold Miles replied.

"Really," Jack said.

He could feel the weight of his own revolver resting on his right hip, and he could read the young detective's mind like a newspaper. Who in that town would be more able than a rogue cop to manoeuvre someone into a position of helplessness, maybe hand-cuffed and down on his knees? That would explain Jack's interest in the dead man once the tell-tale finger showed up. That would explain his attempt to destroy evidence, or maybe his attempt to move the body to a safer place.

"That's interesting," Jack said, unsnapping his holster and pulling his revolver out.

Harold Miles's eyes opened a little wider, but that was all.

Jack turned the long-barrelled revolver over in his hands. "What kind of weapon was it?"

"We don't know yet."

"But you know he was shot close up?"

"Two or three inches away. Powder burns."

"Surprised you could tell, the corpse being as far gone as it was."

"Not that difficult. It looked like someone had sprinkled some pepper around the entry wound."

Jack held out his revolver to the young detective. "Want to test it?"

Miles hesitated but just for a heartbeat. "Of course not."

Jack smiled. "I understand, detective. Everyone's a suspect at this point. No offence taken." He slowly put the revolver back into its holster and kept smiling. He knew he had to be very careful now. The game was on.

• • •

Jack watched from a distance. Miles had gathered a small army together. A line of slow-moving men worked their way through the trees and bushes and along the riverbank by the empty grave, looking for the murder weapon.

The river had filled up from yesterday's rain, and the water was rushing by mud-coloured and angry-looking. Two cops stood waist-deep in it, bracing themselves against the fresh current, searching the bottom with long-handled rakes.

Jack made a half-circle around the search area, walking through the trees to the river's edge. No one seemed to pay any attention to him or even notice he was there. He began to plow through the tall grass downriver. He stepped over freshets, waded across an over-flowing creek. His feet were wet again. So were his pants.

Jack stumbled, almost pitched over on his face. He was trying to go too fast over the rough ground. And he was feeling a bit light-headed, too. After the meeting with Harold Miles, he'd allowed himself only two hours of fitful sleep.

The mayor had called just as he was leaving the house to let him know he'd had a talk with Miles, too. "We'll let the OPP handle everything from now on. That's the protocol, isn't it, Jack?" the mayor had said.

"Whatever you say," Jack had replied.

He was in a race, that was the thing. He had to keep pressing on. The sky was washed pale by the rain. The heat of the past few weeks had disappeared. The river was gurgling and swishing by.

What did he know that Miles didn't know? Not much. He knew the thin line of blue clay between the heel and the sole of the dead man's shoes hadn't come from the reddish mud in the grave. But Miles would have noticed that, too. He wasn't stupid.

Don't make that mistake, Jack said to himself, and then again, so it would stick. Don't underestimate Harold Miles.

That was Jack's problem. He knew it. His wife had told him enough times. He underestimated people. His own son, for one.

Jack stumbled again, touched down on one knee, struggled back up on his feet. "Goddamn it to hell," he said.

He had to calm down. He could feel his heart racing.

"What do I know that Miles doesn't?" This time he asked the question out loud. The river seemed full of voices. Jack was ready to listen.

Execution-style. Execution-style.

That was the key to the whole thing. Jack had known this as soon as the young detective had opened his mouth. But of course Miles knew this, too. He just didn't know enough about the town to know what he knew. Not yet.

A bullet in the back of the head. Seemed just the kind of summary punishment you might expect from the DPs, given who those people were, given what they must have experienced.

And Jack knew one other thing that Miles didn't know, at least for the moment. He pushed on through the grass.

He knew where to look for the blue clay.

FRANCE, 1944

CHAPTER TWENTY-ONE

• • •

Nuns descended on Adele like a flock of grey birds, covering her in a blanket and leading her through the crowd while all the time remaining grimly silent, making it plain that they were simply doing their duty, distasteful as it was.

They covered up the other women, too, some similarly naked, others clinging to scraps of garments. Lucille Rocque's face was covered in blood.

The nuns hurried them toward a parish hall on the other side of the square. A surly-looking group of men was already gathering by the door. A shaky old priest told the men to go home and ushered the women in. He locked the door behind them. "Fetch the charity boxes!" he cried out. His surprisingly vibrant voice rang through the bleak room. "Fetch some rags!"

Adele fell on the floor.

"Can't you stand?" a sister asked. Adele didn't answer. After a while, the nun went away.

Someone had wiped the blood off Lucille's face. Both her eyes were swollen and from where Adele was huddled under her blanket she could see that Lucille's nose looked almost translucently red.

Adele got up and sat down on a chair beside her.

"Fucking turd-eaters," Lucille muttered.

Adele stared at her, not sure what she was talking about. Something terrible had happened, something unclear.

A young sister came along. She was handing out rags. "You must try to wipe off the paint. Scrub hard. You must pray to God that it comes away."

Adele reached up and touched the top of her head. Her hand looked black.

"I can't rub. My head hurts too fucking much," Lucille complained. She began to dab at the top of Adele's head. Adele couldn't feel a thing.

After a while the old priest came along, dipped a rag in a bowl of wood alcohol and cleaned off the rest of Adele's paint. Now and then he looked down at her. Adele closed her eyes. She had no idea whether the liquid felt cold or hot, whether it stung. She clutched her blanket close to her so that he couldn't see anything.

"Confessions begin in twenty minutes." His voice boomed out over her head as he addressed the room. "No exceptions. See that door? Go through it into the church!"

Adele felt his warm breath touch her ear. "In your deepest despair," he whispered, "remember Mary Magdalene."

Once he was gone, Lucille whispered, "Do you want to go to confession?"

Adele shook her head.

Some of the women began to file through the side door into the church. Lucille led Adele over to the charity boxes and held the blanket up as a screen while Adele dressed in the first thing her hands touched, a faded housedress spotted with bleach. It felt strange to be naked underneath the flimsy dress. She pulled on a pair of scuffed open-toed shoes.

"One more thing," Lucille said and wrapped a paisley-patterned bandanna around Adele's head. She covered her own bald and battered head with a lime-coloured hat.

They made their way to the back of the hall in small stages. The nuns were busy gathering up dirty paint rags and blankets and leading women to confession. As soon as they were looking the other way, Lucille unlocked the back door.

A soft light was just beginning to turn the sky pink. Adele could still smell the bombardment, she could see wisps of smoke still floating in the air.

They followed a path through the priest's vegetable garden and crept behind the back of the small church next door. Some distance away, on a quiet side street, a man was standing under a tree. Groups of people were passing the front of the church along the square.

Lucille and Adele began to walk away down the side street, expecting to hear shouts, expecting to be chased and run to ground at any moment.

• • •

Adele dreamt of Manfred. It was winter and he was carrying buckets of steaming concrete through the wind and the blinding snow. His face was an icy mask. His hands were black.

Adele woke up and saw Lucille sitting at her tiny table in the windowless kitchen. She was on Lucille's couch again. Her bandanna had come loose and was lying across her arm. She put her hand up to her head and touched the cool stubbly skin.

"It's only a fraction of what's happening to Wilhelm and Manfred right this very minute," Lucille said.

Adele got up and stood by the kitchen door. Lucille was smoking a cigarette. Her one eye was completely shut. Blood encrusted her nostrils. Her nose had a white spot in the middle and was leaning over to one side.

"I think your nose is broken," Adele said.

Lucille shrugged. "I'm not worrying."

Adele walked over to the mirror hanging above the sink and looked at herself. It was a shock. Some girl with a bald head and enormous eyes was looking back at her. She could see paint gleaming in this girl's pores like a plague of blackheads. Who was she? Not Adele Georges. Not a citizen of Rouen. Not French.

No one.

"It'll grow back," Lucille said.

"No, it won't," Adele replied. She huddled on the couch again. Her heart felt dead. Her skin felt covered in ice. Her lungs laboured to breathe.

Spat upon. That's all she could get her mind around. Refuse. Waste. Anathema. Yes, that was the word Father Salles would use. That was the very word.

They hid in Lucille's rooms all that day and at two o'clock in the morning Adele went home. The city had turned off all its lights. In the distance the sky flashed and rolled with the thunder of heavy artillery. Evidently the Germans had not withdrawn very far.

Adele hurried through the empty streets guided by glimpses of rooftops and the ghostly shapes of trees that flickered occasionally out of the dark. She was still wearing the housedress and the paisley scarf. Lucille had given her a pair of pink panties several sizes too large. She had to pin the waistband, but still just the feel of them was a kind of comfort.

She knew that all that mattered was getting through the next two or three days because that's what Lucille kept telling her. The madness out on the streets would dissipate. People would have to go back to thinking about themselves. Everything had been disrupted. There was no food, no work, no money. Bombs were falling.

Adele had remembered her cache of money behind the foundation stone.

"We'll need it," Lucille had said.

Adele crept up the back lane and pushed open the wooden gate. She looked toward the house. Each faraway flash seemed to move the house toward her and then it would recede into the dark again. She stood there for a long time watching it appear and disappear. She wanted her father. This emotion came in a rush and filled her heart.

She hurried through the garden but instead of stopping at Old Raymond's cottage, she continued on toward the kitchen door. She could see that Madame Théberge had covered the inside of the windows with bedsheets in obedience to a black-out order. She wondered if Jean and Bibi were sleeping through all the bomb flashes, the far-off rumble of guns. She knew that they wouldn't be. She knew that they'd be lying in their beds terribly frightened. They needed her.

Adele tried the door. For the first time in her memory, it was locked. She moved along the porch toward the window. A sheet was draped over it but it had been pulled aside. Her mother was standing there.

"Mother," Adele said, and wondered if she could hear her through the glass and if she knew what had happened to her. Of course she would know. There would have been a rush to inform her. All the neighbours. Father Salles. And Madame Théberge went out every day to search the shops for food, she never missed a day. Someone would surely have told Madame Théberge and she would have told her mother.

Madame Georges was staring at her as if she'd just stumbled on a burglar and didn't know what to do. Adele could see her mouth working nervously, her thin fingers pressing against her cheek.

"Mother, please let me in."

Her mother didn't move and then she shook her head.

Adele took a step back, and as if she were a child again, as if she were showing off an accidental wound, she reached up and took off her bandanna.

"Go away," Adele could hear her mother say, "get away from here!" Her mother reached up, closed the sheet and disappeared.

Adele went back to Old Raymond's cottage. She knelt down, felt for the loose stone and pulled it out. Through the years she'd hidden everything precious in this hollowed-out spot – a toy she'd stolen from René, glass and paste jewellery, a photograph of a certain boy.

She felt in the dark for her small roll of bills, found them, put them in her dress pocket and without looking behind her, did what her mother had told her to do. She walked away.

• • •

Two other women from the excursion to La Bouille snuck up the stairs to Lucille's rooms the next morning – Bridget the teenager, who now had two blackened eyes, and the woman called Maddy, carrying her sixteen-month-old daughter.

Lucille's nose had turned blue overnight but she could still breathe through it. Bridget said that her father, on seeing her bald scalp, had taken her by the neck and had punched her and punched her. She gazed at Lucille's nose and asked her if it was all right.

"It's not broken," Lucille said.

Over the next three weeks the women settled into a routine, with Lucille's twelve-year-old brother arriving at odd hours to run errands for them and bring them scraps of food. Because the ration system had broken down, everything had to be paid for in cash. Adele had the most money so they used her money to pay for most everything.

Adele passed the time standing in the kitchen staring in the mirror. The slightest covering of fine black hair was beginning to show, as soft as Maddy's little girl's hair. This seemed particularly strange to Adele. Her hair had always been springy and thick to the touch.

Early one morning the women woke to the sounds of shouting. They crept across the front room and, pulling the curtain a little aside, looked down into the street below. Some men were running past their building. Others were gathering in the middle of the street. A kind of rumbling thunder began to fill the air, it vibrated the walls and floor.

French flags appeared in the apartments opposite, people leaned out their windows, Lucille's brother came bursting in through the door.

"What is it?" Lucille demanded.

"Soldiers!" He danced around the room. "Different ones, new ones!"

Adele could see a tank approaching along the street. Some boys were riding on the front of it and two young women were sitting on the edge of the turret beside a grinning soldier. Another tank appeared covered in flowers and excited youngsters. A jeep full of young women and soldiers passed by.

"Who are they?" Adele asked.

"Canadians!" Lucille's brother yelled, jumping up and down on the couch and almost beside himself with excitement. "Canadians!" He opened the door again and disappeared back down the stairs.

"We've been liberated," Maddy said, apprehension in her voice.

Bridget crumpled to the floor, tears streaming down her face. Lucille bolted the door and began to push the sofa in front of it. Maddy picked up her child and retreated into Lucille's bedroom. Adele remained by the window, looking down into the street.

The party lasted for three days, at least as far as the women could tell and from Lucille's brother's daily reports, but none of the celebrants came looking for them. It was as if Lucille's rooms were empty, as if they didn't exist.

On the fourth day Adele came in from the kitchen to make an announcement. "Manfred would have run away as soon as the fighting started," she said. The rest of the women were sitting in the front room in a cloud of cigarette smoke discussing their changed circumstances. Maddy's child was entertaining them, banging a spoon incessantly on the bottom of a pot.

"He'll be in Paris. I'm meeting him there," Adele went on.

The women looked a little startled. They glanced at each other. "No one could have gone anywhere in all that fighting, Adele," Maddy said. "Besides, the Resistance is everywhere now. It would be impossible to hide."

"Everyone's carrying guns," Bridget added.

Maddy picked up her child and settled her on her lap. "Just pray that he stayed with the regiment and that they managed to retreat safely. I pray that's what Ernst did."

"Jon would have stayed. He said he was looking forward to a fight. Better than building scaffolds every day." Bridget puffed furiously on her cigarette.

Lucille's round face looked suddenly flushed. "Why do you think Manfred would have run?"

"Because I asked him to."

All the women looked at Adele.

Lucille's face turned a darker shade. "You asked him to?"

"He hates war. It makes no sense. Or do you think it does?"

Lucille got up off the couch.

"The best thing to do," Maddy said, "is stay where we are and pray that Germany surrenders."

"We could pray that Germany wins," Bridget said.

"No, we can't pray for that."

"But if they win, they'll come back to us. If they don't, who knows what will happen? You don't know what will happen. No one knows." Bridget looked close to tears again.

Lucille's voice sounded harsh and dangerous in the small room. "Wilhelm didn't run. He's not a deserter. Do you know what I pray for? I pray that most of the men weren't asked by their girlfriends to run away and leave the rest to be slaughtered."

"Manfred is in Paris," Adele said.

It all made perfect sense. Manfred had been poised to run on his next leave anyway, so why would he have stayed when the fighting started? And in the confusion, amid all the exploding fire and smoke and terror, who would have cared about one soldier? He would have moved at night and hid during the day.

That's as far as Adele wanted to think. That's all she wanted to know. He had kept his end of the bargain. He had gone to Paris.

Adele picked up some scissors, walked over to her bedsheet where she'd left it crumpled in a corner and began to cut off a long strip.

"What are you doing, dear?" Maddy asked.

"Making a bandage." Adele carried the strip into the kitchen and, checking herself in the mirror, began to wrap it around her head. It was a struggle, trying to make it look like a dressing on a wound, trying to cover every inch of her bald head.

"Why are you doing this?" Lucille had followed her in.

"So no one will know who I am."

"But why, sweetheart?" Maddy insisted.

"I'm going to Paris."

Lucille rolled her eyes at the other women. "That must be quite the head wound," she said.

Maddy handed the baby to Bridget and began to help Adele. She wrapped the cloth more tightly and secured it with safety pins.

"There's no chance that Manfred is in Paris." Bridget was looking red-eyed and very cross. "He's either with the regiment or he's dead."

"No," Adele replied blithely.

"I think we should all stay here a littler longer, Adele," Maddy said, "but it's true, you know. Soon we'll all have to do something. I can't keep the baby hidden up here forever."

"They'll kill us!" Bridget cried out.

Lucille was looking exasperated. "The longer we wait, the better it will be. I thought we'd all agreed to this. We said we'd at least wait until our hair grew out."

Adele went back to the front room and began to cut off another strip. The women followed her and watched in silence. She began to wrap her left arm in a make-shift sling. Maddy relented and helped her tie it around her neck.

"Stop helping her," Lucille said.

Maddy shrugged. "She's going to go."

"Are you going?" Lucille asked Adele.

"Yes."

"Why don't you wait until your hair grows out? Then you won't have to wear those stupid bandages."

"I can't."

"All right then … Jesus!"

Lucille stomped off into her bedroom. A few moments later she came back with a raincoat. She thrust it at Adele. "Take it."

"Thank you," Adele said.

"You've gone crazy. You know that, don't you? You're off your head." Lucille went in to the kitchen and began to rummage through the cupboards, making a great deal of noise.

"I'll tie this again," Maddy offered, undoing the sling.

Adele pulled on the raincoat, not caring that it was at least two sizes too big, just wanting to breathe fresh air, just wanting to leave. She was weeks late. Poor Manfred, waiting all this time. Weeks and weeks.

Maddy stuffed a pair of extra socks into a pocket of the raincoat. Adele added her own extra pair of underwear and a sweater she'd bought using Lucille's brother as a go-between. Bridget wrapped the paisley bandanna around her bandaged head.

"It will look more natural," Bridget said.

Lucille came out of the kitchen with some bread and a piece of cheese wrapped in a bit of newspaper. Her eyes were shiny.

Adele kissed her cheek. "After I find Manfred, and when it's safe, I'll write."

"Sure, okay," Lucille said, and whispered in her ear, "You're sick, Adele. You've become sick."

"No," Adele said.

The women hugged her and Adele hugged each one back. They knew she was taking the last bit of money she had left from her job, the last bit of money any of them had.

Adele went out the door and down the stairs. She couldn't remember having climbed them the last time because she didn't want to remember the last time. She remembered instead climbing them with Manfred after the dance, holding up his weight, glancing at his sweet ravished face.

Adele pushed open the outside door and walked down the street. By the time she'd reached the first corner, she was limping.

FRANCE, 1944

CHAPTER TWENTY-TWO

• • •

Adele decided she'd follow the main railway line out of the city. That way she wouldn't be seen by anyone but tramps and drifters. A crew of workmen was repairing the tracks. Adele circled around them. Soon there were bomb craters everywhere and shattered boxcars and wild tangles of rusting steel. Everything towered over her. The water in the craters looked dangerously deep. It was impossible to pick a clear way through.

When she saw a sandy path leading up a steep railway embankment, she struggled up it and found herself at the foot of a narrow street. The back gardens were strung with lines of laundry. She was still far from the outskirts, in a district of factories and workers' row houses. Adele limped along, hot now under Lucille's over-sized raincoat. Children began to appear at the doors. Two dogs ran toward her to investigate.

A woman with wild-looking hair, bushy and grey, asked her who she was looking for. A massive crater that must have obliterated at least two homes gaped behind her.

"I'm trying to find the road to Paris."

"It's a long walk from here."

"I'm fine." Adele smiled bravely, limping along. Some of the older children fell in step with her.

"When you reach Lucerne Boulevard, turn right," the woman called. "The Paris road is two miles from there. Ask someone to give you a ride."

"I will."

An older girl pulled at Adele's sleeve. "What happened to you?"

"A bomb," Adele replied.

She found Lucerne Boulevard and limped the two miles to the Paris road. She was still inside the city. No one spit at her. No one called her names. Men doffed their caps. Women smiled sympathetically. Adele smiled back at everyone but she didn't know how she should feel.

Ahead of her, a large green army truck was sitting beside the road that led from Rouen to Paris. She could see the legs of a soldier sticking out from under the motor. Another soldier was sitting high up in the cab, the door open, eating something out of a can.

"Hello, Mademoiselle," he called out in very bad French as Adele limped by.

Though it was September, the day was as hot as the middle of summer. Sweat was running under her bandages and under the raincoat. She walked up to the truck.

The soldier's pale blue eyes lit up.

"Hello," Adele said.

"Do you speak the English?" he asked in his broken French. His face was lean, his eyes small. He had red hair.

"No," Adele said, trying to recall her school's conversational English class. "Thank you very much," she added in English.

The soldier smiled. "You're speaking English now."

The man under the truck scrambled out, oil gleaming on his face and hands. He wiped his face on his sleeve and grinned. He looked younger than the soldier in the cab. "Hello," he said.

"Hello," Adele replied.

"She's real friendly," the redhead said.

Adele saw the men exchange glances. "Canadian?" she asked.

The man in the cab laughed. "Hell no, honey. I'm from Philadelphia. This potato-head here's from Idaho. The United States of America. Americans. You've heard of us, haven't you?"

Adele could see a line of sweat trickling down his face.

"Americans, yes." Adele smiled what she hoped was a winning smile.

"Jesus," the young one murmured, scratching his thatch of blond hair with an oily hand. "She's half all right, isn't she?"

The soldier in the cab put his can of food aside and stepped down on to the road. "What happened to you? Did you hurt yourself?" Everything was in English now, aided by sign language. He patted his forehead and bent his left arm like it was in a sling.

"Yes." Adele smiled again. "Paris?"

"Paris?" The older soldier looked down the road as if he expected to see it. "You want to go to Paris?"

"Paris. Yes." Adele turned to the younger one. He was just standing there grinning stupidly at her.

"Hell, you're in luck then," the older one said. He picked up Adele's free hand and led her toward the back of the truck. "That's where we're going. We're going to Paris."

The younger one followed behind. "I don't know, Kelly, we're not allowed. We'll get skinned alive."

The older soldier turned back with a broad and friendly smile. "Don't use my name and shut your trap." He squeezed Adele's hand. "Let's go to Paris."

Adele looked into the soldier's face, into his eyes, she tried to read his mind, his soul. The soldier reached up and yanked on a steel lever. The tailgate crashed down.

"Sorry," he said. He gestured toward the opening under the canvas top and eased himself up on to the gate.

"We're going to get skinned alive," the younger soldier repeated.

The older one ignored him. "Get my coat out of the cab," he said.

The redheaded soldier reached down for Adele. She put her good arm around his neck and felt herself being lifted up with almost no effort at all. He set her down carefully inside the truck so as not to hurt her bad leg. This gesture reassured her. The truck was full of stacked wooden crates.

"Chow. Rations," he said, gesturing toward his mouth, "You know ... eat?"

Adele nodded, though she wasn't exactly sure what he was talking about. It was even hotter under the canvas than on the road; everything was bathed in a bright yellow glow.

The man began to shove the crates around, hurrying to make a narrow alleyway. He cleared out a little room at the front, just behind the cab. "Snug as a bug in a rug," he said.

The other soldier loomed up behind carrying an army coat and looking concerned. "What if some brass stops us? Jesus, I don't know. We're late as it is."

The redhead took the coat, spread it down on the bed of the truck and smoothed it out. He motioned for Adele to sit down. The coat reminded her of Manfred's coat. She smiled and shook her head.

"We'll be in Paris in no time," the soldier said.

. . .

The road to Paris wasn't there. Once upon a time it had been gently rolling and paved, graced with avenues of trees and quaint stone bridges. Adele had travelled it several times before with her father and René in their shiny blue touring car.

Looking out the back of the truck, all she could see was a muddy trail receding behind her like a gash in the earth's crust, and a line of flayed trees. Bomb craters were scattered everywhere, so were abandoned tanks and upside-down trucks and the blasted remnants of artillery pieces. Rough plank bridges spanned gullies and streams.

The truck wound its way through the debris, gears grinding against each other, creaking and bouncing and shuddering. Adele held on to the crates and swayed about in the narrow passageway. Eventually she sat down on the soldier's coat. That was worse – every bump lifted her up and smacked her down again. She squeezed through the crates to the side of the truck and hung on, swaying there and looking out a tear in the canvas.

The villages along the road were unrecognizable. In some places only a single wall remained standing for the length of the main street. In others, blackened shells of gutted buildings seemed to crowd forward, towering over the truck. Groups of ragged children tried to keep up, running alongside and holding out their hands for candy or food. Some of the rubble was still smouldering. The stench in the air made Adele's eyes stream.

On the edge of one village, the truck creaked to a stop and the engine died. Adele could see the younger soldier climb down from the cab holding on to what looked like an oily watering can. He disappeared from sight.

She could hear the scrape of metal, some cursing or what sounded like cursing, more bangs on metal, a crash. The soldier got back into the cab, the engine turned over and everything began to vibrate again.

Adele made her way back to the little room the redheaded soldier had made. She felt half-roasted in the bright yellow light. She took off her raincoat and laid it down over the army coat. Her dress was sticking to her skin. She curled up on the coats, closed her eyes and tried to get used to rocking back and forth. Her arm was slick with sweat, and she could feel sweat trickling down her neck. The road seemed smoother, though, and the truck seemed to be moving faster.

She tried to imagine what Manfred would look like when he first saw her walking down St. Augustine Street. Would he be angry that she'd taken so long? No, not Manfred. His eyes would go red with emotion like they always did. He'd smile his smile, his arms would hold her so tightly she could almost feel them.

"What happened, Adele? What happened to you?"

She couldn't form a reply. She couldn't imagine one. It was beyond being late. It was beyond the public beating in the square. It was beyond anything she knew.

She was flying over Rouen. She could see the park. The river. Everything shimmered below her as if she were flying over a sea and looking down at the ground through water. The air began to turn misty. It began to fill with snow. She lost the horizon.

Adele woke up.

The truck had stopped again. The redheaded soldier was standing in the passageway. Before Adele could lift her head, before she could say a word, he was on top of her.

Adele kicked and tried to crawl away. She could feel his hand digging between her legs. She screamed. He battered her head against the side of a crate. She twisted away and bit his face.

"Jesus Christ Almighty!" he cried out. Adele could taste blood, it was streaming out of his cheek. His hand flew up to stem it. Adele scrambled away, forgetting her bad leg, her wounded arm, and crawled down the passageway.

She could hear him scrabbling after her. She could feel his hand grip her ankle.

"Let her go or I'll brain you, Kelly, I swear to God I will!"

Adele looked up to see the blond soldier straddling the tailgate and swinging an oily wrench in the air.

"She fucking bit me!" the redheaded soldier screamed.

Adele rolled over the gate and landed hard on the road. She got up and began to run, running back toward Rouen, running until she couldn't run any more, until she couldn't breathe.

CANADA, 1946

CHAPTER TWENTY-THREE

• • •

Jack stumbled into the river, regained his balance and gazed up at the cliff face. It towered above him, mud-brown and foreboding.

In years gone by and perhaps as recently as yesterday's storm, sections along the topmost edge had given way, sending trees cascading down toward the water. Some of them had hung up halfway to the river, jammed into small ravines, suspended in tangled, dead heaps.

The water swirled around Jack's knees, tugged at his legs. He stood there motionless, waiting until his breathing calmed down, until his heart stopped racing.

This was a good place to fish when the river was lower and calmer, at least that's what Jack had been told. Bass and pike. Use a minnow and a bobber.

Jack wasn't much of a fisherman, never had the time for it, and his father hadn't been one, either. Just a hard-rock miner. Just a drinker. A fierce and dangerous man in his cups, a tirelessly sarcastic one when he was sober.

Jack waded to the edge of the cliff and put his hand on a scale of caked mud the size of a dinner plate. He tried to get a foothold, managed it, and hauled himself out of the water. This was what he and his son had done over twenty years before. Or at least, had attempted to do.

He'd taken Kyle fishing because Ruth had complained that he didn't take enough interest in his son, that they never did anything together. Jack had ignored her for some time, but one day he saw a man and a small boy fishing along the river and it woke up something painful inside himself.

He'd asked Dickson Smiley, who was still working with the police force at the time and who was supposed to be a good fisherman, where a likely spot might be.

"For what?"

"For fishing."

Dickson looked a little surprised. "What kind?"

"Any kind."

"Well," Dickson said, looking as much amused now as surprised – just the thought of Jack Cullen fishing was funny, "if you're interested in bass or pike, Jack, you could try the Devil's Elbow."

Jack knew the spot, a sharp bend in the river a mile or so upstream from the town, but he thought it was more a swimming hole than a place to fish.

"Both," Dickson assured him.

Early the next Saturday morning Jack borrowed two poles from Dickson, who'd rigged them up and even supplied Jack with a pail of minnows, and he and Kyle struck out for the river.

Kyle hadn't seemed that thrilled when Jack had first mentioned going fishing, and now he was lagging behind as Jack strode along beside the railway tracks. It was the shortest way to get to the Devil's Elbow, hike along the tracks and then take a left turn. A path, worn smooth by countless kids, young lovers and tramps, wound through thick scrub willows to the base of a hill and around both sides to the river's edge. In the summer, at normal water levels, there was a sandbar at the centre of the cliff, a good place to get a suntan and go swimming or, apparently, to fish.

Kyle was fifty yards behind by the time Jack reached the opening to the path, though the boy was only carrying a fishing pole. Jack stood there waiting, an incoherent and unreasonable rage boiling up inside him. Kyle didn't want to go fishing, he didn't want to go anywhere with his father – he couldn't have made it more obvious.

"Step on it!" Jack barked back down the tracks.

Kyle looked a little startled, shaken out of some day-dream.

Jack didn't want to be there either. He felt ridiculous walking along with a slopping pail of water in one hand and a fishing pole in the other. There was something phony about it, as if he were pretending to be someone he wasn't.

Jack hurried down the path and into the scrub willows, finally waiting at the base of the hill where the path split left and right so that Kyle could see which way he turned. Birds flitted about in the thickets. The sun was lifting over the hill and the morning was turning hot. No sign of Kyle. "Jesus Christ."

After a while Jack retraced his steps along the path. He heard a thrashing in the bush. Kyle had got his pole stuck in some branches, the line wound hopelessly around, the bobber bobbing ridiculously a few feet over his head.

"What the hell happened?"

"I don't know." Kyle was looking at the pole as if he'd never seen one before.

Jack grabbed the heavy braided line and whipped and yanked but it wouldn't come free so he took it in both his huge hands and snapped it. Kyle was watching closely now. Jack did the same thing to the line at the bobber and hook.

"I'll tie it back on when we get to the river," Jack said and tried a smile. Kyle didn't say anything. Jack turned and walked away.

As they stood beside the river, Jack could see that he'd taken the wrong path. The sandbar, smooth as the back of a fish, breached the river about fifty feet away but they were standing downstream. There was no chance of floating a minnow past it and Jack had never cast a bait in his life. Dickson had said to fish off the sandbar.

Jack peered into the water. The river was always a thick muddy colour. "We could take our boots off and wade. It's not deep here."

Kyle looked dubious.

"We have to fish off that sandbar."

"We could fish here," Kyle replied.

"What's the matter, don't you want to get your feet wet?"

Kyle looked up the cliff face to the over-hanging clumps of trees that looked poised to crash down.

"Kids go swimming off that sandbar all the time," Jack said, meaning, What the hell's wrong with you?

Kyle looked listless, his shoulders slumped forward, his chest hollow.

"Stand up straight."

Kyle remained Kyle – he didn't even seem to notice what Jack had just said.

"Look," Jack tried to soften his voice a little, "if you want to keep your feet dry we can just climb over there."

The muddy wall of the cliff was cracked and baked and it wasn't exactly straight up and down. There seemed plenty of ledges and footholds. Kyle continued to stare up at the tangle of trees.

"Give me your pole," Jack said, "I'll show you."

Kyle handed over the pole more quickly than he'd needed to, Jack thought, the fastest thing he'd done all day. With the minnow pail in one hand and the two poles in the other, Jack began to traverse the face of the cliff. He was about ten feet above the water and for such a big man was picking his way along quite easily. "Watch what I'm doing and step where I step," he called back to Kyle.

The mud began to break away from under the edge of his heavy police boots. He could feel himself beginning to slide a little. He put his uphill hand on the cliff for balance, the one holding the poles. He crouched there, stuck, unable to proceed forward or retreat backwards. A trickle of water from a spring meandered past his face. The cakes of mud gleamed wetly in front of him.

He decided to try one more step. He took it and began to slide down toward the water. He let go of the bucket but kept hold of the poles. A ribbon of blue clay appeared, grooved out by his boots, moving fast past his startled face. Jack landed in the river, falling hard among some submerged stones. When he stood up the water was hardly covering his boot tops.

Like something out of the funny papers, Jack thought to himself, like a goddamn cartoon.

Dickson's pail was upside down. One of his poles had snapped in two. Jack looked toward Kyle. He hadn't moved an inch. He was pretending not to have noticed. He was standing there like a frozen deer looking off across the river.

Jack had felt a blind and wild rage coming on; something painful had come loose in his chest. He'd picked up Dickson's pail, waded back, climbed up the bank and walked past Kyle without a word or a look. The fishing trip was over.

Twenty years ago. Jack could still remember every detail of that day, the flitting birds, the look of the sun in the trees, the silver threads of water trickling down the cliff. Kyle's ten-year-old face. He'd only been ten years old.

Jack lowered his head, closed his eyes, until Kyle's face disappeared.

He took another cautious step across the mud flakes. He dug his heel in, chipping the mud away. Underneath Jack could see the blue clay again.

The cliff was a wall of blue clay.

FRANCE, 1944

CHAPTER TWENTY-FOUR

• • •

A dele tumbled down into the ditch and crawled behind a tangle of bushes. She tried to lay still. Finally she mustered up the courage to look back down the road. There was nothing to be seen but dust and a shimmer of dancing heat. The army truck had disappeared.

Adele pulled herself out of the ditch and began to walk toward Paris again. As she approached the place where the truck had stopped, she could see Lucille's raincoat lying on the ground. She put it back on and rearranged her arm sling. She stood in a kind of trance on the road.

. Her head was throbbing where the soldier had hit it. She felt a burning scrape between her legs. She thought that she might just stand there forever.

Manfred was waiting. He was on St. Augustine Street. Her feet began to move of their own accord.

After walking two or three miles, she heard a loud banging and rattling coming up quickly from behind her. A man sitting on top of a wagon was trying to rein in a large black horse. Adele moved to the side. As the man swung past, he looked down at Adele's bandages and pulled up. The horse tossed its head, sweat and foam flew, the bridle jangled.

"Where are you travelling?"

Adele looked up at him. He was wearing a sweat-stained fedora, his face was covered with a grizzled beard. She hesitated. The black horse stamped its feet impatiently.

"Where?" the man said again.

"To Paris."

He reached a large hand down to her. "No sense walking."

Adele gave him her hand, and it disappeared inside his. He helped as she lifted herself up the step and on to the wooden bench beside him. "Go on," he said to the restless horse.

They rode together mostly in silence until they reached the dingy edge of the city. The sun was beginning to set behind the flat roofs on a long line of factories. The man, pointing to a corner, told her that she could catch a bus from there to the closest Metro station. All she had to do was be patient, eventually a bus would show up.

"Good luck," he said and pressed a few coins into her hand.

All the people riding in the subway carriage were looking at her. Adele turned away and studied her reflection in the dark rushing window.

At a stop near the centre of the city the carriage began to fill up with American soldiers. Spontaneous applause broke out. Men patted them on their shoulders. An old woman pushed forward and kissed them on their cheeks. One of the soldiers sat down beside Adele.

"Hello," he said.

Adele didn't answer.

It was dark by the time she found her way to St. Augustine Street. She was surprised that it looked just the same as before, cobblestoned and narrow, the rows of houses still neat and prim-looking as if the ravaged villages she'd passed through were in another country, as if the latest round in the war had never happened.

She walked the length of the street, expecting at every moment to see Manfred step out from a shadowed doorway or a dark cellar step. She practised what she would say. "I'm all right," she would say. "The bandages don't mean anything," she would say.

Adele walked back on the opposite side of the street, the side Madame Bouchard's *pension* was on and then she walked the street twice more.

She told herself not to be disappointed that Manfred was not there at precisely that moment. He'd be working. He'd have to have found some kind of work to survive, though it would have been difficult. The Resistance was everywhere. That's what Maddy had said, because that's what Lucille's brother had told them, and anyway they'd read it for themselves in the newspapers he used to bring up to Lucille's rooms. Collaborators were being hung in the streets. Captured German soldiers were being beaten to death.

But not Manfred.

Adele rested on a window ledge hidden under a winding staircase three doors down and across the street from Madame Bouchard's. Hours passed. Traffic dwindled to almost nothing. The hot day had become a cold night. A wind moved between the buildings, swept over the cobblestones.

She knew she had only enough money to last a day or two if she was forced to find her own place. But Manfred would have a room by now. He would have some money.

Adele nodded off and then woke up in a panic, certain Manfred had walked right past and hadn't noticed her. She hurried up the street looking for him. She ran back the other way. There was no one in sight.

She came back to her spot and began to think that the reason for the delay was that Manfred must work at night. The more she thought about it, the more certain she became. It would be much safer for him to work at some obscure job through the night, which meant he would have to search St. Augustine Street during the day.

The lamps went out in all the houses opposite. She decided to wait another hour, perhaps two, just to make sure, and then she'd find a place to sleep. She'd return at daybreak.

It was three in the morning by the time Adele left her post and took a room on a shabby street several blocks away. The room she rented had no key, just a bolt on the inside of the door. A cord hung down from a bare light bulb. There was a cot and just enough room to get undressed. No dresser. No chair or mirror. And no window.

I've rented a grave, Adele thought.

She wondered if she'd run out of air during the night. She wondered how she would know if she did.

Soon she was asleep and dreaming of the redheaded soldier. They were riding in the truck cab together, moving incredibly fast.

"Manfred misses you," he said in perfect French. "He had to work today."

"Yes," Adele replied.

She could see the blond one's face. He was looking in the window, his mouth moving soundlessly, his hair whipping in the wind.

"Everyone knows who you are," the soldier said.

Adele woke with a start. She felt blindly for the cord and pulled the light on. She had no idea what time it was. Perhaps only an hour had passed or perhaps she'd fallen hopelessly asleep and it was the middle of the morning.

Adele got up, secured her bandage and put on her arm sling. She hurried down the narrow stairs and out into the street.

It was still dark outside.

• • •

Adele limped up and down St. Augustine all the next day. People began to take notice. Women shaking out mats stared at her. Men passing by on their bicycles looked back at her. A group of boys began to follow her along, whispering and giggling and limping.

Adele retreated to her window ledge. By late afternoon she told herself that she must leave long enough to find a café and eat, but she couldn't make herself leave. She didn't know Manfred's schedule.

The sun finally set behind the houses. Adele curled up on her ledge. She didn't feel hungry any more. The lamps began to come on in the windows across the way. The street lamps came on. Light blurred in Adele's half-closed eyes and spread out everywhere. She felt as if she were falling into some darkness, but Manfred was walking in light. He would find her. She should have no fear. No fear.

She felt herself slipping away from consciousness.

She felt something wet pressing against her face.

Adele opened her eyes. She saw another pair of eyes.

Adele lurched up.

A dog was sniffing her. She could see a man standing in the shadow of the staircase.

"Hello," he said.

"I'm waiting for someone," Adele managed to say. "He'll be here soon."

The man held up something. Her head bandage was dangling from his hand. "Horizontal collaborator."

"Pardon?"

"That's what they call women like you."

Adele ran.

The dog barked and ran after her, nipping at her ankles, jumping at her sleeve. She raced across the road, aimed herself toward a dark opening between two houses, ran into the alleyway and into a sudden, brilliant flash of light.

Adele was in a dark place. She wondered if she was in that same airless room again. She put her hands out to feel for the walls. Was she standing up or lying down? She couldn't tell.

"Not too bad," a voice said.

A narrow stream of light appeared. It was coming in through a window high up somewhere. She started to climb a ladder up through the dark. A man's face materialized above her, moving very close. "Nothing to speak of." His eyes looked blind. She felt pressure on the top of her head. She could feel black paint dripping down. "Scalp wounds bleed like water fountains. Highly effective. Blackjacks. Knuckle-dusters. People get hysterical, think they've been killed."

Adele tried to study his face. Deep lines ran down his cheeks from the outer edges of his nose to the corners of a turned-up mouth. His eyes were white. Big horse teeth.

He looks like a giant marionette, Adele thought.

"Your bandage would fool most people, I suppose. Dead give-away to me."

Adele looked down at her lap. She was sitting on a bench. Light from somewhere was falling all around. Her bandage was dangling in front of her eyes. She could see that now it was soaked in blood.

"Never run in the dark unless you have a plan. Always figure out your escape route in the daylight." His marionette eyes, round and glassy, weren't white now. They were looking straight at her.

Adele's skull felt like it was ballooning out. Some sharp pain was coming, though it was still far off, like a distant storm. She tried to blink it away.

"Try to stay awake," the marionette said.

Adele fell asleep.

There was something in front of her. A rough plank. Adele watched it for some time. It had been painted blue but that must have been a long while ago. The dusty paint was curling up; she could see the plank's grey grain beneath. The air smelled musty. She seemed to be lying on a bed. She tried to turn her head but a sharp pain pushed her back. Someone's warm breath was feathering her neck. She turned again, more slowly this time, dreading the face she might see. The dog was staring at her.

Adele raised herself up on an elbow. The man was sitting across the room on the top of a small table, his legs drawn up to his chest. He was watching her.

The room seemed to be made of wood, like the inside of a large crate washed faintly blue. Adele's throat felt parched. "Where am I?" she managed to whisper.

"Can't tell you," the man replied.

Adele searched his face. Horizontal collaborator, he'd said, but he didn't look full of hate. If anything, he looked slightly bemused.

"Can I have some water, please?"

The man shook his head. His hair was fair and wispy except for a large crescent bald spot at the front. "Never give water to a person with a head wound."

Adele hesitated. "I don't think that's right."

"Yes, it is."

I shouldn't argue with him, Adele thought to herself, he could be insane. Besides, her head was beginning to pound again. "But I'm thirsty."

The man shrugged as if to say that he wouldn't be held responsible for any unfortunate consequences and slid in a disjointed way off the table. Adele could see that he was quite tall and remarkably skinny. Dressed in a stained black sweater and rumpled black pants – there didn't seem to be much to him at all.

He glided over to a sink that was hanging precariously off a wall and turned on a creaking tap. Eventually a small stream of water trickled out. He held a tin mug under it and crossed his long legs to wait.

"My father's a doctor, that's how I know," Adele said, and then she asked, "How did I get here?"

"I carried you. Robber helped."

"Robber?"

The dog barked.

"How did he help?"

"By opening the doors. He's trained."

The man turned off the tap and came back to the bed with a half mug of water. "Let's hope your father was right."

Adele drank it down. It felt warm and tasted tinny. Her head pounded faster.

"My name is André Dupont. What's yours?"

"Adele Georges."

André's bright eyes danced. "I hope you don't mind, I used that make-believe sling of yours to bind the wound."

Adele could feel a cloth wound tightly around her head. She reached up to touch it.

"You ran into the corner of a brick wall. Since your father was unavailable, I stopped the bleeding."

"My father is a doctor, I wasn't lying."

"Everyone lies," André said.

Adele could feel something rising up inside her. It felt like rage. "Why didn't you just leave me alone? I wasn't hurting you!" Emotions ambushed her, tears burned her eyes. "I wasn't hurting you!"

André looked alarmed. He rubbed his long bony chin.

"I wasn't hurting you!" Adele screamed at him. Tears were streaming down her face. The pain in her head was on fire. "I wasn't hurting you!"

Robber jumped off the bed and sat under the table.

"I'm trying to help," André said.

"But why did you take off my bandages? That's despicable. Why did you do that?"

"It's my business to be curious. And exceptionally perceptive."

"You're despicable."

"I saved you from bleeding to death."

"No, you didn't!" No one did, Adele thought.

Adele lay down again. Her mother was standing behind the window, her mother was telling her to go away.

André leaned against the wall. "By the way, I can find you work."

Adele waited for a moment. She concentrated on breathing. The pain in her head was beginning to retreat to a middle distance. She looked back at André. His shiny brown eyes grew even more large, his mouth pulled up in a hopeful, ridiculous grin.

He's trying to make me laugh, Adele thought.

"I have nothing against you. I collaborated with the Germans. Why not? It worked out for me, it didn't work out for you. That's life, isn't it? You're in a bad spot, sleeping on the street, hungry, penniless."

Penniless? Adele looked for her raincoat. It was draped over the only other piece of furniture in the room, a pink wing chair.

Adele got off the bed. The wooden room rolled like a cabin at sea. She lurched toward her raincoat and felt inside both pockets. "Where's my money?"

André continued to smile his lunatic smile. He opened up his hand to reveal her pitifully small roll of francs.

"If you're any kind of a human being, if you have any decency at all, you'll give me back my money!"

"Well, that settles that," André said, slipping her money inside his pocket.

Adele began to pull on her raincoat.

"Where are you going?"

"Anywhere but here."

André brought the roll of money back out. "I'm not a robber. Did you think I was a robber?"

Adele snatched it out of his hand before he could change his mind.

"That won't last long."

"Long enough." Adele put the money back inside her raincoat.

"You still need a job. I've helped lots of girls from the country find work."

"I'm not from the country."

"Are you from Paris?"

"No."

"Well?" André walked over to a neutral corner and sat down on top of a garbage can as if to say, You can leave any time you want, I'm not stopping you.

"You still need a job. You don't have to do it forever. Just for now. A room comes with it. You can sleep in as late as you want. And there's no danger. A doctor comes to examine all the girls once a month. That should please you. The only problem is, you look like a hard case right now. It would be best if you stayed here for a day or two, until the swelling goes down. Are you as young as you look?"

"I am not a whore."

"Who said you were? I didn't say you were a whore. I just said I could get you a job in a brothel. That's completely different."

Adele could feel her knees beginning to bend without her permission. The room swayed.

"You need a drink," André said. He got off his garbage can, rummaged around in a pile of clothes and pulled out a bottle half full of a colourless liquid. Twisting off the cap and trying to look sympathetic, he carried the bottle over to Adele.

"What's in that?"

"When I have the sniffles, it makes me feel better. Why don't you sit down?"

Adele felt for the pink chair.

"Just try it."

Adele reached out for the bottle and took a sip. It was bitter. It burned going down. It tasted faintly of plums.

"Have another one."

"It's too strong."

"I'll have one." André retrieved the bottle and took several gulps. His prominent Adam's apple bobbed up and down. He closed his eyes. "Excellent," he said.

Adele sat down. "What is it?"

"Eau de vie de mirabelle."

"That's what I thought. Plum liquor. My father, the doctor," Adele said pointedly, "drinks eau de vie on occasion."

"Does he?" André began to sink down as if someone unseen had loosened his strings. He landed on the floor. Adele could see his bony white knees poking through two holes in his pants. "Suddenly everyone's been in the Resistance for the past four years, blowing up bridges and assassinating Germans, and to prove it, they've been running around beating up girls like you. Are you absolutely sure you wouldn't like to work in a safe and beautiful brothel?"

"Will you be paid a fee if I do?"

"Perhaps."

"You're unspeakable."

"Then don't speak to me."

Robber came out from under the table and put his head in André's lap. André took another drink. His Adam's apple bobbed. He shuddered.

"I'm meeting someone," Adele said.

"Oh?" André replied.

"We arranged to meet in Paris. It's just a matter of time."

"Good," André said pleasantly.

They sat in silence for some time. "What kind of dog is that?"

"A water dog. I found him in the river." André put the cap back on the bottle.

"How did you find him?"

"We were unloading a boat. I heard a sound like a cat and I turned my light on. There were five puppies, four lying on the seaweed, dead. He was washing around in the water mewing." André looked at her more closely. "Don't be sad, Adele. There are hundreds of girls just like you. You haven't done anything wrong."

Adele clenched her jaws. Her head began to hurt again. "What do you do for a living?"

"I'm in merchandise. Not me, but I work for people who are. I do whatever they want me to do, more or less. No violence, though. I hate blood. I really do. You have no idea how upsetting it was for me to have to look at your head." As if to prove how upsetting it had been, André took the cap off the bottle again and had another drink.

"You said you were a collaborator."

"Well, it was difficult to work with the Germans, they're so honest. Mainly we do our work in the black market. We have a whole new source of supplies. I'll show you."

André levitated off the floor and crossed the room to open a small wooden door. Robber trotted out. André beckoned for Adele to follow.

When Adele got up off the chair, she had to hold on to it a moment longer for support. She walked out into a narrow white-washed stone hall-way. André was unlocking a set of iron doors at the far end. He and Robber disappeared inside. A light went on.

Adele stepped through the doors into a large vaulted cellar piled full of crates that looked just like the ones in the redheaded soldier's truck. *UNITED STATES OF AMERICA* was stamped all over them.

André and Robber were busy climbing to the top of the pile. "American quartermasters are much easier to deal with than German ones," André called out. "They understand what life is all about."

The two of them, man and dog, sat down on the topmost crate with the same happy expressions. It almost made Adele want to laugh. "Are you supposed to be showing me all this?"

"I wanted to. I think we could be friends."

"I have to go back now." How long had she been away from her window ledge? Manfred could have come and gone.

Adele turned quickly, and the room tilted.

"You're too weak to go back."

Two days with almost no sleep and no food, yes, Adele thought. "Do you have anything to eat?"

André grinned down at her with his crazed marionette smile. He opened up his arms to encompass all the crates in the room.

France, 1944

Chapter Twenty-Five

• • •

Adele sat in the pink chair while André heated up a can of American stew on his battered hot plate. She ate it out of the can and fell asleep before she was finished. When she woke up, she was lying on the bed under a faded quilt.

The little wooden door opened. André and Robber came in. "Good morning," he said.

"Is it morning?"

"Nine o'clock." He came over to the bed and lifted her bandage up a little, took a look and made a face. "The thing is, you need stitches."

"I don't need stitches," Adele said. Something about the confidence of André's touch alarmed her. She felt under the quilt to see if her clothes were all on and all in the right places.

André noticed. He looked slightly hurt. "Robber and I slept in the other room." He picked up the kettle and drifted over to the sink. "I'll make some tea."

"Then I'll have to leave."

"To meet your friend?"

"Yes."

André turned on the tap. A trickle of water came out and splattered into the kettle.

As they drank their tea, Adele thought about the day ahead. She decided to change her strategy. Instead of sitting on her window ledge for most of that morning, she'd watch for Manfred at the end of the street where there was a cluster of shops. She thought she'd be less conspicuous waiting there.

She fashioned a new arm sling out of one of André's shirts, having fished it out of the pile of clothes on the floor. Apparently there were two piles, one for dirty clothes and one for clean but she couldn't tell the difference. André didn't complain even when she began to cut it up. She left for St. Augustine Street. At noon André showed up with Robber and gave her some bread, cheese and a piece of spiced meat. When she thanked him, he shrugged and went away.

Adele began to walk the length of the street again. The same boys began to follow her again. She walked away from St. Augustine Street until they gave up, and then she came back and stood by the shops. When it started to get dark, she moved to her familiar ledge under the stairs. She huddled there all night. Manfred did not appear. By morning she felt half-frozen and could hardly stand. By noon the taunting boys were back again.

To get rid of them, Adele had to walk a long way away from St. Augustine Street. She sat down on a bench in a tiny park. It looked barren, the grass brown and dry. Exhaustion crept over her. The air felt cold and gusts of wind blew through the trees, rattling the leaves.

Adele got up and crossed the park to a screen of bushes growing along someone's garden wall. She pushed between them and sat on the ground. The cold was a shock – it crept all through her. She pulled the extra socks out of her pocket and put them on her hands. She leaned back against the wall. Cold knifed through her raincoat, and her head began to throb again. She could hear the wind high up in the trees. She looked up. The branches were tossing, tossing.

By the time Robber found her, the daylight was fading and Adele was still curled up beside the garden wall. The dog bumped her face and tried to lever her up with his muzzle. She could see André ambling his way across the park toward her. From her perspective, he looked like he was defying gravity, walking like a large fly along an upright wall of grass.

Adele sat up.

André was wearing a frayed tweed overcoat that he'd obviously found somewhere, or stolen, because it didn't fit. It stopped well above his knees, which were still peeking out through the holes in his pants.

"I guess you haven't found your lover yet," he said.

Adele barely reacted. Horizontal collaborator. Of course he knew. He'd seen her shaved head.

"There's not a German soldier for a hundred miles except for the dead ones," André said. He squatted down beside her and balanced there, all legs. He took a bottle of plum liquor from inside his coat and offered her a drink. Adele shook her head. He took a gulp from the bottle. "That job offer we discussed. It's still open."

Adele got to her feet and began to walk unsteadily across the park. André and Robber fell in step beside her.

"You're still not interested?"

"No."

At the street, Adele turned left.

So did André and Robber. "Where are you going now?"

"To find a room. I will get a respectable job and I will watch for Manfred every night."

"Good for you. You'll become famous. People will write songs about you."

"Shut the hell up," Adele said.

André and Robber continued to walk along beside her. "The thing is, I need money."

Adele gave him a look.

"For the room last night, you see. And for the food."

"How much?"

"All you have."

"I need it. I can give you half." Adele fumbled in her pocket for her roll of franc notes.

André sighed. "Giving your money away just like that. You see? You can't look after yourself, you're a simpleton from the country."

Adele began to walk away again.

"You're different from what I expected," André said.

Adele turned back. "What do you mean, different from what you expected?" For the first time since she'd been forced to meet him, André seemed unsure of himself.

"You're a bird of a different feather, that's all."

"What's that supposed to mean?"

André shrugged his bony shoulders. "I can get you a room."

"Yes. And a doctor comes with it every month."

"No. I don't mean that. Forget that. This is different. I'm talking about a private room in a suitable building."

Adele gave him a long look. "Suitable for what?"

"For a young woman in your situation. That's all," André said.

André and Robber led Adele through a series of narrow streets into an increasingly gloomy maze. Buildings leaned uneasily against each other, the narrow roadway tilted downward at an increasingly sharp angle. Adele could smell a familiar pungency in the air not unlike the park in Rouen, but here the river's hidden presence was much stronger. Drying seaweed and slops. Decaying fish in standing water.

They turned a corner into a small square. Shop stalls cluttered the way and though it was almost dark and there were no street lamps, crowds of people were still milling about picking over the few articles for sale, bargaining in languages Adele couldn't understand. They looked darkly foreign and hungry and took no notice of the tall man with the wispy clown hair or the girl with the head wound or the scraggly dog.

André opened a battered door into a tall wooden building. The air inside smelled of everything imaginable. Adele stood in the dark foyer and tried to separate them out. Cabbage. Urine. Spices. Mould. And most pervasively, the thick smell of cooking oils.

"Give me your money," André demanded.

Adele handed over her small roll of francs. Shouts and screams were coming from somewhere above their heads.

"Stay here." André and Robber disappeared up the stairs.

Three young dark-skinned men with black liquid eyes burst in through the door joking and laughing. As soon as they saw Adele, they came to a stop and brazenly took in her pale face, her bruised forehead and bandages, her stained, bulky raincoat. They ran up the stairs in a torrent of foreign words and laughter.

A plump potato-faced woman came through the door carrying something very large wrapped in a cloth bundle. She gave Adele a furtive look and clattered noisily up the stairs in wooden shoes.

People kept coming and going until Adele began to wonder if André had gone out a side door with her money. Just as she was sure he had, Robber appeared on the stairs. André was looking down at her from out of the dark. A tiny woman was standing beside him, barely visible.

"Madame says that everything is settled," André announced, "top floor."

Adele began to climb the stairs. The higher they climbed, the stronger the smells.

"You'll like this place," André said.

The room had a skylight of four dirty panes of glass supported by a rusting iron frame. Adele loved the skylight. Everything else was a disappointment. For one thing the skylight was the only window in the room, and it looked like it leaked because rivers of brown stain ran across the ceiling and down the walls. Pieces of ancient wallpaper clung precariously to yellowed plaster. There were no closets, just two hooks screwed into the back of the door. A small cupboard painted a faded yellow sat in one corner and an intricately wrought bronze light fixture, looking like it had been stolen from a better building, stuck out of a wall. The only other attraction was a stained mattress lying on the floor.

"For the mattress you pay extra," the woman said in a startling loud, guttural French.

"No, thank you," Adele replied.

"Filthy woman." Her dark eyes blazed.

Adele's heart shrank.

"Not you," André said, "she means the woman who had this room before you."

Adele looked back down at the stained mattress.

"No," the woman said, shaking a brown admonishing finger in Adele's face.

"I don't want the mattress," Adele said, "I'm a seamstress."

"Follow now." The woman left the room and headed down the hall. André unfolded himself and landed on the floor by the cupboard.

Adele's new landlady stopped at a door with a hole bored through the middle of it the size of a man's fist. She swung it open. A thick wave of revolting smells went up Adele's nose.

"Toilet," she said.

The communal kitchen was at the other end of the hall. The small stove was covered with splatters of food; a garbage pail sat beside it full of grease. The tour was over. The woman disappeared.

Adele went back into her new room, closed the door and sat on the floor opposite André and Robber. "How long am I paid up for?"

"Two weeks."

"How can that be?"

"It's cheap, and perhaps I contributed a little something."

"Thank you, André."

André nodded.

"I have an electric plug over there." Adele was beginning to feel slightly encouraged. "I could cook in this room. I could heat up water to wash in. I don't need much. A small table. Two chairs. A bed."

"Just in case your boyfriend shows up?"

"He will."

André pulled his bottle out and took a sip.

"Do you think there's a way to open that skylight for some fresh air?"

"I don't know."

"Could you take that disgusting mattress downstairs and give it to the landlady?"

André eyed it. "Yes."

"We'll need some kind of heater once it gets cold. Oh André, you don't know. This is the secret room Manfred and I talked about. This is it!" Adele looked around, amazed more at the vision in her mind than the room itself. She got up and pulled out the drawer in the cupboard. Everything would need to be cleaned. "Who are these people who live around here?"

"Turks and Algerians were here first. Then Poles, Belgians, Dutch running from the Germans." He paused. "You said you're a seamstress. I can get you a job."

"How?"

"I have influence."

Adele turned and smiled at him, a radiant smile. "I've given you no reason to be so helpful."

"That's all right," André said.

• • •

André kept his word. He found Adele a job in a small building that had once been someone's house but now was owned by a textile factory. Foreign women sat at tables sewing elastic bands and ribbons and splintered pieces of whale bone into all manner of underwear and foundation garments. Apparently the foreman of the place had owed André a favour. All Adele had to do was be brave enough to go out in public without wearing an arm sling and prove to the foreman that she could run a sewing machine.

On her first day a supervisor asked her what had happened to her head. She was still wearing her head bandage. She told him the story that André had given her, that she'd been hit by the German sniper fire that had sprayed the streets during the early days of the city's liberation. Her story swept through the building's small rooms and soon all the women were nodding at her in approval.

Sometimes she'd work twelve hours, other times she'd come to the house at six in the morning to be told there was nothing for her to do that day. She continued to wear her bandage covered by a new scarf she'd bought at one of the stalls.

She purchased a used hot plate. André dragged in pieces of furniture he'd picked up from somewhere, including a cleaner-looking and wider mattress. The only time she used the toilet with the hole in the door was the quick moment it took in the morning to empty out a commode.

She lived for Manfred. She felt his hands helping her get up in the morning, he accompanied her to the house she worked in, he sat beside her. Whenever she worked less than twelve hours she huddled on the window ledge on St. Augustine Street. She reasoned that Manfred had been sick or he'd had an accident at work. That was why he hadn't come for her and that was why he was sure to appear at any moment.

Winter arrived and she waited under different quarters of the moon. Sometimes the night sky seemed like hanging crystals and she could see to the end of the universe. Other nights clouds scuttled over the rooftops and snow fell. Every night felt endless.

One frigid evening Adele was sitting in her room staring at herself in a mirror. She knew she couldn't go on wearing bandages forever and she did have a persuasive white scar left over from the brick wall, but how could she explain her hair? She couldn't believe how slowly it was taking to grow, it was only two or three inches long. Most women were wearing their hair gathered up high on the sides. Her hair was turning thick and wiry again. It looked like a short unruly hedge.

There was a furious banging on her door. "Adele, let me in!"

Adele put down her mirror and slid back the bolt. André was standing there, wispy hair standing up and blood running from his nose.

"What happened?" Adele cried out.

André didn't reply. He made his way over to the far corner of the room, put his back against the wall and slid slowly to the floor. Robber limped in after him.

"André, what happened? Tell me! Did you have an accident?"

"The police are after me."

Adele grabbed her cooking pot, hurried down the hall to the kitchen, and filled the pot with water. She had to knock to get back into her room, for André had bolted the door behind her. He took his time unlocking it and when she came in, he sank down on the mattress.

There were blood splatters on his coat and on his hand where he'd tried to stem the flow. "I knocked one of them over," he said.

Adele sat on the floor beside him, soaked the edge of a towel in the water and washed off his hand and dabbed at his face.

"And then I tripped." He held up his other hand to show her a scrape as proof. The top of his nose was also scraped. "If it hadn't been for Robber, I wouldn't have gotten away."

"Good Robber," Adele said.

Robber seemed subdued and hardly managed a wag of his stubby tale.

"He bit one of them. If they catch him, he's dead."

"And what if they catch you?"

"They'll put me on trial with all the others. The black marketeers. The collaborators. Maybe they'll shoot me."

"You're just a petty thief, André. They won't shoot you."

André looked slightly insulted. "They might."

"How did they find out about you anyway?"

"They found Monsieur Talleyrand's American Army rations."

"Monsieur Talleyrand?"

"He's the big man."

"How did they find the rations?"

"That remains unexplained."

"Did they catch Monsieur Talleyrand?"

"No. He's after me, too. And all the people who work for Monsieur Talleyrand. It's not a good situation." André began to feel in his overcoat for his bottle of eau de vie. He found it, propped himself up and took a drink. "They think I informed the police about their hiding place."

"Why do they think that?"

"I have a theory." André seemed to be feeling better. He crossed his legs and offered her a drink.

Adele took the bottle and drank deeply. Over the past weeks she'd developed an appreciation for his cheap eau de vie, for the warm fire it invariably spread through her body and particularly for the dreamless sleep it seemed to produce.

"There's a certain police inspector who is in Monsieur Talleyrand's pay. I believe he's the one who accused me of going to the police and trading information for money, and now you see, all those crates are in the hands of the police. Do you think the police will return them to the American Army or Monsieur Talleyrand. Ha! They will sell them themselves. Monsieur Talleyrand will receive nothing." André looked frightened. "Francois Savard. He fell out of favour with Monsieur Talleyrand. Do you know what they did to Francois?"

"Don't tell me," Adele said.

"They cut out his eyes with a pen knife."

Adele put her head close to his. "They won't find you here," she whispered. "You can stay here as long as you need."

André was watching her face closely.

Robber crept over and put his head in Adele's lap.

"You, too," Adele said.

That night Adele slept on her mattress and André slept under his coat on the other side of the room. Robber curled up by the door, intent on listening to all the comings and goings in the hallway.

Just as Adele was about to fall asleep, André said, "Guess what?"

"What?"

"My real name isn't André Dupont."

Adele felt a foreboding creep through her. She was awake now. She waited for him to say his real name. He didn't. "What is it then?"

"I don't know."

"How can you not know?"

"The nuns picked out a name."

"You were brought up by nuns?" .

A frosty glow came through the skylight. She could see the outline of André's dark figure lying across from her but she couldn't see his face.

"André Dupont was a thirteenth-century friar. Franciscan," he said.

"You were an orphan?"

"You have to have parents to be an orphan. I was a foundling. Just dropped out of a tree like a pear."

"How did that happen?"

"How did I drop out of a tree? I'm not fishing for sympathy."

"How did the nuns find you?"

"Sister told me I was found on their doorstep wrapped in a blanket and with a little wool hat on. Sister was very young and very beautiful."

"She was?"

"Yes. Sister Marie was. Sister Agnes wasn't. She was old and a dragon. She told me I'd been found under a wooden box in an alley. Of course I chose to believe Sister Marie until I was about the age of seven. That's when I discovered she'd told all the other children the same story. Each one of us had arrived on their doorstep with a little wool hat on our heads."

"I'm sorry," Adele said.

"I'm happy for the way it happened."

"Why?"

"I have no ties or obligations like I would have had if I belonged to someone. There's all sorts of things you have to do and all sorts of things you have to feel. What if your mother dies?"

Adele hadn't thought about her mother for a long while.

"I'm as free as a bird," André said.

. . .

André was afraid to be seen in the building so Adele had to let Robber out for walks. André wanted her to dye Robber's hair so he wouldn't be recognized. Adele said that in their squalid quarter there were any number of stray dogs that looked just like Robber. André said he doubted that very much, but since they didn't have any dye on hand and since he wasn't sure where she might procure some, the subject was dropped. Robber went out without a disguise. Nothing happened.

In some ways it was nice having André in her room. She fussed over the scratches on his nose and hand, fussed over the fact that he ate too little and drank too much, in fact was quite drunk most nights by the time he fell asleep.

And in some ways it wasn't so pleasant. Though he didn't know where to purchase dye, he did know where to send her to get eau de vie and soon Adele was spending half her money buying him a bottle almost every day. It wasn't the money that bothered her, though. Sometimes he just got progressively sleepy but on a few nights he saw things that weren't there. He said they were shimmering and beautiful. It was on those nights he would end up crying and Adele would have to hold his head in her lap and rock him to sleep.

And there was the question of modesty and the toilet. Adele was forced to use the hell-hole down the hall now, and when she dressed and undressed she had to do it under her blanket. André told her she didn't have to dress and undress that way because whether she was nude or clothed it made no difference to him.

Adele asked him why he was always watching her then.

André said where was he supposed to look, it was such a small room, and besides, if he averted his eyes it would mean that he was attracted to her, but by looking at her, just as he might look at Robber or a chair, it meant just the opposite.

"I have no sexual interest," André said.

"What's that mean?"

"It means I have no interest in sex."

"There's no such thing."

"Yes, there is," André said.

Adele continued to dress and undress under her blanket.

One night when she'd had a few too many sips of eau de vie herself and was lying on her mattress staring up at the moon through the skylight, she asked André why he thought he was the way he was.

"What way is that?"

"No interest in sex."

André was lying in his dark corner with his long legs flung over the seat of Adele's only chair. He'd been complaining about a sore back. Adele could tell by her wrinkled blanket that he was making a habit of sprawling out on her mattress when she was working or when she was away at night waiting for Manfred.

"I know why," Adele said, "because you didn't have anyone to teach you how to love." A quarter moon suspended itself just above the skylight. "You didn't have a father."

"You don't know anything about anything."

Adele waited for him to say something more but he didn't. She felt ashamed. It was none of her business. Why was she trying to drag him into such a conversation? She knew why, because she felt like being cruel. It was January. The nights were freezing on St. Augustine Street. She had a room but Manfred wasn't in it. Instead, André, the marionette, was in it.

"You're wrong, you know," André said. "I loved Sister Marie."

A few clouds raced by. The moon seemed to be going a thousand miles an hour. The room and everything in it was going a thousand miles an hour. Adele stretched her hand out for the bottle and took another sip.

"One day she explained how the world worked."

Adele was thinking that nothing tasted as good as plum liquor but you had to make sure you had enough of it. It was lighting little bonfires all through her blood.

"I went looking for her one day. Sister said to me, "'Are you trailing after me again?' She was praying in her special place in the garden. She held my hand. She said that I was very precious to her. I said she was very precious to me. She said that when she looked at me she didn't see me at all, she saw the face of Jesus. It was the same with all the sisters. They didn't see us, she said. They washed us and fed us to touch Jesus."

The moon began to look a lot like Simone Ducharme. Adele could hardly believe her eyes.

"I left the orphanage then. I lived on the streets. I had to do a great many things on the streets. I can't tell you what they were."

"How old were you?"

"Ten."

"How could you survive, how could you find work and food and a place to stay if you were only ten?"

"I can't tell you."

Simone Ducharme was flying through a veil of milky clouds. She looked serene. She was going a thousand miles an hour.

"I grew up knowing everything about everything. There's nothing I don't know, and now I prefer to live on the edges and regard the world and everyone in it with amusement and contempt."

"André?"

"What?"

"Is your back sore?"

"Yes."

"You can come over here."

André crawled over to her.

"Lie down beside me," Adele said.

André stretched out on the mattress. Adele rubbed his back. "Does that feel better?"

"Yes."

"I'm sorry for everything that's happened to you," Adele said. Simone Ducharme was peeking through the skylight. Snow was falling inside the room.

"You don't know what happened," André said.

"Try to go to sleep, André."

Adele curled up beside him. André remained stretched out, motionless, and they slept like that all night long.

In the morning Adele went to work. That evening she took her familiar place on St. Augustine Street.

The night was cold and she soon got up because she was freezing. She walked down to Madame Bouchard's and stared at the closed front door. And she had a revelation.

Adele rushed back to her room in the teetering old building. André had to unbolt the door – he hadn't expected her to return so soon. He was in his underwear and looked half-drunk and half-asleep. She'd never seen such a baggy pair of underwear or such a pair of long skinny legs in all her life.

"Put your pants on."

André stood there scratching his head and looking around for his pants.

"Manfred should have been on St. Augustine long before now. But if he had to leave Paris because it was too dangerous to stay, he wouldn't have left without telling me what he was doing."

"But he couldn't tell you what he was doing if you weren't here," André reasoned, coming somewhat to life. Robber was using his pants for a bed. André pulled them out from under him.

"That's right. That's absolutely right. And the only person we have in common in all of Paris is…?"

André staggered a little, trying to put on his pants. "Is what?"

Adele's face seemed transfused with light. "Madame Bouchard! There's a note waiting for me at Madame Bouchard's! I know there is! Why didn't I think of this before?"

André kept his face turned away.

Adele went on. "Manfred said she was too dangerous but if he was desperate enough he would have had to trust her, anyway. She said he was the only one with a soul!"

André sat down on the chair. He was beginning to look distraught. "When are you going to see her?"

"As soon as it gets light."

"Don't do it."

"I have to!"

"Manfred is still right. She made a lot of money off the Germans. All her neighbours will know this. She'll be living in fear. She'd never be stupid enough to hold on to a message from a German soldier. She'd use her head, unlike you. And if you knock on her door and ask her that question, she'll turn you in to the local vigilantes!" André was shaking. His face had gone completely white.

"What is it?" Adele asked.

André put his head down between his bony knees. "Manfred didn't need to leave a message with Madame Bouchard. You and Manfred have someone in common besides her."

Adele touched André's wispy hair. Her fingers were trembling. She touched his shoulder. "What do you mean?"

"How do you think I knew where to look for you? How do you think I knew who you were?"

"You took off my bandage."

"No," André said.

Adele couldn't breathe. She couldn't breathe.

"He paid me to watch for you. It was too dangerous for him."

"Oh God," Adele said. She could feel her whole body begin to tremble.

"This tall German officer, he arranged for Manfred to hide in a house owned by Monsieur Talleyrand. Unfortunately you were late and didn't arrive before the Germans had to leave. His friend was going to get him back into Germany. That was the plan. Easier planned than done, don't you think, in all the confusion and bombing?" André looked up at Adele – he looked almost hopeful.

Adele sank to the floor. "Why didn't you tell me he was in Paris? Why didn't you tell me he was alive?"

"I don't know that he's alive."

"But you didn't tell me anything."

"I needed you to stay here. I wanted you to stay. At first it was business. And then, it wasn't." He dared another glance at Adele. "You missed him by several weeks."

"You didn't tell me!" Adele screamed.

André got up and began to circle the room. He walked across the mattress and around the chair and table.

"When did he leave Paris? In August? That's months ago. Months and months! When were you going to tell me?"

André walked across the mattress again in his aimless journey.

"You betrayed me!"

André let out a moan. "But I love you." Huge tears trickled out of his eyes and ran down the grooves in his face. They wet the corners of his mouth.

"How could you say you love me and not tell me?"

"Because I love you!" André dropped down on his knees. He was still almost as tall as she was. "I love you." He wrapped his arms around her waist, pressed his face against her breasts. "I love you!"

Adele could feel his hot breath all the way through her coat. "Stop it! Don't!" She wrenched herself out of his grip and backed against the wall. She looked toward the cupboard searching for something sharp or heavy.

André was watching her. "Look at me. What's wrong with me? Can't you see me?"

"André, please, don't go on like this."

"Do you see me, Adele? Or do you see Jesus? Is that who you're seeing after all this time?"

"No. I'm seeing you!"

"Then love me!"

"I do love you! I love you. You're my family, you're the only person I have. But I don't love you like you want me to love you!"

"But I don't have a family."

"You do now!"

André stood up. He started rubbing his head as if he were waking up all over again. "Everything's fine," he said. As if to prove it, he picked up a bottle of eau de vie from off the floor and took a long drink. He held the bottle out to her, but Adele shook her head.

André sat down on the chair and began to pull on his shoes. "I'm going to take Robber out." He pulled on his overcoat.

"Aren't you afraid to be seen outside?"

"I don't think so."

André walked out into the dimly lit hallway. Adele could hear him clumping down the stairs and the click of Robber's paws as he followed him.

Adele closed the door and bolted it. She wondered if André could hear the bolt as it slipped into place. She didn't care. She lay down on the mattress and pulled the blanket over her coat. There was no source of heat in her room except for an electric heater André had found.

Manfred was alive. He'd been alive in Paris. He must still be alive wherever he was. She lay there feeling successive waves of happiness sweep over her and waves of dismay. How could André have done what he'd done to her?

She didn't know what she'd do when he came back. She wasn't at all sure she'd unbolt the door. She'd been a country bumpkin, all right, just like he'd said, perversely blind and stupid. She'd been getting undressed under her cover with him sitting not ten feet away, and cooking his suppers, and talking with him and listening to him far into the night. And holding him when he cried. And falling asleep so close to him that if they'd stretched out their hands they could have touched each other's fingers.

They'd become each other's best friend, she'd thought, and she'd spoken to him about Manfred almost every day and he'd stayed silent for months and months. And let her sit out in the cold. And let her continue to suffer.

Adele decided that when he returned she would open the door a crack and tell him to move down the hall to the kitchen. He could turn the stove on for heat. If he refused, then she'd move down the hall herself. The next day they'd have to discuss what to do. He'd have to find a job, despite Monsieur Talleyrand and his men, and he'd have to find a room of his own. And he would have to tell her everything he knew about Manfred. The officer who was hiding him had to be Lieutenant Oberg. And they were heading back to Germany. Was that where he was now? What had Manfred actually said to André? She had to know every word.

Adele waited a long time to hear approaching sounds in the stairwell. Finally she got up and turned off the light. She stared at the heater's single working coil glowing in the dark. She waited to see shadows under the door, hear a faint knock. She waited all night.

Snow covered the skylight when she got up in the morning. She pulled off her coat despite the cold and changed for work. She avoided looking at André's abandoned corner, his rumpled sheet and pile of clothes.

When she pushed open the building's decrepit front door she half-expected to see André and Robber standing in the snow waiting for her. There was no one in sight.

• • •

Adele continued to work at the factory house and watch her hair grow out and save as much money as she could. She looked for André and Robber every day. She was sure he had fallen into the hands of Monsieur Talleyrand and she'd been the cause of it. Her anger melted away.

Why had she been so mean, so thoughtless? Why hadn't she been more gentle? Why hadn't she talked to him and allowed him to explain his feelings, and then she could have told him that it was impossible for him to act on what he felt, but that she still loved him, that she would love him forever.

Adele wandered down to the river to look for André and Robber among the smells and misery of the waterfront. She walked tirelessly far and wide. Had his eyes been put out, was he begging blind somewhere on the puddled streets? Was he dead?

By spring Adele had discarded her head bandage and was wearing a dark purple tam pulled down over her ears. The streets were warming and the stalls were full of crocuses and daffodils and discarded piles of old winter clothes. Something almost unimaginable was in the air. The end of the war was in the air.

The women in her quarter were laughing and joking among themselves, looking at old dresses and coats, fingering material and bartering in various languages. Moustached men in shirt sleeves stood in clusters smoking their pipes. Children raced around in giddy circles.

Adele climbed up the stairs. She stood in her room and looked at it for a long time so that she might remember André and Robber forever. She packed a cardboard suitcase with her few clothes. She pushed the corner cupboard away from the wall and took out the money she'd saved. She couldn't make herself wait any longer.

She would follow Manfred. She would travel into Germany.

CANADA, 1946

CHAPTER TWENTY-SIX

. . .

J ack stared at the blue clay clinging to the heel of his boot. He looked across the cliff face. If the river had been at its normal depth, he would have waded downriver looking for any sign that someone had scrambled across the steep bank, but the water was too high and running fast.

Perhaps he was late, anyway. Perhaps the torrent of rain the previous day had washed the tracks away.

He'd been right, though. There was no question that the clay he was staring at was the same colour as the thin clay line caught between the sole and heel of the dead man's shoes. Jack tried to control his breathing. His legs felt weak, braced against the sheer drop of the cliff. He had to figure everything out and he had no time to waste.

The man had been buried in a hurry, in fact, more hidden than buried, under no more than six inches of soil. It had been broiling hot for the last while. Part of the body had been dug up by feral dogs, and the air had got at it. Maggots were all over it. He could see the open gut again. Smell it. Jesus.

Jack slid back into the water. He waded knee-deep to the near bank and pulled himself out. His chest was heaving. How long had the man been dead? Two weeks, three, four? Bodies decayed at different rates of speed depending on all sorts of things. You didn't have to be a hotshot wet-behind-the-ears OPP detective to know that.

Jack looked up the steep hill in front of him. He'd have to climb along the edge of the cliff and search every damn inch. He'd have to climb down the other side. He'd have to examine the path leading out to the railway tracks.

He looked downriver at the tumbling brown water as it raced around the Devil's Elbow. He didn't have a thousand men like young Harold Miles. He only had himself.

• • •

Jack limped along beside the railway tracks heading the opposite way from town, heading back toward the Broome farm.

He'd climbed the hill, he'd scrambled through brush and brambles, he'd half-killed himself and he hadn't found the murder weapon or a suspicious piece of torn clothing or splatters of brain that were still somehow clinging to a trunk of a tree. But he had begun to wonder about something. Why would a person carry a body half a mile up the river to bury it? Why wouldn't the murderer, or murderers, bury it close to where it fell?

The solution was simple enough but it gave Harold Miles the strong hand again. The man had crossed the cliff face, yes, maybe he'd even slid all the way down it if he were agile enough and desperate enough, but he hadn't been killed there. He'd been caught and murdered close to where the grave was, exactly where Miles was searching.

Jack hurried along. His feet were still squishing inside his boots from wading in the river and he'd pulled a muscle somehow on the inside of his left thigh. It felt like he'd been shot.

He still had the big card to play, but it wouldn't last long. Miles had been around the town for a night and a day. He'd be talking to everybody. He'd be on to the DPs soon enough.

Jack had parked his own car, a maroon 1937 Studebaker he kept in immaculate condition, near the wooden railway bridge. He could see it now, shining like a faraway dream.

• • •

Jack stood in his bedroom and looked in the mirror.

It had been almost more than he could manage to make himself pull on a checkered shirt and brown slacks and loafers. He hated wearing civilian clothes, it felt like he was in the wrong skin.

It was better this way, though. The mayor had told him to stay out of the investigation. He would be, if he wasn't wearing a uniform. He'd be on his own time, a private citizen who had the right to talk to anyone or look at anything. And anyway, uniforms made the men out at the DP camp nervous.

He didn't have time to eat. For all he knew Miles and his posse were already out there. He didn't have time to call down to Constable White or Constable Westland, either. He was supposed to be covering for one of them that afternoon but he couldn't remember which one. He had the duty sheet somewhere in the house. It was usually up on the nail by the phone in the kitchen. In fact it was always up there but for some reason, lately, things had gotten a little out of order.

He decided to leave his revolver at home. He couldn't imagine anyone out in that camp having the nerve to shoot him, but if they did the last thing they'd see would be his hands going around their neck. Just the thought of it gave Jack a familiar rush of pleasure.

What would people say? Took a bullet in the gut and kept going, wrung the bastard's neck like an unwanted chicken.

It was a childish emotion. A childish thought. He'd been having them forever.

Jack left the house, opened the door of his Studebaker and sat behind the wheel for awhile. His leg still hurt. He was still breathing too fast, panting like an old dog. He touched his forehead. His fingers came away shiny with sweat. Maybe he should have lain down first. The secret to taking naps had always eluded him, though. Whenever he tried, he'd just lie there wide awake and stiff as a board.

He would try again. He'd come home for a nap after he talked to the head man out at the camp. And he'd eat, too. And he'd go up to the hospital and visit Ruth. He had to get his life straightened around. It felt like it was unravelling somehow, like a ball had fallen out of his hands and he was trying to reel it in by a goddamn thread and it just kept spinning away, getting smaller and smaller.

Jack drove through the town. He eased the car over a railway level crossing and past two large coal bins and a water tower. He continued on by a factory with lumber piled high behind it and pulled up. That was as far as the road went. He could have driven along a bumpy trail beside the railway tracks right out to the DP camp – he'd done it before with the town cruiser but he wasn't driving the town cruiser. He was driving his Studebaker. He'd walk – it was only a few hundred yards.

The head man was waiting for him, standing on the path that led up the slope to the shantytown just as if Jack had called ahead to make an appointment. He was a sharp little bastard, Joe Puvalowski was. He had good English, he was prickly, and when one or more of the men ended up in jail it was never their fault, it was just a confusion. Joe liked that word, confusion. Usually the reasons weren't very complicated anyway. They'd gotten themselves blind drunk and couldn't walk as far as the camp or they'd gotten into a fight with some of the locals and needed the protection of a jail cell for the night.

Jack and the head man had always managed to work things out, and afterwards, particularly when he was sitting in Jack's office and therefore in close proximity to the mayor, Joe Puvalowski would want to discuss jobs. There seemed to be a confusion: they were promised jobs by the prime minister of Canada and the King of England. Where were the jobs? They'd crossed half the country and no one would talk to them. They'd go up to the factory doors, caps in hand, and ask for anything. The worst jobs. Anything at all. And lately they'd even being threatened and chased away.

Jack had explained, more than once and with more patience than he usually exhibited, that any new jobs were going to the town's returning soldiers, which was only right and fair, and that the men should be patient – their opportunity would come.

And over and over again, Joe's dark face would flush, his wiry grey hair would tremble, he'd pull a worn piece of paper from the shabby hand-me-down suit he always wore when he came into town, and he'd point with a stubby finger. "Here, it says the bearer of this paper, he must be given a job."

"Given priority, wherever possible and reasonable. That's actually what it says, Joe."

"We were promised," Joe would thunder, clenching his fist and waving his paper in front of Jack's face. And Jack would allow Joe Puvalowski to do that, his hard grey eyes looking into Joe's excitable black ones, and once again he'd wonder what kind of sights the man had seen, what godforsaken things had he seen?

"How's it going, Joe?" the chief asked, limping up the path.

"Not good." Joe's face was dark as a thunderstorm, his mass of wild hair trembling.

Jack looked past him. The ramshackle camp seemed a little messier than usual, some clutter of wood and corrugated tin strewn around, a water barrel turned upside down.

"What's not good?"

Joe was staring at the chief's checkered shirt.

"I'm off duty, more or less," Jack explained.

A cluster of men was standing beside the low door of the first shack. They were wearing the same kind of clothes as the dead man, shiny pants either too long or too short, an odd assortment of faded shirts, pants held up by suspenders or looping belts or rope, any kind of shoe.

"You're too late, Mister Jack," Joe said.

"Am I?" Jack could hear the sound of his own blood in his ears. A muffled beat. A whispering. He gritted his teeth and walked up the slope.

The men, wiry and small, pinched-faced and roughly shaven, gave way. Jack looked inside the first shack's door.

The air smelled of unwashed bodies and drifting smoke. In the far corner two men sat on a rough bench. Coals beneath a makeshift stove smouldered in front of them. They stared back at Jack.

Harold Miles was nowhere to be seen.

"Your friends have been here already," Joe said.

Joe had come up behind him. Jack stepped back out the door. "No friends of mine. How many?"

"Two bosses, dressed like you. Four in uniforms. Pushed things over. Pulled things apart." Joe's voice began to rise. "Put us in a line. Here. Right here." He was pointing toward the top of the path. "Lined us up. Searched us."

"For what?"

All the men's eyes turned to Jack. They were frightened, Jack could see that now. No doubt Miles had wanted them to be frightened. No doubt the

172

young bastard had known exactly what he was doing.

"Brought back memories, did it, Joe?"

The blood in Joe's face darkened another shade but he didn't answer.

"They were looking for a gun. A murder weapon. Didn't they tell you what they were looking for?"

"I know what they were looking for," Joe said.

"Without them telling you, you mean? You knew before?"

Joe glanced at the other men. "We know nothing, Mister Jack. It has nothing to do with us."

Jack grinned. "One of the fellows out here got himself murdered and you don't know anything about it? Is that what you're saying?"

Joe thought this over for a moment. "The young boss, he took our papers. He said no man leaves until he says. We have nothing to do with this trouble. People jump off trains. They jump back on. Do I keep a record, do I write down in a book? This man in the ground, these men who do such a thing, how would I know? And the boss, the big boss, he says this happened many weeks ago."

"How many weeks ago?"

Joe shook his head.

"Did he say?"

Joe shook his head again.

No goddamn forensics for me, Jack thought. He put his big arm around Joe's shoulder and led him off a little distance from the rest of the men. "This little prick you're calling the boss, do you know what I think he's thinking? I think he's thinking you'd have a hard time throwing away a gun, given all the things you've been through. A gun would be too important to someone like you. He thinks you've hidden it."

"They didn't find a gun because we don't have a gun!" Joe's hair quivered.

Jack picked up the lapel on Joe's suit coat. He ran his huge thumb up and down its frayed edge. "You and I, we're friends. Do you know what that means? It means you'd be a lot better off telling me what happened than talking to that young cop."

"The boss said, if we want our papers back don't speak to nobody but him."

"Did he?"

"Who is the big boss here? Who is the commandant?"

"I am."

"It's all a confusion."

"There is no confusion," Jack said.

Joe tried to look away but the chief of police was twice as large as he was and standing right in front of him. "We want jobs and no trouble. No more trouble. We have done nothing. None of us. This I swear."

"Tell me what you know, and I'll get your papers back."

Joe shook his head again, but slower this time.

"What are you afraid of?"

"This is not our country."

"And?"

"We don't know what will happen."

"Nothing will happen. We have laws here."

Joe shook his head a third time. Jack could see that he was settling down into a stony silence. He let go of his lapel.

"Think about it. I'll give you a minute," Jack said.

The chief walked slowly through the camp pondering his options. There wasn't much point in searching for the murder weapon, not now. And if Joe continued to refuse to talk there wasn't much he could do about that, either. Confiscating their landing papers had been a smart move. That's all they owned in the world, they wouldn't be going anywhere. Miles could take his time, talk to each one of them separately, wave their papers in front of their noses and threaten to light a fire to them if they didn't tell him everything they knew. Of course most of the men couldn't speak English – that might be a problem. But then Miles would have a translator. Miles would have everything.

Jack limped up the grassy hill behind the camp. He looked back over the dingy collection of makeshift shacks, past the railroad tracks and the scrub bush angling down toward the river. Clouds were scuttling along the far horizon. The storm the day before was becoming a memory. A shaft of smoky sunlight lit up a distant hill.

How far was Miles ahead? He had the forensic reports, if not in his hands, then soon – it had only been two days. And maybe he'd found something out there by the gravesite, but not the murder weapon. If he had, he wouldn't have been searching for it in the camp. The truth was, probably, Miles didn't know anything more than he did.

Joe Puvalowski was standing at the bottom of the hill watching him. Jack could see the other men moving about, picking up debris around the camp, trying to put things back together. About thirty yards across the face of the hill from where Jack was standing, he noticed a tarpaulin lying on the grass, a few boards strewn around, and what looked like a man-sized hole dug into the slanting ground.

Jack crossed the hill. As he got closer he could see that the tarpaulin was actually someone's old awning, no doubt hauled there from the town dump, the alternating green and white stripes long since faded into a general mildew grey. The boards nearby were dark and still wet from the rain. Soaked newspapers, empty tin cans, and a soggy shirt were scattered around the opening into the hill.

Jack got down on his knees on clumps of grass the colour of old straw and looked into the entrance to the cave. He glanced back down toward the camp. The head man had disappeared. He stuck his head inside the hole. The passageway was just large enough to accommodate his shoulders. Curiosity, as it usually did, got the better of him. Lying down on his belly and with some effort, he managed to wiggle forward. He could feel the walls widening out, the floor sloping down a little.

He crawled in a little farther until he could make out a hollowed-out space in deep shadows. It looked just large enough to accommodate all of him. Jack wiggled in, rolled on to his hip and sat up.

The raw red earth above his head and to all sides of him was within easy reach. He looked back out the tunnel. All he could see was a piece of sky as grey and mottled as the awning.

A groundhog's view of the world, Jack thought to himself. He leaned back against the wall. This is the way it ends, the way it must look going down into the earth.

He closed his eyes. It wasn't a half-bad place to be, hidden away from everyone. And from all the things you ever did and all the things you ever thought. All the unnecessary pain. Caused and received. Forgotten by everyone. Far, far away.

Jack felt a tiredness deeper than his bones, deeper than his soul. He stopped breathing. He strained his ears. He couldn't hear a thing.

He opened his eyes. The grey sky was still there.

Jack backed out of the hole and immediately cracked his knee on something hard under the piled-up clumps of grass. He scrabbled about and pulled out a can of beans. There was a can of something else, too. When he pushed the grass aside, he could see the label had come off. A large Mason jar was nestled beside it. Jack picked it up and screwed off the top. A pungent smell he couldn't identify assaulted his nose. He tipped it over and a thick blue mould riding on an amber liquid poured out on the ground.

He tipped it a little more. Something dark slipped out of the jar's mouth the size of a child's liver. Jack poked at it. Now he recognized the smell. It was unmistakable. Plums.

"They were already here."

Jack looked up. Joe was standing a few feet away.

"Who were?"

"Those other police. They looked here, too."

"What did they find?"

"They found nothing."

"Is that so?" Jack struggled up on his feet and became aware by degrees that his sore leg was still killing him. He nudged the jar with the toe of his shoe. More plums oozed out. He looked toward the entrance to the dugout cave. "What do you use this for? Storage? Is it a root cellar? This your refrigerator, Joe?"

"That's right," Joe said.

FRANCE, 1945

CHAPTER TWENTY-SEVEN

• • •

Adele boarded a train heading for Strasbourg. Manfred had told her that when he'd first been sent to France he'd been stationed there. It was on the doorstep to Germany. It seemed the logical place to go.

Through the window, Adele watched the city streets turn into muddy laneways and muddy laneways turn into green countryside. And Manfred was alive. He was alive.

Adele closed her eyes. She listened to the tracks clattering beneath her. Sunlight streamed in through the window, it warmed her face. Manfred was alive.

To Strasbourg, to Dresden, to Ringstrasse. That was Manfred's street. He'd told her about it and about his family's drafty apartment in an ancient stone building. The rooms had immensely high ceilings and deep casement windows where he'd curled up on cushions to read and to dream. He'd been happy growing up there, he'd said.

I'll learn some German phrases, Adele thought to herself, I'll walk through the streets of Dresden, I'll find Ringstrasse. And in every shop along the way, I'll ask, "Do you know where the Halder family lives?"

And what if he isn't there? What if his German father, his Polish mother open the door with tears in their eyes? "Manfred is dead."

Adele kept her eyes closed and willed that thought away. Manfred had escaped from Paris, and the war would be over soon. People hardly bothered to watch the lazy lines of bombers that continued to fill the sky. Everyone was feeling safe. She'd find work in Strasbourg. She'd wait the war out.

She concentrated on the sound of the train, the warmth of the sun. She dozed off and on.

"Do you know that we have changed the spelling?" Manfred's voice was soft and close to her ear. "It is Strassburg now." He spelled it out and shook his head and laughed, as if to say, Why is the world so mad?

Yes, the world was mad. And where were they? Lying in the long grass close together where no one could see them.

"It is illegal to wear a beret there. Too French. Francs have been outlawed, marks are the legal currency. It is forbidden to speak French in shops and schools and churches in Strassburg. You do not know this?"

"Nien," Adele said, watching the play of light and shadow on his lovely face.

"We are re-Germanizing it. We have deported two hundred thousand mongrels into Vichy France. Only people with German ancestors, German blood, can stay. You see how clever we are?"

They were so close that Adele could feel his warm breath on her lips. His eyes overwhelmed her.

The train lurched, the wheels began to squeal. Adele woke up.

She was passing a factory that seemed to stretch out forever. All the windows were thrown open and for some inexplicable reason people were leaning out waving at her. She began to hear sustained blasts from factory horns and from shrill steam whistles. The town's market square slowly appeared. People were running this way and that. They were hugging each other. Children raced toward the slowing train waving tiny flags.

The train shuddered and stopped. Billows of steam passed by Adele's window. Passengers were pushing down the aisle, climbing down off the carriage, flooding across the tracks.

"It's over, it's over," a red-faced man cried out as he passed Adele's seat, "the war is over!"

Adele looked out the window again. Passengers were walking around, staring up at the sky. They were hugging and laughing and crying. Townspeople came running up to greet them.

Adele climbed off the train holding on to her suitcase for safe-keeping. It couldn't be true. Not so soon. Not like this. She was in a dream.

Some stranger grabbed her and kissed her. "The war is over!" he cried. Tears were streaming down his face.

Adele kissed him back.

Everyone was kissing everyone. Everyone was crying. Adele reached up for the next face, and the next one. The celebration lasted for two hours, and at the next town people were all over the tracks again and factory whistles were blasting and the train stopped and the passengers crowded off. It went on like that into the evening and all the next day.

Adele continued to carry her suitcase around at every stop, her blouse stained with celebratory wine, her mouth bruised with kisses. She laughed and cried with all the rest. She felt both free and a fraud. No one knew who she really was.

The train pulled into Strasbourg on the second day just as the light was beginning to fade from the sky. Adele walked away from the station and along a boisterous street. People were still celebrating. She wondered how long the party would last. She needed to find a room and get out of the clothes she'd been wearing for the last two days. She needed to sleep. She decided to turn into the first affordable-looking hotel she passed. This took several more blocks.

In her hotel room, Adele put her suitcase down and looked out the window. Below her shabby room people were still milling about in the street but in a kind of dreamy euphoria now. Strangers drifted into each other's arms and danced slowly to phantom music under the glowing lamps. All along the street a forest of blue and white flags hung from every window and every lamppost.

Adele was about to turn away and crawl into the bed when she noticed three trucks lined up in a courtyard across the way. Large red crosses had been painted on their doors and roofs. Some young people were busy carrying cardboard boxes toward them.

Adele flew down the hotel stairs. She ran across the street and approached a young woman who was struggling with a large cardboard box stamped *MEDICAL SUPPLIES-FRAGILE*. She'd had a wild hunch. She'd seen the endless lines of bombers flying into Germany.

"Can I help?" she asked.

"This one's heavier than it looked." The woman smiled. Her pleasant face was flushed. A few strands of light brown hair had escaped from under her Red Cross cap and were sticking to her gleaming cheeks.

Adele grabbed one end of the box and studied the woman more closely. Perhaps she was a year or two older than herself, but no more. "What's in it?"

"A ton of vaccine. Please be careful."

They lifted the box up into the back of the first truck in line. A young man came out from under the canvas top. Even in the gathering dark Adele could tell that he was strikingly handsome. "Nicely done, Char," he said, "only nineteen more to go."

"Who's counting, the devil?" Char brushed her hair away from her face.

"No, Maurice is." The young man picked up the carton and disappeared under the canvas again.

"I can help you – I don't mind," Adele said.

The woman offered her hand. "Charmaine Blanchot, Char for short."

When Adele shook Charmaine Blanchot's hand, it felt strong and sure of itself.

"Adele Georges," Adele replied and immediately regretted having used her family name. She had no right.

Adele followed Char toward the open doors of a narrow building. Other workers were going in and coming out.

"Do you live near here?" Char asked.

"I have a room across the street."

And the war was over now, and her father had been freed and was walking in Rouen under the plane trees … he was opening the front door. "Where is Adele?" he'd say.

"You've been having a good time." Char was smiling at her, glancing at the wine splatters on her blouse, her bedraggled look. "Everyone has been celebrating. It's wonderful, isn't it?"

"Yes," Adele said. They climbed up the stairs. "All these preparations, you must be going somewhere?"

"To Weimar. Well, a work camp near Weimar. Maurice was there last week. This is his second convoy."

Adele tried to make a mask of her face, she tried to hide her leap of joy.

In the brightly lit interior of the building, cartons marked with red crosses were stacked against one wall. A thin man in an ill-fitting threadbare uniform, stoop-shouldered and lantern-jawed, paced up and down in the crowd of workers.

"Be alert. Follow instructions as indicated," he called out, his deep funereal voice easily overpowering the shuffle and chatter. "Medical supplies, stack number one to truck number one. Food supplies, stack number two to truck number two. Clothing and other personals, stack number three to truck number three."

Adele looked around at the faces. Most were as young as Char or herself but a few were middle-aged or older. Three women in grey caps, immaculate blue blouses and starched grey skirts were sitting at a long table checking over voluminous lists.

"Our nurses," Char said with a note of pride, picking up a lighter carton in the medical stack. Adele picked up one, too, and they walked back outside. Char seemed determined to continue to help load truck number one. Adele thought she knew why.

The same young man reached down and took the two cartons. Char smiled up at him and once again brushed the stray strands of hair away from her face.

They walked back to the building. "There seems a lot of people for three trucks," Adele said.

"Not everyone's going. Most aren't. They have families so they can't leave their jobs. I'm sure they all would if they could manage it. Anyway, we have two personnel carriers with benches in the back."

"When do you leave?"

"Tomorrow morning at six o'clock."

"I've come to Strasbourg to look for work."

"From where?"

"From Paris."

"You've come a long way. Isn't there work there?"

"I couldn't find any. I would like to work here. I mean, with you. Go to this camp near Weimar. Do you think that's possible?"

"But this isn't work. I'm a volunteer. Most of us are volunteers."

"I would like to volunteer."

"Do you have any training?" Char looked at Adele more closely.

"In what way?"

"Well, for example, I'm a nursing assistant."

"I can work hard. I've worked long shifts in factories. I'm much stronger than I look."

Char smiled. "Well, the truth is most of our work is just basic kindness, anyway."

Kindness. Adele had a vision of André standing out in the snow. "I'm willing to do anything, the dirtiest jobs, whatever it is, it doesn't matter."

"You don't have to convince me. I'll introduce you to Madame Sarraute."

Madame Sarraute, the oldest of the nurses, hardly bothered to look up at Adele. When she did, she stared at the wine stains. "Are you drunk?"

"No."

"Are you sure?"

"Yes."

"I can't afford to take on an untried person. You have never worked with us before and the place to start is not inside Germany. I don't need a hysteric on my hands."

"I'm not a hysteric, Madame Sarraute," Adele said.

"How do I know? How do you know? That's the point. I'm delighted you want to help. Join the organization, by all means. Charmaine will give you some material to read. You must learn basic first aid, and you can work here on rolling bandages and sorting out goods and putting relief packages together. If that all works out well, then we can take you out into the field at a later date." Madame Sarraute went back to her lists. The interview was over.

Adele couldn't think of anything more to say in her own defence, so she turned away. The man with the lantern jaw was standing right behind her.

"Hello," he said.

Char took Adele's arm. "Adele Georges, Maurice Caillaux, director of the Red Cross, Strasbourg chapter."

Director Caillaux bowed a little. "And how old are you, Adele?"

"Nineteen."

"Do you like children?"

"Yes."

"How do you know? You don't have any of your own?"

"No," Adele felt herself blush a little, "but I have three brothers and I've looked after the two younger ones all my life."

"Have you worked with other people's children at all? Groups of children?"

"Yes," Adele lied, "at church and at a school near our home where I helped the teachers. I read stories and played games and things like that."

"Do you have any other skills to offer?"

Nurse Sarraute had come around the table to join them. She didn't look pleased.

"I'm a seamstress." Adele had no idea why she'd said that but she was instantly glad she had. Director Caillaux's cavernous eyes brightened.

"We could use a seamstress."

"Surely, Monsieur le directeur," Nurse Sarraute interjected, "it's not wise to take an untried person to such a place. I'm quite certain there are people in Weimar who can sew."

"I understand. However, I think Adele may bring something to the children only such a young and may I say unthreateningly diminutive person can supply. A freshness of spirit that tells them that they must go on living. They must try. They must."

A shadow of deep feeling passed over Director Caillaux's homely face. For a moment Adele wasn't sure that it wouldn't overcome him.

"I will do my very best. I promise you, Monsieur Caillaux," Adele said.

He took her small hand and held it firmly. "Six o'clock tomorrow morning, Adele." Nurse Sarraute was giving him a terrible look. He turned to her. "You know as well as I, Elaine, we need all the help we can get." He released Adele's hand and bowed again, this time to all three ladies, and went back to calling out orders.

Nurse Sarraute turned her cold gaze on Adele. "We'll see. You must read all the material Charmaine will give you. You must stay up all night until you understand it."

"Yes, Madame."

"Bring practical clothes and as few items of toiletry as you can manage. Be prepared to eat sparingly and sleep rough."

"Thank you, Madame."

Nurse Sarraute moved back around the table shaking her head.

"Congratulations," Char whispered.

Henri Paul-Louis was sitting on the edge of Adele's empty bed. René was holding up a lighted candle. "How can I forgive her?" her father said.

Char touched Adele's arm. "Are you all right?"

"I'm all right," Adele said.

. . .

After the trucks were loaded, Adele and Char walked a long way to a small cellar café close by the building where Char and her family lived. It was late in the evening, and they were both half-starved.

There was something faintly boyish about her new friend's face and her whole person that Adele found attractive. Char walked with a little swagger for one thing, her grey eyes perfectly candid, her nose generous, her mouth quick to smile. Most of all, she seemed completely at peace with herself.

Over steaming bowls of soup and chunks of bread, Char told Adele about her large family. Despite living in only three rooms, they all got along with each other. This seemed highly unlikely to Adele.

"And your parents? Do they live in Paris? What are they like?" Char asked.

"They're dead." The words seemed to come out of Adele's mouth of their own accord. "My father died in the first month of the war. Near Arras. He was a doctor in the medical corps – I don't know where he's buried."

"Oh, I'm sorry, Adele."

"My mother died of shock."

Char's mouthed dropped open a little. She looked dismayed. "That's so awful!"

"Yes," Adele said.

"No wonder you had to look after your little brothers. Where are they now?"

"At an uncle's."

As soon as she returned to her room at the hotel, Adele crossed the hall to the toilet and peeled off all her clothes. She looked at herself in the mirror. Her hair was curling into its usual black mass of contradictions. No one had remarked on its shortness. It now covered the nape of her neck and her ears. It also covered the scar on her forehead. It looked almost normal.

Adele sank into a tub of water as hot as the hotel could muster and stayed there until another resident rapped on the bathroom door and told her she was taking too long. Back in her room, she checked a map she'd bought at the station in Paris. Weimar was more than two-thirds of the way to Dresden. It seemed a miracle.

Adele sat in the middle of the bed surrounded by the books and pamphlets Char had given her. She knew at some point she would sneak away from the Red Cross and walk alone through carnage and death toward Dresden. French but no longer French. Anathema to both sides. Perhaps she'd be stoned. Or hung inside some broken building.

Adele curled up on the bed. She thought of Char, her self-confidence, her free-limbed gait. But then Charmaine Blanchot was a good girl.

She would have been a good girl, too, if she hadn't met Manfred Halder. She knew why she'd said that her father was dead. To think that he was alive and that he knew who she was was unbearable.

Adele could hear music coming from the street below. People were still celebrating. She sat up and picked up one of Char's books. It seemed to weigh more than Simone's books all put together. She opened it up. The words shifted and fell off the page.

• • •

At five in the morning Adele woke up. She looked out her window toward the courtyard across the street. It sat empty under its lonely lamp. Char had warned her that the trucks would be taken away to a staging area and not to think that she'd missed the convoy.

185

She tried to read Char's books again. Light began to creep into the sky. At half past five she packed up her suitcase.

Adele crossed the street and sat on the steps of the Red Cross building. After a while some young workers she recognized from the night before began to arrive. They had their Red Cross caps on and canvas packs slung over their shoulders. Adele knew her cardboard suitcase looked stupid. She knew she looked stupid. The others nodded at her but no one came over to talk.

Char was one of the last to arrive, carrying an extra-large pack and striding purposefully into the courtyard. She glanced around the assembled crowd. Adele knew who she was looking for but he hadn't arrived yet.

Char came over to her.

"What should we do with your books?" Adele asked.

"We can leave them here once Maurice unlocks the door." Char took another look around. "How'd the reading go?"

"I didn't get through everything."

"Of course not. Not even Madame Sarraute could expect that."

Two personnel carriers rumbled into the courtyard. The young man from the night before came running through the gates and despite being late was the first to climb into the back of one of them. Char climbed into the back of that one, too. "Come on, Adele," Char urged from one of the two benches inside, "hurry."

Adele reached out for the metal railing and pulled herself up into the truck.

"Adele Georges," Char said, "this is Pierre Savard."

"I'm pleased to meet you," the handsome Pierre said. He held out a smooth white hand from across the aisle. "You've decided to come with us."

"Char is the one who made this possible," Adele replied, lightly touching his hand and trying to deflect his attention to where Char obviously wanted it to go.

Char smiled. "Not me. You did it yourself, Adele."

"I hope you won't be sorry," he said.

It took an hour to reach the staging area, a factory with only two walls left standing and gutted by bombs. The personnel carriers pulled up in front.

The three trucks from the night before along with two larger ones were lined up waiting.

The young workers clambered off the benches and out the back of the carriers – it was a last chance to stretch their legs.

Char opened up her pack and lifted out two large boxes of pastries, courtesy of her mother and her great-aunt. It didn't take long for everyone, including the drivers and mechanics and the nurses to gather around. Nurse Sarraute marched up to Adele. "Put this on," she said, handing her a grey cap.

Adele pulled off her purple beret. She was sure her hair looked wild.

"Go on," Nurse Sarraute said.

Adele put the Red Cross cap on. Her thick hair resisted.

"You'll have to pin it." Nurse Sarraute's face softened for just a moment. "Do your best," she said.

The convoy rumbled across the Rhine. Adele was sitting opposite Pierre Savard again, holding on to the railing behind her for support, her new cap perched precariously on the top of her head with the help of two borrowed pins.

Pierre leaned across the aisle. His hair was curly and so black it looked blue. His skin was absolutely smooth and cream-coloured, his eyes green. He had perfect teeth. His chin was strong, too, but his bottom lip stuck out a little like a petulant child's. This one flaw came as a relief to Adele.

The truck rocked crazily.

"It's a pontoon bridge," Pierre shouted at her. "It was built by the American Army three months ago."

Adele nodded.

"General Patton pissed off it. Did you see the photograph?"

Adele gave him a look.

"No, really, it was in the papers," Pierre said.

At first the road into Germany reminded Adele of the road between Rouen and Paris, except for all the people walking along it, streaming toward the French border and the checkpoint the trucks had just passed through.

"Workers," Pierre told her, "forced labour. They're coming home. Some aren't French citizens, though. They're afraid to go back to their countries because of the Russians."

Char joined in. "They've been displaced from their homes, their families, their whole lives. There are refugee camps all along the river. Everyone has to be processed."

Adele nodded and watched the ragged line of men recede behind her. The convoy began to wind its way through a string of German villages. Some of the larger buildings were roofless and windowless, but as in France the general shape of each community remained intact. Women were sweeping the streets, men were shoring up walls and stringing electrical lines from house to house. A hot wind was blowing dust everywhere.

Deeper into Germany, in the larger towns, the scale of the destruction increased. Men and women and groups of children began to appear from crevasses and crude shelters looking like Bedouins in a desert. No hands were held out, no shouted requests for food. They stood on the piles of bricks and the ridges of debris watching the trucks pass by, their faces the colour of ash, their clothes dust-caked and unravelling.

When they reached Stuttgart, it wasn't there. A vast plain of chalky rubble had replaced the city. The occasional church spire or wall stuck out like grey fingers of warning.

The trucks stopped. The three nurses and Maurice Cailloux had been riding in the cabs of the two leading trucks. Maurice climbed down and called out for the young workers to join him. The nurses stayed where they were.

The air was hot. The smell of death was overwhelming.

"This is central Stuttgart," Maurice announced.

Iridescent bloated flies swarmed all around them. Obese rats waddled across the bricks and stones. They scuttled past the workers' shoes, they slipped down into holes and crevices.

Adele knew what lay beneath her. She could see it as clearly as if she were looking at a photograph. Acres of lightless caverns. Broken chairs. Windows. Vast storehouses of decaying men and women and children.

"Take a moment to look around. I want you to remember Stuttgart when we reach Buchenwald," Maurice said.

"Why?" Char was holding her nose and looking with a kind of desperation up a hill of bricks and splintered boards.

"To see what God has put up with," Maurice said, "on all sides from this terrible war."

Adele's eyes were running from the horrendous stench. She could feel Nurse Sarraute watching her.

"I don't understand," Pierre said. His face looked blotched and flushed like a spanked child's.

The young workers held their hands over their mouths and noses and gazed across the chalky plain. They might as well have been standing on the moon.

"It's not possible to understand," Maurice said.

CANADA, 1946

CHAPTER TWENTY-EIGHT

• • •

"They sure made a mess," Jack said to Joe Puvalowski, looking over the boards and clothes and tin cans strewn across the slope, at the awning and the opening into the ground, "those other policemen."

Joe nodded. He knew what was coming.

"Damn shame the way they took your landing papers away. High-handed. I'll get them back. All you have to do is tell me all about it."

"About what?"

"About that dead man. But not here. We'll go down to my office. We'll write it out."

Joe stuck his hands in his jacket pockets. He was going stony again. "Why us?"

"Because the dead man came from here. Didn't he?"

"Why not you? Why not those police?"

"What about those police?"

"You want to ask questions? Ask yourselves. Always it is us." And now Joe was shaking his fist, as he always seemed to end up doing, shaking it in the chief of police's face. "Missing apples, chickens, we get blame! You know this. Wash on a line. They come to us. This time, no. No!" Joe's hair shook, his jaw stuck out, he thundered. "We do not lower ourselves to touch such a man!"

Joe headed down the hill. "Ask yourselves, Mr. Jack!"

Jack stood there watching him. He'd forgotten his throbbing leg. He'd forgotten the grey sky, the railway tracks leading off into the distance.

Such a man, Joe had said.

• • •

The late afternoon sun was coming through the lace curtains and fossilizing Kyle's memorial room in amber. Jack leaned against the door frame and looked over the table of photographs, the ribbons, the letters home to his mother.

He picked up the photograph of Kyle in his Royal Hamilton Light Infantry uniform. Twenty-four then. Twenty-seven at Dieppe.

Jack closed his eyes. It was as silent in his house as it had been in that hole in the ground. Despair was in his house, it was padding soundlessly from room to room.

Such a man, Joe had said. Ask yourselves, Mr. Jack, he had said.

Was the murderer some man from town then? Was that what he'd meant?

Jack had figured too much time had gone by, over two, maybe three weeks, more than enough for whoever had fired that shot to jump a freight and disappear. But if he lived in town, why would he run? He wouldn't. He'd stay put, go to work, carry on just the same as before. Day to day.

Jack could feel his pulse quickening.

So the DP had gotten himself into trouble in town. Maybe he molested a child. That would fit with the other men not wanting to touch him. That's what Joe had said. Bellowed it, actually.

Jack couldn't get the idea of an execution out of his mind, though. It was possible someone could have snuck up behind the man or he could have slipped and been lying helpless on the ground, but all Jack could see was the man on his knees, his hands tied behind his back. And bang. Something military about it.

A soldier's child had been molested? A soldier's wife? Was that it? Or something else? Something to do with overseas and prisoner-of-war camps and someone recognizing the DP walking through the town as big as life. Something to do with military justice. Revenge.

Jack looked down at his son's photograph again. All of Europe was shrouded in mystery as far as Jack was concerned. A mass of lightless flames. A terrible darkness. Kyle rotting on a beach somewhere, food for the seagulls, white bones now.

He held the photograph in an iron grip.

He tried to remember how long it had been since he'd visited his grandson. He couldn't recall.

• • •

The Studebaker pulled up in front of the house. Jack sat there for a moment. No one ever used the front door, and now it was too overgrown with bushes to see it. The truth was, the house was in a condition of disrepair, sinking down into the uncut grass like it had given up.

Jack got out of the car. A kind of smoky dusk was settling down over the town. He leaned against the front fender. The air felt warmer than it had all day – it was going to turn back into a heat wave tomorrow. He could hear a radio playing from inside the house.

Jack walked around to the back and rapped on the screen door. He rapped louder against the sound of the music. Dorothy's face appeared through the door like a face on a movie screen.

"Jack," she said.

"Just thought I'd come over."

She wasn't opening the door.

"To see George."

"All right. He isn't here right now. He's playing somewhere." Her face disappeared.

Jack opened the door and walked up the two inside steps into the kitchen. Dorothy was already sitting at the table rolling cigarettes. She had a contraption that made six cigarettes at a time. Dirty plates were piled high in the sink, dirty pots on the stove. She kept her head down, her hair hiding her face. She picked up a razor blade and began to slice through a slot in the machine.

Jack turned the radio down. "You don't mind, do you?"

Dorothy shrugged and made four more passes with the razor blade. Six cigarettes rolled out of the machine. She picked up one, struck a match and lit it. Smoke drifted in the air.

He always felt awkward in her house, the rooms were too small, the ceilings too low. "When's he get home?"

"When the street lights come on."

"They're on," Jack said.

She looked up at him. Her hair had a honey-coloured cast to it. His grandson's hair was darker. He didn't look a lot like her, not so far, anyway. George had a thin, pensive face like Kyle's. Dorothy's face was fleshy, almost bruised-looking, but not unattractive. In fact there was something about it that was downright seductive. Kyle hadn't been a complete fool.

"Do you want a drink, Jack?"

Jack could see she had one for herself. She hadn't bothered to turn on any lights. It was more than half-dark in the room.

"Sure." He hadn't eaten all day. He hadn't even thought about it until now.

Dorothy got up and went over to the sink. A bottle was sitting there. "Rye and water okay?"

"Skip the water."

"All right." She reached into the cupboard for a glass, picked up the bottle. "Why don't you sit down?"

Jack sat down on a kitchen chair opposite her side of the table and facing a little toward the back door.

"How's Ruth?" Dorothy asked.

"The same. Well, worse."

"I've been meaning to get over to see her."

"Right. She'd like that."

Dorothy handed him almost half a glass of rye and sat down again.

"Cheers," Jack said and reduced the rye by half in one long drink. When he put down the glass, Dorothy was staring at him.

"What's the occasion, Jack?"

"What do you mean?"

Dorothy picked up her glass and sipped at it. She lifted her smouldering cigarette from the ashtray and took a puff. "I haven't seen you for such a long time. That's all."

"Oh?"

"Last Christmas. You came over with Ruth."

Last Christmas, Jack thought, Jesus. "I guess that's why."

"Why what?"

"Why I'm here." Jack tried his pleasant smile on her. She always seemed a little uneasy around him, he didn't know why. He'd never given her any trouble, not even when she'd got herself pregnant so Kyle would have to marry her. He was only twenty-two. She was all of twenty-eight. Ruth had almost had a fit.

"She's just a factory girl," Ruth had said. And then the baby had come and Ruth had changed her tune. She was crazy for the baby. And then Kyle went way. And then he was dead.

"Are you busy these days, Jack?"

"What?" Jack had been drifting.

"You must be."

"Why?"

"A body was found, wasn't it? Out on the river? Everyone's talking about it."

"It's out of my jurisdiction. I called in the Ontario Provincial Police. They're looking after it."

"Do they know anything?"

The screen door opened and closed with a slap, and nine-year-old George was standing on the steps to the kitchen.

"Your Grandfather Cullen is here," Dorothy said, though this seemed obvious enough to Jack. In fact her announcement was down-right irritating.

George's hair was sticking up, his face was shiny. He'd been running and he was still trying to catch his breath.

"Hi there, George," Jack said.

George stood there looking a little startled and slightly perplexed, an expression not unlike one of his father's. He stared back at Jack.

"Say hello," his mother said.

"Hello," George said.

"You're not running from anything, are you, George? You haven't done anything? I don't have to arrest you, do I?"

George shook his head. He crossed the room and circled well around Jack before dashing down the hall.

"Come back and talk," Dorothy yelled after him.

"I will," George said from somewhere.

"He's getting his new baseball glove to show you." She didn't sound particularly convinced of it. "He's crazy about that glove."

Jack nodded.

"Show your grandfather your baseball glove," Dorothy called down the hall.

Jack looked back toward the screen door. Why the hell had he come over in the first place? He couldn't actually remember.

"The man was murdered, wasn't he?"

Jack nodded. It didn't surprise him that everyone in town was talking about it, with Harold Miles setting up shop right there in the Arlington Hotel and his men all over the goddamn place.

"They don't know anything," Jack said. He looked back at Dorothy.

Once again and with some intensity, she was staring at him.

GERMANY, 1945

CHAPTER TWENTY-NINE
. . .

The convoy turned down a narrow lane and pulled up behind a screen of trees. It was time for lunch. A Spartan meal was laid out on folding tables, but no one was hungry. Pierre, Char and Adele went for a walk.

"What do you think, Adele?" Pierre asked.

"About what?"

"About what happened in Stuttgart."

Char answered for her. "All that bombing is the reason the war is over. We were fighting for our lives."

"We were under occupation, we weren't fighting for our lives," Pierre replied.

"My father was," Adele said. She could feel her nerves unravelling, twitching under her skin.

"Adele's father was a soldier," Char explained. "He was killed in the first month of the war."

"I'm very sorry," Pierre said.

"And her mother died of grief."

"Oh, no." Pierre looked doubly sorry.

Adele clenched her teeth. "It's all right."

"Doubt and guilt never fed anyone." Char sounded upset. "We don't have time for such things. It never clothed anyone or nursed anyone, either. Everything has been wrong and nothing has been right. That may be true, but still, the war is over and now we can be of use."

"We've been bombing women and children for over two years, Char," Pierre said.

It was almost dusk by the time the trucks rattled across a plank bridge over a wide river. They pulled up along the edge of a woods. Gathering everyone around him, Maurice explained that though they were only forty miles from Weimar, because of all the shattered machines of war clogging the road and the bomb craters and uncertain bridges, it was too dangerous to push on in the dark. They'd spend the night there.

After a skimpy meal, the drivers and mechanics put up two tents, a large one for the nurses and a smaller one for Maurice. As for themselves, they were happy enough to curl up in the truck cabs.

Since the night was promising to be clear and the sky was already filling up with stars, the young workers voted to sleep on groundsheets in the open air. Char and Adele lay their bedrolls down beside each other. The warmth that had followed the convoy all that day was disappearing. A swampy smell of decay, coming from somewhere deeper in the woods, crept coldly over them.

"What do you think of Pierre?" Char whispered once they had settled in.

Adele had been lying there thinking about Dresden, wondering what it must look like. Did it look like Stuttgart? Was all of Germany a charnel house?

"He's very honest with his feelings," Char said.

Adele couldn't bring herself to look Char's way. Frivolous and mindless and foolish feelings in the midst of other people's horrors and nightmares – it reminded her too much of someone she knew. It reminded her of herself.

Char chatted on but as Adele wasn't answering she soon gave up and fell asleep. Adele continued to lie there wide awake, feeling nothing but a smothering confusion. She could hear her father. "Be of service to other people. That's the most important thing," he had said. She could see his kind face. And all she was doing was looking for Manfred.

When Adele woke up the next morning, the first thing she saw was a dazzle of dewdrops sparkling all around her. Her hair felt wet, her bedroll freezing. She looked over at Char, who was still asleep, the early morning sun just beginning to colour her face. She looked as innocent as an angel.

They reached Weimar before noon. It had been bombed, too, but not devastated. On the outskirts gutted buildings stood side by side like rows of haunted houses. Deeper into the city nothing seemed to be touched at all.

The trucks didn't stop in Weimar but drove straight through and began to climb a series of rising hills. After a few miles, they slowed to a crawl.

Adele smelled the camp before she saw it – it smelled like an open sewer. Soon they were passing by barbed wire fences and watchtowers and long wooden buildings. The trucks pulled through a wooden gateway, rattled into a dusty compound and stopped. Adele looked out the back of the truck. Some men were sitting along the edge of a veranda in front of a large central building. They looked for all the world like a row of cadavers.

An officer poked his head around the canvas opening into the truck. "Welcome to Buchenwald, we've been waiting on you folks," he said in English. "Good to see you all."

His heartiness seemed wildly out of place to Adele.

"We're pleased to be here," Pierre responded, also in English. Char smiled. Pierre was a man of many talents.

They began to climb out of the trucks. Maurice came hurrying up, and he and the army officer walked off together. A few of the men who'd been sitting on the veranda began to step haltingly across the yard.

"French?" the one in the lead asked.

"Yes." Nurse Sarraute had climbed down from a truck cab and was positioning herself between the advancing men and her workers. "I remember you. Do you remember me? We've come back to help."

"Many have left. Not us."

"I know."

The young workers tried to avoid staring at the men's bone-like arms, yellow skin stretched like parchment, skull faces, but they couldn't.

"Sweets? Chocolate?" One of the men held out an emaciated hand. The others crowded in aggressively. "Cigarettes?"

"Yes, of course. As soon as we get organized." Nurse Sarrutte turned away and, clapping briskly for her flock to fall in line, walked across the compound toward a smaller building. The young workers hurried to follow her.

A large American flag was hanging listlessly from a flagpole. The dusty yard was full of army trucks, stars and stripes painted on their doors. Groups of soldiers were lounging around. As the young women filed by, the soldiers pushed their caps back off their foreheads and smiled.

Adele turned away, shielding her face with her hand as if the sun had suddenly struck her eyes.

They filed through a double screen door into the foyer of a small infirmary. Nurse Sarraute, with the help of Pierre's translation, began an animated discussion with a blond army nurse as to where the supplies they'd brought should go and how best to deploy her people. The smell inside was almost as powerful as the smell outside, and now it was mixed in with the sharp odours of disinfectants and medicines.

Half-dead men in nightshirts, eyes and faces expressionless, shuffled past Adele and the rest of the young workers. They didn't seem to be going anywhere in particular, just a restless, endless circling up and down the narrow halls.

A naked man, his ribcage protruding grotesquely just under translucent yellowish skin, came up to Adele and stared at her as if he were trying to remember something that had happened a long time ago. Adele took a step back. Char picked up his hand. "Can I take you somewhere? Can I take you back to your room?"

"Third door on the left," the army nurse called out in English, "try to make him keep his gown on."

"Third door on the left," Pierre translated, "try to get him to put his shift back on."

Char nodded and with the naked man teetering beside her, she walked off down the hall.

"Adele," a voice called out.

Adele turned to see Maurice poking his long solemn face in past the screen doors. He motioned to her.

By the time she'd caught up to him, he was some distance away from the infirmary, striding toward a small building sitting on top of a knoll.

"The people here are the in-between men. That's what I call them, anyway," he said to her as she caught up. "These are the men balanced between life and death. The Americans stumbled on this place a few weeks ago. Twenty thousand souls were packed into these buildings, though apparently the Germans had marched off another twenty thousand two days before. The Americans gave them food. Some died just from that. And some died because they were going to die anyway. Most of the healthier ones have left, trying to find their way back home."

Adele could see a group of tiny old men with yellow faces sitting on the wooden steps of the building. As she and Maurice drew closer, the men stood up and stared. Now Adele could see that her eyes had played a trick on her. They were children.

"Good day, boys," Maurice said, walking up and smiling broadly. "Who speaks French?"

None of the children answered. A few looked down at their tattered shoes but most stared straight at Adele with deep, enormous eyes.

More yellow faces peered out of the gloom of the building.

"Come now," Maurice insisted, "I know some of you are French. Speak up now."

A boy of about ten, wearing leather breeches and with an American soldier's cap on his head, stepped forward. Though his stick-like legs were caked with mud and his skin was stretched in creases across his face, unlike the men in the infirmary, his eyes were full of light. "I speak French."

"Who else?" Maurice asked.

A few others put up their hands.

"These are the orphans of Buchenwald," Maurice said. "There used to be about nine hundred but most have already been shipped to Switzerland or America. We're trying to find places for everyone. There's only these few left."

"What about their relatives, they must have relatives?"

Maurice stared at her. "No," he said.

The boy who had spoken up moved closer to Adele. When he smiled, Adele could see that his teeth were rotting. "What's your name?" he asked.

"Adele."

"Are you going to stay with us?"

Adele looked at Maurice. Maurice nodded and walked away.

The boy took her hand and led her through the door of the building. The other children shuffled in after them. It seemed dark at first and then Adele began to make out rows of crude plank beds stacked to the ceiling. There seemed hardly space enough to crawl between the layers, even for the smallest child.

"You can sleep here." The boy led her to a bunk with a little more head space. Adele sat down on the edge of it. The boy took off his cap and sat down beside her. Some pieces of his hair stuck up in random tufts; the rest of his head was bald.

"My name is Étienne," he said.

"Hello, Étienne." Adele was feeling desperate to make some kind of normal conversation. "And can you tell me your last name?"

Étienne pushed up his ragged sleeve. Bright blue numbers were tattooed on the underside of his wrist. "A-4133," he said.

All the children crowded around and pushed up their sleeves and showed Adele their numbers.

"That's not your last names," Adele said. She touched the numbers on Étienne's wrist. They felt raised under her fingertips. She glanced at him.

Étienne was watching her, his eyes like two beams of light.

. . .

Over the next few days Adele discovered that she didn't have to do everything on her own. The Americans had arranged for selected citizens of Weimar to come up to the camp to do the dirty work, as a kind of punishment or, at least, as a penance. On her first day, two middle-aged women arrived to scrub the floor of the barracks.

The nurses from the infirmary made periodic visits, and some of the Red Cross workers did as well, especially Char and Pierre, but it was Adele who had been given the job of permanent nanny. She slept with the children, organized their meals, demanded that they bathe regularly, led them in gentle exercises, sorted through a mountain of donated clothes, altered everything to fit on a clattering old sewing machine, moved from bunk to bunk quieting the children who had bad dreams, the criers and the screamers. Sometimes she was up half the night.

For the first time in a long while Adele felt like she was of some use. When she'd first tried to organize a game no one had moved. They'd just stood there as if to play was as foreign to them as if she'd asked them to fly. Lost little Ukrainian boys. And Czechoslovakian, Polish, Belgian, French.

She'd decided to divide them into three groups depending on their size and to play games that required no language. She'd thought up variations of hide and seek for the little ones, games of tag for the middle ones, football for the biggest.

As the days went by, the boys began to find their smiles, and then they began to laugh. The big ones crowded around her eager for the next game, the middle ones organized secret competitions to see who could hold her hand the longest, the small ones began to follow her around the camp like a clutch of ragged ducks.

Étienne became Adele's lieutenant. He did any job she asked him to do. He kept order in the barracks. He ate beside her at the table. He slept on the bunk above her.

One night, when the other boys were supposed to be asleep, he hung upside down from his bed and peered down at her.

"Go to sleep, Étienne," Adele whispered. She could see him quite clearly. She always left the light on just inside the door. Behind the circle of children, rows of empty bunks receded into the dark. Étienne's tufts of hair were hanging down like long ears.

"You look like a bat," Adele said.

Étienne smiled. "Do you know what my real last name is?"

"No."

"Adler."

"Is it? That's a nice name, Étienne."

"Étienne Adler."

"Where do you come from, Étienne?

"Auschwitz."

"I don't know it."

"It's in Poland." Étienne watched her for a moment, the downward flow of blood making his face go red. "They marched us through the snow."

"To Buchenwald, you mean?"

Étienne swung down and landed on Adele's bunk. He sat cross-legged by her feet. He pulled the bottom of her blanket up over his lap. "My brother died."

"I'm sorry."

"My father didn't die. He died here."

"I'm sorry."

"My mother died in Auschwitz. My two sisters died in Auschwitz."

Adele could see his hand moving up and down under her blanket, his pinched face falling into a kind of trance.

"Please don't, Étienne," she said, reaching out and gently drawing him down beside her, covering him up with her blanket. "Try to go to sleep. There."

"They sprayed my father with water," Étienne said. "It was night but they had big lights on. I could see. There were other men, too."

"Sleep, Étienne," Adele whispered.

"He was covered in ice. Then they sprayed him again until he could hardly walk. They sprayed him again. Then he fell down. Then a doctor came. He looked at him and all the other men. Then they sprayed them all again. When they were frozen, they lifted them and took them to the hospital."

"Why?"

"They were trying to find out something."

"What?"

"I don't know."

Étienne tried to turn his small body toward her. She could feel him shaking. She wanted to say, "It's all right, Étienne. She wanted to say, "It's over now," but the words stuck in her throat.

"Shhh," she said.

•　•　•

When they could, on most evenings, Char and Pierre and Adele went for short walks outside the perimeter of the camp. It helped to walk out under the high wooden entrance gate and lose sight of the shuffling men for awhile.

"According to Maurice," Pierre said, giving another of his lectures, "this camp was specifically designed to provide slave labour. Men and boys to Buchenwald. Work them to death. Ship in a new supply and do it all over again."

"I know," Char said.

"They had their own munitions factory here, before it was bombed to smithereens."

Adele felt like the grey air in front of her was solid, as if she had to push a way through.

"The Jews usually went straight into the incinerator, though," Pierre said.

Adele sat down abruptly on the slope of the hill.

"What's the matter?" Char sat down beside her.

"I don't know. I'm tired."

"That's not a big surprise, Adele. Running after those kids all day." Pierre sat down on her other side.

A kind of darkness was falling all around. The stars were falling. Everything was so cruel and hopeless. Adele choked off a cry and put her head between her knees.

"Adele?" Char said.

Pierre touched her arm. "What is it?"

Adele didn't answer. They made her keep her head down for two minutes. Pierre timed it on his watch. Char rubbed her neck and told her to keep breathing. After a while Adele put her head back up.

"We can stay here a little longer if you like," Pierre said.

They sat on the hillside for a long time, looking down the dark slope in front of them, looking toward the faint, far-off lights of Weimar.

• • •

It was Étienne who told her about the bodies. They were running the crematorium day and night but they couldn't get through all the bodies so they had to leave them piled up on wagons.

"They were naked. The American general made the people in the town come and look."

Étienne was standing in front of Adele. The other boys were watching from their tiers of bunks. It was a strange bedtime story Étienne was telling. Adele sat on a chair under the light and continued to sew a button on a shirt. She wondered if she should change the subject.

"Everyone from the town, women too, they all had to come up here and look. '"See what you've done?' That's what the general said. And other people came from a long way to see the bodies. They came from America. They took pictures. They took pictures of us, too."

Étienne fell silent. Adele glanced at him. He was looking back at her, his bright eyes full of anticipation. He crept closer and touched her shoulder as if he were trying to wake her up.

"What is it, Étienne?"

"One night we went again to look." He turned to the other boys. Adele turned toward them, too. They were still paying attention, their luminous eyes fixed on Étienne. Only two spoke French, but they all seemed to understand, they all seemed to be remembering the walk through the dark to see the bodies.

"They didn't smell," Étienne said.

"They didn't smell?"

"No. And a blue light came down from the sky. And the bodies stood up."

Adele felt a bolt of electricity race through her.

"The light woke them up," Étienne said.

The children murmured in agreement. They were all nodding their heads. They had all seen this.

Adele got up from her chair. She knew that they were waiting for her to answer Étienne's silent question. How could that be? How could the dead come alive again? Adele wasn't going to argue with them. They had seen what they had seen. "The bodies woke up because God was there."

She hadn't meant to say that, not exactly. She had meant to say that their souls were leaving their bodies because they were going to Heaven, their bodies were dead but their souls were not.

The boys continued to stare at her. They were waiting for something more.

"They had defeated death. You see? They didn't die, after all." Adele turned to Étienne.

Étienne was looking up at her as if she'd come down from Heaven herself just to tell him that. "Yes, Adele," he said.

All the children went to sleep more easily that night, even the habitual screamers – it was the best night they'd ever had. In the morning Étienne was gone.

Adele got dressed and ran through the camp looking for him. He didn't appear in the mess tent for breakfast. He wasn't sitting on his bunk with a mischievous grin when they returned.

Adele made a game out of it, sending the children through all the buildings looking for Étienne's hiding place. He didn't appear the rest of that day, or that night, or the next day, either.

Adele sat on her chair by the open door paying almost no attention to the other boys. Of course Étienne was getting stronger. No one was holding him in the camp against his will. He was actually eleven years old. He was free to walk out the gate. But where would he go? There was nowhere for him to go.

She knew why he'd left. It was because of what she'd said. He'd believed her when he hadn't believed his own eyes, when he hadn't believed himself. Étienne had pushed out the door to look for his dead parents because she'd told him that they weren't really dead. They were alive somewhere.

She had made a terrible mistake. What was it that André had said about running away from the orphanage, about living on the streets? He was forced to do such terrible things he couldn't even tell her what they were.

Adele sat by the open door for several more nights. She felt like she was dying. Étienne did not come back. The other boys were upset at Étienne's disappearance, too. Adele no longer thought of leaving the camp to travel to Dresden. She'd wait now until all the children were safely assigned to new families and new homes, until all their paperwork had come through, until the very last one of them had left the camp forever.

She tried to feel better. She tried to feel like she had when Étienne was there. She worked twice as hard as before, she invented new games for the children to play, she sat up all night with anyone who cried or had a temperature or as much as moaned in their sleep.

One day she installed a new boy in the bunk above her head. He was one of the other two French speakers. His name was Simon.

"Are you asleep yet?" he said the first night.

"Not yet. Are you?"

"Yes." This was to become their little joke. Simon repeated it to her every night and then he'd fall asleep. Adele couldn't fall asleep, though. She couldn't get rid of the feeling that she had failed Étienne, that she had failed everyone she'd ever known. And the red-headed soldier had come back into her dreams.

• • •

The boys, all twenty-three of them, were being examined by a doctor in the infirmary. This happened every week and took most of the day. Char and Pierre came into the waiting room and asked Adele if she wanted to go into town. Another worker had volunteered to watch the children.

"No," Adele said.

Char looked disappointed. "You must take a break."

"Maurice said to make sure you go along. It's an order." Pierre was trying to look stern.

"Come on, Adele." Char picked up her hand and began to drag her toward the door. Most of the children were playing among themselves. A few were watching her. Simon was watching her.

"All right," Adele said.

Two jeeps were waiting outside. One was full of American nurses sitting on each other's laps, talking and laughing. The other one was empty except for the soldier driving it. Adele got into the back. Char and Pierre climbed in. Two more nurses came running up to join them.

They had no trouble finding the most raucous beer garden in town because the street in front of it was swarming with soldiers and with quite a few young women, too. A few days before, Pierre had translated a poster that had been tacked up outside the mess tent. It had said that all Allied soldiers were strictly forbidden from fraternizing with the local population. The order didn't seem to be taking effect.

Adele looked at the young women's faces. They seemed familiar, their anxious smiles, quick forced laughter, the fear of no future in their eyes. She knew them well.

Adele sat down with Char and Pierre and the American nurses at a long, beer-smeared table. Giant porcelain steins, white froth spilling over their tops, descended from somewhere. One landed in front of her. She picked it up and took a drink. It had been too long since her body had felt the warmth and comfort of alcohol. She'd missed it. The beer tasted bitter, though. She took another drink. And another one.

They were sitting in a courtyard and despite the absence of a roof the noise was deafening. Everyone was shouting at everyone. Soldiers came over, leaned across the table, chatted with the nurses. Adele remained frozen, unresponsive to any look they were sending her way.

Bright faces were everywhere, mouths going up and down, a bedlam of sounds that seemed to Adele to become one giant rush, like a building on fire, like a giant tumbling wave. Nurses. Soldiers. German girls, too. They smiled too much, the German girls, they hurt Adele's heart the way they puffed on their cigarettes, bony shoulders sticking out of thin cotton dresses.

"Dresden."

The word came through the storm of sound like a strike of lightning. And again "Dresden."

Adele looked for the source. A large soldier was sitting at a table talking to some other soldiers and shaking his head. His hair was blond, and he had a big face to go with his big size. One of the other soldiers had his arm draped around a German girl.

"Dresden?" Adele called out, looking directly at him.

The big soldier looked back at her. She expected to feel the fear she always felt when she had to have anything to do with soldiers. He smiled across the tables.

"Have you been to Dresden?"

"I do not speak French," he replied in the most terrible French possible. And smiled again, a broad, warmer smile this time. He got up, circled around his table and sat down opposite her.

"Hello. My name is Alex. I am a Canadian."

He seemed determined to speak unbearable French. He held out a large meaty hand. It seemed a strange, foreign thing to do. Nevertheless, since it was there, Adele shook it and tried to smile.

"Adele," she said. She looked up the table toward Pierre. He and Char were looking back at her like two Cheshire cats.

"Will you translate for me?"

"Of course," Pierre said.

"He was talking about Dresden. Ask him if he's been to Dresden."

"My friend would like to know if you've been to Dresden," Pierre said in English.

The Canadian looked at Pierre, then turned back to Adele. "Are you going there?" he asked in English.

"What did he say?"

"He asked if you're going there."

"Tell him I have a relative who lives there and I'm worried."

"She has a relative who lives there and she's worried."

"Worried about what it's like there?"

"Yes, I suppose," Pierre said.

"If she's thinking of seeing for herself, tell her not to go." He touched Adele's hand and shook his large head from side to side.

"What is it?"

"He says not to go there."

Adele could feel her heart beginning to race. "Why not?"

Pierre turned back to the soldier. "Why not?"

Though he was speaking to Pierre, the soldier leaned closer to Adele. His blue eyes held hers. "Tell her there was a fire there. Tell her it was bombed by incendiary bombs. It caused a great fire. The pavement melted. Everything turned to lava. Bricks and steel and glass. People. We've just been there. It's like nothing anyone's ever seen before. There is nothing left of Dresden."

"He says the city was fire-bombed. It melted. There's no one left there," Pierre said.

"Don't go there," the soldier said.

"Don't go there, Adele," Pierre said.

Adele was rocking a little on the bench. There was no air to breathe.

"Tell her the Russians have taken over. It's their sector. They own Dresden now. No one comes or goes without their say-so. And the Russian soldiers – what they're doing to the women – tell her she doesn't want to go there."

"The Russians are there now, Adele. No one can go in or out. You'll just have to hope your relative is safe."

"Yes," Adele said. And "Thank you," she said to the big soldier. And though there was no roof, the air had disappeared. She got up from the bench and walked away.

It took Char half the street to catch up. They walked along together for a little while.

"Are you all right?" Char asked.

"I just needed some fresh air."

"I'm sorry about Dresden. About your relatives."

Adele nodded.

"Where are we going?"

"For a walk. I just want to walk by myself."

"Are you sure?"

"Yes. Sorry."

"That's all right." Char stopped. "Don't be long, Adele. We'll be waiting."

Adele kept walking and turned at the first corner. She crossed several more streets. After a while she got tired and sat down on some steps. She began to notice that, unlike the others, this street had been bombed. The row of buildings across from her was a pile of rubble. One wall, three storeys high, remained standing.

She could see large patches of variously coloured wallpaper still clinging to it. Splintered window frames. A remnant of a curtain hanging down. Families had lived there. Cooked supper. Children had played in those rooms. Argued. Laughed. What were their names? What had they thought and dreamt? What had they hoped for?

Where were all the families?

A dog came over the top of a pile of rubble and began to pick its way slowly down through the bricks. Adele could hardly believe her eyes. When the dog walked stiffly out on to the street, she stood up and called out, "Robber!"

The dog ignored her.

"Robber!"

It stood there exhausted, its legs splayed out a little. Adele could see now that it wasn't Robber. It had the same whiskered, hairy face, but it was slightly smaller and it had mange. A patch of bare grey skin ran across its flank and down its back leg. She could see that it was shivering.

Adele began to cry.

FRANCE, 1945

CHAPTER THIRTY

• • •

I
t was obvious to everyone except Adele that she could no longer look
after the children. Her voice shook when she talked. Her hands shook.
Char spoke to Maurice, who spoke to Nurse Sarraute, who brought
another Red Cross worker up to the children's barracks to replace her. She
insisted that Adele spend the night in the nurses' residence. Obviously Adele
hadn't been sleeping, so she gave her something so she could sleep. Adele was
surprised by this, but she didn't argue. She did what Nurse Sarraute told her.

That evening Maurice climbed up the dormitory stairs to see her. Adele
was sitting by a window looking over the lights of the camp.

"Can you continue with your work?" he asked.

Adele thought about this for a long moment. She shook her head.

"You did an excellent job. I am so very pleased with you."

Adele closed her eyes.

The next day Nurse Sarraute accompanied Adele back to Strasbourg.
She made it clear that she wasn't making a special trip just for her – she had
to return anyway.

After two days of mostly strained silence, they rattled back across the
Rhine. As soon as the empty truck reached the first busy intersection, Adele
asked the driver to stop. She told Nurse Sarraute that a girlfriend of hers
lived nearby, and she wanted to spend some time with her. Adele picked up
her suitcase and opened the door. She climbed down from the truck and
was surprised to see Nurse Sarraute following her. They stood on the street
together, the truck idling noisily.

"Don't be disappointed in yourself," Nurse Sarraute said. "It was unconscionable of Maurice to put you in such a situation. The truth is you surpassed our expectations."

Adele didn't feel a thing. "Thank you, Madame," she said.

"There are so many jobs to be done right here in Strasbourg. When you feel up to it, you must come around to see us."

"Yes, Madame."

"Why don't you keep this?" Nurse Sarraute put her hand in her pocket and pulled out Adele's grey cap. Adele had left it lying on the bed in the dormitory.

"Thank you."

Nurse Sarraute climbed back into the truck and Adele walked away.

She still had some money left from Paris hidden in the lining of her suitcase so she took a small room in the first *pension* she came to. It was at the back of the house and overlooked a walled garden.

Adele put her suitcase down and lay on top of the bed.

It seemed to get dark very suddenly. She wasn't sure whether she'd fallen asleep or not. She could hear someone climb the stairs and pass her door. She could hear another door opening and closing. She wondered how long it would take to die if she just lay there, getting thinner by the day, drifting. Her new landlady would be sure to come tapping. "Are you still in there, dear?" she'd say.

Manfred was dead.

Adele got up and dragged the dresser in front of her door. She pulled down the blind and lay down on the bed again. She went over some other ways she might kill herself, faster ones. She could buy a rope and hang herself, she could buy rat poison, she could buy a knife, get in a bath and slit her wrists. She could jump from a high building. She could walk into the Rhine. There were so many ways.

Dresden had melted, Manfred was dead, and she couldn't touch her feelings. Just a terrible weight in the centre of her chest. And in her soul. And some kind of pain that seemed to be nowhere in particular and everywhere.

Adele got up again and pulled the dresser aside. She went down to the street and found a place that sold liquor, where she bought a bottle of eau de vie de mirabelle. She returned to her room and drank until the pain went away and she passed out. The next day she went to a café around the corner and ate some bread and cheese. She returned to her room and finished off the bottle.

She continued living this way for several days, eating very little and drinking a lot. She avoided thinking about anything. She avoided looking at herself in the mirror.

One day she realized she was out of money.. She walked down the hall and drew herself a bath. She made it as hot as she could. Steam covered the mirror, dripped off the walls. Without taking off her clothes, she slipped under the water. She could feel her hair fanning out, her stupid hair. She opened her eyes. The ceiling above her rippled, it looked like it might dissolve. She was standing outside the world looking through a window. The room was full of water now, the world was filling up. All she had to do was take a deep breath and drown. Her father was there, his face was right in front of her. "Don't, Adele," he said.

Adele lurched up, gulping for air.

She sat there for a long time. She thought of the in-between men shuffling endlessly up and down the halls of the infirmary. She thought of Étienne, his starved face and random tufts of hair. His bright, lively eyes despite all he had seen, all he had suffered. And what had happened to her? Nothing in comparison. She looked at her dress clinging to her legs, her hands wrinkling in the water. She felt like a coward.

Adele changed her clothes and walked three miles to the train station and from there retraced her steps until she found the hotel she'd stayed at when she'd first arrived in Strasbourg. She crossed the street, walked through the courtyard and pushed through the doors.

A woman who looked to be in her sixties and who was dressed in civilian clothes was sitting at the front desk. Other women were working farther down the room at several long tables.

"My name is Adele Georges. I would like to work here. I have worked for the Red Cross before. I was in Buchenwald."

"Adele Georges?" The woman had a pleasant face and the purest of white hair tied back in a bun. "Yes, I think I know the name." She began to look through a stack of well-worn cards. "Before Nurse Sarraute returned to Buchenwald she said to expect you. Here we are." She picked out a card.

"How did she know I'd come back?" Adele was surprised.

"She didn't, she just said she hoped you would. You can start off sorting those clothes donations." She indicated two bulky cartons sitting by the door. "And making up relief packages, if you like."

"I need money."

The woman frowned. "I'm afraid this is all volunteer work. You should know that."

"Until I find paying work, I mean. I wonder if you could lend me some money?"

The woman studied Adele for a moment. "How much do you think I should lend you?"

"Just a few francs. I need to eat. I think my landlady will give me some time on my room."

The woman put Adele's card carefully back in the box. "All right," she said.

Adele dragged the cartons to the back of the room and began to sort through them. She tried to think of what to do next. She could get a list of tailors from someone. She could go from shop to shop and ask if they needed someone to sew. She separated the clothes into male and female piles. And adult and children.

Some of the clothes were nothing more than rags and they all needed washing. Who would give away such disgusting things? Who did they think they were giving them to?

"All these clothes have to be washed," Adele yelled out, her voice ringing through the room, startling everyone.

Adele forgot to eat that night, even though she now had the older woman's money in her pocket. She drank herself to sleep instead. The next morning it took all her strength to get dressed. She didn't bother brushing her hair, but she went back to the Red Cross – she didn't know what else to do.

Within a few hours Adele had washed the clothes that were washable from the previous day and had hung them out to dry on a line strung up for that purpose behind the building. When they were dry, she gathered them up and brought them inside. She got out the ironing board and was almost through her ironing when she heard a pair of boots marching across the hardwood floor.

Adele looked up.

The big Canadian soldier from Weimar was approaching her. He had his soldier's cap on at the prescribed regulation angle. He looked official and serious. When he saw that she'd noticed him, he took off his cap and smiled his broad open smile.

"Hello once again, Adele," he said in his halting French.

"Hello."

He glanced down at a page in a book he was carrying. Adele took the opportunity to study his soldier's face. It seemed innocent enough, but then how could anyone tell?

"I am very glad to see you once again. I am sorry I upset you." Again in painful French. It was obvious he had been rehearsing. There were several tabs sticking out of the pages of his book. "My name is Alex. Do you remember me?"

"Yes."

Alex turned to another marked page. "Would you like to go to a store and eat?"

"Pardon?"

"Would you like to go to a store and eat?" His face flushed a little. He looked back down at the page.

Adele put her hand over the book and pointed up at a clock on the wall. It was only a few minutes past eleven o'clock in the morning. Besides, she was still feeling ill from the eau de vie of the night before. "No," she said.

"Oh," He said something in English that Adele didn't understand. He smiled again.

Adele went back to her ironing.

Alex touched her bare arm. It felt strange to be touched like that. He was pointing at the clock and then he tapped his wristwatch. It had a small wire cage over the crystal. And then he pointed toward the door and nodded hopefully.

Adele didn't understand. She shook her head.

Alex sat down on a chair and crossed his one leg, pointed to the door again, pointed to the clock, pointed to her.

He would wait for her. Outside. That's what he was saying.

Adele smiled a little.

Alex smiled, too. His face seemed to hold a generous spirit, perhaps because of its broad boyishness. His cheekbones flared out in a not unattractive way. He stood up. He was almost twice her height and three times her width, but his size didn't seem a threat. It had the opposite effect – it seemed reassuring somehow.

"Yes. All right," Adele said.

Alex looked extraordinarily pleased. Before she could change her mind he turned away, walked past the other workers, past the woman at the desk and out the door.

Adele went back to her work and tried not to think about what she'd just said. She finished her ironing. She brushed several suit coats and pants. She decided to get a damp cloth and try ironing them. The next time she looked up at the clock it was almost one. She went into the toilet and looked at herself in the mirror. She tried to bring her hair under some control by flattening it with her hands, but it didn't work. Her eyes looked so tired and desperate. Had they always been that way? She rubbed her cheeks and lips but she couldn't coax any colour into them.

Why am I primping, she thought to herself.

She thought of Manfred.

She thought of her father.

Adele pushed out the front door, half-expecting the Canadian to have disappeared. He was sitting on the courtyard wall. They stood in the sun and looked at each other for a long time. He opened his book and began to fumble through the pages. Adele pointed across the street at a café beside the hotel. She walked across the courtyard and out the gate as if she were in a hurry.

After they settled themselves, Alex ordered a bottle of wine. With the first glass Adele's hangover disappeared. Halfway through the second, she felt almost instantly drunk. The busy room seemed to be turning slowly. People floated by. The sun poured through the window.

Adele picked up his book. It said "French-English Dictionary and Common Phrases" in both languages on its bright blue cover.

Alex had taken off his soldier's cap. His blond hair, though still short, was beginning to grow out a little. Perhaps because the war was over, Adele thought. She knew who he was. He was just a typical soldier trying his best to get a girl into bed. Any girl. Any bed. That's what they did. And when that didn't work, they'd rape you.

Alex touched her hand. He didn't seem to have any inhibitions about touching, but as accessible as his face seemed to be, his touch felt complicated.

"You. Char and Pierre. To Strasbourg. Red Cross," he said.

"So that's how you knew where to find me," Adele replied.

Alex began to thumb through the pages trying to figure out what she'd just said.

Adele wondered what Char and Pierre had told him. Particularly Pierre with his fabulous English. That she'd failed? That she couldn't go on? That she was in a vulnerable state?

Adele ordered veal. It was the first substantial meal she'd had since the mess tent in Buchenwald. Alex ordered the veal, too.

He pointed to his book again, to the word for *relative, kinsman, one's family*, and said, "Dresden?"

Adele nodded and looked away.

Don't touch my hand again, she thought, please don't touch my hand. He didn't. When she glanced back at him, he was looking appropriately sad for her relatives in Dresden, and then she wasn't so sure. For a brief moment his face looked haunted by its own thoughts.

After lunch Alex walked her back across the street to the Red Cross building. "May I see you again?" he said. He'd found this expression quite easily – it was one of the ones he'd marked in his pages.

It was a question to dread. Adele had been dreading hearing it for the last half-hour. And dreading not hearing it. What could she do with herself? She'd be loathed by anyone who ever found out what she'd done, who she really was. She'd be loathed by this man too, if he knew.

There was no answer to his question and there was no answer to her life. Adele ran up the steps and disappeared through the door.

She finished her ironing, her folding, her sorting and packaging. When she came out, Alex was gone.

She walked back the three miles to her room. She took out her bottle and sat on the floor by the window watching the shadows darken, the walled garden slowly disappear.

She tried to picture Alex reaching tenderly for her, but all she could see was the red-headed soldier, his face and hands, and feel her head smashing up against the crate.

"I can't do this," she said. The room was dark by now and no one answered.

Adele didn't go to work the next day. Or the next. And she was afraid to leave her room long enough to buy another bottle in case her landlady wouldn't let her back in. She knew she had to look for a real job soon. She hadn't eaten since her meal with Alex.

On the third morning she promised her landlady the week's rent would be paid the very next day and she went back to the Red Cross. She would let the gods decide.

The woman at the desk told her that Alex had been looking for her for the last two days. She asked if there was anything wrong.

"I'm very hungry."

"But dear, I can't give you any more money." The woman seemed more worried than annoyed.

"I know. I mean, I can't seem to eat."

"Do you have a doctor?"

"Yes," Adele lied, "I'm seeing him. I have an appointment for tonight."

That day, Adele worked later than everyone else except for the caretaker. She helped him sweep up the floor. Although it was past seven before she left, Alex was waiting for her by the gate.

"Hello, Adele," he said. His face seemed to glow at the sight of her. "Would you like to go to dinner?" He managed to say this without referring once to the book he was still holding in his hand.

"No," Adele said. She went up on her toes and kissed one of his flaring cheeks. Then she kissed the other one. She walked toward the hotel across the street and Alex followed her.

"Get a room," she said to him in French.

He seemed to understand.

Adele stood in the small lobby and watched him pay for a room. She tried to feel nothing.

They walked up the stairs to the third floor. Alex unlocked a door and they went inside.

Adele crossed the room and closed the curtain.

Alex turned the light on.

Adele turned it back off.

Alex put his book and cap down on a chair. Adele wondered if he'd proceed now to undress her in a disinterested, matter-of-fact way, as if he'd just picked up a street girl, as if he were preparing to pay her a few francs.

He was just standing there, a gentle smile on his face. Adele picked up both his hands. They were large and warm. She held them against her face and closed her eyes. She could feel the soft brush of his lips on her forehead, on her nose, her lips. His lips felt as warm as his hands. Warmer.

She began to unbutton his shirt.

His hands went around her waist.

The bed creaked – it made a ridiculous amount of noise, but it didn't seem to bother Alex. After a while it didn't bother Adele, either.

She had thought that just the sight of his naked body would kill her, but it hadn't. She'd had no idea how to get undressed herself, so he'd done it for her. He was tender, like some powerful animal who for some inexplicable reason had made the choice to be tender. He had a swirl of hair on his chest, and his white comfortable belly was wide and round. Warm skin pressing on warm skin, Adele had forgotten how wonderful that had felt.

His face, floating above her, still looked a little surprised. Grateful. She was giving him a gift, a surprise gift. A gift. She could feel him deep inside. She could feel his breath on her cheek, his mouth on her neck, his hand in places even Manfred hadn't dared touch. She didn't pull away from him. She didn't care. It didn't matter any more.

The bed rattled and seemed to move across the floor. Adele clung to him, dug her fingers in. The room dissolved. "Oh God," she heard some woman say.

"Ohhhh, Jesus," she heard some soldier say.

They lay quietly together afterward. A faint light was sneaking in through the curtains. Adele touched his broad nose. His full lips. "I think we broke the bed," she said.

"Pardon?" Alex replied, smiling sleepily. He looked tired.

Adele smiled and shook her head. It was nothing. She continued to watch him and wonder why she wasn't feeling despair. That feeling had become familiar enough, cold and relentless in its pull, like a whirlpool. An endless falling into nothing.

Adele brushed her hand over Alex's chest, trailed it down his belly. He shifted on his hip. She could feel him responding under her hand.

"I'm starved," Adele said.

• • •

They saw each other almost continuously after that evening and took no precautions. Adele knew that Alex would have used a condom if she'd only asked, and she didn't want to become pregnant. She wondered if he thought she was trying to trap him. She wasn't. She just couldn't think about her future or any normal life at all.

Alex was waiting for his regiment to receive orders to proceed to England and then return home. Meanwhile the woman at the Red Cross helped Adele by giving her an acquaintance's name and she got a job in a garment factory. She learned how to cut out patterns. Days went by. Weeks. Almost every evening Adele and Alex met in that same hotel room and afterwards they ate in various cafés and pored over his dictionary. When Adele found herself laughing, it seemed a violation, a deep betrayal of all the things she'd seen and all the things she'd done, but she couldn't help it. Usually they had only a few hours together, because Alex had to report back to his barracks by curfew. But one night, when he was on a two-day leave, they stayed overnight at the hotel.

This was the first time they'd actually slept together. Adele woke up before Alex did. He was snoring softly, his face looking gentle in the early morning light. His blond hair was beginning to curl.

He looks like an exhausted bull, Adele thought to herself, a young, handsome one. Her heart felt warm but she didn't want to call it love. Love depended on a future. Love meant hope.

Alexander Mason Wells. That was his name. He'd written it out for her. He was twenty-five years old and he came from a small town in Canada called Paris.

"No!" Adele had said.

"Yes," Alex had replied.

After a great amount of page turning, he'd managed to explain to her that only three thousand people lived there and none of them, as far as he knew, were French.

"Why do they call it Paris?"

"There are two rivers there. One big one, one small one. There are plaster of Paris beds. They named the town after the plaster of Paris beds." It had taken some while to communicate all this.

"That seems very strange," Adele had said.

Adele watched the morning light creep across Alex's face. He was in an artillery regiment. He was a gunner on a twenty-five pounder, whatever that meant. What did it mean, because occasionally and just for a fleeting moment, something troubled and troubling moved through his eyes? She'd seen him tremble once, standing outside a café, a great shiver passing through his whole body. It took only an instant and there seemed no reason for it at all.

Adele felt an impulse to move closer to him and kiss his closed eyes but she didn't want to wake him. She lay still and wondered what kind of dream he was dreaming. He had landed somewhere in Normandy over a year ago. Was it near where Manfred had been stationed? Had he fought past the village of La Bouille? Was he one of those soldiers who had paraded through Rouen? Had he looked up at a certain window, the only window on the street where there were no flags and no one waving?

Adele closed her eyes and rested against her pillow.

Alex stopped snoring. She listened. She couldn't hear him breathe. She opened her eyes. He was still there.

• • •

Alex and Adele were sitting at an outside table watching strangers go by and sipping wine when Alex said, "My regiment is leaving Strasbourg."

A thin stream of sunlight was dancing on the table. It was turning the wine in Adele's glass blood red. Adele couldn't take her eyes off it.

"When?"

They spoke in English now. They had discovered that Adele had a facility for learning a new language that far eclipsed Alex's. The blue book, Adele had pointed out to him, could be used either way.

"Two days." Alex held up two fingers helpfully.

The wine pulsed in her glass. Adele tried to marshal her thoughts. Alex was going away.

"We travel to Le Havre first. And then England. And then home."

"Oh," she said. Of course he was going. He had to go.

"*Je t'adore.*" The one phrase he had down pat. He said it again. "*Je t'adore.*"

Adele looked away. Where had she been all these weeks? Where had her mind been? This was not news. He was a foreigner. He was leaving.

Adele turned back to him. "I love you, too," she said.

Adele got up and gave him a quick kiss on both his cheeks. Almost unable to breathe, she said, "Goodbye" and walked off the terrace and down the street.

That was the way to do it, she told herself. Clean and fast. Like a knife. And then it was over. She could imagine him sitting there, his book still in his hand, saddened no doubt by this inevitable moment, but relieved as well. They'd had an intense affair but it was over. And that was that. She knew that he was already looking forward to going home.

Adele began to run.

She came to the bench by her bus stop and sat down. Now that she was working she'd been taking the bus back and forth to her room. Looking up, she saw Alex jogging along the street toward her. His face looked flushed. He collapsed on the bench and pushed his cap to the back of his head.

"I had to pay the bill," he puffed, "the cheque." He made writing motions.

Adele looked the other way.

"Adele," he said, "please, Adele. You misunderstood." He nudged her with his elbow.

Adele shook her head. Just go away, she thought.

He nudged her again. He dropped something into her lap. A small velvet box. Royal blue.

"Marry me, Adele. I want you to marry me."

Adele opened the box. A thin gold band shone up at her.

Alex took the ring from the box, picked up her hand, and slipped the ring on her wedding finger. It fit.

Her bus stopped in a cloud of dust in front of them. Two people got off, three people got on. The bus drove away.

"Marry me?" Alex said.

"I want only for you," Adele replied in English. The strange foreign words felt like they were tumbling over in her mouth. Burning.

"What?" Alex looked puzzled.

"To be happy," Adele said.

"I will be."

"No, you won't. Not with me."

"Yes, I will!"

Adele smiled at him. She knew she loved him. She did love him. But he didn't know who she was.

Alex put his arm around her shoulders. It was a familiar feeling to her now. It felt indispensable.

"Adele," Alex said, "you have to answer me."

He was indispensable.

"Yes," Adele said, "yes."

CANADA, 1946

CHAPTER THIRTY-ONE

• • •

The heat wave had returned. No matter the time of day, the sun seemed suspended in the high noon position. It blazed down on Jack's head and followed him around. It was following him now as he walked back toward the police station. He was determined to ignore it.

He had just been investigating a crime at Johanna's Dress Shop. Johanna herself had been in the washroom at the back. She'd heard the bell jangle over the front door as someone had come in and she'd hurried things up as best she could but apparently she hadn't been fast enough because before she was finished she'd heard the bell again. It had taken her only a few minutes to realize that something was missing, the mannequin closest to the front door and all the clothes it was wearing.

"Who would do such a thing?" Johanna had asked.

"I guess that's why I'm here."

"And in broad daylight."

"That's peculiar, all right."

Jack continued to walk through the sun-bleaching heat along the main street. Jesus Christ, he said to himself. He'd give the case over to the mayor's nephew. Maybe between him and his fucking uncle, they'd solve it. Jack had better things to do with his time.

The previous evening he'd gone over to the Legion Hall. It was a rare appearance for Jack. He was better known there, or at least more warmly regarded, as the father of a fellow serviceman killed in action than as the chief of police. Some of the young men in the boisterous room had graciously come over and had sat down with him to keep him company. After a few beers, Jack had brought the conversation around to the dead man he'd found out along the river. No one had known anything about how that man had gotten there. And no one had shifted their eyes or cleared their throat or shuffled their feet.

Some of the other men hearing the drift of the conversation had come over to the table.

"Where would I get a list of the men who were in POW camps ?" Jack had asked.

"Try the armoury in Brantford," one of the ex-soldier's had offered. "They should have a record of most everyone."

"Or the War Office in Ottawa," someone else had chimed in.

And not a whiff of anyone hiding anything.

Jack turned off the main street, pushed through the side door of the town hall and walked down the stairs to the police station. Harold Miles was standing there going through the papers on his desk.

"Hello, Jack," he said, just as cool as a December breeze, "I was looking for a note, since the place was empty."

Jack took off his cap and hung it up, as always, on the top hook of the halltree. He took off his jacket and put a hanger through it and hung it on the second highest hook, as always. And almost immediately he regretted doing this. He was sweating like a hog underneath.

"A note about what?"

"When you or somebody else might be back in the station." Miles was dressed in some kind of seersucker shirt the colour of a Popsicle, like he was planning to go to the beach later.

"Unfortunately, unlike some people," Jack said, unbuckling his holster, "we don't have a surplus of manpower around here." Jack pulled open the bottom drawer of his desk and put his revolver inside it.

Miles moved away a little. "Lucky to be in a basement this time of year," he said. He leaned against the other desk, the one used by either White or Westland depending on who was on duty. "How's the case going?"

"Which case is that?"

"I hear you were out talking to Joe Puvalowski the other day." Miles smiled. He wasn't much shorter than Jack. His neck was thick enough, his bare arms looked strong.

Jack measured him with a side-long glance. He'd go toe to toe with him, he'd go toe to toe with any man alive. "Is that right?"

"He said that you said they could depend on you to get their landing papers back."

"Oh yeah?"

"Do you know what I think? I think we're working at cross purposes here, Chief."

Jack could feel the familiar hit of adrenalin jolt his heart, could feel it being pumped into every place it needed to go. He'd been feeling that feeling all his life. It was his stock in trade. "Do you have a problem?" he said.

Just like always, Jack could see everything before it happened. One more word of disrespect, followed by a left fist coming in low and crashing into the solar plexus hidden under that seersucker shirt. The young man would try to respond, nothing would work, not even his breath. A hand on the back of his neck. The office wall coming up fast. And that would be that.

Jack didn't want to think beyond the broken plaster, the welt of blood, the young detective sliding slowly down the wall. It was all going to be so goddamn immensely satisfying.

"I need your help," Miles said.

Jack's heart was pumping too fast, it couldn't reverse gears, he could feel his eyes bulge. "How do you figure that?"

"You obviously have some kind of history with Joe Puvalowski. He trusts you. Maybe you can get something out of him. And you know the town. You've been asking the same questions I've been asking but you know these fellows. You can read them. Am I right?"

Jack sat down on his swivel chair and rolled it back and forth a little, waiting for his heart to slow down. "What kind of fellows?"

"The soldiers back from overseas. We're both thinking the same thing, Jack."

"I haven't come up with much to this point." He looked at Miles. "How about you?"

The young detective was looking steadily back at him. "I thought I'd send you my notes, the lab reports, everything we've got. If you've got the time, I'd appreciate you looking them over. Maybe you'll come up with something we haven't. We'll have a supper meeting. On me. Could you do that for us, Chief?"

Let him think he's fooling you, Jack thought to himself.

"That'll be just fine," Jack said.

FRANCE, 1945

CHAPTER THIRTY-TWO

• • •

Adele and Alex sat on the bench by the bus stop and made plans. The pages in the blue book flipped madly back and forth.

"You'll want to get married in Paris," Alex said. She'd already told him the same story she'd told Char about her parents. "So your brothers and relatives can attend."

"My brothers are out of the country. They're with my uncle. He's a diplomat."

"You'll want them to attend, though."

"It won't be possible for them to return before you leave for England. It really doesn't matter. I don't want any relatives to attend."

"Oh," Alex said.

"We're not close."

Alex accepted this and explained that he would need written permission from his commanding officer to marry. Once he'd received this, he would travel back from Le Havre to Strasbourg. They could be married in Strasbourg, Char could be her bridesmaid.

"I don't think so," Adele said. The last thing she wanted was to have Char putting together a trousseau and organizing a luncheon. "We'll get married where you are. In Le Havre."

"All right," Alex said. He told her that after the wedding he'd have to go back to Canada with his regiment. Adele would follow later, on a different ship. "I hear the ships are all fixed up nice for the brides. It'll be fine. And I'll be there when you arrive – I'll meet you in Halifax."

Adele nodded, though she wasn't sure what he'd just said. It didn't matter. She would make him happy. He would never be sorry about his decision, she swore to herself.

Two days later Alex left with his regiment for Le Havre. A week later a letter arrived saying that Alex had everything arranged. An army chaplain would marry them in two weeks' time. He enclosed a money order in case she wanted to buy some clothes and for her train ticket to Le Havre. He'd already found her a place to stay. She could come now. Come soon, he wrote.

Adele stretched out and put the letter on the pillow beside her. She tried to imagine the mattress settling down from his weight, tried to imagine tipping toward him as she always did, his big friendly face right in front of hers. She could see him smiling. She could feel his love for her all the way from Le Havre. And her love for him.

That night Adele dreamed of Manfred. He was cradling her foot in his lap and painting her toenails a ruby red. He looked as young as he had that first day bending over his work at the Domestic Population Bureau of Information. His dark hair. Delicate arching eyebrows. Sweet beautiful face. Water was sloshing around her body. Steam dripped down from the walls. She could feel every stroke of the tiny brush. Her toenails gleamed.

"You found a most excellent room," he was saying. "Do you like living together?"

Adele tried to touch his arm so he'd know how glad she was to be with him, but she couldn't move.

"Do you love me ?" Manfred asked.

Adele tried to speak but her mouth couldn't make a sound. The water felt cold. It was creeping up her face.

The next morning Adele packed her suitcase, cashed the money order and caught a train for Le Havre. This time the tracks were uncluttered with people celebrating and the trip was speedy. The train pulled into Paris in the middle of the first night. All she had to do was wait for the connecting train to Le Havre later that morning.

Adele curled up on a bench inside the massive station, her suitcase safely beside her, and tried to sleep. She was facing a tall row of doors that led outside. She wondered what would happen if she pushed one of them open. She wondered if André and Robber would be standing there. She knew they wouldn't be. The Paris air would smell familiar, though, and her heart would ache.

She wondered what Jean and Bibi were doing. They'd be asleep, of course. It was the middle of the night. And her mother would be asleep. And Madame Théberge.

And René? Where was he?

And her father? How could she leave and not know whether he'd been released? Perhaps he was already home. What would it matter what he thought or what he might say? Just to know he was alive. It would mean everything. How could she leave forever and not know?

And there was something else. There had always been something else. It had been there from the first day Alex had walked into the Red Cross. It had followed her to work, ridden beside her on the bus, sat with her in her room and watched the garden disappear. A ragged, war-ravished, nagging thought. What if Manfred wasn't dead? She had pushed this improbable possibility back down into the dark, rejected it each time it had surfaced, because Alex was her love and her escape.

Adele looked up at the milky glass dome high above her head. A bird was flying inside the building. It circled around and around.

• • •

Rouen looked half-asleep and in a grey mood when Adele climbed off the train. Clouds scuttled over the rooftops, and the light seemed diffused and murky.

She hurried along through the familiar streets, her collar pulled up, turning her face away from anyone she passed. She hadn't expected that she'd feel so afraid.

A new enterprise had moved into the empty dress shop below Lucille's apartment, or what had been Lucille's apartment over a year ago. A jumble of bicycles and bicycle parts was visible through the shop window. It was only seven-thirty, and the shop's door was still firmly padlocked.

Beside the window, the outside door to Lucille's stairway looked even more worn and paint-blistered than before. Adele gave it a push and it swung open. She climbed the narrow stairs and knocked on the familiar door, anticipating all the while that she'd be confronted by a disgruntled stranger.

The door opened a crack. One of Lucille's almond-shaped eyes peered out at her. "Holy Mother of God, I don't believe it. Look who's back."

"Hello, Lucille."

Lucille opened the door a little wider and saw Adele's suitcase. "You can't stay here."

"I don't want to." Adele could see a man sitting on the couch wearing a pair of faded blue undershorts and nothing else. A skinny woman in a pink bra and white panties was standing right in front of him. Adele didn't recognize her. The man was scratching his chest nonchalantly and puffing on a cigarette. He turned to look at Adele looking at him. The woman collapsed on the couch. Adele could smell the sweet, languorous smell of alcohol.

"Did Manfred ever show up here?" she asked, not knowing what answer she hoped for, but needing a final answer, nevertheless.

"You're still not looking for him, are you? Christ, that's pitiful." Lucille let the door swing open some more. She was holding a faded dressing gown tightly to her neck – she looked naked underneath. "They're all dead. Wilhelm and Manfred and all the rest. Anyway, they might as well be. They'll never come back here."

"I know. I just wanted to make sure."

"Why would they come back here? The war's over. It's all over!"

"Yes."

"Jesus Christ, Adele, haven't you got over him yet?"

"I am over him, Lucille," Adele said. "I just felt I needed to know."

An older man, a hairy expanse of gut suspended over his rumpled pants, appeared in Lucille's front room. He picked up a bottle from the table and disappeared from sight again.

"I have my own business now," Lucille said by way of explanation. "You take advantage of whatever you can. Right?"

"Right."

"I'm taking advantage of my reputation."

Adele kissed Lucille on her cheek. "I'm so glad to see you. I missed you."

Lucille's face collapsed a little. "Where's my raincoat?"

"I lost it somewhere."

Lucille wrapped her arms around Adele. They hugged each other for a long time.

"I have to go back to work," Lucille said.

• • •

Adele made her way down to the river. It was invisible behind a screen of mist, but she knew it was there. She could hear the deep sonorous horns of fishing boats and barges as they moved out of their moorings and felt their way along the far shore. The benches in the park were too wet to sit on. All the trees were silvery and dripping.

She walked down to the wall over-looking the water. Manfred had thrown his cap through the air at just that spot. "I have a plan," he'd said. "We will run away."

Adele shivered. She was only ten blocks from her house.

She looked down at Alex's ring. It looked fragile on her hand, but it also looked like some kind of defence against the world. She decided to leave it on.

The back laneway seemed the same as always. So did the neighbours' houses. Over the wooden gate, Adele could see that the vegetable garden had been recently cultivated, the flower beds weeded and in order, even the tangled masses of vines sprawling over the arbour had been pruned back.

She pushed the gate open and hurried through the gardens. Who had put everything in order? There could only be one possible answer. Henri Paul-Louis. She ran towards the porch and opened the kitchen door. A tall woman was standing at the sink washing dishes.

"Simone?"

"Oh my God," Simone cried out, her eyes widening behind her steamy glasses in surprise.

"What are you doing here? Where's Father? Is he home?"

"Oh my God," Simone said again. Soap suds dripped off the pot she was holding up in front of her. "Adele. No. He hasn't come home. No one knows."

Adele could feel her heart falling, falling away. "No one knows what?"

"Anything. Anything more than before you left. He hasn't been found. Oh Adele, my God, you scared me."

For the moment Adele didn't know what more to say. She just stood there clutching her suitcase, feeling lost.

"René's been travelling all over trying to find out about your father. He went to the mass graves near Arras and searched through a mountain of personal belongings they'd picked up off the battlefields. There was nothing of your father's there, nothing to indicate one way or the other."

Adele came into the room and sat down at the table. She could feel her hand twisting convulsively at her ring. It slipped off inside her pocket.

"He was looking for your father's watch, or family photographs he might have been carrying, anything to prove he'd been buried there."

Adele nodded.

"René says that when he can find time he'll start searching again."

"When he can find time?" Adele looked more closely at Simone.

Simone turned away and put the pot back in the sink. She splashed around in the water for a moment. "It came as such an enormous shock."

"What did?"

"Everything. What happened to you. What you did. And that we were best friends and you didn't tell me. You betrayed everyone and everything." Simone kept her back to Adele. "Was he that German clerk?"

"He's dead."

Simone turned around. "I'm not judging you, Adele. At least, I try not to. I can imagine how terrible everything's been. It's just that I didn't expect to see you. Not like this. The door flies open and there you are. I'm not prepared!"

"I'm not staying, " Adele said, "I have a train to catch."

Simone sat down at the table. She dried her hands and picked up a package of cigarettes. She took one out and lit it up. Her fingers were trembling. "I heard what happened in the square. Your hair. The paint. Everything."

"I don't want to remember," Adele said.

"No. I guess not." Simone took another puff. "I'm sorry, do you smoke?" She pushed the package toward Adele. Adele pushed it back.

"No."

"René got me started and I can't stop."

"Oh?"

"Your mother's here."

"I assumed she would be. And you're what? The hired help?"

Simone's cheeks reddened a little.

"I thought you'd be a nun by now."

"Well, as it turned out, I didn't have the aptitude for it."

"How could you tell?"

Simone blew a stream of smoke halfway across the room. She pushed a stray bit of hair off her forehead. Her shoulders didn't seem as hunched as the last time Adele had seen her. She'd gained some weight. "Well, I guess because of you. I was so shocked and I was so glad you'd been punished. I was thrilled, really. I really did hate you. And then one day I looked at myself and I realized how far away I was from that person I thought I might become. Full of sweetness and grace and all that. Actually, I knew I couldn't make it." Simone looked across the table at Adele. "I'm studying to be a teacher."

"Simone, you're with René, aren't you?"

Simone examined her cigarette closely. She smiled. "Yes."

Oh my God, Adele thought, and once again she could see pieces of Monsieur Ducharme's brain flying through the dark.

"We don't see each other that often, though. He's very busy."

"Are you in love?" Adele managed to ask.

"Collectively, you mean, or just me?"

"Collectively."

"I don't know."

"Has he said he loves you?"

"Of course. It just takes getting used to, that's all. I wasn't exactly the most pursued person in our school. You remember that, don't you? All the boys chased you. No one chased me. René's the first one. And he's so handsome and so worldly. I just have to trust myself. I'm foolish. I know."

"I never thought of René as worldly."

"He is now. So many things happened to him."

"Does he talk about them?"

"Not really. He works in Paris. He works for the Department of Justice. He has his own office in the main building on St. Charles Square. I visited it."

"My brother?"

"Yes!"

"How did that happen?"

"Because of the Resistance. Because of all the retaliation against collaborators. Summary trials and shootings and hangings."

Adele felt a familiar panic.

"The provisional government had to regain control. They hired people like René who knew all the important people in the Resistance to try to restore order. René was a negotiator and now he has a good job there. They want to send him to law school."

"Who do?"

"His superiors. He's extremely busy, but he tries to come home every other weekend."

"To see you?"

"And his mother."

Adele had forgotten. She turned toward the hallway, half expecting to be greeted by two familiar, grinning faces. "Where are Bibi and Jean?" Adele got up from the table.

She should have brought presents. What was she thinking? She should have gone to a shop first. She moved toward the hall.

"Adele." Simone was standing, too. "They're not here. They were here for a little while. During the summer. They go to a boys' school in Orleans. She had to send them away."

"Why?"

"Because," Simone said. Her long pale face looked even more strained. "It was impossible for them here. They were being bullied every day, called terrible names. And beaten up."

Adele didn't have to ask why.

Simone stood rigid as a post, her cigarette smouldering in her hand.

"That's why it's so quiet in here," Adele said.

Adele walked down the hall. She looked into the parlour. It was empty.

She crossed toward the west wing. Madame Théberge was nowhere in sight. A blessing, Adele thought. One small blessing, anyway.

The adjoining door from the west wing to her father's office was open. Adele could see her mother sitting at Henri Paul-Louis' large desk. She seemed to be engrossed in a book. She was sitting very straight with her knees together as she'd no doubt been taught to do by the nuns in some long-ago school. Her hair had turned red again and was pinned up in soft curls. She was wearing a soft blue crepe dress and white shoes. Her face was made up as if she was about to leave for a social engagement.

Adele stood in the other room and watched her. After a moment, Madame Georges sensed her presence and turned. Her calm expression didn't change.

"Hello, Mother," Adele said, coming up to the open door. "How have you been?" She was about to depart for a foreign land and a new life, and she was determined to remain above everything now, all the old hurts and pains.

Madame Georges looked back down at her book and began to read aloud. "'When we were baptized in Christ Jesus we were baptized in his death. In other words, when we were baptized we went into the tomb with him and joined him in death, so that as Christ was raised from the dead by the Father's glory, we too might live a new life. But we believe that having died with Christ we shall return to life with him. Christ, as we know, having been raised from the dead, will never die again. Death has no power over him any more. When he died, he died, once for all, to sin, so his life now is life, with God, and in that way, you too must consider yourself to be dead to sin but alive for God in Christ Jesus.'"

She looked back at Adele. "I have no idea what I just read."

"You don't?"

"No. I do it to please Father Salles." She closed her book. "He wants the leading church ladies to be engaged in theological study. It seems very important to him and so I do it. I do it for him."

"I see."

Madame Georges arched her pencilled-in eyebrows and stared up at Adele as if there were some significant message in what she'd just said and she wanted to make sure Adele had received it.

Outside the house, the morning sun must have made an appearance because the blind covering the window seemed to glow. Adele could still smell the sharp smells of medicine in her father's rooms.

"Kiss me," her mother said.

Adele went around the desk and kissed her lightly on her forehead. She's still mad, Adele thought.

"I've been expecting you. I didn't know when but I knew you'd return." She looked up at Adele. "You have more hair now than the last time I saw you."

Adele could feel tears pushing into her eyes. She fought against them. Her mother's bony hand clutched her arm.

"I am so sorry I didn't love you more, dear."

Adele couldn't hold them back, tears ran down her cheeks and caught her by surprise. Madame Georges looked like they'd caught her by surprise, too, and confused her for the moment.

"You look like you're getting along," she murmured, looking away. "You look well. You must have made a life for yourself." She rose from the chair and retreated around the desk. She began to brush invisible wrinkles out of her silk dress. "I'm afraid I have to ask you a favour." She seemed to be addressing the wall. "René is going to have a brilliant career in government. He has everything it requires except for his family background. I am trying to repair this the best I can. I have always done for others, though you may not believe this. Henri Paul-Louis. Father Salles. René."

She turned to Adele. Adele had forgotten how terrifyingly depthless her mother's eyes could look.

"The Bible says it's a good thing to be the servant of others. So I am asking you, begging you, to do the same. For the sake of your brother's future. All your brothers' futures. Don't open old wounds."

"You want me to leave?"

Madame Georges shook her head. "No. Not if we could go back in time and undo everything, but we can't. You know, Adele, I could see that there was something wrong when you were very young and I didn't do enough. A better mother would have tried harder."

Adele felt like she was going to fall. "What do you mean?"

"I mean your strangeness of mind. If only I had addressed it at the time, the unnatural attraction you exhibited toward your father. The great regret of my life."

Adele knew she was going to fall.

"Unseemliness of thought leads to unseemliness of action, which leads to perversity and to all those German soldiers." Suddenly Madame Georges looked terribly upset. "Please go away, Adele!" She walked stiffly toward the open door and disappeared.

Adele stood there looking at the shelves full of well-worn reference books, at the locked dispensary cabinet, at her father's black leather valise gathering dust on the window sill.

She knew at that moment, for an absolute certainty, that he was dead.

FRANCE, 1945

CHAPTER THIRTY-THREE

• • •

Simone had gone outside.

Watching through the kitchen window, Adele could see her moving about. She pushed open the door.

A small orange cat, its sides bulging out, was purring and rubbing up against Simone's legs. Simone tore off bits of bread and dropped them into a soupy mixture in a tin bowl. She kept her face down. "How did it go?"

"I just wanted to see her one last time."

Simone nodded and scratched the cat's ear. "Mischa is pregnant again, maybe this time she'll get to keep them."

"What happened to her before?"

"Madame Théberge followed her around until she found the kittens."

"Did she eat them?"

"No." Simone looked up at Adele a little warily. "She put them in a sack and drowned them in the sink."

"Well, maybe she'll follow her again."

"I don't think so. Madame Théberge is not here. She's gone back home to Bretagne."

"Really? Why?"

"René didn't think she was a good influence on your mother. And she was beginning to act like she owned the house."

"So he kicked her out?"

"He asked her to leave."

"René can be very ruthless. Do you know that?"

"He can be decisive. He's very protective."

Simone looked as innocent as if she were standing in the Garden of Eden. For some reason Adele felt like waking her up. "In a way, you remind me of my mother."

"Oh?" Simone said guardedly.

"Just that you both have this remarkable gift for thinking exactly what you want to think. I'm sure it's an admirable quality, Simone. For instance, Mother thinks I'm dirt. You think René's an angel." Adele looked away. She didn't want to turn into some bitter and bloody-minded person. She really didn't. "Who's been working in the garden?"

"René hired a gardener." Simone's voice sounded colder than before.

"Did he?"

"He likes things to be neat. That's why I come over in the mornings, just to help out. I'm still living at home." Simone began to untie her apron. She looked anxious to escape. "Adele, I have to go to class now. Will I see you later? When's your train leaving?"

"Immediately." Adele felt like something was burning inside her chest.

"Where are you going?"

"I do have some friends, Simone. They live in Le Havre. I'll be staying with them."

Simone kissed her lightly on her cheeks. "Write us, Adele." Simone went back into the house and closed the door carefully behind her.

Adele had left her suitcase in the kitchen. She thought she'd wait a little while to retrieve it, at least until Simone had had a chance to retreat out the front door. With any luck her mother might retreat out the front door with her.

Adele sat down on the edge of the porch. She'd made an inquiry about the schedule when she'd first arrived in Rouen. There was only one daily train from Rouen to Le Havre, and it had left ten minutes before she'd arrived in Rouen. She'd have to stay somewhere until tomorrow.

She wasn't sure where to go. The thought of staying with her mother made her feel ill – and she wasn't sure her mother wouldn't call the police, anyway. She could try going back to Lucille's, but she didn't seem to have any room. She could stay in a hotel – Alex had wired her enough money, or she could be frugal and sit up overnight at the train station. The more she thought about it, the more the station seemed impossible. What if someone recognized her? And a hotel seemed almost as risky.

She reached into her pocket and put on Alex's ring. It seemed to calm her a little.

Where else? Old Raymond's cottage was a possibility. She looked toward it and for the first time noticed that it was missing its roof. It looked like a bomb had hit it. Now she could see that everything had been neatly removed, roof, rafters, floorboards. All used for firewood, no doubt. Madame Théberge, before she'd been forced to leave, had evidently gone into the heating business.

Adele wandered around the gardens. Whoever René had hired had done a very good job. René was staking his claim to everything. It was René's house now.

Adele pushed open the kitchen door. She listened for Simone's voice, her mother's voice. She looked through the downstairs' rooms. She climbed the stairs. The door to her mother's bedroom was closed. She tapped on it. There was no answer.

She knew from long experience that a non-answer did not indicate that her mother was not there. She certainly wouldn't respond unless she wanted to. Adele felt like pushing the door open. She wasn't sure why, maybe to scream.

Adele pushed open the door. The room was empty.

She walked along to her old room. She was surprised that her bed was still there. So was the ridiculous picture of the blue boy. He was still riding his rocking horse.

She lay down on the bare mattress. She'd been awake all the previous night.

She could see Simone and her mother scurrying away from the house, arm in arm, making plans not to return until it was safe. Where would they go? Over to Madame Ducharme's gracious mansion, probably. Clever René. Always smarter than she. Always.

She wondered what Alex was doing at that very moment. She tried to see him. He seemed a long way away.

She wished, more than anything else, that she had something to drink.

She slept for several hours. When she opened her eyes, though it was the middle of the afternoon, the room was full of shadows. She got up, stepped out into the hall and listened. If anything, the house seemed more silent than before.

Adele couldn't make herself think of going anywhere else. Her mother might not return that evening or she might. It really wouldn't matter. They would still manage to avoid each other, either way. They had long practised doing just that. And right now her old room seemed the safest place to be.

Adele went downstairs, nibbled on a sausage she found in the icebox and made herself a tea. She would stay one last night. It seemed a satisfying and fitting thing to do, in a way, a kind of memorial evening. She'd been happy in that house, a long time ago.

The light was fading from the window and Adele was sitting in the kitchen looking through one of her mother's magazines when she heard the front door open. At first she thought her mother had returned, or perhaps Simone. René walked into the kitchen. He was wearing a dark grey suit and carrying a leather briefcase and he had a Paris newspaper tucked under his arm. Adele thought he looked completely bourgeois, almost silly, but still there was a leap of alarm in her blood.

"Hello," she said.

René put the newspaper on the table and his briefcase down on a chair.

"Who called you to come home, Simone or Mother?"

"Both," he said. He took off his suit jacket, folded it carefully and laid it over the back of the chair. His hair was neatly cut, his face cleanly shaven.

"Did you come all this way just to make sure I leave?"

"I understood that was your plan. But you haven't gone. Why haven't you?"

"I didn't want to."

René smiled a very tight smile.

"I'll leave tomorrow. Early. My train leaves at seven o'clock."

"All right," René said, "I'll be staying over, too." He sat down at the table. "Have you eaten?"

"A little."

He nodded. He seemed undecided about something. He studied his hands for a while. "I'm sorry about how things turned out. You were very young. Foolish." He looked up at her. "As impossible as the situation is for you here in Rouen, and obviously you can't stay, I want you to know that in some ways, I forgive you."

"You do?"

"We've all been through a lot," René said.

And the bloody-mindedness came back, and the rage and the despair. "René, are you with Simone now?"

René smiled a little. "Yes."

"Tell me something. I've been wanting to ask you this for a long time. Did you murder her father?"

René's face turned dead white. He rose from his chair in a very slow and deliberate manner. "You can stay here by yourself tonight. Make sure you're gone by tomorrow morning." He began to gather up his suit jacket, his briefcase, and newspaper.

"How does it work, René?" Adele asked. "Is it a special pleasure for you, having murdered her father, to make love to her?"

Adele didn't see René's hand coming but she felt it. It caught her across the mouth and knocked her off the chair. She fell backwards and hit her head on the floor.

When Adele opened her eyes, René was standing over her.

"Adele," he said. He leaned down and looked like he was about to cry. "Adele!"

Her voice had gone away. She couldn't speak.

"Her father was the enemy. The enemy! And I do feel condemned for eternity. And I do owe Simone everything I can give her. And I've fallen in love with her. It's all mixed in together. And this is my life. Can you understand all this? Is it too complicated for you?"

René was walking in a snowstorm. Flakes of snow were melting on his hair, in his silky beard. Her lovely lost brother. She could see him reach down and touch her mouth. She could see blood on his fingers.

"Go away," her brother said.

• • •

Lucille opened her door. Adele was standing there with a dish cloth pressed against her mouth. Her blouse was streaked with blood.

"Adele!" Lucille said.

"Can I come in?"

Lucille nodded. Adele walked past her into the room and eased herself down on the couch. A young man was sitting in the kitchen at the table. Lucille went in to him, kissed his face, ruffled his hair, whispered in his ear. Adele knew what she was saying, that he'd have to leave.

He took his time getting to his feet. When he passed Adele, he glared down at her as if she'd conspired against him. He didn't seem to care about her bloody face.

Lucille closed the door after him. "I'm not worried," she said. Her pillowy breasts were almost falling out of the top of her dress. "He'll be back."

Lucille hurried into the kitchen again. Adele could hear water running. Her jaw had stopped throbbing. It felt like a large bee had stung her on the mouth, nothing more.

Lucille came back with a wet cloth. "Let's see." She moved Adele's hand away.

Adele could feel the warmth of the cloth as Lucille dabbed at her mouth.

"It's stopped bleeding. It could use a stitch. Or two." She began to wipe off Adele's chin and neck.

"I have to change my clothes."

"Yes."

"I have a change of clothes in my suitcase."

"You went home, didn't you?"

Adele nodded. Her mouth began to throb again.

"Who hit you?"

"I don't know."

"All right," Lucille said, "let's have a drink." She got up and poured two generous glasses of gin. "Everyone's drinking this stuff these days."

Adele had trouble swallowing. She dribbled and the alcohol stung.

"That's good, it's sterilizing the cut," Lucille said. "Want to look?"

"No."

Lucille handed Adele a silver compact from off the table. The round mirror was smudged with rouge. Adele could see a half-inch of flesh yawning open on her lower lip. It was holding a bloody clot in its small mouth. She pinched it shut and then let it go. It opened again.

"Quit playing around with it, you'll start it bleeding." As Adele's hands moved from her mouth, Lucille suddenly gasped, "Where did you get that ring?"

Adele pulled her ring off and handed it to Lucille. "I'm getting married."

"You're not!" Lucille examined the thin gold band. "It's beautiful, Adele."

"So's he." Adele smiled. It hurt to smile but it was worth it.

"Mother of God, Adele is getting married. Who to?"

"A Canadian."

She told Lucille everything she could think of. About Alex. About her plans. She'd been thinking about training to be a nurse in Canada. Canada was untouched by the war. It was difficult to imagine such a place. No one had been driven crazy there and everything would look brand new. She'd had some experience with the Red Cross. She thought she could use that. Her father had been a doctor. Had she ever told Lucille that?

Lucille nodded. "Lots of times." She wanted to see some photographs of Alex. Adele didn't have any. She wanted to hear all about the wedding arrangements, every last detail. Adele didn't know any. She knew where she was going, to a town called Paris in Canada, if Lucille could imagine such a place. And she knew Alex. She talked about Alex.

Adele fell asleep on the couch, and early the next morning she caught the train to Le Havre.

When she arrived she called the telephone number Alex had given her. Twenty minutes later Alex, dressed in his parade uniform and looking flustered and pleased, hurried in through the station door.

"Why didn't you call from Strasbourg? Why didn't you give me some warning?"

As Adele stood up from where she was sitting, Alex's eyes lit on her mouth. His expression changed.

"Jesus Murphy, what happened?"

Adele had looked at herself in Lucille's kitchen mirror first thing that morning. The cut on her lip had filled in with a dark spongy clot, and the surrounding flesh had turned yellow. Her jaw was swollen.

"I fell down the stairs in Strasbourg," Adele said in well-rehearsed English.

"Jesus." Alex touched her cheek so gently she could hardly feel it. "I'm sorry. Does it hurt? Pain?"

"No."

Alex made sewing motions. "You're going to need stitches."

"No."

Adele reached up and kissed him. "You see?"

"Oh God, Adele, God, I missed you." It was more a sigh than a statement.

"I missed you," Adele said, and meant it with all her heart.

Alex walked Adele to a small house beside the river. The open sea was just beyond. They sat in a tiny room full of doilies and knick-knacks and shared a pot of tea with the proprietor, an elderly hunched-over lady with bones as slight as a bird's. If she noticed Adele's mouth she didn't let on. Her son had died in the Great War. She showed them photographs of a smiling young man in uniform, she showed them a posthumous medal.

As soon as she tottered off to do some shopping, Alex led Adele up to the room he'd rented for her. They made love. Alex seemed desperate with desire and Adele clung to him as tightly as she could, even though the room swam in her eyes, even though her mouth was being jarred again and again.

Alex moved up the wedding arrangements by a week. They only had to wait two days. The army tent was baking in the sun. The air was close and sweltering. Alex had a soldier friend stand up with him. The soldier's girlfriend was standing to Adele's right. Other soldiers were standing at the back. Alex had given Adele a small bouquet of flowers. She could feel them trembling in her hands. After an agony of twenty minutes, the chaplain pronounced them man and wife. And then she had to sign some papers. They'd gone through a civil ceremony earlier that same day with the same best man and bridesmaid in Le Havre's town hall. Adele felt exhausted.

The chaplain shook Alex's hand and turned to Adele, took her hand in his and called her Mrs. Alexander Wells. She was now the responsibility of the Canadian government, "until we deliver you safely to Alex in Canada."

Alex whispered in her ear, "The army won't let you out of their sight. You're like a handle-with-special-care package, this-side-up."

Adele smiled, assuming that whatever he'd said was intended to be amusing. When the wedding party came out of the tent, more of Alex's friends set up a great cheer and threw their caps in the air. It took four of them to lift Alex off the ground and bounce him up and down. They clustered around Adele and kissed her on her cheeks. After that everyone piled into three jeeps and headed toward Le Havre.

Along the way the soldiers began to tease Adele about how she came by her split lip. Alex translated. Adele smiled and shook her head as if to say that it was a funny accident but that it was a secret.

Alex said, "It wasn't me."

Adele held on tightly to Alex's arm.

More girlfriends joined them for their wedding supper in a waterfront café. The Canadians made speeches that none of the Le Havre girls could understand, and the Le Havre girls made ribald comments that the soldiers couldn't understand. She and Alex held hands under the table. Most everyone got drunk.

Alex, gently weaving from one wall to the other, carried Adele up the stairs. In a room overlooking the sea, lost in the sounds of the rolling surf, they officially consummated their marriage and fell asleep.

The next morning they had breakfast in bed and went for a walk along the sea wall. The wind was up. Soon their faces were wet with spray.

Green waves rose and fell, rose and fell. Adele stared down into them. Alex took her in his arms as if he were afraid she might fall. He kissed her. His lips felt soft and warm and salty.

"Thank you," Adele said.

"For what?" His face was soaked and gleaming.

For this last chance, she thought to herself.

Adele touched his lips with her tongue. "Salt."

Alex did the same to her lips. They braced themselves against the wind.

This is what I can do, Adele thought, I will make you happy.

Three days later Alex left Le Havre, shuffling up a gangplank with the rest of his regiment. They were to be shipped across the channel to

Southampton and from there they'd sail to Canada.

Alex had been right, the Canadian government or at least the army did treat her like a package. Two weeks later, she was shipped to Southampton where she joined a hundred English war brides, some with babies, and put on a train to London. Once there she had to fill in copious forms at the Canadian Wives' Bureau. Finally they were all put on another train and transported north through rain and fog to Glasgow.

Adele wrote to Alex, and some weeks later she received a three page reply that took her half a morning to translate. It was mostly about how much he loved her. He said that he was busy trying to find just the right house to rent. He said that his family could hardly wait to meet her.

On the fourteenth of February, the SS *Sharpe*, a coastal steamer refitted to accommodate eight hundred women and several hundred children, nosed carefully out into the cold spray off the Firth of Clyde. The brides slept in swinging hammocks, a hundred and fifty to a room, ate at long, rolling tables, and got sick together in the heads, two aft and three forward. It took the *Sharpe* only twelve days to sail into Halifax harbour though it seemed much longer. Most of the women had been getting ready to disembark for the last three days but a few were homesick and refused to get out of their hammocks. By the time the city, clinging to a series of high, snowy hills, slowly appeared, almost eight hundred women and all the children had pulled on their heavy winter wear, some of it bought for them courtesy of the Government of Canada, and had assembled on the decks.

Adele could see a large crowd on shore. They were frantically waving flags. The women began to wave back. Adele found herself waving, too, though she knew Alex wouldn't be there. She'd received a wire on board ship:

> DEAREST. STOP. CAN'T MAKE HALIFAX. STOP. BUSINESS.
> STOP. RED CROSS WILL LOOK AFTER. STOP. ARRANGE
> MEET IN QUEBEC CITY. STOP. LOOKING FORWARD. STOP.
> LOVE, ALEX.

She'd taken the wire back to her hammock and read it over and over. She'd concentrated on the words DEAREST and LOOKING FORWARD and LOVE.

A band played the women off the ship to the tune of *Here Comes the Bride*. A few of the pregnant ones became hysterical with laughter. In a flurry of hugs and tears the women and children rejoined their husbands and met their husbands' families. Adele pushed through the crowd and made her way up a long flight of stairs to the Immigration Building.

She was put up in a rooming house close to the railroad station. Though the radiator made a sound like a gun going off from time to time and was as hot as a stove, there was a deep frost on her window. She put her hand on it. Eventually it melted away. She could still feel the gentle roll of the ship in her body. Outside, billows of smoke rose from a ragged line of houses overlooking the harbour. Adele put her face against the window. Canada seemed more like a dream than a place.

The next morning, while Adele was trying to deal with a meal of bacon and eggs, her Red Cross worker appeared in the dining room. With a cheerful "Good morning" and a beaming smile, the young woman handed Adele another telegram.

DEAREST. STOP. TAKE 15:10 TRAIN. STOP. ARRIVES
TOMORROW 11:45. WILL BE THERE. STOP. LOVE, ALEX

All the world was white. Adele had never seen so much snow in all her life. The occasional farmhouse peeked out from the endless drifts like a small boat swamped in a storm, and when the train glided through deep forests trees passed her by like clouds.

She wasn't travelling alone. The train was full of brides, a few she recognized, most she didn't. Whenever the train stopped, and it seemed to stop at every hamlet, some nervous woman got off and all the other women rushed to the windows to see what kind of reception she'd receive.

Sometimes a crowd of people were waiting and there were hugs and kisses all around. At other stops, the brides anxiously watching from the train sensed a skepticism, even a stony hostility in the waiting family. Sometimes the greeting between wife and husband was only cordial or painfully awkward. At one stop, just a wind-blown crossroads, there was only a horse and a cutter and a lone husband standing there.

Returning soldiers haunted the train, moving restlessly up and down the aisles. A few of them swayed wildly as they passed by, struggling with a missing leg or a missing arm. When Adele first saw them she was struck with the unreasonable fear that if they'd only glance her way they'd know what she'd done, particularly the badly wounded ones. She avoided their eyes.

At five o'clock in the afternoon on the second day, the train crossed a long iron bridge and swung into the heart of Quebec City. Some of the women were staying on until Montreal. It was Adele's turn to descend the steps under their watchful, hopeful, critical eyes.

Trying to control her nerves, she picked up her suitcase and climbed down from the train. As soon as her foot landed on the station's platform she could see Alex. He was pushing through the crowd, running through the billows of steam. He swept her up in his arms. She almost disappeared inside his open overcoat. She knew this must look very funny from the train windows but she didn't care. He was covering her face with kisses. She kissed his face back.

Most of the women had been complaining on first seeing their husbands that they looked two sizes smaller out of uniform. Alex didn't. He looked even bigger, his suit jacket unbuttoned under his overcoat, a broad expanse of white dress shirt showing.

"I missed you so much," Alex was saying.

"I missed you," Adele replied, "I missed you."

They made love in the front seat of his father's car – they didn't even get out of the parking lot. It didn't really matter because the windows steamed up fast enough and soon they were hidden inside their own private cocoon. He had some kind of funny-smelling cologne on. He had a wide blue tie with yellow diagonal stripes on. It ended up flung over his shoulder.

Afterwards, puffing happily, Alex said, "I guess we still work."

Everything had taken Adele by surprise. Her infinite delight in seeing him. Her immediate comfort in being in his arms. Her electric response to his first intimate touch.

Adele rested her face against his face.

"Welcome to Canada," Alex said.

CANADA, 1946

CHAPTER THIRTY-FOUR

• • •

The Ontario Provincial Police notes were delivered to Jack by two o'clock that afternoon. Harold Miles's detective partner dropped them off in a burgundy cardboard file secured with a red cord and a tassel.

Jack nodded a curt thank you and ignored the file until Constable White showed up for work at four o'clock, at which time he buckled his gun back on, pulled on his jacket and his cap, tucked the file under his arm and drove up the hill to his house.

He set the file down on the kitchen table. He knew what those notes represented. Just enough rope to hang himself.

Jack crossed the room and looked out the window. He could see a car parked down the street but it was his neighbour's car. And just beyond it three girls were skipping double-dutch despite the heat. There was no one else in sight, but that didn't make him feel any calmer.

Jack sat down, unwrapped the cord from the file and spread the papers out.

He was still a suspect despite Miles's talk about the soldiers in town. The kid's face was so transparent he might as well have had it written across his forehead. *The chief of police is a suspect.*

But what was his game? Set up some plausible piece of evidence in those notes that could only point to one person. And then what? Wait for the doddering old fool to try to hide or destroy it and by doing so incriminate himself.

Jesus Christ, Jack thought. He glanced toward the window again. He could feel sweat running down his sides. He didn't used to sweat.

Jack got up and opened the door to the refrigerator to cool the room down. He took off his cap and his jacket and loosened his tie but he left his revolver on. He sat down again and stirred the papers around. Extensive search of the grave area. Upriver. Downriver. Even a little hand-drawn map. One thing you could say about the prick, he was thorough.

Location: undetermined where the fatal shot was fired.

Murder Weapon: not recovered, most probably a .38 calibre revolver, possibly a .45.

Jack touched the polished wooden butt of his own .45 to make sure it was still on his hip.

He read on.

Average depth to bottom of grave, two feet.

And a speculation. *Perhaps the victim had been buried to be found.*

What the hell does that mean, Jack thought, that someone was trying to frame the Broomes? It seemed unlikely.

Jack turned to the lab report.

Subject: male between ages of twenty-three and twenty-eight. Five foot ten. Weight approximately one hundred and forty pounds. Two missing molars. Teeth generally uncared for. One gold filling. Details and impressions circulated to local dentists. To date, no matching file. White skin. Black hair. Black eyes.

And more drawings, but not by Miles this time. A precise measurement of the position of the head wounds, a relatively small entry point to the left side of the back of the head and a massive exit wound over the right eye.

Minute traces of lead on brain tissues and bone. Neither the spent bullet nor the empty cartridge, to date, have been found. Victim had been dead for approximately seventeen days and had been in the grave site for approximately the same length of time.

There it was then. Seventeen days.

Additional note: a dog or dogs unidentified tore into the body cavity approximately one week before the body was found causing some damage to the intestines. Believed to be incidental to and not connected to the murder. Fourth and fifth fingers on right hand missing, probably rodent depredation.

And a list of clothes, brown tweed jacket, plaid shirt and so on. Notes on the various soil types.

This was more interesting. Jack's eyes sought out what he already knew would most likely be there.

Small quantity of fine-grained clay, blueish-grey, found against the heels of both shoes. This clay did not appear in the soil or in the subsoil of the gravesite, nor was it found in the immediate vicinity of the gravesite.

Nothing in Miles's notes about conducting a search at the Devil's Elbow, though.

Jack turned over another page. The analyses of the stomach contents. Apparently there hadn't been much to analyze as there were just a couple of notations.

Small meat residue, most probably cured pork, ingested within twelve hours of death. Some fibre strings, non-citrus in nature, found in the stomach and the pylorus. Most probable identification: plums.

Jack got up. He closed the refrigerator door. He looked out the window again. His neighbour's car was still there. The girls weren't skipping any more, though.

Jack wasn't seeing the street, anyway. He was staring at the hole in the ground, the mounds of dried grass, empty tin cans, soggy shirt, the plums sliding out of the jar.

A man the others wouldn't lower themselves to touch living apart from the rest in a hole in the ground. Who the hell was he? The town wasn't saying. And the problem was, the town didn't seem to know.

Jack went back to the table and checked Miles's note.

Perhaps the victim had been buried to be found.

That still felt all wrong. No, it was a shallow grave because it was a desperate grave. An unplanned-for grave.

But maybe not all that unplanned. Why would you bury the body near the site of the murder? Wouldn't it be smarter to separate the two just in case the body was found? Why give the police anything more to work with than you had to?

Which probably meant there was more than one man involved. It would take two to carry a body.

So where was he murdered?

Jack moved to the cupboard and took down a bottle of rye. He unscrewed the cap. He needed a celebratory drink because it was obvious. The man had died at the last place he'd been standing.

The Devil's Elbow.

CANADA, 1946

CHAPTER THIRTY-FIVE

• • •

Alex started the car and pulled out of the parking lot. Since the train had been five hours late and there was talk of a storm coming, he thought they'd better be on their way. Otherwise they could have taken some time to explore the city.

"The folks are planning a big party. Everyone's all excited to see you."

"How far is it?"

Adele had been speaking nothing but English for several months now. Alex couldn't get over how well she spoke. Every time she said something, his face glowed.

"About five hundred miles or so."

Five hundred miles or so. That seemed like a long way. But it had been a long way from Halifax, too. An abundance of space, Adele thought. There would be more snow. More forests. The odd farmhouse. This didn't seem to be a particularly comforting thought but they were in the middle of a busy city now.

She glanced at Alex. He looked more or less the same as she remembered. The skin under his eyes seemed darker, though. And there was something about his smile. It wasn't so much at ease with itself. It appeared quickly enough, just as open and unguarded as always, but it went away just as quickly.

He's nervous, like I am, she thought. She wiggled her hand up his sleeve. She squeezed his arm.

"God," he said, "I'm glad you're here."

"How big a party?"

"At our place? Big. Everyone."

Almost all the money Alex had given her was still in her suitcase. She'd gone out one day in Glasgow with a few of the other women and bought herself some winter clothes, staying within the allowance of the Canadian government. All she could find for the money allowed was a bulky sweater, heavy stockings, a wool hat, black boots made out of rubber and a brown tweed coat with a fake fur collar. She'd thought Alex would be pleased with her thrift, that he would see how thoughtful and careful she could be, a beginning promise that they could work together, that they could build a life.

Alex was driving an expensive-looking car. His family must be rich. Adele wished she'd spent more money.

Alex drove slowly through the city streets. The car was a deep maroon colour outside and an even deeper maroon inside. The seats were wide and plush. Adele could hardly hear the motor at all. It reminded her of her father's touring car except her father's car had been bright blue with cream upholstery.

Adele looked down at her drab coat and her rubber boots and her heart sank.

"I took a room just outside the city, once I found out the train was going to be late," Alex said. "I thought we could have a nice meal, go to bed early." There was that smile again. "And we could get an early start tomorrow."

They drove out of Quebec City. The snowbanks seemed remarkably high on either side of the highway. It was getting dark, so Alex put the headlights on. After a few more miles, he slowed the car down, turned on to a narrow road and parked in front of a large building. It looked like a picture of a hunting lodge in the Alps.

"This is it," he said.

Alex drank a bottle of wine at supper. Normally Adele would have helped but she only felt like one glass. She kept a wary eye on Alex – he hadn't used to drink so much – and busied herself talking French to the waiter. Alex had told her to take advantage of the opportunity.

"When we cross into Ontario tomorrow it will all be English. Except for you."

The room he'd booked upstairs was small and felt chilly. Alex closed the door and busied himself checking the radiator. After he was done, they stood there looking at each other. For the first time that day they felt shy.

"I can't believe you're actually my wife. I can't believe it."

"Why?"

"Because you're so beautiful."

"No, I'm not."

They made love in a bed that was hardly wide enough to contain Alex. Afterwards they touched each other's hair and gazed into each other's eyes as if they'd just miraculously appeared in the same room, as if they weren't sure the other one was really there.

"*Je t'adore*," Adele said.

Alex began to shiver. And then he began to shake.

"What is it?" Adele held him closer.

"Nothing. Don't." Alex's breath was coming in little gasps. He sat up on the edge of the bed. "It goes away."

Adele rubbed his shoulders. She rubbed his neck. Alex held his face in his hands. Slowly the shaking subsided. He lay down again. He kept his back to Adele. "I'm sorry," he said.

Adele got up and turned the light off. She pulled the blanket over his shoulders, then got into bed beside him and put her arm over him, felt for his hand. She found it and held it tight.

"How long have they been? These shakes?"

"Not long." Alex hadn't looked at her since he'd sat up on the edge of the bed.

"Do you take medicine?"

"I don't need it."

Adele was sure he did. She kept her arm around him and her fingers entwined in his until she fell asleep.

The road to this new Paris seemed to wind through every town and city in the whole country. And when it didn't, when they were out in the open, there was nothing but snow to see, drifting snow crossing the road in front of them like a huge white flood.

Adele waited for Alex to bring up the subject of his shakes. He seemed in a good mood, talking about his hometown. He made jokes. He kidded her. He held her hand with his right hand and drove with his left. He didn't mention his shakes.

That night they stayed in the tiniest cabin Adele had ever seen. There were two rows of them stuck out behind the proprietor's house – it looked like a town for dwarfs.

Their cabin had a sink, an icebox, an iron bed and just enough room left over to turn around. Alex switched on the electric heater and soon it was too warm. There seemed no middle ground – the only setting was red hot and their one window wouldn't go up. In a moment of inspiration Alex opened the door and kept the heater on. He gazed out the open door. "It feels like I'm back in Germany living in a tent," he said.

Alex twisted the top off a bottle of rye he'd stowed in the car's glove compartment and mixed two drinks with a little water. Adele had never heard of rye and didn't like the taste of it in the water, so she tried it straight. It was strong and made her eyes water, but it went down. They sat on the bed together.

Adele asked him about their rented house.

"I haven't found one yet. There's a real demand with so many fellows back from overseas." He took another sip of rye. He leaned back against the wall. "There were a couple of places but I didn't think they were right. The thing is, I'm having a hard time making decisions these days." He seemed to be talking to the ceiling. "I thought I'd wait for you."

"Where are we staying?"

Alex took another sip. "With my parents. Just for now. They have an extra room."

Adele tried to smile pleasantly. "Alex, we have to stop somewhere. I need new clothes."

"Sure."

"Why didn't you come to Halifax?"

"Well, it's a long drive."

"You said you would when we were in France. And in your letter."

"I know, but like I said in the telegram. Business, Adele. You know." Alex studied his drink. He put his hand on her leg. It felt warm. "I wasn't sure."

"Sure about what?"

"That I'd make it. I wasn't even sure I'd make Quebec City." Alex looked out the open door. The light fell across the snow. Everything was sparkling outside. "Anyway, I did."

Adele could hear Alex breathing now. She leaned her head against his shoulder. "We will see about the medicine when we get to your home."

"No, we won't."

"Yes, we will," Adele said.

There was still some rye left in the bottle by the time they fell asleep that night and Alex didn't get the shakes. The next day they stopped in Toronto so Adele could shop. Alex called his father from a public phone. Adele could hear a sharp voice crackling like static on the other end of the line. Alex put his hand over the receiver.

"Apparently that storm's finally coming. He says we should hurry." Alex winked at her. "Take your time."

They approached Paris in a snowstorm. Alex had to keep getting out of the car to push snow off the windshield so the wipers could slap from side to side. As far as Adele was concerned it didn't matter whether the wipers were working or not, it all looked the same outside to her, a ghastly whirl of white. The wind rocked the car. She had no idea how Alex knew where the road was.

"It's not that good," Alex kept saying.

Good? No, Adele thought. She tried to concentrate on the fact that Alex had been a gunner on a twentyfive-pounder, he had survived the war. She decided that the best thing for her to do was to keep her eyes closed. She hadn't been of much use anyway, sitting on the edge of her seat and staring out the windshield in disbelief.

The wind seemed louder with her eyes closed. It seemed to howl like something gone mad. She tried to think of somewhere else. She drew her legs up and rested her head against the side of the door.

"I'd put my arm around you but I'm afraid to let go of the wheel," Alex said. It was a joke. His voice was soft.

Adele smiled. She kept her eyes closed.

"The old man will be dying a thousand deaths," she heard him say. "He'll think I've put her in the ditch, for sure."

English words. A sea of English words. She could feel herself drifting.

Seagulls were circling, bright white specks against a startling blue. An ocean rolled lazily in, the waves bronzed, sizzling across the sand. Water rushed against Adele's bare feet. Everything felt warm. Everything sparkled like fairy dust. A boy with leather breeches was standing in the water. He looked half-starved. She knew she had seen him before.

"Étienne?"

Alex nudged her awake. "We're home."

Adele rubbed her mouth, she'd been dribbling. "I have slept."

"Oh yeah," Alex said playfully, "I could tell."

Adele pushed the thought of Buchenwald and Étienne, Étienne who had run away, out of her mind.

She looked out the window. They were driving down a snowy hill into a street of shops. The houses beyond were built on a hill and though it was still snowing, now the snow was falling as soft as feathers.

"It's beautiful," Adele said.

His family lived at the far end of the town. The car had to climb two steep hills to get there. Luckily there was a layer of sand on the slippery road.

Alex pointed out his house. It was made of yellow brick and looked very squared-off and as solid as a fort. It was the largest house on the street. Someone had thoughtfully shovelled out the drive. Alex pulled in, stopped the car and turned off the motor.

"From Strasbourg to Paris," he said.

Adele looked toward the imposing house. "I should have kept on my new clothes." This had been a decision that had seemed to take a long time, at least it had to Alex, given the impending storm. Should she wear her new outfit out of the shop and have nothing different to put on for the party that evening or should she save it? She'd decided to save it. Now she was furious with herself and almost sick with a sudden wave of nerves.

The front door opened and a woman almost as large as Alex came out on the veranda beaming a welcome. She was wearing a lovely dress.

"That's Mother," Alex said.

Mrs. Wells came down the steps and waded through the snow despite the fact that she didn't have any boots on. Alex got out of the car.

Adele followed him.

"My God, you're the cutest thing I've ever seen," Mrs. Wells said, embracing Adele in her strong bare arms. "I'm so pleased for Alex, I can't even begin to tell you. Gordon, Gordon!"

A man with sandy red hair appeared at the open door. He was noticeably smaller than Alex's mother and he seemed to have the kind of eyes that could look right through a person. For the first time since she'd stepped outside the car, Adele felt how cold it was.

"Hello," he said.

The party turned out to be a roast turkey dinner served on tables laid out in the dining room and the adjoining living room, as the front room was somewhat curiously called. A large blue paper banner hung between the two rooms with gold letters spelling out WELCOME HOME ADELE.

In her new black suit and sheer nylons, in her patent leather high heels, with her deep eyes and pale face framed by her blazing black hair, her lips and cheeks enlivened with lipstick and rouge, Adele looked strikingly beautiful. Alex thought she did, anyway. He couldn't keep his eyes off her.

The dinner was for family and relatives and close friends of the senior Wellses. Alex's friends were to arrive later.

The dinner was a success and almost entirely because Adele looked so pleased to be there and was so friendly with everyone despite a bit of awkwardness with the language, and laughed so easily and throatily for such a little thing, and kissed Alex at all the right times during the toasts. By the time dessert was served, she'd charmed everyone in the house except for Alex's father. He sat at the head of the larger of the two tables in the dining room, quiet and small and watchful.

Soon after dessert Alex's friends arrived. They brought in a burst of laughter, a gust of cold air and the aroma of rye whiskey. Everyone else was perfectly sober. The senior Wells didn't believe in alcohol. Adele had discovered this when she'd raised her wine glass during the first toast and had been ambushed by the thin, watery taste of some kind of fruit juice. Her throat had seized up for a time.

Alex introduced Adele to his friends, about twelve in all, excited young women as well as men. Apparently they'd all been friends since their earliest days in school. The men seemed forthright and friendly. "Welcome to Canada, Adele," they said.

"Alex is wonderful," one of the women whispered to her while the rest of the women nodded their heads in agreement.

One man was standing off a little from the rest. Alex led Adele over to him. "This is my blood brother, Johnny Watson. Johnny, this is my wife, Adele."

"Any wife of Alex's is a wife of mine," Johnny said.

Adele laughed. "Pardon?"

Alex laughed, too, and wrapped his arm around his slight friend's shoulders and squeezed him tight. "You don't know what a blood brother is, do you? When we were small, we nicked ourselves with a knife and mixed our blood."

"We saw it in a movie," his friend said.

"Johnny and I went through the whole shebang together. The war," Alex added by way of explanation.

"Almost the whole shebang. Until the end."

"We were each other's good luck charm. That's what I always said, didn't I, Johnny? Caen, Verrieres, Falaise. Jesus. How come we didn't die?"

"Maybe God didn't want us. A couple of ugly toads like us," Johnny said.

"So many others died." Alex's eyes were beginning to redden. "Shit," he said.

Adele slipped her hand into his.

"I saw most of France," Johnny said.

Adele wasn't sure whether he was trying to deflect attention away from Alex's show of emotion or not, but he didn't seem particularly concerned by it. In some subterranean way, Adele thought to herself, he seemed pleased.

"I didn't meet you in France, though."

"No."

"If I'd known Alex was getting married, I would have been there."

"They split us up in Germany," Alex explained. "I didn't know where the hell you were, pal."

Adele didn't think Johnny looked convinced that Alex didn't know where he was, even though his black eyes hadn't left her eyes.

"Nothing could have kept me away." He leaned a little toward Adele. "I had a French girlfriend. From Tours. I had lots of them, actually."

"Not like Adele," Alex said.

"No, that's for sure." Johnny picked up Adele's free hand. "Alex is my best friend. That means you are, too. Anything you ever need, any help at all, you can count on me. I want you to know that."

He didn't seem drunk. "Thank you," Adele said, though he made her feel somewhat uneasy. As soon as it was polite to do so, she took back her hand.

After the guests had left, Adele helped her new mother-in-law and her three sisters-in-law wash up the dishes. She didn't have to, for Mrs. Wells had made it clear that she could go right up to her room and rest, she'd had such a long day, but Adele had insisted on helping.

The eldest sister, Deborah, who was even taller than her mother but thin and quite glamorous looking, was concerned about both the night drive back to her out-of-town home and the silk sleeves of her blouse, so she hardly helped at all. Adele felt uncomfortable with this sister because of the height difference and her smart clothes, and because, when she was first introduced to Adele, she'd unnecessarily bent her knees a little.

Betty, the youngest, seemed the happiest. She was the mother of two children. The middle sister, Grace, was short and plump and had a sour face that looked just like her father's. Apparently she was childless and worked at the family store. Unlike her older sister, who maintained a kind of regal inscrutability, Adele could tell at a glance what Grace was thinking, that the world and everyone in it were continually conspiring against her, and now Adele, this foreigner, whom everyone was making such a fuss over and whom she'd been eyeing sideways all evening, could be added to the list.

"Where have the boys got to?" Betty asked, looking out the kitchen window into the dark.

"What boys?" Deborah said.

"Our husbands."

"You know where they are," Grace said, whacking a pan against the edge of the sink more violently than necessary to dislodge some left-overs, "Behind the house, standing in the snow drinking."

"I'm sure they're not," Mrs. Wells Senior said, smiling encouragingly at Adele. "They're out walking, getting some fresh air."

Later on, upstairs in a large and chilly bedroom at the back of the house, Adele pulled off her new clothes, changed into her nightgown and crawled under a pink eiderdown. She felt exhausted. Alex was nowhere in sight.

She turned off the lamp and lay in the dark. After a while she heard Mr. and Mrs. Wells talking in the hallway. She could tell that Mr. Wells was refusing to whisper, though she couldn't make out what he was saying. She heard the toilet flush and then the house became very silent. She fell asleep.

Adele was bounced awake by Alex climbing clumsily into bed. She couldn't see him but she could smell the alcohol.

"Sorry. It was Johnny's fault." He rubbed her arm for a moment. "Did you like everyone?"

Adele thought, No. "Yes," she said.

"You looked great."

"So did you."

"We won't be living here for long. I'll get looking for a house right away."

The air in the room was thick with the smell of alcohol. Adele could see the rain-stained skylight above her head. She could hear André stumbling around somewhere in the dark.

"Alex. Please. Don't come to bed any more stinking of drink."

"What?"

"Don't come to bed any more. Stinking of alcohol."

Alex fell silent. Adele wondered what he was thinking. His arm wrapped around her. He drew her close against his wide stomach, his furry chest. He felt warm and comforting.

He didn't answer her.

CANADA, 1946

CHAPTER THIRTY-SIX

• • •

J ack waded into the water. Though it was as warm as a bath, it felt cool in comparison to the sweltering air that pressed in all around him. The sun blazed right above his head – it didn't seem to matter that it was after five o'clock.

He surveyed the situation, his bare feet sinking into the muddy bottom. The river had receded to its late summer levels after the downpour of almost a week ago. It rippled gently around the Devil's Elbow. The deeper water off the cliff face looked dappled and still as a millpond. The sandbar had appeared again.

Jack was standing on the downriver side, his police boots and black socks sitting on a rock behind him. He could see the crime unfolding. The hunted man in his hand-me-down clothes and his cast-off shoes cutting across the clay bank, his assailants closing in, dragging him down into the river, forcing him to his knees and blowing his brains out. A bloody trail of debris floated down the river and around the Devil's Elbow. One of the men tossed the gun into deeper water. They picked up the body and splashed up the river looking for a place far enough away to bury it.

As simple as that.

A brown ribbon of dry riverbed outlined the far shore. A band of seared grass covered the far bank. Just beyond Jack could see a thick tangle of cedars. He tried to peer into the dark shadows underneath their sweeping boughs. He turned and looked up the cliff face. Harold Miles could be watching. It could be a trap.

Jack looked across the river again and picked out a dead pine tree. That tree would be his first line of direction. He'd planned it out. Criss-cross at set intervals, feel the bottom with his bare feet and work upstream. He knew he could wade across quite easily from where he was standing. He knew it would get deeper the farther along the cliff face he went. He would worry about that later when he got there.

He looked around again. There was no one in sight.

Jack started across the river, dragging his feet along and out to both sides. The sun followed him. Light was bouncing all around him.

He tried to think things through once again. If Miles and his men had already searched the Devil's Elbow, if they'd found the murder weapon, if those notes had been a lie and now Miles and his men were following him, what would it look like? It would look like he'd panicked and he was trying to find the weapon he'd thrown away. That's what it would look like.

Jack stepped on a submerged rock. His foot slipped, his ankle scraped on something sharp, he stumbled a little. The water was seeping up his thighs, climbing his wool trousers like a wick in a kerosene lamp. He regained his balance and pressed on. The river began to cool his privates. He hit his foot on another rock – it hurt like hell. "Jesus Christ," he said.

Jack limped up on the far shore and looked back across the river. He could see his boots and socks sitting there on a bleached rock. They looked lonely.

He took off his dark blue jacket and laid it down on the bank a small distance farther along. All he had to do now was aim himself a short distance above where his boots and socks were and cross the river again. And then move his boots and socks up river and so on.

He felt a little winded, though.

He studied the trees on the high ridge above the cliff face. There wasn't a breath of air over there. Nothing was moving, not even the topmost branches. He checked behind him. He could barely see the cedars over the top of the grass. He could smell them, though, their pungent leaves turning rusty red in the blazing sun.

Jack took his police cap off and ran his hand over his head. His short silvery hair was soaking wet. He dropped the cap on top of his jacket and started to wade back.

"Fuck," he cried out. He pulled his foot out of the water. His big toe was bleeding. He reached down and felt around. Now he was soaking himself up to his chin. His tie was floating in front of him. He pulled up a tin can from the bottom and tossed it downstream so he wouldn't step on it again. He continued on, leaving a wispy trail of blood behind.

When he reached the halfway point he stopped. Light danced in his eyes. Dragonflies droned by like miniature rainbows. Swallows were chasing insects right past his face. He stood there for a long while.

By the time he'd reached the shore, his feet were killing him but his toe had stopped bleeding. He sat down below the cliff face. The cut looked white and puckered as if that part of him had already died. He stilled his breathing and listened for a rustling in the brush piles hanging above him. He couldn't hear a thing. Just insects. The river had come alive with a black mass of insects.

Jack got up, picked up his boots and socks and placed them farther along the shore and waded back into the water. He aimed himself upriver from his jacket and cap sitting on the other side. The water was soon lapping over his waist, pushing against him.

Jack staggered out on the other side, moved his jacket and cap again and started back the other way.

Back and forth. The water went past his chest. Back and forth. It crept by his arm pits. By the time it had topped his shoulders, his breath was coming in little sing-song whines and he was heading toward the middle of the sandbar. He couldn't swim.

"Kyle," he said.

The strangled sound of his own voice startled him. It skipped away across the water like a flat stone. He could hardly see anything any more, reflected light had bleached his eyes. "Kyle."

His foot hit something. Whatever it was seemed to scuttle along the bottom. It had felt hard. Jack went under water for the first time in his life, his hands grabbing at nothing, and then at mud and clay. And then he had it. He had it in his hand. He came boiling back up.

Black and malignant-looking, short of barrel and thick through the handle, he recognized it right away. The soldiers called them souvenirs.

He was holding a German Luger in his hand.

CANADA, 1946

CHAPTER THIRTY-SEVEN

• • •

The next morning Alex had to go to work. He asked Adele if she'd like to see the store. She said she would. Apparently his father was already there. Up at six o'clock and arrive at the store by seven, that was Mr. Wells's routine.

Up some time later and take a cab to work was Alex's.

As it turned out, the cab company had only the one cab and Alex had a standing order to be picked up at eight-thirty, though the cab was rarely on time. Four passengers were already sitting in it when Alex and Adele climbed in. Alex introduced her to everyone, including the driver, and then settled back in his seat and closed his eyes. He looked pale and hungover.

The cab drove through the snow-packed streets, bumped over some railroad tracks and pulled up in front of a factory with piles of lumber stacked at the back. A middle-aged woman struggled out of the cab and went in through the front door.

On the other side of the tracks, Adele could see several ragged looking men walking away from the town.

"More DPs," a large man sitting in the front seat, snug in a fedora, scarf and long overcoat, observed.

"Or just hobos," the driver replied.

"DP's," the large man insisted, "hobos don't shave. These fellows are trying to get jobs. Your job and my job."

"They can have my job," the driver said. The other passengers chuckled.

Adele stared out the window. She'd seen ragged men like that before, long lines of them shuffling along the road toward the Rhine. She hadn't expected to see them again. She glanced at Alex. His eyes were still closed.

The cab came back along the tracks, turned down a steep hill, and pulled up in front of a large factory. The remaining passengers got out, except for Adele and Alex. Adele looked out the window – she could hardly believe her eyes. Steam was pouring out of the side of the building. An iron footbridge spanned a frozen raceway and a line of women were walking across the bridge. If Adele had seen the blitzkrieg widow and the button-eyed woman among them, she wouldn't have been surprised. She looked away.

The cab stopped on the street with the shops. "Don't mind Turnbull," the driver said to Alex as they were getting out, though he was looking sympathetically at Adele, "he doesn't know what he's talking about."

Alex looked displeased. "Adele isn't a DP," he said and slammed the door.

"DP. What is that?"

"Displaced Persons. Refugees from Europe. Stupid assholes." Alex looked like his headache had grown worse.

"Stupid assholes?"

"Not the DPs. The people in this town."

Alex pulled out some keys and they turned in at a shop. Gold lettering across the glass on the door proclaimed, *Arthur Wells & Son*. It was past nine o'clock. Alex didn't need his keys, the door swung open.

Alex grimaced. "Great," he said.

Arthur Wells & Son was surprisingly long and narrow and dark, with worn wooden floors that slanted dangerously toward the middle of the building. Adele could see rows of shelves sagging under the weight of every kind of hardware anyone could imagine and just as many rows of labelled wooden drawers. Barrels full of nails and spikes and brooms and mops cluttered the aisles. The air smelled sharp and tinny.

Alex pulled off his coat and put on a green cloth smock to protect his shirt. Before he turned his face away, she could see he looked embarrassed. Adele noticed the plump sister staring down from a perch above an office at the back like a lookout on a ship.

"Good morning," Adele called out, waving up at her.

Grace nodded glumly.

Mr. Wells came out of the office and looked at his watch. "Ten past nine."

Alex didn't reply.

"Good morning," Adele said for both of them.

"It would be if Alex ever got here on time," his father replied and disappeared back into his office.

"Charming, isn't he?" Alex said.

At Alex's suggestion Adele went sightseeing along the main street. The sun was climbing into a cloudless blue sky. She turned her face up to it and was surprised not to feel any heat. The new snow from the day before was reflecting the sun brilliantly, though, hanging over rooftops and off rolled-up awnings. The cold air pinched her nose in a not too unpleasant way, but it made her want to sneeze.

It took her five minutes to reach the end of the street. She crossed over and took more time looking at the shops coming back the other way. When she re-entered the store, Alex had a customer, a weathered-looking man wearing a corduroy hat with ear flaps and with a hammer hanging off a loop in his baggy overalls. Alex dipped a large metal scoop into a barrel and with a loud clatter poured some nails on a scale.

"Hello," Adele said.

The man smiled. "Hello there."

"Alex, I can help. What can I do?"

"Is this the new missus, Alex?"

"I think it must be," Alex said.

The man took off his hat. "My name is Walter Jack and I'm very pleased to meet you. You've come a long way."

"Thank you. Yes. My name is Adele Wells. You have a very beautiful town."

"Oh, it's all right, I guess, as long as you don't mind people knowing everything you think and everything you do."

"How was your walk?" Alex asked, pouring the nails from the scale into a large paper bag.

Adele began to unbutton her coat. "It was fine but I'm ready to work now."

"There you go, Alex, you've got yourself a helpmate."

"I don't want you working here."

"What's Grace doing?"

"She does the books. That's different. We'll talk about it. Later." Alex aimed a smile in her general direction and secured the bag with a strip of tape.

"You can help me anytime," Walter Jack said.

Adele wandered about the store for a while feeling awkward and useless. She found a rag in a storeroom and started to dust.

"We have someone come in and do that at night," Alex told her. He suggested she go home and rest up – the gang was going tobogganing after supper that evening.

Adele took the same cab back up to the house. When she arrived, Mrs. Wells was pitching a bucket of soapy water out the side door. "Just doing the kitchen floor, dear," she called out.

"I can help."

"It's all done, dear. Go in the front door."

Adele was taking her boots off when Mrs. Wells came hurrying down the hall. "My goodness, you weren't downtown very long. You couldn't have seen anything."

"I saw the store," Adele said.

Mrs. Wells took Adele's wool hat and her dowdy coat and put them in the closet. "But there's lots more stores. There's really some lovely ones. There's a wonderful store with old-fashioned linens and there's three dress shops. Alex didn't show you around?"

"He had work."

She led Adele into the front room. "I'll take you downtown next time, dear, and we'll go into all the stores and I'll introduce you to everyone."

Adele sat on a settee by the front window. Mrs. Wells sat down on a chair opposite her.

"How do you find Alex?"

It seemed a strange question.

"I mean, you haven't seen each other for four or five months. I was just wondering if Alex seems the same to you now as he did in France. That's all." Mrs. Wells looked anxious and hopeful all at the same time.

"In France," Adele said, "Alex was a soldier. He was, for a long time, a soldier."

Mrs. Wells nodded vigorously. "A year in Canada. Two years in England. Two years in Europe. We were so afraid."

"You have such a beautiful house here. You have such a beautiful town. It is difficult for anyone here to know."

"That's what I keep telling Gordon. Alex has been so restless. I think he missed you."

Adele smiled. "Alex is good."

"Yes, he is. He is so good! But he's not good, you know? It's his nerves. Have you noticed?"

Adele shook her head.

"No? Well, perhaps he's better now that you're here." Her eyes began to glisten. "I badgered and badgered until I finally got him to go see Dr. Jerrison. He gave him some pills but Alex said it was an insult and refused to take them. He said they were for crazy people. Gordon said he didn't need them, either. All Gordon ever says is that he should pull himself together, that there's lots of other men home from overseas and there're not falling all over themselves." She looked dismayed.

"I will see that he takes his medicine," Adele said.

"But I don't want to cause trouble, dear." Mrs. Wells brushed at her tears. "Maybe you should wait for a while."

After the floor dried, she made a pot of tea and they talked in the kitchen, but not about Alex. She wanted to know everything about Adele's family. Adele told her about her father's life in politics. She told her that her two young brothers were travelling with their uncle, the diplomat. Mrs. Wells seemed very impressed. At eleven o'clock she told Adele she had a meeting of the Women's Missionary Society. She was the chair and so it was unavoidable.

"I won't be long," she promised.

Adele watched her go down the front walk and get into a friend's car that had great plumes of exhaust floating up behind it. She watched her drive away.

She wandered through the downstairs' rooms. She sat on the settee again and flipped through a magazine. There were so many colourful advertisements, so many things to buy.

She went upstairs and looked out her bedroom window. The neighbours had a large backyard with a gazebo in the middle. Everything was covered with snow. She thought about Alex. She wanted to tell him the truth, who she really was, what she had done and everything that had happened to her. She wanted to do that more than anything else in the world.

• • •

That night Alex took Adele tobogganing out at the local golf course. They drove out with Johnny Watson and his girlfriend in Johnny's old car. All the gang was there waiting for them on the third hole.

The moon was full, so it was almost as bright as day and Adele could see for miles. Farm lights winked at her in the far distance. Long shadows lay across the snow. It was fun careening down the hill, everyone shouting and screaming, sometimes falling off and rolling over and over. Adele got snow down her neck and in her ears. It wasn't so much fun walking back up the hill.

Some of the men had silver flasks inside their coats, others just bottles. Everyone drank. Alex drank. Adele took a sip or two. She began to notice that Johnny was placing himself in a way that blocked her off from Alex. He seemed to have forgotten that his girlfriend was there, a tall skinny girl who, perhaps in retaliation, was out-drinking all the men.

She heard Johnny tell Alex a joke. It was probably a joke, though no one else could hear it, certainly Adele couldn't, but Alex laughed. So did Johnny. He leaned in to Alex and grabbed his arm, just to hold himself up, his sharp face creased in a grin. It must have been a good joke.

Adele began to feel chilled. The fun was seeping out of the occasion. She was relegated to tobogganing down the hill with some of the other women. Alex seemed to be more interested in drinking. Johnny began to turn his attention to her.

"Are you cold? Are your feet cold?"

"No. Thank you."

"How about your hands. You can put them in my pockets."

"No, thank you."

"Having a good time? Enjoying yourself? Fun?"

"Yes."

"That's great. You like fun. You're used to having fun, I bet."

They were standing halfway up the hill. Adele had stopped to rest and Johnny was standing much too close to her. She looked for Alex. He was far ahead, pulling a toboggan up the snowy slope.

Johnny's black eyes were relentless. "You know, you seem familiar to me."

"No," Adele replied.

He put his face close to hers. "I know who you are." His hand touched her between her legs. He turned away and started up the hill.

Adele couldn't move. Alex had to come back down to get her.

"Are you all right?"

"I want to go. I'm tired."

Alex looked disappointed. "So soon?"

"I can walk home."

"No. Of course you can't walk home," Alex said.

Alex went over to talk to Johnny. Johnny looked like he was commiserating with him. Alex came back and said Johnny wanted to stay but he'd given him the keys to the car. They drove back toward town.

"I thought you'd get a kick out of it," Alex said, "tobogganing."

Adele didn't respond.

Alex let her off at the house and drove back to the golf course. He had to give Johnny back his car. Adele got in bed, pulled up the pink eiderdown and waited for him to return.

She tried to think of all the places she'd lived in since she'd met Manfred, places where Johnny could have met her, but it didn't make any sense. The only people who knew what she had done were living in Rouen.

Except for André. But that didn't make any sense, either. How would he know André?

Lucille? What if he'd been a customer of Lucille's? He looked like he could have been. And what if Lucille had told him about her? But how would he know who it was that Lucille was talking about? How could he know, here in Canada, that it was her?

Because she had made the mistake of telling Lucille who Alex was. All Lucille had to do was mention Alex's name.

No. It wasn't possible.

After what seemed an unnecessarily long time, she heard Alex clumping up the stairs and along the hall. He came into the bedroom still looking disappointed.

"Did you come back with Johnny?"

"No. He wanted to stay. I got a ride with Ray and Nancy." He sat down on the edge of the bed. "Adele, did something happen?"

This is my chance, Adele thought, I'll tell him about Rouen, I'll tell him everything. The words wouldn't climb out of her throat. They wouldn't appear. "No. I was just cold."

"I thought you were having fun."

"I was." Adele grabbed his hand and kissed it. "I was!"

Alex's expression changed from disappointed to worried. "Are you all right?"

"Yes."

He lay down beside her.

She kissed his nose. She smiled at him. "Johnny Watson is your blood brother."

"I guess."

"You have known him a long time."

"Since about six or seven. His father died in a mill accident. It made Johnny kind of special. At least I guess I thought it did."

"You were with each other through the war?"

"Until the end."

"Were you in Rouen?"

"No. Why?"

"Was Johnny?"

"I don't know. Why?"

"I just heard there were a lot of Canadian soldiers there. That's all. Nothing."

"The thing you have to know about him, Adele," Alex seemed to take a deep breath, "he lived through twenty-four hours of hell. Twenty-four hours under fire. Direct artillery bombardment." He took another deep breath. "We both did. Do you know how we survived?"

"No."

"By crawling under the corpses of our friends and staying there for twenty-four hours."

Adele expected to see him begin to shake but he didn't. She covered him up with the eiderdown. "I will never ask you again," she said.

That Sunday night, despite the tobogganing fiasco, Alex decided it would be a good idea to try skating on the river. Adele just had to remember to dress more warmly this time. Most of his friends were there, including Johnny Watson and his girlfriend.

Adele waited until Johnny turned those dark eyes of his on her, and when he did she gave him a look that would split a stone. He turned away and stayed his distance.

Some of the men were busy building a roaring fire in an iron barrel. The women were already gliding around over the ice. They disappeared into the dark, came back into the firelight, disappeared again.

Alex tied on Adele's skates and held her up and guided her around and around. It wasn't as easy as tobogganing. Soon she could feel sweat running down her forehead from under her wool hat. Her ankles began to ache. Ray, who belonged to Nancy and who was a better skater than Alex, took her other arm. They picked up speed. All Adele had to do was keep her skates straight and be swept along through the dark.

"Now you're officially a Canadian," Ray said, laughing.

"She was officially a Canadian the first time I laid eyes on her," Alex said.

"I am a good French woman," Adele declared. She had no idea why that came out. The air was cold, her eyes were tearing up from the bite of it.

Ray and Alex laughed.

"I can attest to that," Alex said.

After a while Adele's feet began to feel numb. Alex took off her skates and rubbed her toes. He rubbed her hands. He rubbed her cheeks. She was sitting on a log by the barrel of fire. Sparks were flying everywhere.

Johnny Watson was still keeping his distance. His tall girlfriend was drunkenly practising pirouettes.

"Let's go home," Alex said.

"What will your friends think?"

Alex smiled. "Who cares?"

The wooden bed in their room made a ridiculous amount of noise. Alex had told her the first time they'd made love on it that his father had rigged it up that way to try to get them to move. Adele hadn't been sure whether he was joking or not. The senior Wellses' bedroom was at the other end of the hall but Adele knew they could hear every sound.

The Wellses had gone to bed by the time Alex and Adele had arrived back home, and Alex's veins were bulging out on his forehead trying to make love and restraining himself at the same time. It made Adele want to laugh.

"Don't worry," she whispered, "don't worry."

"All right, I won't," Alex said.

The bed began to bang and bang.

. . .

Adele woke up to discover Alex wasn't there. She assumed he'd gone down the hall to the toilet. She lay there waiting for him to return. After a while she turned on the bedside lamp. The clock said three-thirty.

She sat up and listened for any kind of sound. She couldn't hear anything.

She got up and moved as silently as she could along the hall past her in-laws' bedroom. She pushed open the door to the toilet. He wasn't there.

Adele went down to the kitchen. The refrigerator motor was whirring in a dark corner. She walked along the downstairs hall. Light from a street lamp was streaming in through a small window above the front door and casting shadows on the walls.

The front room was empty. So was the dining room. She went back into the kitchen and stared at the cellar door. It was firmly closed.

She looked out the window.

Alex was standing in the driveway in his pyjamas. Adele crossed the room and leaned against the window. He had one hand on the front of his father's parked car and he was looking off toward the gazebo in the neighbour's back-yard. Random flakes of snow were drifting down. He was in his bare feet.

Adele slipped on her boots and pushed the side door open. She walked along the path to the driveway. When she got close, Alex turned to look at her. His face was bright red and running with sweat. His eyes were bulging. His pyjama bottoms were soaking wet.

"Get down," he said.

"Alex, come into the house."

"Get down!"

"Please!"

Alex turned back to look at the neighbour's yard. He turned to her. He looked like a man trying to wake up.

Adele began to shiver. "Please, Alex. Please."

He walked past her and back into the house. Adele followed after him, afraid to touch him or say anything more.

Alex thumped slowly up the stairs, walked down the dark hall and crawled into bed. Adele tugged off his pyjama bottoms and began to dry him off with an extra blanket. She could hear her in-laws' bedroom door open, she could hear someone creeping down the hall.

"Is everything all right, dear?" Mrs. Wells's voice sounded frightened on the other side of the door.

"Yes." Adele turned off the light.

Mrs. Wells seemed to hesitate. Adele wondered if she'd come in to see for herself. After a moment she heard the sound of retreating footsteps and a door closing.

Adele got into bed and put her arm around Alex. She couldn't see his eyes in the dark, she couldn't tell whether they were closed or open. His body felt warm. Her body was freezing. Light was beginning to creep in through the window before she could fall asleep. An hour later Alex got up and started to dress for work.

He didn't say anything about the night before. Adele didn't know whether it was because he was too ashamed or he couldn't remember. He pulled on his clothes, had his breakfast and climbed into the cab.

Adele didn't mention anything to Mrs. Wells. Mrs. Wells didn't ask her anything. They avoided looking at each other.

Adele went down into the basement and did a load of wash, including Alex's pyjamas and the blanket. When she came back up the stairs, Mrs. Wells was kneeling on the kitchen counter wiping down the cupboard doors.

"Those pills," Adele said.

"What pills, dear?"

"The pills you said Alex would not take. Where are they?"

Mrs. Wells stopped working. "He threw them out."

"He needs them."

"He won't take them."

That afternoon Adele sat in Dr. Jerrison's small stuffy waiting room with three mothers, their numerous coughing children and several old ladies.

Dr. Jerrison, a very thin man whose glasses sat slightly cock-eyed on the end of his nose, finally ushered Adele into his inner office. She sat down in front of his desk and told him the purpose of her visit. Dr. Jerrison rested his chin on the tips of his fingers as he listened.

"It's unusual to write a prescription for a patient, in absentia," he said. "However, since I recall that I had the pleasure of whacking Alex's bare bottom when he first came into this world, this must give me certain proprietary rights."

He went to a cabinet, took down a large bottle, and began to measure out a quantity of small yellow pills. "I can name you ten young men in town who should have this prescription filled. I hope Alex doesn't think he's the only one this time. If things get worse, let me know."

"Thank you," Adele said.

Mrs. Wells was down on her hands and knees waxing the front hall when Adele returned. "Did you get them?" she asked.

"Yes."

Mrs. Wells began to buff the floor furiously. "I'm not going to tell Gordon a thing."

Alex was mostly silent at supper that evening. His father was completely silent, his florid face turned blotchy white from some kind of pent-up rage. Adele assumed it was because of Alex's misadventure the night before. As soon as his parents left to go to a church meeting, Alex got up from the table, walked over to the closet and took out his overcoat.

It was Adele's night to do the dishes. She was standing by the sink trying to think of something to say to stop him from going off to one of the town's taverns when he pulled a glossy magazine from the inside pocket of his coat.

"Look at this," he said, sitting back down at the table.

Adele dried off her hands and leaned over his shoulder.

"Dinnerware," Alex announced, flipping through a catalogue full of brightly coloured photographs, "Melmac. This stuff's unbreakable. It's made of a new material called melamine – it's the coming thing."

Adele looked down at pictures of plates and cups and milk and sugar sets all deeply and richly coloured. Some of the larger bowls were asymmetrically shaped in graceful, swooping curves. They were really quite smart.

"Plastic is going to revolutionize the world. We could sell these things in the store. The old man says no, let the department stores sell them." Alex sounded exasperated. He looked up at Adele. "I was talking to their traveller. Melmac's already selling like wildfire all over the United States. It's brand new here."

Alex walked over to the sink and began to rattle some dishes together. "No more danger of cracked plates. Melmac dinnerware won't break, chip or fade, it's as modern as tomorrow and it will last forever."

"I'll buy one," Adele said and wondered if this display of energy and spirit was meant for her benefit, if it was somehow to make up for the previous night.

"I could go out on the road, Adele. I could leave the store."

"Yes, this is good," Adele said.

They spent the night sequestered in their bedroom, Alex writing down columns of figures, Adele waiting for the right moment to talk about the pills.

He'd already had a conversation with the traveller about joining the company. The pay to start would be a weekly twenty-dollar draw against five percent of everything sold. They were looking for a representative west of Paris. Woodstock to Windsor, Alex said. He'd be getting in on the ground floor.

"The ground floor?"

"The ground floor of a sure thing," Alex said.

He continued to work on his figures. "We don't have a car but that's not a huge obstacle. I can travel by train for now."

Adele got up and took the pill bottle out of her sock drawer. She climbed on the bed and handed it to Alex. "You'll need these," she said.

Alex stared at the bottle. His muscles began to bunch along his jaw. "Where did you get them?

"Dr. Jerrison."

"When?"

"Today."

"You went into Dr. Jerrison's office, in broad daylight, and asked for some crazy pills?"

"They're not crazy pills."

"Jesus Christ, Adele!" He got up so quickly his pen and papers went flying off the bed. "How many people were in his office?"

"One or two."

"I'm not crazy, Adele! Goddamn it!"

"No. I know you're not. But to do this work you will have to feel better. That's all. Those pills will help."

"They won't help. I'll feel like an invalid if I take these pills. I won't be able to do anything. Vets in hospitals take these things, not me!" Alex tossed the pill bottle back at her. It hit her in the chest and hurt.

Adele picked it up off the bed, opened the top and rolled a few pills into the palm of her hand. "You take two at night, two in the morning and you don't drink alcohol any more."

"Is that right?" Alex said, "And who the hell are you?"

Adele got off the bed. She stared at him for a moment. Alex's eyes looked bloodshot.

"I am your wife." She held out the pills. Alex didn't budge. "I am your love," Adele said.

Alex's face seemed to break. He looked away.

Adele waited. She knew this was the moment of all moments. This was her life.

Alex held out his hand. She gave him two pills.

"Do you want water?"

Alex tossed the pills into his mouth and swallowed them. "I feel better now."

Adele smiled. "You will."

Adele felt transported. She felt like her heart was going to break. She felt grateful to God.

CANADA, 1946

CHAPTER THIRTY-EIGHT

• • •

Winter melted away.

Water trickled across the sidewalks, crows cawed from high up in pine trees and the sun actually felt warm on a person's face. It felt warm on Adele's face, whether hanging up the wash in the backyard of her mother-in-law's house or on one of her solitary walks through the town. She could feel its invisible fingers warming her blood, touching her heart. She felt extraordinarily happy.

Alex had written the Melmac company in Toronto and they had written back saying that they were very interested in his background in merchandising and that they would be interviewing applicants sometime in May. He should contact them again the first of May.

For Adele the most important thing was that Alex was feeling better. Though he'd had two more episodes of shaking he'd kept on with his pills and he hadn't gone missing in the middle of the night. And though he still took a drink now and then, and still stopped off after work every once in a while with his friends, particularly Johnny Watson, he was careful not to drink too much. And he began to use condoms.

At first Adele had found it upsetting because his fumbling around with them and his boyish look of concentration putting them on had reminded her of Manfred, but she knew why he was doing it. He still didn't feel well enough to have a child, but at least he was feeling well enough now to do something about it. All Alex had said the first time, sitting on the edge of the bed and not really looking at her, was "Just for the time being."

In France and now in Canada Adele had thought it was a miracle that she hadn't become pregnant. And then she'd begun to worry about it. And then she'd tried to put it out of her mind. It was a good thing not to bring life into this deranged world, not after what she'd seen, not after the children of Buchenwald. And Étienne.

But that was why she wanted children, too. One child, anyway. Because of Étienne.

Alex wrote the Melmac company at the end of April for an appointment. Three weeks later he received a reply. They weren't taking on any additional representatives at this particular time. They'd hold his name on file, though.

The next Friday Alex wanted to go to a dance in Preston. They hadn't gone to any of these popular out-of-town dances before because Alex had said he wasn't that keen on them. Adele had danced with him in Le Havre the night of their wedding and so she knew why he wasn't keen – he wasn't a very good dancer.

"Why?" Adele asked.

"To celebrate."

"Celebrate? Yes, what?"

"My lifelong career at Arthur Wells and Son."

They went with Johnny Watson and his girlfriend in Johnny's old car. Adele had thought they were going with Ray and Nancy – she was almost sure Alex had told her that.

Johnny was driving too fast, the car seemed to careen around every curve. Adele's body shifted against Alex. She wished he'd say something to Johnny and she wished he'd put his arm around her, but he just sat there. Johnny's girlfriend was leaning against her door, looking angry. Apparently she and Johnny had had an argument.

Johnny pulled a bottle out of his jacket and took the cap off. He seemed to be driving with one finger. Adele could see him watching her in the rear-view mirror. They hadn't spoken since the night of the tobogganing, he hadn't dared come close enough, but now there he was. Johnny Watson. Her husband's blood brother.

Johnny took a drink and handed the bottle over the seat to Alex. "We're going to have a good time tonight." He looked over at his sour girlfriend. "Whoopee."

Alex took a drink.

"Pass it to Adele."

His mirrored eyes were burrowing into hers. "I'll wait. Thank you," Adele said.

"You're welcome," Johnny said.

Alex handed the bottle back but Johnny's girlfriend intercepted it.

"I thought you weren't talking."

"I'm not." She put the bottle to her lips and took a long drink.

"It's going to be some night," Johnny said.

Alex danced with Adele for a while. He liked to dance the slow numbers and sit out the fast ones. Adele liked the fast numbers.

A very competent twelve-piece orchestra and a singer Alex called a crooner were providing the music. Multi-coloured balloons were strung across the ceiling and two spinning globes like impossibly huge diamonds sent refracted light whirling through the darkened hall. It seemed as if each man had brought a bottle in a plain paper bag and was busy mixing drinks under the long tables. This seemed very peculiar to Adele, that drinking at a dance should be made illegal.

They were sitting with all of Alex's friends and a few people Adele hadn't met before. Alex was drinking more than he usually did. At first she wanted to tell him to remember his pills, but then she thought of Melmac and decided not to.

She loved the brassy sound of the music, she loved the smooth sound of the crooner in his white tuxedo and the imploring way he held out his hands just for her, or so it seemed, she loved the whirl and the blur of it all. Some of the other men began to invite her to dance since Alex seemed increasingly disinterested. Alex didn't mind. Every time she came back to the table, she kissed his cheek and he squeezed her hand.

"Dance with Johnny," he said.

"That's all right, I'm tired." Adele smiled apologetically across the table at Johnny.

"Come on, Adele, Johnny's the only one you haven't danced with."

It was almost midnight. Johnny got up out of his chair. His eyes seemed slightly glassy and just as intrusive and unblinking as always. He bowed.

"Come on, Adele," Alex said.

Adele got up. Johnny came around the table and took her hand and led her out on to the dance floor. He put his other hand around her waist and smiled down at her. She'd been watching him dance with the other women. He was a good dancer.

Adele kept her eyes on his chest. She could feel him pulling her gently into the music. Her feet had to move. His feet moved with hers. She tried to keep her distance.

"It's been a good night, hasn't it?" Johnny said.

Adele didn't reply.

"Good music, good friends, good cheer. Just enough to drink."

Adele didn't reply.

"You've worn Alex out."

Adele didn't reply.

"Hello down there," Johnny said.

Adele looked up at him. He was still smiling. How could he be so ignorant, Adele wondered. How could he not know that she hated him?

"Adele?"

"Yes?"

"I remember now."

Her body froze, his dark eyes were piercing into hers.

"In Lyon. Two candy bars and a package of cigarettes. For the privilege of fucking you up your sweet little asshole." He was still smiling.

Adele stopped, not completely sure that she'd heard what she'd just heard, and then she pushed him away and walked off the dance floor. By the time she got back to the table her face looked like someone had broken it.

"What happened?" Alex said.

Adele shook her head. She was trembling.

"Did he say something? Did he do something?"

All Adele could manage was to stare dumbly back at Alex. She couldn't sit down. She couldn't move.

Johnny was sauntering back to the table as if nothing had happened. He had his hands in his pockets and a sleepy smile on his face. Alex got up. His chair clattered to the floor behind him.

"Did you say something to Adele?"

Johnny looked shocked. "What?" he said.

Alex reached out, grabbed him by his jacket, jerked him forward and hit him in the mouth all at the same time. Blood sprayed across his face. Alex hit him again. Women screamed. Men scrambled to hold on to Alex. Johnny grinned through the blood. Alex began to swing him around. Johnny clung to his arm, grinning and grinning. His mouth was full of blood. He smiled at Alex.

Alex dropped him on the floor and pushed through the crowd and banged out the door.

Adele followed him out into the parking lot. She found him in the dark, leaning over someone's car fender. His white shirt and best suit were spotted with blood. His shoulders were heaving.

"Oh Jesus," Alex moaned, "he didn't fight back. He didn't say anything." He looked at Adele. He looked bewildered.

"He touched me," Adele said.

"Where?"

"Between the legs."

After someone took Johnny to the local hospital to get fixed up, and after some standing around, Ray and Nancy drove Alex and Adele home. "He'll be all right," Ray kept assuring Alex.

Alex was slouched in the back, his hand covering his eyes as if he were sick or ashamed. Adele was sitting on the other side of the car – there seemed to be a mile of seat between them. Nancy hadn't asked her what had happened. No one had asked her. It was just as well. God only knew what Johnny would say in rebuttal.

Adele stared out the window and watched the night rush by.

Ray and Nancy dropped them off in front of the Wellses' house. The lights were on in the kitchen even though it was late. Alex stood in the driveway staring at the side door, swaying a little in the dark. Adele hadn't realized how drunk he was. "I can't go back in there," he said. He started off down the sidewalk.

Adele followed him, past the neighbour's house, past the next house. "Where are we going, Alex?"

Alex didn't reply.

It was near the end of May and the night was pleasant enough. They walked through pools of lamp light and under rows of dark maple trees for three blocks. Alex turned into a playground, weaved around swings and teeter-totters and a sand box, and collapsed down on a bench.

Adele sat down on a bench opposite. There was one lamppost inside the playground. A swarm of insects with translucent wings were flapping around it and throwing huge shadows across the grass. Adele had noticed these same insects clinging to the screens in her in-laws' house a few nights before. Mayflies, Alex had called them.

Alex stretched out on his bench and rested his head on his arm. A full moon sailed over the rooftops. A car went by.

Adele looked up at the light again and at the flapping swarm going around and around. The air was beginning to feel chilly. She thought of Johnny Watson. He didn't know who she was or anything about her. And yet how he must hate her, loathe her, to say such a thing. But why? Because she had come between him and Alex? Because he had been driven half-mad by the war?

The night cooled off and the mayflies disappeared. Adele felt frozen.

• • •

It seemed to Adele that she'd just fallen asleep when Alex touched her on her shoulder. It was dawn but the sun was still screened behind the tops of the trees.

"I'm going home to change. And to tell the old man I've quit my job."

Adele pushed herself up. Droplets of dew covered her bench. Her light jacket and party dress felt damp. "What are we going to do?"

Alex sat down beside her. "I won't have any trouble finding another job."

"Where?"

"Anywhere. In one of the factories, I guess. And I know a fellow who has a house to rent. I was talking to him about renting it once I got the Melmac job. I'll talk to him again."

"I'll get a job, too."

"I don't think so."

"Yes. In one of the factories."

Alex looked away. He looked in pain. "I'm sorry, Adele."

"Why?"

"For Johnny. What he did. I'm sorry."

Adele wrapped her arms around him and held him with all her might. His face felt warm against hers. After a while he disengaged himself and got back up. "Maybe I can rent that house today."

"I'll stay here," Adele said. "I'll talk to your parents later. You hurry, your mother will be worried."

Alex started off across the playground.

The sun began to climb above the trees. The air felt warmer. Eventually she left the bench and sat on a swing. She didn't feel hungry, she felt empty. Johnny Watson had emptied her out. She was light as a shadow, swinging softly. Her hopes and dreams, all light as a shadow. She tried to fight off a familiar feeling, the falling away into despair, the endless falling.

The dew disappeared. The sun climbed higher. A woman came into the playground pulling a little girl in a wagon.

"Good morning," Adele said.

The woman seemed surprised to see her there, and a little uncertain. Adele thought she must make quite the sight. Her satin dancing shoes. Dangling earrings. Hair standing up on end.

The woman lifted the little girl out of the wagon. "Morning," she said. She helped the child climb up the ladder on the slide. Adele had an impulse to walk over and stand at the bottom of the slide to help catch her, but she thought better of it.

Two boys rode across the grass on battered-looking bicycles. They hopped off, jumped on a teeter-totter and began to bounce up and down, keeping their bright, curious eyes on Adele all the while.

Adele wondered if they'd seen her from a distance and had come across to investigate. They didn't seem particularly interested in playing on a teeter-totter. Up and down. Up and down. They seemed too old. Perhaps they'd been talking to Johnny Watson and were exciting themselves. Up and down. Up and down. Perhaps they could smell her Boche cunt.

Two young mothers were pushing baby carriages along the sidewalk. They turned into the playground.

Adele got off the swing and walked the other way.

"Adele!"

Alex was hurrying across the grass toward her. He'd changed his clothes and combed his hair. "So much for Arthur Wells and Son," he said, coming up to her, "let's go get some breakfast."

They went to a tiny restaurant near the railway crossing where Alex ordered ham and eggs with toast and Adele ordered a coffee. Alex had already talked to the man about the house to rent, he had the key in his pocket. Adele could hardly believe it.

"Hurry, Alex, finish eating," she said.

Apparently Mr. Wells had shouted at Alex for some time and then he'd left for work. Mrs. Wells had cried. Adele could only imagine what they'd thought of the blood all over his shirt and suit jacket. And what they thought of her.

She watched Alex munch his food down. He seemed happier than he'd looked in days. She was determined to feel happy, too. She'd gotten to know most of the town from her walks. This area they were sitting in was called the Junction and was a bit run down. They were within a few blocks of their new house.

"Come on, Alex," she said.

They walked for a short distance until Alex stopped in front of two little wooden houses. They looked nearly identical and equally shabby. A mass of shrubs had grown up wild around the front of one of them, the other one was more open to the air. Adele could see that this house, the one on their left, had a cracked front window.

"Which one is ours?"

"The one on the left," Alex said.

He unlocked the back door and they walked up two steps into a small kitchen. The cupboards were painted a dark yellow and it looked like someone had scratched them with a nail. Alex turned on a light switch. Nothing happened. They walked through the rest of the house – two bedrooms, a hall closet, a dusty loft under the eaves and a front room. The front room had worn hardwood on the floor. The bedrooms and hall had only rough planks. The kitchen floor was covered with a sheet of wavy green linoleum.

"Where is the toilet?" Adele asked.

"Out back."

Adele looked out the kitchen window. She could see a little hut sitting in the middle of some bushes at the end of a path. Such arrangements weren't unheard of in Rouen but she'd never used one.

"What do we do at night?"

Alex grinned. "That's up to you."

Adele turned on the tap in the kitchen sink. After a suspenseful moment, water came out. She felt grateful.

"I'll get the town to turn the power on," Alex said. "We won't have hot water in the house until they do. And we'll need some other things, right?"

Adele nodded. The house was empty – they'd need everything. "Stove, icebox, bed, chairs, table."

Alex headed toward the back door.

"And a broom and a mop and a pail," Adele yelled after him.

Alex waved and went out the door.

Adele walked through the house again. It wasn't all that bad. On second inspection she was beginning to feel it could be made quite cozy once it was scrubbed and freshly painted and some colourful rugs laid down on the planks, pictures hung on the walls, curtains on the windows. The only thing she really hated was the huge space heater in the front room. It was shiny and painted brown and took up at least a third of the available space. She thought she'd paint it the same colour she'd paint the walls, so at least everything would blend in. Right now the walls were covered by a faded wallpaper of blue and violet flowers.

She went back into the kitchen and looked out the window. She could just make out the back corner of the house next door. A woman was hanging up washing. She looked to be in her thirties and more than amply endowed, from Adele's perspective, her honey-coloured hair long and a little wild around her soft face. A cigarette smouldered in the very centre of her mouth. She was talking to someone – Adele could tell this because her cigarette kept bobbing up and down. A boy came into view, brown-haired and so slender he looked like a little wood sprite. He held some wet clothes in his arms.

Adele eased the window up just an inch or two, she didn't want to draw attention. She could feel the warm May air move by her, caress her, fill the kitchen with the faint scent of lilacs. She could hear the woman's voice.

"Careful, George," the woman said, "don't drop anything."

Mrs. Wells arrived before noon. Her woman friend had driven her over. The back seat of the car was full of Alex and Adele's clothes and bed sheets and pillows and towels. The trunk was full of food. Adele helped Mrs. Wells and her friend carry everything into the house. "We don't have an icebox yet."

"I know, dear, Alex dropped by and told me. For now, I've just brought you non-perishables."

Mrs. Wells pulled a rag out of her pocket and began to wipe down the kitchen cupboards with cold water. She didn't stay long. When she left she hugged Adele. "Please ask for help if you need any."

Adele knew what she meant.

She carried the clothes into the larger bedroom, the one with a closet, and hung them up. She washed down the tiny closet in the hall as best she could. When it dried, she put everything else in there. She thought about going next door to ask her neighbour if she could borrow a broom but decided against it. It didn't seem the proper way to meet.

It was almost dark by the time Alex came home. Adele was sitting on the floor in the front room. He was carrying a new broom, a mop, a pail, and a box of soap. And that was all. He sat down beside her. He looked tired in the faint light that was seeping in through the cracked window. He smelled of alcohol.

"I've got things organized," he said, sitting down beside her. "We're going to use Ray's dad's truck. Everything's coming tomorrow."

"When are the lights going to come on?"

"I had to put down a deposit. The town will reconnect the power the first of the week."

Adele knew he'd gone around to see Johnny Watson. It wasn't in Alex's nature to stay away – he'd want to make sure he hadn't killed him.

Adele wondered what Alex had said. Did he say, "You touched my wife." Did he say, "That's the end of our friendship." Did he say, "Johnny, I'm sorry."

She wondered what Johnny Watson had said.

"Your mother brought us some left-over chicken. She brought you your medicine."

Alex sighed. He rested his head against the wall. He picked up her hand and held it in his lap.

"One thing, Adele." He turned his face toward her. It looked uncertain and smudged in the dark. "I promise you. This is as far down as we go."

They slept beside each other on the floor. It took a long time for Adele to fall asleep. She stared out the window at the street lamp across the road. The light caught in the crack in the window and made swirls on the glass. It looked as if some people had gathered on the front lawn and were holding up candles. She wondered if they were looking for her.

Alex got a job in a factory, just like he'd said he would, and as the days went by the house in the Junction began to look more like a home, as Adele had thought it would.

Mrs. Wells dropped off numerous pots and pans and an old kettle and everyday dinnerware. Alex purchased a new bed, a used stove and an old icebox. His friends dropped off furniture. Adele cut and sewed and hung curtains, and hunted through the shops for colourful scatter rugs.

Mr. Wells did not make an appearance. His absence didn't seem to bother Alex. He came straight home from work every day, dusty and tired, his hands increasingly calloused, but looking pleased with himself. He drank very little. He took his pills. He didn't shake.

A few days after they'd moved in, the woman next door had arrived at the back door carrying a bouquet of flowers in a pretty glass vase. Adele knew she must have purchased the flowers – they couldn't have come from her garden, she didn't have one.

"Hi, I'm Dorothy. I thought you might like these."

"I will find something," Adele said, lifting the flowers out of the water.

"No. It's for you. The whole thing, it's a house-warming gift."

"Oh." Adele felt inordinately grateful. "I am pleased," she had said.

One morning, just after Alex left for work, Dorothy arrived at Adele's back door with a steaming pot of coffee and her cigarettes. After that they made it a morning ritual, either Dorothy coming over to Adele's or Adele travelling over to Dorothy's place. She worked for one of the factories down-town. Her front room was her sewing workshop. A truck dropped off cartons of unseamed socks each morning and picked up the finished ones Wednesdays and Fridays.

"It's called piecework."

"I know," Adele said, "I have done the same."

"Oh? Where?"

"In Paris."

Dorothy laughed. A silly coincidence. Adele liked her very much.

"I'm sure that Paris is a lot more interesting than this Paris," she said, puffing on her cigarette. She seemed to always have a cigarette stuck to her lips, even when she was rolling more of them in her machine. "How far is Paris from Dieppe?"

"I'm not sure."

"My husband died at Dieppe. He was a soldier."

"I am very sorry. So many bad things happened."

Dorothy had large brown eyes to go with her honey hair. They looked enormously sad. "Yes," she said.

One day Dorothy suggested that Adele buy a used sewing machine. They could work together in her front room. The factory was running two shifts, so there was more than enough work to go around. And it would be fun.

Adele thought that was a wonderful idea, in fact she'd been thinking about the same thing. Alex seemed to think it was okay. He liked Dorothy, he liked teasing her. Whenever Alex talked to her, she just smiled and said, "Is that right?" She seemed more at ease with Adele. When they were alone, she talked all the time.

Adele bought a used machine and they worked side by side with the radio blaring and Dorothy smoking up a storm. At ten-thirty they'd break for coffee and Dorothy would roll more cigarettes. At noon George would come home from school and the three of them would eat lunch together because Alex took his lunch to work. Sometimes Dorothy would provide the food, sometimes Adele would bring food over from her house, most of it surplus from Mrs. Wells, who kept building up their supplies. George went back to school at one. At two-thirty, Dorothy and Adele would break for a glass of rye.

Adele adored George. He was like an older and quieter version of her younger brothers. The first week in her new home he'd helped her construct a clothes line from her back wall to a nearby tree and afterwards he'd found a sturdy wooden box for her to step up on. He was always asking to run errands for her. He even offered to paint her house.

"You're too young."

"No, I'm not."

"All right. But only after you paint your own," Adele had said. "Your mother might not like it, otherwise."

June turned into July. The small house broiled in the sun. Alex bought a fan for the front room and a smaller one for their bedroom. He told Adele that there were all sorts of new gadgets coming on the market. Electric orange juice makers and coffee makers and mixing machines, a whole slew of home appliances. He was thinking of a selling job again. He'd been talking to another traveller – he might make an application.

One morning just before Adele was ready to cross over to Dorothy's place to start work, Dorothy came through the back door wearing a faded bathrobe and dilapidated pink slippers. "I'm not working today," she said.

"Are you ill?"

"No." She leaned against the counter and played with her hair. "Well, the truth is I have some company." She blushed and fished around in the pocket of her bathrobe for a cigarette. She pulled one out and lit it up.

"Company?"

"A man. You know," Dorothy replied, and then in a rush, "Do you want to take the day off, too? Or we could carry your machine over here for the day. We could easily do it. Whatever you like."

Adele smiled. "A man?"

"God knows it's been a while." Dorothy smiled. "I want to make the most of it."

Adele decided to wash her floors. At noon she heard Dorothy's screen door slam shut and George laughing. She looked out her kitchen window. George was climbing high up in his favourite tree. Adele could see a man climbing up after him, pretending to grab at his feet, playing with him. George let out a squeal and climbed higher.

Adele recognized the man right away. It was Johnny Watson.

She closed the window. She locked the doors. She raged around inside her house. When Alex arrived home from work, she asked him if he knew.

"No." Alex looked surprised and a little defensive. "Not until now. I just saw his car parked out front." He put his lunch bucket down on the table and sat down.

"He can't be next door," Adele said.

Alex began pulling off his work boots. "Johnny and Dorothy," he said, as if his brain was just beginning to register the idea. He smiled a little.

"Make him leave!" Adele said.

"How would I manage that?"

"I don't know how!" Adele went into the bedroom and slammed the door.

Alex followed her in. Though it was past six o'clock, the temperature was still close to ninety. Adele had the fan set on high. She was sitting in front of it, her hair blowing around.

Alex sat a safe distance away on the bed. He didn't say anything, he just sat there.

"I was so sick I didn't make supper."

Alex nodded. "That's all right. I'll make it."

"Alex, what are we going to do? I can't live here."

"Well, wait for a few minutes, anyway. You don't even know if he's going to move in."

"He'll move in. Oh God, what's wrong with him? Why is he like this?"

"It's too bad he picked Dorothy."

"Too bad he picked Dorothy?" Adele felt hopeless. "He picked her on purpose!"

"Maybe it won't work out," Alex suggested. After a while he got up and went out into the kitchen and began to make supper.

Normally, after they'd had their meal and it started to get dark, they'd take their kitchen chairs out into the backyard and sit out there to cool off. Sometimes Dorothy and George would come over to join them.

Adele wouldn't go outside.

Alex shrugged and stayed in, too. They sat in the front room. Alex's face began to shine with sweat, and drops of sweat were running down his bare chest. "We'll just have to see what happens," he said.

Adele refused to pack Alex's lunch the next morning. Johnny's car was still pulled up on Dorothy's lawn. Alex started off for work and Adele watched him disappear down the street. A half-hour later Johnny got in his car and drove away. Adele waited for George to go off to play and then she crossed over to Dorothy's house.

Dorothy was still in her bathrobe. "Are you early or am I late?" she said. She was sitting at the kitchen table drinking a coffee. Her face looked even softer than usual. She held her coffee mug in a languid sort of way.

"Where is your friend?"

"He went to work." Dorothy smiled to herself, as if her mind was somewhere else.

"When does he come back?"

Dorothy looked up. "You know him, Adele. He says he's Alex's best friend. Johnny Watson?"

"Yes. Is he coming back?"

"What a question. Of course he's coming back."

"I can't work here any more." Adele felt wretched – she felt like she wanted to cry.

"Why not?"

"Because."

Dorothy reached for one of her cigarettes. She lit it up. "Why?"

"Because of him. I can't be around him."

"Well shit, Adele, why don't you just come out and say what's on your mind?"

"Did he tell you Alex had to hit him? Did he tell you why?"

Dorothy got up from the table, her face flushed now, her movements no longer languid. "I don't give a shit why. I don't want to hear stories, I don't want to hear anything. Shut your mouth or get out!"

Adele turned and went back out the door. Five minutes later she came back in and asked for her sewing machine. Dorothy nodded but didn't help.

She leaned against the wall, her arms firmly crossed, smoked a cigarette and watched Adele struggle across the kitchen carrying the machine.

"I'll say one thing for you, you sure have one hell of a nerve, Frenchie," Dorothy said.

Later that morning Adele walked down to the factory and asked the foreman if he could drop off her share of the piecework at her house from now on. He said he guessed that would be all right.

Adele had made up her mind. She was feeling quite fierce about it. Johnny Watson was not going to defeat her.

When it had become obvious that Johnny had moved in next door, Alex went over to talk to him. He came back and told Adele that he'd made it clear that he didn't want him speaking to Adele or getting anywhere near her. Johnny had promised that he wouldn't. And Johnny had said that he was deeply sorry for any misunderstanding.

"There was no misunderstanding. I understood everything," Adele said.

"I know. He touched you."

"Doesn't that make you angry?"

"Yes. Of course it does," Alex said.

Johnny began to haunt her. He'd stand in Dorothy's backyard and stare at her kitchen window for the longest time. He'd make a big show of staying on Dorothy's property whenever he saw Alex, pretending to shout hello over an invisible fence. He took her place with George, the youngster rarely came to visit her any more. But the worst was having to walk down to the privy at night, hurrying through the dark, flinching at every noise. She resisted using a commode, on principle. She made Alex install a huge bolt on the inside of the privy door.

Adele's front room filled up with boxes of unseamed socks. She worked furiously during the day and sometimes long into the night. She didn't want to fall behind what Dorothy was doing.

One day she and Dorothy happened to go out into their backyards at the same time. Dorothy waved hesitantly toward her. Adele, caught off guard, waved back. Dorothy smiled and went back into her house.

Johnny began to give Alex a ride downtown. He'd back off Dorothy's lawn, stop in front of the house and honk the horn.

The first time he did that, Alex looked out the front window and then back at Adele. "I gave the guy eighteen stitches and cracked a bone in his nose. What do you think?"

Adele didn't know what to reply. It was a long walk down the back hill to where Alex worked. The summer was still boiling hot. It was a longer walk home. Against her better judgment she said, "All right."

The next day Dorothy crossed over into Adele's yard to show her where there used to be a vegetable garden, lost in weeds now, just in case she was ever thinking of putting in another one. Adele wasn't. A few days later, in the middle of a rainy afternoon, Dorothy rapped on Adele's back door. She was carrying a bottle of rye and two glasses in her hand. Adele felt she had to invite her in. The subject of Johnny never came up.

Mrs. Wells was Adele's only other visitor. She dropped a letter off one day that had been delivered to her house for Alex. It was from the Melmac company, Adele could tell by the printing on the envelope.

As soon as Alex arrived home Adele put it in his hand. The company had had a change of plans. They'd decided to expand into south-western Ontario after all and wanted to get started in time for the Christmas season. They wanted Alex to come to Toronto right away for an interview.

Alex gave out a whoop and lifted Adele up in his arms. "At last! We got a break! A break! A break!" He rushed to get out his papers and pencils and sat at the kitchen table adding up columns of figures. He wouldn't hear of Adele serving him supper. Instead he insisted they eat out. They walked over to the restaurant near the railway crossing hand in hand. As soon as they'd returned and closed the outside door they made love. They didn't even make it as far as the bedroom. Alex didn't use a condom, and Adele didn't complain.

Afterwards Alex went back to his calculations and Adele sat down in the front room to work on her socks. Shortly after midnight Alex said goodnight. Adele looked in on him. He was sprawled out naked across the bed, the fan whirling away, hugging his pillow. The Melmac Man, Adele thought. The sheer bulk of him shining in the dark made her smile. She closed the door softly.

It was one o'clock. Since she didn't feel tired, she decided to work a little longer. The familiar whirr of the sewing machine weaved and drifted through her thoughts. Alex will be a great salesman. They'll move away from Johnny Watson and rent a house with a basement and a furnace and an inside toilet. She'll walk to the hospital and make inquiries about becoming a nursing assistant.

The curtain on the front window lit up.

On their way home they'd noticed some lightning off to the east. Every once in a while a quarter of the sky had whitened in a great blotch. Alex had called it heat lightning and said because it was heat lightning it wouldn't rain.

But now Adele could hear individual drops of rain hitting the roof. She could hear approaching thunder. She continued to work. Rain began to clatter down. The lightning grew brighter outside her curtain, the claps of thunder seemed closer.

Adele's work light flickered and went out. Her machine whirred one last time and died. She sat there waiting to see if the power would come back on. It was pitch black in the room. Lightning flashed again and for a moment she could see the piles of cartons. The space heater. They disappeared again. The rain thundered down.

Adele got up and opened the curtain. It was just as black outside as inside. The street lamp across the street had gone out. No lights in any of the neighbours' houses. No lights anywhere.

Another flash. She could see water pelting past her face like a silver screen. It went dark again. Another flash. Adele peered out through the rain.

A man was standing in the middle of the road.

Adele froze. She waited for another flash. It arrived like a blinding spotlight. The man was gone.

Adele hurried to the front door and pulled it open. The street lit up and then plunged into darkness again. She splashed out onto the road. Another flash and a row of houses came and went. Adele began to run, certain she was about to crash into something unseen. Lightning flashed. The street appeared in stark relief. She aimed herself down the middle of it, and everything went black again.

She ran until she reached the main road through the Junction. She could see the man splashing away toward the railway tracks. She began to run after him. The man stopped.

Adele could see him, and then she couldn't see anything, and then she could see him again. He was wearing some kind of tweed jacket, drenched now, hanging heavily off his narrow frame. She approached him. He was holding his one shoulder higher than the other, as if he were trying to protect himself from something. His dark hair was roughly cut.

She could see the bones in his face, his ghostly white skin. She came up to him.

"Adele," he said.

She leaned against him and he put his arms around her and her legs gave out and she sank to the road. The man did, too, and they huddled there in the streaming rain.

The headlights of a car swung out of a side street and swept slowly over them.

"Manfred," Adele said.

CANADA, 1946

CHAPTER THIRTY-NINE

• • •

I t was after eight o'clock in the evening and the police station was empty and so was the town hall. Jack had sent Jock White home, saying he'd work a double shift since he hadn't been as consistently available as he should have been over the last little while. Jock had looked both surprised and grateful – no one liked pulling the long night shift.

Jack turned the weapon he'd fished out of the river over in his hand. *Parabellum Luger*. Under the lamp on his desk, he could see the name etched in the black steel just above the grip. He slipped the empty eight-cartridge magazine back up into its hollow handle. It made a satisfying metallic click as it locked into place. Five live cartridges lay on his desk, 9x19mm, pressed into their brass cases. Jack figured that would make the pistol approximately a .38 calibre, not quite as powerful as his weapon but more than adequate to do the job.

It felt balanced in his hand and surprisingly heavy. It had the look of an efficient machine.

Jack pointed the gun toward the front door. He pointed it up toward the mayor's office.

There was no way Miles was going to get his hands on it, no way he was going to hear anything about it. No supper meeting for Miles. Besides, it was way past supper time.

Jack opened his weapons' drawer, slipped the Luger inside, put the five cartridges in with it and locked it up.

It could be a coincidence, of course. Jack had pondered this. But who the hell would throw a perfectly good Luger away, and at that precise spot?

No. He had the murder weapon, all right, though any fingerprints on it other than his own would have been rubbed off on the river bottom a long time ago. Seventeen days ago.

A minimum of six bullets in the magazine and one fatal shot fired, or maybe seven bullets and two fired, or eight and three. Up to two rounds banged off while they were chasing him, then, the empty cartridges ejecting somewhere. And then the killing shot, the empty cartridge kicking out of the gun and sinking into the water. There was only one question left. Only one that counted. Whose gun was it?

Jack thought of Joe Puvalowski.

● ● ●

The sun had finally given up following Jack around and had fallen out of the sky. It didn't seem much cooler, though. Jack drove up the hill to the Junction with all the windows in the cruiser rolled down, over the tracks, past the factory and continued on along the rough trail beside the railroad tracks.

He loved his Studebaker, he didn't give a damn about the town's cruiser. The headlight beams began to wave and jump around in the dark, the muffler bumped and scraped along the ground.

Hope it falls off, Jack thought.

Just before the DP camp he caught a glimpse of himself in the mirror. "Hello, Jack," he said.

The headlight beams caught a scruffily-dressed man crossing the tracks. Jack braked and switched the spotlight on. "Get me Joe Puvalowski!" he yelled out the window. "Joe Puvalowski! Now!"

The man, caught like a fugitive in the harsh stream of light, looked gratifyingly frightened. He disappeared.

Jack waited where he was, switching off the spotlight but keeping the motor running and the headlights on. If Joe didn't show, he'd walk up to the camp but he'd prefer to have Joe sitting beside him in the car. From long experience he knew it would work better that way.

After a while Joe Puvalowski sauntered out of the night and peered in through the open window. His swarthy face didn't look particularly intimidated. "You have our papers?"

"Get in."

"Why is that?"

"Just to talk. We're not going anywhere. That's all." Jack leaned over and opened the door, swinging it wide. Joe got in the car but left the door open.

"Excuse me," Jack said, leaning over him and slamming the door shut. In the green glow from the dashboard, he gave Joe a dead-cold look. "I have something of yours." He opened the glove compartment and pulled out the Luger.

Joe straightened up. "What is that?"

"Your gun, Joe. The one you used to execute that guy you didn't like who lived in a hole in the ground."

"You're a crazy man," Joe said.

"You mean he didn't live in that hole in the ground?"

Joe hesitated.

"What part have I got wrong, Joe?"

Joe looked back out the window. Jack glanced past him. He was sure most of the men in the camp were standing close by. He couldn't see a thing.

"Joe, where you come from, if I didn't like what you just said, I'd shoot you right in the head and not blink. Wouldn't I?"

Joe turned to look at him.

"It's different here." Jack turned off the motor and killed the headlights. He could barely see Joe now but he could hear him breathing. "In this country you want to get involved. That's what we call being a good citizen. Tell me who used the gun, you'll not only get your papers back, you'll get a good job in town. I guarantee it."

"This is not my gun," Joe said.

Though Jack couldn't see it, he could imagine Joe's chin thrusting out, his hair beginning to shake in indignation, like always.

"Whose gun is it?"

"I don't know."

"Who was the man in the hole?"

Joe shifted around a little and then seemed to settle back against the seat. He let out a long sigh. "Not one of us. Not Polish. His accent not that good."

A long, heavy silence.

Come on, Jack thought, come on.

"A German."

"A German?"

"He said he'd been a clerk. That's all, some minor clerk somewhere. We voted. He could stay, but he could not live with us. That was how it was decided. It was a wrong decision."

"Why? Because of what happened?"

"Yes."

"Is that all? Joe?" Jack waited.

Joe stirred a little.

Jack stopped breathing.

"There was a French woman," Joe said.

CANADA, 1946

CHAPTER FORTY

• • •

A dele held Manfred's face in her hands. "Oh God." She clung to him, kissing his mouth, his eyes, his nose. Their faces were wet with rain. It streamed down their cheeks, it was turning warm. Manfred touched her face.

After a while Manfred said in his faltering French, "We cannot stay this way."

"Manfred, how did you come here?"

Manfred began to get up. He lifted Adele up off the road. He looked around, took her hand and pulled her toward the tracks.

Adele let him.

They cut across an empty cinder yard and hurried toward the dark shape of some sheds. The lightning was receding to the west. The rain was beginning to ease. By the distant lightning Adele could see a row of bins and the glint of coal. Manfred stepped under a slanted roof and leaned against the rough board wall. Adele began to shiver. She had only a sleeveless blouse and skirt on and she was soaked through.

"This is a miracle," Adele whispered.

"It's just me," Manfred said.

Adele snaked her arms beneath his jacket and held him tight. He was soaked through, too. "How did you find me?"

"Your friend Lucille. Remember? You gave her the name of your husband-to-be. You wrote it down if she ever wanted to write."

"You went to Lucille's after I was there?"

Manfred smiled. It was a smile to break someone's heart. It was breaking Adele's heart, anyway.

Adele rested her face against his chest. "I am married, Manfred."

"Lucille told me what the people in Rouen had done. She told me how you'd been looking for me. This husband-to-be did not matter. I thought, what else could you do? You were only escaping."

"And now? What do you think now?"

Adele could feel his rough hand touch her hand, she could feel his fingers brushing against her fingers.

"I think I was a madman in a madman's dream. Go home before your husband misses you."

"No!" Adele could feel her tears again. "No! You can't do this! I will come back tomorrow, I will meet you tomorrow."

"You cannot."

"I will!" The desperation in her voice startled her. "Tell me where you're staying, Manfred. Tell me or I swear to God I'll kill you."

He smiled again. "Where am I staying? Ah well, I have excellent accommodation." Manfred looked down the tracks.

Adele knew where he was staying. "I will meet you there tomorrow."

Before he could answer, Adele had pulled away and was running back across the cinder yard toward the road.

The street lights came back on before she'd turned the corner to her home. She hurried along praying to Christ Jesus and Holy Mother Mary every step of the way, praying that Alex had not woken up, that he had not seen her chasing after Manfred, that he was not standing by the door waiting.

She came in the back way. It was dark in the kitchen. She couldn't remember if the light had been turned off before the storm or not. She could see a glow coming from the front room. She slipped out of her soaked shoes and walked down the hall. The fan was still whirling noisily in the bedroom. She opened the door. Alex was sprawled crossways across the bed, still hugging his pillow.

Adele went into the other room, pulled off her clothes, hid them under her dirty clothes pile and rubbed herself down until she stopped shivering.

She crawled in beside Alex. She had to lie crossways too, because she was afraid to wake him. The room felt cooler since the storm. She pulled a sheet over herself but left Alex naked and undisturbed. She lay there listening to his breathing. She tried to organize her thoughts.

The next morning Adele made Alex his usual breakfast and waited for him to go to work. Johnny honked his horn. Alex told her for the third or fourth time that he'd be calling the Melmac company as soon as he could from the public phone in the post office downtown.

"Wish me luck."

Adele kissed him hard.

Alex's blue eyes opened in mock surprise.

"Good luck," Adele said.

He went out to meet Johnny. Adele watched the car disappear down the street. She waited to see if Dorothy might come over carrying her coffee mug and her cigarettes. She didn't. Adele began to gather up some food to take out to Manfred. Just after nine o'clock the factory's truck pulled up and delivered a supply of unfinished socks to both houses. She made herself wait until ten o'clock, when Dorothy would be sure to be immersed in her work.

The air outside felt heavy, almost steamy with floating layers of suspended mist. Adele hurried through the back streets with a sack of groceries over her shoulder, skirting puddles and keeping her face down. She cut through a field of weeds and began to walk along a rutted makeshift road beside the railway tracks.

Almost immediately she could see Manfred standing in the distance waiting for her. He began to walk her way. His brown tweed jacket looked disreputable in the daylight – so did his pants and he was definitely carrying one shoulder lower than the other. Adele's heart ached.

"Good morning," he said, "what have you got there?" His smile was almost as boyish and just as heart-stopping as it had always been.

"Food. I thought you might want some food. I prayed to God all night, Manfred. I haven't prayed for such a long time. I thanked Him that you were alive. I thanked Him that you found me."

Manfred took the sack from off her shoulder. "I prayed, too. I am thankful that you have discovered such a good life." Manfred looked down the railway tracks as if he were expecting to see a train. "Thank you for the food." He picked up Adele's hand and held it. "You must return home now. It is not good for us to be seen together." He dropped her hand and simply said, "Goodbye."

Manfred began to walk back the way he'd come. Adele followed along after him.

"Go away," Manfred said.

"Where are you going?"

"Back to where I live. I will be leaving this afternoon."

"How?"

"By train. I have a reservation."

"We have to talk, Manfred. You can't come all the way to Canada just to say hello. You can't just go away." Adele caught up to him and took him by his arm. "You're stupid, you know, if you think I'm just going to give up. Don't you remember what I'm like? Don't you remember anything?"

Manfred looked away. "I remember," he said.

Adele continued to walk along beside him. "I looked for you for so long."

Manfred didn't reply and he kept his face away.

They walked together until they came to a path leading from the tracks. Adele could see a group of men dressed almost as poorly as Manfred standing on a slope in front of a collection of huts. They were staring down at her.

"This is where I live," Manfred said.

The men began to walk toward them. Adele didn't think they looked very welcoming. A short older man with bushy hair pushed himself to the front. "We don't want trouble here," he said in English.

Adele turned to Manfred and continued to speak in French. "What's the matter?"

"You should go now."

"Why don't they want me here?"

"It's not you they don't want here," Manfred said.

The older man came a step closer. "You go back to town. That's a good woman. This is not a place for you."

"I'm not leaving," Adele said to Manfred.

Manfred began to talk in a language Adele didn't understand. The bushy-haired man waved his arms around and spoke in the same language. The other men gathered around and continued to glower.

Manfred seemed to be staying surprisingly calm given the situation, Adele thought. She didn't remember him being calm.

"Come on, Adele." He took her hand and they began to skirt around the camp. He led her through a field of wild grass and up the side of a hill. Adele looked back. There were more men now. They were all watching.

Manfred stopped in front of a faded awning and pulled it aside. There was a dark opening underneath. "Socks only," Manfred said, standing on a soggy piece of cardboard. He kicked off his worn shoes.

"What is this?" Adele said, and thought, Please don't say it's where you live.

"I'm staying here. Just for now." Manfred knelt down and began to back into the hole, dragging the sack along after him. "If you don't mind tight spaces you may enter."

Manfred disappeared from her sight.

Adele looked back at the men. They were obviously waiting to see what she'd do. She pulled off her shoes and looked inside the hole. "Manfred?"

"Come on," Manfred said from somewhere under the ground.

A light flickered down the passageway. She could see his shoes tied with odd looking pieces of twine. She could see his pant legs. Adele crawled inside.

Manfred was sitting on a pile of grass in a little room. Adele wiggled by his feet and sat down beside him. The grass felt soft and dry and smelled sweet. It rustled when she moved. A candle was flickering on a small plank shelf. Another plank held a few cans of food. An old coat was stuffed in one corner. Her sack of groceries was sitting on top of it.

"If that candle falls we'll burn to death," Adele said.

"It won't fall."

"I thought you lived with those other men."

"As it turned out my Polish is not as good as I thought it was. Anyway, I am grateful to them for this place. They have much reasons to hate me."

"But you didn't do anybody any harm. You didn't fight."

Manfred's eyes caught hers in the soft light. "Everyone fought. Back in Germany everyone did. Boys thirteen years old manned machine guns."

"Manfred, how long have you been living here?"

"It's not so bad as it looks. It's cool in the day. It was dry last night."

"How long?"

"Five days."

It was impossible. Like an animal.

"I saw you last night. You and your husband."

"Did you?"

"When you left your house together. And when you came back. You looked very happy."

He was giving her one last chance. She had spent the night weighing everything, weighing her heart. She knew what she had to say. "Yes, we are happy." The words seemed to tear at her throat.

After a moment, Manfred said, "I am glad."

When Adele dared to glance his way, his eyes seemed full of light. "We should go back outside, Adele. The men might be getting the wrong idea."

They sat on the grassy slope in front of Manfred's shelter. Adele had made two cold roast beef sandwiches, the bread cut extra-thick and lathered in mustard. Manfred ate them both. A breeze had come up. It was blowing the grass in waves in front of them. The men had grown bored and had disappeared.

Adele nibbled on some crackers and a sliver of cheese to keep Manfred company though she didn't feel hungry. She opened up a jar of her mother-in-law's plum preserves. Manfred seemed to like them.

"You don't smoke any more?"

"I would if I had some."

"I will get you some money."

Manfred shook his head.

"I am so sorry I was late getting to Paris!"

Manfred nodded. He gazed out across the countryside for a moment, and then he got up on his feet. "Let's go for a walk," he said.

They circled around the camp again, crossed the tracks and made their way down to the river. Manfred led her to a large slanting willow with a bough suspended over the water. Manfred walked out on it balancing himself. Adele followed him. They sat down together. Manfred seemed pleased that she was there. Adele felt enormously pleased, too, that he was pleased. The river slipped beneath their feet.

"Manfred? What happened to your shoulder?"

"Shrapnel. Nothing to speak about."

"No?"

Manfred shook his head. "No."

"And after the war? What happened after the war?"

"I went home to Dresden. It was not good in Dresden. No one was there."

I know, Adele thought, I know.

"I tried to cross into Poland. I had aunts and uncles in Poland. I thought perhaps there might be some small chance my mother and father had fled there. The Russians arrested me. Held me in a camp. One day they put me on a workers' train to their country but I got away. I went back to Rouen instead." Manfred broke off a small branch and began to pinch off the leaves. "After that I returned to Germany carrying your address in my pocket. There were Displaced Person camps everywhere. A very stupid idea struck me. I could pass for Polish. I could apply to come here."

Light from the water was dancing on his face. It reminded Adele of La Bouille. We will be the New Europe, she had said. Some place deep inside Adele was bleeding. She could feel it. Manfred started to drop leaves into the river.

"The head man in the camp, he has English. We made a deal. He would go to the post office and find where Alex Wells lived, and I would leave this place. As it turns out you lived not far from here."

Adele was fighting back tears.

"Your husband doesn't know anything about me, does he?"

"No. Manfred, you can't leave. You have to let me help you."

"I don't need you to help. Do you think I've survived this long, not to be able to build a life here in this land? Everyone has money here."

"You don't. Not right now. You can't even speak English. I have money."

"I don't need any."

Adele got up abruptly and almost fell in the water. She knew what she'd do, though, she'd return with every cent she'd saved from her piecework and stuff it in his pockets. And wherever he went he'd have to write her. He'd have to swear that he would tell her where he was staying.

Adele climbed off the branch and hurried back up the slope to the railway tracks. When Manfred caught up, she told him what she was going to do.

He shook his head. "That's not why I came here."

"I know. It doesn't matter."

"I can't do it."

"For me, you can."

"I cannot accept."

"You don't have to accept. Just wait for me!" Adele didn't trust herself to kiss him. She turned and hurried away. When she looked back Manfred was still standing beside the tracks.

The sky had settled down so low it seemed to Adele all she needed to do was reach up to touch it. A random drop of rain fell on her face. She stumbled over some rough ground.

She had always known this moment would arrive, the moment to tell Alex the truth. She had waited for it for over a year and now it was here. If she found just the right words, he would be sure to understand. Alex understood war. He understood desperation. He might even help Manfred. He might help him get a place to stay. And a job.

Adele left the rutted trail and waded back through the field of weeds. When she reached the street, she began to run.

CANADA, 1946

CHAPTER FORTY-ONE

• • •

"A French woman?" Jack asked.

Joe nodded.

"How does she fit in?"

"She visited the German. They talked in French. We knew this much but could not understand."

"What did she look like?"

"Like she would bring us trouble."

"How old was she?"

"Young. I don't know. Twenty. The German was carrying a sack of food she must have given. She stayed some hours. The next day the German was gone. That is all we know." Joe looked out the window. "You will give back our landing papers."

Jack looked out the window, too. He thought he saw a shifting in the swirling dark. "Sure."

"When?"

"Soon."

"And my good job?"

"There's only one more thing you have to do." Jack moved his face close enough for Joe to see it. "Keep your mouth shut."

"I know who you mean," Joe replied.

Jack drove back down the rough trail grinning to himself as he bounced along. The German had come a long way just to get killed.

Jack walked down the stairs and into the police station with the Luger

tucked jauntily inside his belt. Harold Miles was nowhere in sight. He slipped
the gun back in his desk drawer and locked it up. All he had to do now was
find a woman who could speak French and looked like trouble. It was
strange, though, that if she was actually from France and was living in town
he hadn't heard about her. Where the hell had he been these last weeks?
Months?

For four years.

Jack forced that thought out of his mind.

Of course, the woman could have driven in from some other town.
She could have come from almost anywhere. The German had been a minor
clerk during the war, Joe had said. And he'd also said, Look to yourselves.
That part was still unclear. Did he mean the woman? Or someone else?
Maybe someone from town had taken exception to that woman bringing him
food, spending the time she did out there, doing whatever she was doing.
In fact, so great an exception that he blew the German's brains out.

There were enough crazies around town to do the job, God only knew.
Soldiers who'd returned home alcoholic. Or half wild. Or broken. Or all three.

Some hadn't made it home at all.

Jack looked at the wall clock. Almost ten. He had the whole goddamn
night to get through.

He looked at the two filing cabinets across the room. He walked over
to the one that held police reports. It was somewhere to start, anyway, something to do.

Jack pulled open a drawer and thumbed through the files. *Drunk and
Disorderly*. Mainly fist fights. And the infamous night when two carloads of
air force vets decided to blast every mailbox in the township off the top of
their posts. And the explosions at the gravel pit. Live grenades. That was a
good one. And a fine for dangerous use of a firearm within town limits. Todd
Westland had written that one up. He didn't describe the weapon, though.
Just wrote *hand gun*.

Fucking idiot.

Jack stopped. He looked back at the gravel pit report. One of the grenade
boys and the dangerous firearm fellow had the same name. Jack continued on.
He pulled out a report by Jock White. Jack remembered this one. Someone

had been shooting beer bottles off a fence in a backyard. Kids were coming home from school. His landlady had complained and the man had received a five-dollar ticket. According to the report, the gun had sentimental value to the accused and so had not been confiscated.

German Luger, Jock had written down. And the man's name and address. The name was the same as in the two previous reports.

One of the crazy ones, Jack thought.

• • •

The town's cruiser pulled up in front of a rambling one-storey house in an area of the town called The Flats. Jack could see a light glowing faintly through the front window. He got out, strode up on the veranda and pressed the buzzer.

After a while an outside light went on and a heavy-set woman opened the door.

"Mrs. Taylor?"

"Oh, hello Jack," she said.

He didn't recognize her but it was always a small and constant source of pleasure to know for certain that everyone in town knew him. Jack took off his cap. "Sorry to bother you this late."

"That's quite all right. You come on in."

Jack stepped in to the carpeted hallway, ducking his head a little to avoid banging it on the door frame.

"Is there some trouble?"

"Just looking after some unpaid fines."

"Oh well, I wouldn't know." She looked a little startled.

"Not you, Mrs. Taylor. A boarder of yours by the name of John Watson. He lives here, doesn't he?"

"Well, I'm not surprised," she said. "And no. Johnny Watson does not live here. Not any longer."

"There was a shooting incident in your backyard."

"Yes, there certainly was, and you can believe me when I say that Mr. Watson left shortly thereafter."

"You wouldn't happen to know where he moved?"

"You bet I do. Just out of pure spite he didn't pay his last month's board and I had to send my husband chasing after him." She pulled out a small drawer in a telephone stand and shuffled through some papers. "Here it is." She handed Jack a torn envelope with an address written on the back.

Jack pulled out his notebook to jot it down. His pencil suspended itself in mid-air. It was his daughter-in-law's address.

CANADA, 1946

CHAPTER FORTY-TWO

• • •

Johnny Watson's car was already pulled up on Dorothy's lawn when Adele reached home. It wasn't quite five o'clock.

He must have gotten off work early, Adele thought. She turned into the path that led to her own back door. She looked up. Alex was watching her from the front window.

Adele slowed down. Her breath caught in her throat.

Why was he home? She waved her hand a little, tried to smile, and hurried around to the back of the house.

The kitchen was empty. The house was silent. She expected Alex to come in from the front room but he didn't. A letter and an envelope were lying on the kitchen table beside Alex's famous blue book. The envelope was addressed to Adele, in care of Alex Wells. Lucille Rocque had written her return address on the top left corner.

"It took me all day to translate," Alex said.

Adele looked up.

Alex was leaning in the front room's doorway now. His eyes were reddened and bruised-looking. His face looked blotched.

"It was addressed to me," Adele said. Her voice sounded thin and faraway. It sounded lost.

"Your friend is worried about you," Alex said.

"Why did you open it?" She knew this was wildly beside the point but she didn't know what else to say. She just needed some time to think. Maybe this was best, that Lucille should write. It was the final push she needed to tell Alex everything.

"She gave the name of our town to the Squarehead," he said. His mouth was moving thickly like he'd been drinking. "Your German. After a while she began to worry. She thought he might try to come over here."

"Alex," Adele said. That's all she could think to say. "Alex."

"I know. You thought he was dead. He's not. So I hear."

Johnny Watson came out of the front room. "Hello, Adele," he said.

"Johnny saw you with someone on the road last night." Alex crossed the kitchen unsteadily and looked out the window. "Down on the road, actually. In the rain."

Adele looked at Johnny. He shrugged.

"Jesus Christ!" Alex bellowed. He was holding on to the sink with both hands.

Adele went up to him but she didn't dare touch him. "I was sixteen. Just sixteen. He was a clerk. That's all. He worked in an office."

"You saw him again today. Johnny followed you out there. Lucille's letter came." Alex's face was pale as death. "My lucky day."

"We were children, Alex! We didn't know what we were doing, the world was mad, we only had each other! Dear Alex!"

"We fought sixteen-year-olds, Adele. Trained by the SS."

"They were the worst," Johnny said.

"Manfred didn't fight!" Adele cried out.

"Oh yeah? Well, that's news," Johnny said. "Never saw one of those. Too bad we couldn't tell that to the boys swimming around in their own guts. 'Don't worry! There's a pacifist Kraut out there somewhere, boys!'" Johnny's face broke into a crooked grin. He strode across the kitchen. "Let's go," he said to Alex and banged out the door.

Alex's head was still lowered. Adele could hear him gasping for breath. She could see he was beginning to shake. She wrapped her arms around him and held him with all her might. "No, Alex, no." She pressed her head against his head until it hurt. "I love you, I love you! Please Alex! Manfred needs our help. That's all it is. He's a good person. He just needs our help!"

Alex's head came up. "Help," he said, as if it were the strangest word in the world. "Help?" He had his hand on the back of her neck, he had it in her hair. "I'll help." Alex swept his arm around and sent Adele spinning across the room. She slammed into the table. It caught her in the ribs. She fell against a chair.

Alex lurched down the steps and out the door.

"Alex," Adele screamed.

Dorothy appeared at the open door, her eyes wide, her hands to her face. "Oh God, Adele. I'm sorry."

Adele pushed by her, ran along the side of the house. She could hear Johnny's car roaring. He pulled up in front. Alex got in.

"Don't," Adele screamed, "don't!"

The car pulled away.

Adele began to run. She headed for the shortcut through the weedy field again, splashing through puddles down the dead-end street, her breath coming in little cries.

She was only halfway across the field when she saw Johnny's car speeding by the factory. She turned and began to run toward a fence and the countryside beyond. She climbed up on the rusty wires and jumped down on the other side. She ran toward the horizon. There was nothing in front of her but sky. Her throat felt scraped and bloody, her lungs flayed. She ran and ran.

She saw a long line of trees and a wooden fence. She climbed the fence and fell on the other side. She stumbled on for a few more steps and sank down to the ground.

Below she could see the circle of huts, and closer to her the awning spread out on the side of the hill. Johnny's car had already reached the camp. He was already walking up the path. Alex got out of the car and leaned against the fender as if he were going to be sick. His blond hair was blowing around in the wind. Some of the men came out to intercept Johnny. They seemed to be arguing with him.

Adele got up and started to run down the hill. She didn't look at the camp, she concentrated on the awning. "Manfred!" She fell on the cardboard in front of the entrance. "Manfred!" There was no answer. She looked back down the slope.

Johnny was pushing his way through the men. He was waving something around in his hand. Alex was walking up to the men now, too.

"Adele!" Manfred had come around the other side of the camp and he was angling up the slope through the wild grass. Adele could tell by his smiling face that, though he'd seen her, he hadn't seen the car pull up.

"Stay there!" she screamed out.

Johnny looked up at the sound of her voice. He stared straight up the hill toward her. Adele could see now that it was a gun he was carrying, glinting a warning in the weak light. Adele ran toward Manfred. "He's going to kill you!"

Manfred grabbed her hand and they turned back the way he'd come, running down into a ravine and up the other side.

"I can't go any further," Adele cried out.

Manfred wouldn't let her go.

They started to run along the railway tracks, heading away from town. Adele was gasping, stumbling, she couldn't breathe. "He won't hurt me. You go. Go!"

"You don't know that," Manfred said.

She was slowing him down. She yanked to get free. He held on. She couldn't go much further. She couldn't feel her legs.

Adele looked back.

Johnny's car was coming along the side of the tracks. Adele yanked furiously at his hand. "Run!"

He still wouldn't let go. She could hear the roar of the car's motor. They stumbled on. A path opened up through some thickets.

"Down here," Manfred said.

They were running under a long canopy of leaves. It felt cool and dark. Adele could hear the car braking behind them and a door slamming closed. They stopped and stood there panting. A second door slammed closed. They ran on until the path branched off in opposite directions.

"You go on. Go on," Adele said, "I'll wait for Alex."

Manfred didn't look convinced.

"Alex won't let him hurt me."

"How do you know?"

"I know. Run. Go!"

Manfred reluctantly let go of her hand, took a last look and disappeared. Adele turned to face the way they'd come. There was no sound of running footsteps. No sound of anything. She stepped off the path and hid herself deeper in the thickets. She told herself that if Alex was with Johnny, she'd step out of her hiding place. And if he wasn't, she didn't know what she'd do.

She peered through the leaves and tried to control the sound of her breathing. She should have seen them by now. Heard them. Heard something. Where were they?

She crouched lower and tried to see behind and to the sides but she was surrounded by a thick wall of leaves. She went back to watching the path. It was cool and felt damp on her knees where she knelt. She listened. There were no sounds.

No bird sounds, Adele thought. Or squirrels. Insects. Nothing. It was as if the world had died. And then she did hear a sound. Before she could turn, Johnny had clamped his hand over her face.

"If you yell, I'll kill you," he said. He braced his knee against her back. "Want to try?"

He began to draw her farther into the bush. She tried to get to her feet. He began to climb up a steep hill. Adele fell to her knees. He caught her by the collar of her blouse and dragged her up over rotting logs and through dead branches, sliding her through wet leaves and pools of water.

"Get up, bitch. Filthy fucking bitch. Get up!"

And bombs had fallen somewhere, acrid smoke, terrible faces, words. "The Kraut fucked you last night, didn't he? Fucked you again today."

Adele could hear a drum. The shake of a tambourine. The fierce young widow. "Buttercup," the button-eyed woman said.

"You filthy fucking bitch!"

She became a dead weight, her blouse half ripped off, her clothes black with muck. She could hear Johnny moaning and panting somewhere above her. She could feel him let her go. He was moving through some trees, clinging to a branch, leaning out into space.

"Oh Jesus," he said. He sounded excited. "Jesus Christ, yes," he said. He swung his gun up and aimed.

The noise was deafening. It reverberated through the trees, the sky, Adele's head. She crawled up the rest of the way. She was on the top of a cliff.

Far below she could see Alex standing knee deep in the river. He seemed to be looking up at her. He looked amazed. She could see Manfred sliding and scrambling across the face of the cliff.

"Don't shoot, goddamn it!" Alex bellowed.

Johnny raised the gun again.

"No," Adele screamed.

The gun roared and jumped in his hand.

Manfred fell and rolled down the muddy cliff and into the river. He got up on his knees. Alex waded over to him and stood in front of him, protecting him.

"You goddamn idiot," Alex was screaming up the cliff face. He started to climb up.

Johnny stared down at him as if he couldn't quite figure out what Alex was doing.

Alex took two steps up and slid back into the river again. He struggled up three steps, digging his boots in, and slid back down.

Johnny began to laugh. He turned to Adele. "He wants you to get fucked again."

Adele ran back down the hill. Over logs. Through dead branches. Sliding. Falling. Tumbling down.

Johnny crashed on top of her.

They slid down hill, Adele screaming and kicking. His weight was pressing her down, he had his free hand around her throat. "Look what I've got," he said. His eyes were opening impossibly wide. Saliva was hanging out of his mouth. His hand was tightening. "This is our break-out day, boys! This is the day we get out of here! Give them hell!"

Adele could feel the cold steel of the gun scraping up between her legs.

"Don't," Adele tried to scream. "Don't."

"Give them hell!" The gun jammed up against her, pushed inside.

Adele did scream.

Alex loomed over both of them, picked Johnny up, and threw him through the air. The gun went flying but Johnny was up in a blur. He kicked Alex between the legs. He held his shirt with both his hands and kicked him again. Alex fell. Johnny kicked him in the face.

"Retreat," he was screaming at the top of his lungs, "get the hell out of here!"

Adele picked up the gun, brought it to within an inch of Johnny's head and squeezed the trigger. A bullet tore through the back and out the front. Blood followed, blossoming out of his forehead, opening up like a slow red fan. Pieces of brain pattered against the nearby leaves. Adele could hear the sound of each piece. She hadn't heard the sound of the gun at all.

Johnny spun away from her and, gentle as a sleepy child, sank down to the ground.

"Oh Jesus God," Alex moaned. He knelt down and picked Johnny up in his arms. Johnny's head lolled to the side. Red foam hung down.

"Oh Jesus," Alex said. He started to walk, then run through the trees. "Oh Jesus!"

Adele and Manfred followed Alex upriver. They walked along the dry riverbed when there was some, and waded through the shallows when there wasn't, waiting for him to slow down, waiting for him to stop.

After a long time Alex climbed up on a bank and sat down. Only his head was showing above the tall silvery grass. They climbed up toward him. He was still cradling Johnny in his lap.

Adele collapsed on the ground facing the other way. Manfred went back to the river and sat down on a boulder. After a while she could hear Manfred's voice. "Tell your husband I didn't mean this. Tell your husband I would never have come here if I had known this."

Adele looked at Alex. "Manfred is saying he wouldn't have come here. Not if he had a chance to do it again. He never would."

Alex stared across the river.

"Don't hate me," she said.

Alex continued to stare across the river.

"I just want to go to sleep," Adele moaned, "please God."

A mist was beginning to rise off the river. The invisible sun was setting behind the clouds. Adele put her head down on her knees. She couldn't believe what she'd done. She thought of her father. She wished she could see him again. She wished he was sitting in his office and she was pushing the door open and she was five years old again and instead of being annoyed, his face would light up. If only she could begin her life again.

"It's not your fault."

Alex's choked voice came from somewhere. Her body felt like it weighed an infinity of days and nights, an infinity of red-headed soldiers, an infinity of running and lying.

"Knew something like this would happen. All along," Alex said.

And the blood fanned out. And his brains pattered against the leaves. Who was she really, deep inside? She thought of Monsieur Ducharme. She thought of René. She had no idea.

"I didn't know what to do," Alex was saying. "We were the only ones left from thirty men. The only ones alive. But I didn't know how to help him. His mother had died. He had no one here."

"I killed him," Adele said.

"But I saw what he was doing. I saw it, Adele."

"I killed him!"

"To protect me. The both of us. He didn't give you a choice."

Adele wished that that were true, wished it with all her being but she knew what she had felt. A wild joy, an exaltation, the moment her finger had touched the trigger.

Alex let Johnny go. His limp body slid slowly down Alex's legs and rolled face down into the grass. The air seemed thick, a gritty darkening grey. Bats flew crazy loops over the river.

"What does he want to do?" It was Manfred again, almost forgotten.

"Manfred wants to know what you want to do."

Alex turned to look at him. "So this is your friend?"

"Yes."

"And all you wanted to do was to help him?"

"Yes."

Alex seemed to study Manfred for a long time. "What happened to the gun?"

"Manfred took it from me. He threw it in the river."

Alex nodded.

"We have to tell the police," Adele said.

"Do we? You wouldn't have a chance, Adele. Not with the police or anyone else." Alex stood up. "Tell Manfred I'll need his help. We have to find something we can use to dig. He's a soldier, he'll be used to that." He looked back toward some trees.

Adele got up. "Oh God, Alex, don't!"

Alex started walking farther up the slope. "Tell your friend he'll have to take off his clothes."

· · ·

It was dark by the time they drove Johnny's car back past the camp. Manfred had taken a long time washing the blood off Johnny's clothes. He was wearing them now and he was driving. Alex was sitting beside him. He'd said that if anyone from the camp were watching it would look like the same two men were heading back to town. Besides, Manfred was proving to Alex that he could drive.

Adele was lying in the back, rocking about, feeling numb and sick. She'd watched them dig the grave. Make their plans. Everything. She'd translated for them. And now she was sick.

They bumped across the tracks. Adele could see Alex signal Manfred to drive down a side street toward the edge of the Junction. As soon as they'd cleared the last house Alex motioned for him to slow down. Adele could feel the car pull off the road, slant down and stop. The motor died, the lights went off.

Alex turned to look at her. She could hardly see his face in the dark. "I'll walk back and tell Dorothy that Johnny lost control. He shot Manfred with that damn Luger of his. We buried Manfred and Johnny's heading out west. He said for me to tell her he loves her, that he'll be calling her as soon as he feels its safe."

Alex turned the ceiling light off and opened the door.

"Give me a few minutes and then sneak back into the house." He looked over at Manfred. "The gas tank's almost full. I've given your friend all the money Johnny and I had on us. He's smart. He'll be all right."

Adele didn't answer. Alex was poised in the open doorway. She knew what he was thinking. He was leaving her with Manfred and he wasn't absolutely certain what she'd do.

"I'll see you soon," he said and closed the door.

Manfred was waiting patiently behind the steering wheel. He and Alex had come to an agreement earlier. It would be Manfred's responsibility to get rid of Johnny's car.

Adele sat up. "Manfred? None of this is going to work. You don't even know where you are. How will you know where to drive? How will you know where to hide a car?"

"It is not so difficult, you know."

Adele could feel his smile though she couldn't see it.

"I will drive in the opposite direction. I will drive all night. And in the morning I will find a place with deep water."

"Will you?"

"Yes. And then I will sink it."

"And then what? What are you going to do? Where are you going to go?" Adele could feel a stream of tears running down her face. "I know what you're going to do. You're going to stay in the car."

"You think I am weak. Is that it?"

"No!"

"You think I can't live without you?"

"No!"

"You don't know me any more."

"I'm so afraid for you!"

"I found you. Didn't I? And you still love me. Is this not true?"

"Yes!"

"This is all I needed to know. Wanted to know. Don't you see?"

"No!"

"Shhh," Manfred whispered, "shhh. Trust me. Adele, I am ready to find a new life here."

"Swear it to me!"

She could feel his hand touch her hair, her wet cheek.

"Wasn't I in Paris waiting? Didn't I come looking for you in Rouen? What have I done that makes you think differently about what I say?"

"Swear it to me!"

"I swear it."

Adele found his lips. She kissed them hard. She fumbled for the door and got out.

They were parked in a field. Adele found the roadway again. She could see the lights of the Junction in front of her.

She walked toward them.

CANADA, 1946

CHAPTER FORTY-THREE

• • •

J ack could tell Dorothy had had too much to drink before she opened the door. It was an instinct first developed as a child by living with his father and then honed to a fine edge by forty years of police work. It had to do with the sound of her uncertain footsteps on the two steps down to the door, the sound of her hand brushing against the wall.

"Holy smoke," she said, "if it isn't Jack. Two visits in less than a week. This must be some kind of record."

"I know it's late. I won't keep you long."

"Keep me as long as you want. I don't care."

Dorothy went back into the kitchen. Jack followed her. A bottle and glass were sitting on the table alongside a green ashtray holding one of her constant, smouldering cigarettes.

"I was working late. Set a record for boxes today. Thought I'd celebrate before I went to bed." Dorothy sat down heavily on a chair. "Have a drink, Jack. Grab a glass out of the cupboard."

Jack opened up a cupboard door.

"The next one over."

Jack found a glass, sat down at the table and poured himself a healthy shot. She was watching him more closely now. Jack had the distinct impression that she knew what he was going to ask before he asked it. He turned his glass around in his hand. Let her stew for a moment, he thought. He took a drink.

"Well, what brings you here?"

Jack looked at her, not unpleasantly, but not pleasantly, either.

"In the middle of the night," she said. "What's the goddamn time, anyway? Excuse my English."

Jack looked at his watch. "It isn't that late, Dorothy. It's not past eleven."

"I go to bed early these days." She picked up her cigarette. She flicked the ash off.

"Do you know a John Watson?"

She studied her cigarette. She put it between her lips. "John Watson?"

"Yeah."

"That's a peculiar question."

"It's just a question, Dorothy."

"I don't think I'm required to discuss my private life with my father-in-law. Or am I?" Dorothy's eyes hardened. "My ex-father-in-law."

"It's a police matter."

"Is it? My life is a police matter? That's good."

"It doesn't have to do with your private life. It just has to do with the whereabouts of John Watson."

"I don't know where he is."

"Why not?"

"I just don't."

"He doesn't live here any more?"

Dorothy got up. She turned her back to him and looked out the window. She didn't seem to be looking at anything in particular. Just smoking. Besides, it was pitch black out.

Jack pulled the Luger out from under his jacket and laid it down on the table with a clatter.

Dorothy turned at the sound. "Jesus Christ," she said.

"Look familiar?"

"No."

"It's John Watson's gun."

"How do you know that?"

"Fished it out of the river."

For just a heartbeat, panic tightened her face and widened her eyes.

It was just long enough for Jack to see it. She went back to the table, butted out her cigarette and lit up another one.

"I have another question for you."

"I'm tired, Jack. Why don't you finish up your drink, pick that thing up and go."

"Did John Watson happen to know a French woman?"

"Is Johnny back?" George was standing in his pyjamas at the end of the hall and staring at the Luger.

"Get back to bed," Dorothy said.

"That's his gun." George came up to the table. "He showed it to me."

"Do you know a French woman, George?" Jack asked.

"She lives next door."

"Go to bed!" Dorothy spun him around and aimed him back the way he came.

Jack got up. "No. That's all right. Come here, George."

"Go to bed!" Dorothy gave the boy another shove and turned on Jack. "Leave us alone!"

"I would, Dorothy, but I can't." He watched George, looking frightened, disappear into his bedroom. "The woman next door and the gun on your table connect up with that body. You know, that body you were asking me about the other day?"

Dorothy leaned up against the hall. She looked suddenly stricken by something.

"Where's John Watson?"

"Looking for work. Somewhere. I don't know where."

"Is he coming back?"

Dorothy stared at her cigarette as if it might have an answer. She brushed her thick hair away from her face. "We may be leaving here. George and I may be going away somewhere else to live."

"Where?"

"I don't know yet."

Jack nodded. "Well, Watson won't be doing anything until he answers some questions. Same with that woman." Jack started for the door.

"She isn't there."

"Where is she?"

"Look, Jack, I don't know anything. I really don't. And I don't believe that's Johnny's gun. He's just looking for work."

He could tell she was lying. He could always tell when people were lying. He stood in the middle of the room and waited.

Dorothy came back into the kitchen. She sat down. "She's Alex Wells's wife. You know, the Wells who own the hardware store."

"Yeah?"

"Ask Alex. He's Johnny's best friend. He'll tell you Johnny didn't do anything. He'll set you straight."

"He's next door. Is he?"

"No. They're somewhere else. It's vacation time for some people, Jack. They're on a holiday."

"Where?"

Dorothy hesitated. "He'll set you straight." She seemed to be convincing herself.

"I'd appreciate that," Jack said. He picked up the Luger and tucked it back in his belt. "Where is he?"

"I think his family has a cottage. I think its near Port Ryerse."

Dorothy looked like she was about to cry. "It's somewhere down there. He'll set you straight."

"All right, Dorothy."

Jack headed for the door. He turned back.

"By the way, you won't be taking my grandson anywhere."

CANADA, 1946

CHAPTER FORTY-FOUR

• • •

Alex had been walking through a nightmare for three weeks. He didn't have any other way to think about it. Adele had told him it would be like that. A nightmare. He'd thought they could get through it. He'd even called Melmac and made an appointment, but when the time came to get on the train he couldn't make himself climb up the steps. He was at the train station, he was all dressed up, but he couldn't move. He couldn't sleep, either. He couldn't concentrate on his factory work. He began to get the shakes again despite the pills.

One night Adele found him crouched in the corner of the kitchen. He was calling out co-ordinates and degrees, he was orientating the heavy guns. It was the same night that the news had travelled around town that a body had been found by the river.

Adele had gone over that moment in the woods a thousand times. The gun landing at her feet, picking it up, taking a step toward Johnny, feeling the sudden searing pain from where he'd brutalized her. And fear. And a rage so deep, so powerful, it had taken over her whole body and mind. And finally, release. That's as close as she could come to describing the feeling. A release from everything and everyone.

Of course it hadn't been any kind of a release and the feeling had lasted less than a second. And now? She didn't even know what now was. She only knew that the life they were trying to live couldn't last. It was her refuge from complete despair, the knowledge that it couldn't last.

Dorothy had stayed closeted in her house, too, thinking whatever thoughts she was thinking.

And the days dragged by.

Alex came home from work early one afternoon, put on a painful show of cheerfulness and said he thought they should go to a cottage his parents owned. It was empty at the moment and Ray would give them a lift down.

"Anyway, I have to get away," he said.

"For how long?" Adele asked.

"I don't know. Until things get better."

Adele nodded.

"You'll like it down there," he said.

● ● ●

Alex was on one of his early morning walks when he saw the chief of police coming along the beach. He'd been sitting in the sand dunes looking over the lake. He recognized Jack right away. Everyone in the town of Paris knew Jack Cullen. He was striding along the edge of the water in full uniform and a long way from where he was supposed to be.

Alex wondered if Jack would notice him or if he'd just walk by. It didn't matter, he'd find the Wellses' cottage soon enough. There was no question in Alex's mind who Jack was looking for.

The chief saw him and walked up to the foot of the dunes. "Morning."

"Good morning," Alex replied.

"You wouldn't know where the Wells' cottage is, would you? Gordon Wells?"

"Hello, Jack," Alex said.

"Well, hell," Jack grinned, "I've seen you in the store. Alex, right?"

"Right."

"I must be getting old."

"That's all right. I've been away."

"Yes. I knew you'd been away. Army, wasn't it?"

Alex nodded.

"Alex, I've got a few questions for you. And I've got a couple for your wife."

334

"Do you, Jack?"

"Yes, I do."

The two men stared at each other. Alex got to his feet. "The cottage is just down here. I think Adele will be up by now."

They walked through the sand. The sun was dancing in front of them, a fiery red ball balancing on the very edge of the lake. "It's been hot," Jack said.

"Yeah."

"It's going to be hot again today. Have you ever seen it so hot?"

"No."

Alex wasn't going to ask the chief of police just what kind of questions he was planning to ask. He was going to stay calm and he was going to wait. He had his story ready. He wasn't sure about Adele, though.

"I understand John Watson's a friend of yours."

"An army buddy. Right. He worked in town for a while but he got bored, I guess. You know how it is. It's hard to settle down. I mean, as a civilian."

"I know," Jack said.

"He went off somewhere. He said he'd write. And away he went."

"Think of that," Jack said.

They stepped from the sand up onto a wooden platform in front of a small cottage. "Just let me check first to make sure my wife's dressed. All right?" Alex opened the screen door.

"Fine," Jack said.

The cottage was on top of a sand ridge in a line of about ten similar cottages. Jack stepped down off the platform as casually as he could and went for a little stroll. He glanced behind the building. He didn't want anyone making an exit out the back. He looked across the lake. Water as far as he could see. The sun had cleared the horizon. It was brighter now, too. Jack could feel the heat of it on his face.

"Come on in, Jack." Alex was holding the screen door open.

Adele had been asleep.

"It's the police chief from home," Alex had whispered to her, waking her up. "This is what we're going to do."

She'd pulled her housecoat on and forced a brush through her hair, and now she was running some water into her mother-in-law's coffee pot. She wasn't sure what she was feeling. As if she were sleepwalking. And frightened, too, but her fear seemed a long way away, it seemed like it was standing outside the cottage somewhere.

Adele turned at the sound of his boots on the floor. She saw a giant of a man, much taller than Alex. He was in a dark blue uniform and despite the heat, he had a cap and a wool tie on. He took off his cap. His hair was silver.

"This is Adele, my wife," Alex said, "Jack Cullen, chief of police."

"Sorry to bother you so early, Mrs. Wells," the policeman said.

"I'll make you a coffee."

"That would be nice. You speak English."

"Yes."

"You're French, though."

"Yes."

"I knew that Alex had come home with a war bride. Heard that from somewhere. But I'd forgotten you were French. Or maybe nobody told me that part."

His eyes had almost no colour. Adele turned away and busied herself making the coffee.

"Sit down, Jack," Alex said.

Adele could hear the chairs scraping.

"Here's my problem." The policeman's rough voice again. "You know the body of that DP that was found up the river?"

"I heard about it," Alex said.

Adele was trying to measure out the coffee. Her hands were beginning to shake.

"I have reason to believe he was a German."

"Is that right?"

"In fact I know he was."

Adele could feel his eyes burning into her back.

"I found the gun he was shot with. I fished it out of the river."

Adele had to turn to face him. She couldn't bear the sound of his voice. When she did, she wasn't surprised to see that his colourless eyes were staring straight at her.

"It belonged to John Watson. And the thing is, the same day the German was killed I have witnesses that saw your wife out at the camp talking to him. She'd taken him food. They'd spent the day together."

There was disdain in his voice and on his face now. It crossed the room, it pressed up against her.

"John Watson was a close friend of yours. He disappears. The German turns up dead. And John Watson's gun is found at the murder site."

"The German was a soldier," Alex said, "and he'd been my wife's lover in Europe some time ago."

Adele could see the old man's face slowly light up. That's what he'd been thinking all along and now he'd been proved right.

"He'd followed her over here," Alex went on – nothing could stop him now. "The thing you have to know, though, Jack. Johnny Watson had fought his way all through France. All through Germany, too. Seen his friends die. Most of them. We'd been together through most of it and he loved me in his own way, do you understand, and he went mad. That's the only way I can explain it. There was this German soldier here, and he went mad."

The policeman wasn't looking at her any more, he was staring at Alex.

"I couldn't stop him. I couldn't do anything about it," Alex said.

Jack continued to stare at Alex. He nodded. "Where is he now?"

"I don't know."

The policeman turned to look at Adele. "You were a French girl. And he was a German soldier. I think there's a name for that."

Adele turned away. She closed her eyes.

"Who buried him?" she heard the big man say.

"Johnny did. I helped." Alex paused. "What are you going to do, Jack?"

"You're still living with this whore? You're still in the same room?"

"Yes," she heard Alex say.

"John Watson is in trouble. You're in trouble, too."

"We were in bigger trouble all during the war, Jack."

A silence fell in the room. It fell across the world.

"Tell her to turn around."

"Turn around, Adele," Alex said.

Adele opened her eyes and turned around.

"The food you took out. What did you feed him?"

"Sandwiches."

"And?"

"Some dessert."

"What?"

"Plums."

The policeman turned from her and looked out the window. "You did, did you?"

He got up from the table. He crossed the room. His massive chest was in front of her. His wool tie. She heard the sound deep in his throat. She'd heard that same sound before.

He spit in her face. Adele didn't bother to close her eyes. It ran hot down her cheek and across her mouth.

Alex didn't get up.

The screen door slammed against the side of the cottage like the sound of a gunshot. The chief of police had disappeared.

• • •

Jack roared back out the dirt road. It was narrow and he was going too fast. Tree branches flew past his open window, they whipped the side of the Studebaker. He'd taken his own car because he wasn't sure that the town cruiser would make it all the way to the lake and back. Normally he'd have cared about his own car, but he didn't care right now. He pressed the gas pedal down. The car shot out of the grove of trees and screeched on to a paved road. Jack rocked against the door. He aimed for the next hill and for the sky beyond.

He couldn't outrun it, a feeling of wild hatred and hopelessness beyond all reasoning, beyond all thinking away. He raced along beside the lake. Finally he slowed down and tried to think about the German soldier's little whore.

He could hardly make out her face but he could see as plain as day Alex Wells sitting there at the table. Just a young man, a kid almost. Shadows under his eyes. Shadows buried deep in his face.

What had he been through overseas? What had he seen?

Jack couldn't imagine.

The problem would be Harold Miles.

Jack didn't know what to do.

A bridge loomed up. It spanned the same river that ran through his own town but the river was much bigger here. It seemed as wide as a small lake. A stretch of white beach fanned out from its mouth into deeper water. And then nothing but lake. Miles and miles of open water all the way to the United States of America.

Jack reached the middle of the bridge and stopped. He got out of the car. Seagulls cried and wheeled over his head. The sun reflected off the water, bounced off the sky. Light leaped and shimmered and surrounded him.

Jack leaned against the railing. The water looked deep and cold straight down. This would be a good place to go fishing, Jack thought to himself. If only his son were standing beside him trying to sort out his line and his fishing pole. Kyle could take all day. He wouldn't mind.

Jack watched some seagulls land on the sand spit. They strutted about.

Looking for my son, Jack thought.

He didn't give a fuck about Harold Miles. A fuck about the mayor. Or the town.

Two Canadian soldiers. Two of our boys.

It felt right. For the first time in years, it felt just right.

Jack opened the door, opened the glove compartment and took out the Luger. There were no other cars in sight. No boats. Nothing but air and light. He began to run beside the railing, his heart felt like it was going to burst, he could hardly see where he was going. He flung the Luger out as far as he could throw. It sailed through the air, glinted back at him and disappeared with hardly a splash.

Jack stared at the spot for a long time. Until he couldn't see it any longer. He slumped his head down on the railing. He slumped down to the pavement below.

"Where's my son?" he said.

• • •

Alex wiped Adele's face off. He kissed her and held her and apologized over and over again. Adele just shook her head. It didn't matter. It had been Alex's plan and who knew, it might even work. It had to do with the chief of police having lost a son in the war.

"I didn't think he'd do that," Alex said.

"It's all right," Adele said. But she didn't feel all right.

They waited for the chief to come back all day, but he didn't come back.

They sat in the sand dunes that night. Alex held her in his arms. The stars seemed particularly close and especially bright.

"Someone somewhere probably knows all the names of those stars," Alex said, "but then again, I don't know. There must be millions."

Alex had hardly let her out of his sight. He'd held her in his arms almost as many times as there were stars, Adele had thought, trying to make up for what wasn't his fault or his doing. Even God couldn't undo what she'd done.

"Does that make us small?" Adele said.

"What?"

"Those millions of stars?"

"I don't know."

"My father used to say it didn't. It made us bigger. That's what he used to say."

The sand still felt warm from the sun. Adele let it run through her fingers. "Why do you think he asked about the food?"

"Let's not talk about it."

"Those plums came from your mother."

"I know."

"She gave me four jars. I gave two to Dorothy."

Alex looked at her. "Oh?" he said.

"Alex, this isn't going to last."

Alex looked out across the lake. "You keep saying that. It's lasted so far."

"I mean, for you and me. We won't be able to do it."

"You know what the alternative is."

"We'll find Manfred."

"No one will believe Manfred."

"It's not so difficult to understand what happened. And the police will listen to you."

"Adele, I can't go over this again."

"You're afraid I'll go to jail."

"I know you'll go to jail."

"And you, as well? You will go to jail?"

"I don't care about myself." And he didn't. She knew he didn't.

"You don't know what will happen," Adele said.

"Lets talk about the stars. Or go back inside."

"I know one thing. Some one thing everyone knows." She knew Alex wouldn't be able to resist the bait.

"What's that?"

"About whether we go to jail or not. It would be better to tell the truth now than after we're caught."

Alex just sat there. He didn't answer.

That night Adele had a dream. She was walking along a beach but it wasn't the beach by the lake, it was much wider and smoother and seemed to stretch out forever, sand and water and a far far distant sky. There was someone standing in the surf. As she came closer she could see that it was Étienne. Foam encircled his thin bare legs, it splashed against his leather breeches.

"What are you doing?" Adele asked.

He had the same patchy hair, the same yellowish skin, the same eyes of undiminished light.

"I'm looking for my family," he said.

Alex got up early the next morning while Adele was still sleeping, and sat in the dunes at the same place where he'd seen Jack the morning before. He half-expected to see him coming along again. He half-expected to see a phalanx of Ontario Provincial Police, too. He knew they'd been in town investigating for the last week, but no one armed with guns came by.

Adele and Alex stayed inside the cottage all that day. She didn't say anything more to Alex because she knew she didn't have to.

They went to bed early that night and although they hadn't made love for a long time, since before that day on the river, they made love that night, and they whispered "I love you" and Adele felt a weight of happiness she thought she'd lost fill her heart.

"What about your plans?" Alex said.

They were lying in each other's arms, their faces close together.

"What plans?"

"Nurses' assistant."

"Oh?" Adele said.

"Your hopes for the future and all that."

"It's all right."

Adele knew what they would do the next day. She knew exactly what Alex would decide. He'd call Ray and Ray would drive to the lake and take them back home. They would find the chief of police and they would tell him the truth.

And she would be who she was. And her history would be what it was. And she would never have to lie or hide again.

• • •

Brantford Expositor — November 24, 1946

The jury trial of Adele Wells (nee Georges), charged with manslaughter in the wrongful death of John Watson, and of her husband Alex Wells, charged with being an accessory after the fact, came to its end today in the county courthouse.

Prior to today's sentencing the jury, citing the right to self-defense and other mitigating circumstances, had found both defendants not guilty of the two serious charges against them, but both guilty on the lesser charges of committing an indignity to a dead body and of obstructing justice.

Today Chief Justice William Hastings, who had presided over the five-week trial, handed down a jail sentence of sixty days to both defendants. Mrs. Wells will be serving her time in the Brantford jail. Alex Wells will be incarcerated in Hamilton.

Despite a country-wide search, Manfred Halder, the illegal German refugee who was at the centre of this affair, has never been located.

• • •

Adele said she liked the prairies best, Alex voted for the mountains but by the time they'd reached the west coast of Vancouver Island, they knew they had finally arrived at the right place.

Alex found a job by the end of the first week refitting and repairing ocean-going pleasure craft at the local marina. Adele busied herself organizing their new home. She would have to wait for a while to look for work. In November, in the midst of the trial, Dr. Jerrison had confirmed what she'd already known. She was pregnant.

The child arrived on a windy April morning three weeks earlier than expected. Alex was already at work. Adele called to tell him that he'd better hurry back to take her into the hospital. She lay down on the bed to wait.

The baby pressed against her, becoming more insistent. Adele smiled to herself. She could hear the sounds of the surf from their modest clapboard house, she could imagine the long lines of waves sweeping in. Sweeping in.

And Étienne.

He was staring at her house. He was splashing toward her through the water.

ACKNOWLEDGEMENTS

• • •

In my background research for this novel, I would like to acknowledge two books of history that I found particularly helpful: *The Guns Of Normandy* by George G. Blackburn and *Occupation* by Ian Ousby.

This novel, quite literally, would not have been written without my wife Judi's continued tolerance of my being locked away in my writing room and for her remarkable insights into the heart of the story.

I have to acknowledge the influence that my artist father Robert had on the roots of this story. I remember very well his illustrations for War Bonds and other paintings and drawings he did during the war and they must have buried themselves deep in my child's psyche, along with all the other influences and memories that go with being a child in a small Canadian town during and just after the Second World War. Mysterious and inexplicable influences seem to reach over the generations. After finishing *Transgression* I learned that my soldier grandfather, who had been gassed in France during the First World War, was sent to a hospital in Rouen – which just happens to be the city I randomly chose to set the first half of this story in.

I'd like to thank my Canadian editor Wendy Thomas for her very helpful notes, and also my German editor Stefanie Hess and my translator Silvia Visintini for their insightful notes prior to the German publication of this novel.

I would also like to thank my first outside reader, Ted Boniface for his enthusiasm, incisive comments and encouragement. Thanks to Jessica Scott of McArthur & Company for all her timely and gracious help in shepherding the book through to its final completion and thanks to Jeff and Manijeh at ASAP Design for their willingness to consult with the author and for their stunning design.

And as always, I am grateful to my agent Beverley Slopen, who continues to inspire, cajole, and keep me on track.